THE LAST FLORIDA BOY

TOM GRIBBIN

Greg,
Old friends are the best friends. Enjoy the ride.

Much love,

Tom

This is a work of fiction. Names, characters, businesses, places, events, locales, and incidents are either the products of the author's imagination or used in a fictitious manner. Any resemblance to actual persons, living or dead, or actual events is purely coincidental.

Published by St. Petersburg Press

St. Petersburg, FL

www.stpetersburgpress.com

Design and composition by St. Petersburg Press

Cover design by: Florida-based firm, Clear ph Design. Art Director: Cledisson Jules

Rear Cover Painting: *Dead In The Water*, by Ron Stansel Art. Used by permission. All rights reserved. See ronstanselart.com

Photography: Rebecca Gast, RockStar Image

Paperback ISBN: 978-1-940300-30-6

eBook ISBN: 978-1-940300-31-3

First Edition

To Sheila, my swimmer, my queen.

Acknowledgments

Bill DeYoung. This project, lying dormant for years, would not have gotten off the ground without your belief, persistence, and support. Thank you for your keen editing and philosophical observations.

Charlie Hudson II, a friend and persuasive leader of men, who encouraged me to write the first word.

Joyce Maynard, author, who maintains that everyone has a story to tell. Joyce was the first to take the time to read and critique my manuscript. Her hand-written comments, on each page, still make me smile. Tough love, not for the faint of heart.

Lee Fugate, premier defense lawyer and valued brother, guided me though the complex legal principles contained throughout.

Michael Edward Hubbard, original Florida boy, with stories of his own to tell, provided me with much technical assistance and historical background.

Bob Duke, elusive and mysterious pilot, worked with me, line by line, to recreate a near-disastrous flight.

Bill Edwards, businessman, producer and visionary. Our adventures together in the entertainment world could fill another book, except I think that I signed an NDA somewhere along the way. Thank you for many years of opportunities, good times and high-rolling experiences.

Ron Stansel, artist and another original Florida boy, graced me with his painting, *Dead In The Water*, on the rear cover of the book. I have become a collector of his fine work.

Amy Cianci, thank you for your tireless work in the publisher's chair, especially for your continued guidance and intellect.

Bob Shoemaker, fellow traveler. Kids Incorporated.

Holly Bourne, author, just as you said.

THE LAST FLORIDA BOY

Prologue

So far so good. I leaned against the stern rail of our boat and listened to the pulse of the vessel's diesel engine. That hypnotic cadence, coupled with the soft rolling motion of a gentle following sea, made me drowsy. This was going to be it for me… my last gig. If we could only complete this run without screwing it up, I was determined to finally quit. I could then afford to. And I could go play some of the world's finest golf courses.

We hadn't had an ounce of trouble since meeting up with the Captain in Jamaica and loading up the ageless shrimper. With our eager crew of four we set out to cross the Caribbean and pass through the Yucatan Channel, skirting Cuba off to our starboard. We planned to avoid South Florida altogether and slide along the traditional shrimping routes into the Gulf of Mexico. Then up the west coast of Florida to meet the unloading crew out at sea.

The whole load had been sold upfront…we just had to pick it up in Jamaica and deliver it to them. As runs go, this had been the simplest ever. Not a misstep or delay at any point along the way. So far.

I ALWAYS LOVED GOING to Jamaica. There was never any trouble on that leg of the trip. The east end of the island, where we always went to purchase our stuff, was inviting...very few roads, and colorfully dotted with remote villages sparsely populated by laid back, yet very entertaining, Rastafarians.

The prevailing tradewinds blew in from the east, the cool winds off the Atlantic Ocean racing along the warmer Caribbean Sea, colliding with the fabled Blue Mountains on that side of Jamaica. Those chilly breezes ran up and across the mountaintops creating one of the rainier pockets in the region. The steady precipitation on those lush mountains produced some of the richest crops in the world. Especially the kind we sought to acquire. Curiously, there were no large-scale suppliers. One had to connect with a tribal leader, who purchased the sticky buds from different small personal patches grown by the ancestors of those bound to the old sugarcane plantations.

When we first traveled to Jamaica years ago, it took thirty to forty small local ganja gardens to supply just three hundred pounds. Luckily, it had become somewhat less difficult for the locals to supply much heavier weight. The villagers, however, were still cane cutters, as evidenced by the machetes carried by many of them. And every once in a while the overindulgence of their overproof homemade rum led to bloody confrontations up in the hill towns.

There were never any guns, though. Guns have been forbidden on the island, punishable by a life sentence in Jamaica's Gun Court, since the Toussaint L'ouverture slave uprising in Haiti in 1791. That slaughter at the hands of rebellious slaves scared the be-Jesus out of the Colonial authorities and led to a crackdown on firearms that continued to the present day. You still wouldn't want to get into an argument with one of the inebriated mountain villagers, however, because those sharp sugarcane-cutting machetes were much more intimidating than any handgun. But all that was between the locals, though. They were always friendly with the Florida boys.

The law never much ventured out to the east end. Maybe because of the lack of roads or usable ports. I guess they preferred to let the wild and woolly locals handle their own affairs. That was also fine with us.

Unlike in Florida, these islanders never built down along the water, preferring to be on high ground and not be inconvenienced by the occasional tropical storm that meandered through their domain.

That left mile after mile of unprotected and unobserved coastline to bring in a boat and load up as much product as you could gather. We never tired of dropping anchor in Discovery Bay…so named because it was where Christopher Columbus discovered Jamaica. But on this trip we met Captain Rodriguez and the ship farther east, out at Port Antonio. While Port Antonio had its own rich history, we were most impressed by Errol Flynn's house in the middle of the bay, on Navy Island. We found it even more interesting that the estate was still owned and used by his family.

Because the Jamaicans are some of the most superstitious people in the world, our crew was able to use a couple of the many coastline caves to stash some equipment and product as we readied ourselves for loading day. Any onlookers nervously grinned, but most openly shuddered when watching us enter or emerge from a cave. I'm not kidding…grown men with thickly-layered muscles squirmed at the thought of confronting the ghosts they believed lived in those spacious caves. It hasn't changed, not even today.

All went according to plan. Little Cyrus was packed, stacked and ready to load on the day our boat appeared offshore. We were shocked. This was the first time, ever, that there had not been some delay with his Rasta boys, who caravanned most of the load down to the coast by mule and cart. We all had a good laugh, Cyrus and his happy barefoot mountain lads included, when we expressed our exaggerated amazement at his efficiency and promptness. Coal black faces with big white grins greeted our surprised looks. And not a machete in sight.

After loading and packing the bales below-decks, carefully distributing the weight in the shrimper's holds, Little Cyrus hefted a case of coconut rum aboard for our journey. We hugged, and when Cyrus waved and said he looked forward to seeing us next season, I didn't have the heart to tell him that this was my last run. The nature of the business was changing and it was time for me to quit.

II.

The boat sailed evenly, and we made great headway. Better than that, the weather had been perfect through the deepwater part of our voyage. And as we rounded the west end of Cuba, we breathed a small sigh of relief. At this point, even if the weather turned bad, which was not predicted by the forecast, the most difficult part of the passage, weather-wise, was behind us. We could make the remainder of the trip in a storm if we had to.

Hilly Burke was nervous though. Hilly had never made a run that was not severely problematic. Everyone called him snakebit. He was probably the only Florida boy who seemed to lose money regularly on gigs...just the stupidest things would happen to him. Once he had a sailboat suddenly sink beneath him in twenty feet of water, in sight of the drop point. Another time his nighttime lookout was knocked unconscious by a flying fish and they missed the rendezvous point altogether. Circling back to reconnect, he ran aground on a high-falling tide, leaving the vessel stuck for most of the day and requiring everyone to abandon the load.

For someone who had never been busted, he was the brokest, unluckiest pirate any of us could remember. And his legendary misadventures provided hours of laughs throughout the Caribbean's many bars and beaches where such stories were shared. We had to agree, though, that Hilly did have incredible contacts in Jamaica, like Little Cyrus, and was able to score primo product at rock bottom prices.

And this load was going to permit me to finally retire...if I wanted to...which I swore to myself I would.

Off in the distance to the east, we could just make out the mountains of Cuba, the tops made visible by the afternoon sun. What a beautiful island...and what a shame we couldn't travel there at will to fish, drink and consort with the most beautiful women in the Hemisphere. There wasn't a one of us who didn't yearn for the wide-open, less political days of Ernest Hemingway.

My eyelids heavy, I reflected on the many beautiful mountains dotting the Caribbean, which was much more renowned for its pristine beaches. But in my opinion it was the mountains that made the region so special. Then...clunk. I opened one eye. Then again, just like that...clunk. There was no sound of the engine struggling, or of a problem with any of the equipment. The engine just stopped running after that second clunk. I sprang to my feet and immediately looked across the deck for Hilly. Had we not been aboard, it would have been amusing. But with the ship adrift in a gentle easterly current there was absolutely nothing funny about the situation.

The Captain came out of the wheelhouse and we all followed

him down to the engine room to inspect the situation. Man, it was dead. None of us could even coax a sound out of the silent engine.

"What the hell...," Hilly began.

There was no rhyme or reason for the sudden failure of the motor. These diesels were virtually bulletproof. Perhaps had we been in rough seas the bilge water sloshing below might have fouled the injectors, but such was not the case. We had no idea what was wrong. We were suddenly snakebit.

We stood in a small circle on the deck. A perfect day...not a cloud in the sky...adrift. It was startling to realize how fast we were drifting eastward. It was too deep to drop an anchor, and while we had crossed paths with a few vessels along the way, there was not a boat on the horizon in any direction from which to get assistance. The Captain reacted first.

He called for Hilly to make a decision. He explained that while still in international waters, we were dangerously close to Cuban waters, and it wouldn't be long before we would clearly be inside Cuba's jurisdiction.

CUBA DIDN'T LIKE smugglers any more than the U.S. did. It wasn't that long ago that Cuba had the death penalty for such crimes. And while that was no longer in effect, their sentences were still harsh, and their treatment of gringos in general was reportedly deplorable in any event. We had to make a decision...immediately, the Captain urged.

We were about one hundred and twenty miles away from Florida. We figured to send out a Mayday for assistance from anyone in the area, outlining our proximity to Cuba and hoping to catch a friendly charterboat or pleasure craft nearby. There was no time to lose.

Our Mayday was immediately answered. "This is the Coast

Guard, Key West." The voice came through 5 by 5, loud and clear, over the radio for all to hear. They requested our position, stating that they were patrolling in the area and could assist us if needed. There was no other response to our Mayday. We all looked at Hilly like he had a dark cloud hanging over him...jinx, Jonah, snakebit.

We had to make the decision together. "Shit, it's either the Coast Guard or the Cubans, make up your minds," the Captain stated flatly. Cuba was looming larger on the horizon.

The Coast Guard, if they could get to us in time, would be required to search the ship, for safety's sake, before towing us. And there was no way to hide the over 20,000 pounds of Jamaican packed below. So our decision came down to this: serve time in a Cuban prison or get busted by the Coast Guard. Put that way, it was unanimous. We immediately responded to the Coast Guard's call, giving them our position and letting them know that we were drifting, rapidly, east toward Cuba. We also confirmed that we were a U.S. documented vessel and required their immediate assistance.

The U. S. Coast Guard is great...fearless when you need them. They informed us that they were coming directly, but they estimated that they were about ninety minutes away from our present position. They also advised us that if we were approached by any Cuban vessels, we should delay and avoid having them board us for as long as possible. It would prove much more difficult for them to assist us if a Cuban patrol boat got a line on us first.

Ninety minutes...maybe even a bit longer...and the coast of Cuba now in plain sight. We were stunned into silence. None of us could see this ending well. Now it seemed we might not even have the option of going to a U.S. jail.

WE TOOK turns looking at our watches and scanning the horizon, as the Captain continued to work on the engine. A very slow ninety minutes, let me tell you. As if to lessen the tension, Hilly jumped up and dragged a small inflatable life raft to the rail. We inflated it quickly and tied it to the bow of the shrimpboat. Hilly jumped in with two small plastic oars and attempted rowing westerly…trying to tow our bulky, heavily laden craft away from Cuba.

He succeeded in turning the bow of our boat away, but it really didn't seem like he was making any headway. We all just continued to drift backward, tied together and pointing west. Again, if we weren't in such peril, it would have been hilarious…the unlucky sailor alone in his tiny dinghy attempting to tow this lumbering, dead-in-the-water, load. But he kept at it and no one laughed.

After a seemingly endless wait, alone and adrift, the Captain suddenly alerted Hilly that a craft was approaching fast. He pointed almost due north, and we all saw it. Hilly tugged on the line and pulled the life raft back to the ship and we helped him aboard.

Due north…that was encouraging. "That's where the United States is," Hilly exclaimed. "If they were Cuban, they would be coming from the east," he continued, pointing over toward Cuba.

As we followed his finger, we all saw another boat coming toward us, fast. "Uh, oh," the Captain groaned. "They must have heard our Mayday too."

The Cubans seemed a bit closer to us, but both ships were approaching so rapidly that we couldn't really tell who would get to us first. As the Cuban ship moved closer, we could see that it was a patrol boat, flying a Cuban flag, and armed fore and aft. The Coast Guard cutter was three times bigger and while it seemed farther away, it appeared to be closing faster. We were adrift in the open sea, watching two government vessels racing each other toward us…neither of which offered an escape from our dilemma. And there we were…wildly cheering for the Coast Guard.

I looked over at a silent Hilly. He shook his head. "Well, we're fucked either way," he muttered.

THE CUBAN PATROL boat reached us first and ordered us to throw a line. Seeing that the Coast Guard cutter was moments away, we ignored their demands. They then attempted to come alongside and tie up. But our ship's bow had swung back around in the current and momentarily frustrated their first attempt. They didn't get another one.

The Coast Guard cutter roared into the mix at a high rate of speed, identifying themselves over the loudspeaker…as if we didn't know who they were…and ordering the patrol boat to "Stand off"…in English and in Spanish. When the Cubans ignored the cutter's orders, maneuvered against the large wake thrown up by the bigger vessel and swung alongside us, the Coast Guard fired an overhead warning shot from their sizable bow cannon.

That noisy concussion caught everyone's attention. Reacting, we all ducked beneath the railing. There was a sudden, momentary standoff until Hilly, thinking quickly, heaved a mighty toss of our bowline to a sure-handed sailor aboard the cutter…who caught it on the first try and tied us tightly to his stern.

The Cubans backed off, but only about fifty feet as the situation remained tense. The Coast Guard briefly inquired about our health and about our food and water situation, and, comfortable with our present physical welfare, secured a longer, stronger towline to the bow of our vessel. They shouted to us to remain steady as the Cubans approached us again. The cutter's bow and bow gunner had now swung away from us, but armed sailors appeared on the cutter's starboard rail, standing ready to protect us as the cutter prepared to tow us away.

Finally, the smaller boat turned around and headed east, back to Cuba. I was standing on the aft rail of the shrimper and caught the steady grin of one of the Cuban sailors. It was as if he sensed our predicament and was laughing at me. My stomach suddenly became seasick and I threw up.

We were now in the hands of the U.S. Coast Guard.

III.

The hull of the large Coast Guard cutter allowed it to plough through the heavy seas at a high rate of speed. If they tied the towline too short, our boat could be sucked under by the wake of their powerful vessel. So the Coast Guard had to rig a long towline and maintain a slow pace as they dragged us along. We figured we were going about 8 knots with approximately fifteen or sixteen hours before we were greeted by Customs in Key West.

Because of the confrontation with the Cubans, and the necessity for us to quickly clear out of the disputed area, the Coast Guard had foregone the safety search of our boat. They were reassured that we were all healthy, with enough food and fresh water to last the time it would take for us to reach the U.S.

So we were not in custody…we were still free men, at least for one more night. Huddled together on the deck of our boat, we desperately attempted to come up with a solution. We worked for over an hour on the engine…with no luck. As the afternoon sun flattened and prepared for its pre-sunset ritual, we abandoned the engine and hashed out our alternatives.

Hilly thought we might jump ship as we got close to land, but the Captain reminded us that by the time we reached Key West, it would be daylight again, and we would be easily spotted and picked up by the Coast Guard, who would be extremely vigilant. "Forget about anyone attempting to leave or approach the ship," he concluded.

"We might as well enjoy our last night of freedom," I offered, pulling out a bottle of Cyrus' coconut rum.

Hilly began to roll a joint from his Jamaican stash. Even the Captain seemed resigned to our fate, taking the bottle from my hand and pouring himself a long dollop into his coffee cup.

"Let's watch the sunset together," he suggested. "No clouds...we might even see a green flash tonight," he added.

Robbie Tannenbaum, the fourth member of our crew, had been relatively silent during the long passage from Jamaica. He was the rookie on the boat and thought it best to work hard and keep his mouth shut. But he couldn't contain himself.

"Are you guys fucking nuts?" he exclaimed, almost shouting. "It'll be dark in a couple of hours. We have all night to dump the load. We can arrive in Key West...empty."

He snatched the joint from Hilly, and the bottle of rum from the Captain's hand and ordered, "Let's keep clear heads. We have a lot of work to do tonight."

"Jesus, Robbie," Hilly responded. "There's 20,000 pounds below. We'll never get all that off the boat."

Robbie tossed the bottle of rum and the joint off the stern and continued, "20,000 pounds, that's right. Okay, that's 5,000 pounds per man."

"That makes me feel better," Hilly spat sarcastically.

Robbie ignored him. "Listen, the bales might be different weights, but they are all about fifty pounds each. So that's about one hundred bales, more or less, for each guy to toss over the side."

The Captain was doing the math in his head, and nodded approvingly. Then he said, "Once the sun goes down, we'll have about ten, eleven hours to work. It might could be done."

I piped up. "That's about ten bales an hour for each man..."

"Fuckin' A," Robbie said. "We can do it, fellas." He paused, and said seriously, "I don't want to go to jail on my first run."

So that was the plan. Hilly joined in, adding, "We need to get rid of every bud, every stem. We can't let Customs find anything at all on this ship."

The Captain agreed. "We can hose it all down once the bales are dumped. We can git'er close enough."

We figured that even if we were busted for some overlooked residue, we'd probably only be looking at something light, like probation, rather than some long sentence for a major load. It was worth the effort, we all agreed. Whew, it was going to be a long and stressful night.

We decided on one glass of rum each. I pulled another bottle out of the case and we settled in to watch the sunset, resting, waiting for dark to fall. The sun set and an almost full moon rose in the periphery of my eye. There was no green flash that evening...so much for good luck signs.

IT TOOK FOREVER for it to get dark. No clouds, a bright waxing moon, and a rather glassy sea didn't make for much cover. Hell, there was enough light to shoot a movie. Luckily, our rising bow and cabin blocked the view of our deck from the cutter. In any event, we went ahead with our plan.

It began roughly, but we became more and more efficient as we began to assume different roles...unstrapping, bringing the bales up on deck, sliding and rolling them to the stern, then dumping them overboard. It was strenuous.

We dumped the first ten bales, then stood back to admire our work. Hilly came up from the hold to join us. Something was terribly wrong. The bales, each encased in rough burlap, were not sinking. They were drifting away in a meandering line in our wake, the bright moon clearly outlining each bale floating in a relatively calm sea.

Hilly went white. "Oh my God!" He ran to the bow of the boat and peered ahead to the cutter. It continued to pound ahead, none the wiser. But it was way too obvious for them not to eventually notice.

"At some point, they are going to spot those bales," the Captain predicted, his shirt already drenched with perspiration.

I didn't want to think about it. "Come on guys," I ordered, "Back to work. Let's just get rid of what we can."

We labored hard throughout the night...lifting, rolling, dumping, cursing. We stopped again for a short breather and looked out from our stern. In the moonlight...bale upon bale of floaters trailing in our wake as far as the eye could see. I couldn't even count them all. "Jesus, it's like Hansel and Gretel dropping the breadcrumbs..."

Hilly almost panicked. "How can they not see..." he whispered hoarsely. "Damn, maybe we should stop dumping for a while and let them float away before we continue."

Robbie jumped in. "Are you kidding? We're not close to even being half-done. We can't slow down. Come on, man, we have to speed it up."

The Captain shook his head. I could tell he was somewhat amused. None of us had ever experienced anything like this before.

"We don't want to be putting into Key West with a mile-long trail of square groupers behind us."

Even Robbie looked defeated. Nevertheless, we went back to work...single-mindedly...harder, faster, with the blind effort of slaves.

It's a story we'd tell for years to come. We worked right up until dawn. No more breaks, no more indecision. Dumping and dumping and dumping, over 20,000 pounds of loosely-packed Jamaican superbud over the side, the many bales all bobbing in our wake. It almost appeared as if they were following us. We hosed and scrubbed and hosed again into the morning hours. Hilly's personal stash was hosed along with the holds and the deck.

At sunrise, we were exhausted. I had never, ever, worked so hard in my life. All four of us lay on the deck, totally fatigued and dehydrated. We could only hope we didn't overlook some small piece of evidence. We all knew that a proper search always turned up something. So as exhausted as we were, we groaned, forced ourselves up and attempted to go over the boat in the daylight. The seas had picked up after the sun rose and bounced us around until we couldn't move anymore. For the next two hours we lay prostrate on the deck, unsheltered from the sun, trying to drink as much fresh water as we could.

THE COAST GUARD cutter signaled two blasts as we approached Key West. The Captain limped into the wheelhouse with Robbie while Hilly and I stood on the bow, searching for signs of trouble. We finally steered into Key West at about 10 a.m., well after sunrise. The cutter didn't take us to the Coast Guard station. Instead, we headed in the direction of Mallory Square, downtown Key West. We found this strange, but we were too tired to speak.

Hilly went below to use the head…we'd been urinating over the side all night. In seconds he was tapping my shoulder, frantic.

"What's wrong?" I asked.

"Come with me, quick," he blurted.

Hilly took me below, where, inside the unused head, sat one bale of pot, tightly wrapped in course brown burlap and strapped with a piece of duct tape. Handwritten on the gray tape was a simple notation in black marker, "60 lbs."

"How in the hell did we miss this?" I exploded.

We could feel the boats slowing down. We were about to dock. I quickly grabbed some foul-weather gear and covered the large bale as best I could.

"There's nothing we can do about it now," I said, too tired to really care.

JUST AS WE climbed back on deck, the Coast Guard was retrieving their towline from Robbie, as Robbie tossed our bowline to the helping hand on the pier.

"Should we tell Robbie?" Hilly whispered.

Before I could answer, a young officer hailed us from the cutter's bridge. "Are you guys alright?" he asked.

"Yes sir," the Captain replied. "You and your crew are really lifesavers."

"That was a tight spot," the officer barked back. "Almost an international incident. We all got lucky, I think."

Robbie added, "Seeing you roar out of the horizon was like watching the cavalry appear."

The officer saluted. "If it's okay, we'll leave you here."

We were stunned. Nobody spoke, and the efficient officer was obviously expecting an answer. Finally, the Captain coughed and found the words. "Yeah, this is great. Uh, thanks."

Suddenly the large cutter wheeled away from us and headed out the channel, picking up speed as it left.

We looked at each other, still stunned…and still exhausted, dehydrated and totally bewildered. We could have kept it all…

Still holding the bowline, Robbie turned around, looked back at us and said, "…fuck."

"Fuck…," I echoed. Goodbye, Pebble Beach, I thought to myself. My golfing retirement would have to wait.

"Fuck," the Captain muttered, his arms hanging limp by his side.

Hilly said nothing. He slumped on the deck, looked at his hands, and started to cry. Snakebit.

It was supposed to be my last gig. Needless to say, we were all back to square-one. So I was not retiring...not just yet. There would be other trips.

But as so often happens in this business, it was to be some lesser offense, a minor mistake coupled with a big mouth, that would eventually lead to my undoing.

Chapter One

It is said in primitive societies that, although we are given a name at birth, a subsequent journey in life determines who we really are. In many tribes, the praise name, or nickname, that a journeyer earns by his deeds on this adventure, is cherished more than the name he was given as a child.

Life affords us...or subjects us to...many travels. But the special journey, that journey which offers us the opportunity to forge a new identity, is rarely provided. And most times, the traveler is not even aware that his fate has been cast along such a road.

My road was River Road. A clay and gravel service road running through the Prison Camp, down along the Alabama River and around the Air Force base golf course.

When I first arrived, and walked around the Camp to orient myself, I found myself walking down River Road. It seemed that everyone was out in the invigorating autumn weather...walkers, joggers, fishermen, inmate philosophers and Air Force fitness freaks alike. And me, in the blue jumpsuit of a newly-arrived prison camp inmate.

The inmates were only allowed to travel about a half-mile down the road, to an imaginary line by the golf course. I was happy that we were permitted to use the road at all. It was incredibly liberating. I knew immediately that I would be spending much of my thirty-eight month sentence out on River Road.

I HAD KNOWN that the Prison Camp was located on the grounds of Maxwell Air Force Base, but I was surprised to see so many non-prisoners sharing the same area.

It was because the surroundings were so beautiful. The river on one side, and a lake on the other. A serene, tree-lined piece of Southern water-land...home for squirrels and rabbits, playground for turtles and beaver, and a stopover for herons, egrets and great flocks of other migratory birds. All with wide grassy shores upon which to sit, fish, play cards, or just dream away the day.

Under threat of disciplinary action, we were forbidden to speak to non-inmates. I could only nod at that pretty little Air Force joggerette. I later found out that she was a Captain. But that was over a year ago, and that's another story.

The relaxing appearance was just one of the things that gave Maxwell Federal Prison Camp its 'Club Fed' reputation. There was no fence around it, and an inmate could wear his civilian clothes after work hours and on weekends. But spend some time there confined and one would discover that, while relaxed, it was definitely not the country club it was made out to be.

Oh, it was civilized, and shiny clean. And the food was good. The population was a mixed bag of tax evaders, pot smugglers, insider-traders, crooked television evangelists, used-car dealers doing a couple of years for setting back odometers, and an occasional celebrity convict. In fact, we had a well-known former big-league baseball player…a fiery but popular guy who turned the Camp's softball team into the scourge of the base intramural league.

Slipped into this mellow recipe was an assortment of erstwhile stock market tippees and would-be wiseguys. All with generally short-term sentences.

Lately, as a result of the so-called "war on drugs," there was an overabundance of small-time, non-violent crack dealers from the big-city streets. Along with the occasional islander…Dominicans, Jamaicans, and Bahamians. The sleepy traditional mix of white-collar offenders was changed by these younger, louder, more aggressive rappers. But not that much. In truth, although not everyone would agree, to me their presence added a wilder, funnier element.

"It could be worse." A phrase to be remembered…more than that, it demands memorization. For no matter what walk of life you come from, if you are forced to do penance for your misdeeds, you must constantly remind yourself of that. It helps you to get by. It helps because in reality it is true. Things could always be worse.

As for myself, I was doing fine. Actually, I was living a very healthy existence. I had plenty of time to exercise and physically I felt wonderful. I had erased years of sedentary living and high-speed partying, and had begun to look at the positive side of my confinement. Frankly, I had been looking for a change of direction for a long time, and if this is what it took to make that happen, I would accept it.

I also found plenty of time to read. Previously, I could always find excuses not to read. At the Camp, however, I tried to read everything…novels, non-fiction, articles, odd periodicals and poetry. Anything.

Of all the activities I became involved in, in the end it was reading and physical fitness that took up my time. I used to be a confirmed television-watcher, but two or three nights of trying to watch TV in a noisy, crowded room cured me of that. In fact, the only fistfights I saw the whole time I was at the Camp occurred there. *Miami Vice* reruns versus music videos.

"Doesn't anyone watch the news?" I grumbled on my final visit to the TV room.

So it came down to reading and working out, a very simple regimen, my only material needs being a dictionary and a good pair of cross-trainers. And I too made a vow to myself that I suspect many an inmate has made. That after I got out, I would continue to read and to keep fit. Mentally and physically, philosophically and emotionally, there were tremendous personal benefits.

Of course I missed my friends and my family. Some days the sadness would come from nowhere and overwhelm me. But, in general, I concentrated on the positive, reminding myself that things could be worse.

Unfortunately, with less than a year to go on my sentence, things began to get worse.

I HAD ALREADY SERVED eighteen months of my sentence. With "good-time" subtracted from the total time, an inmate must serve two-thirds of his sentence before being released. One was also eligible for parole after serving one-third of his sentence. But at my one-third point, I had been denied parole. The Parole Board had reasoned that giving me parole would, in their words, "allow me to avoid effective punishment for my crime," and they demanded that I "do it all."

All in all, I had another seven months to do before being released...when things took an unexpected turn.

AFTER A YEAR OR SO, only a few of my closest friends continued to write or visit. Some, who I had considered to be very close, had long since stopped. Although a couple of people who I had never considered special surprised me by faithfully corresponding. It was something I would always remember.

At first the noticeable drop-off of mail was disheartening, then somewhat hurtful. For no matter how comfortable a confinement one might have at a minimum-security camp, it was confinement nonetheless. The separation from normal life is weird...sometimes I even felt like I had been transported to another planet. And mail from home, no matter how trite or illegible, was a welcome link to real life...and to sanity.

Ultimately, I adjusted to the decline in my mail. I even weaned myself from having to attend mail-call on a nightly basis. However, I still appreciated those friends who continued to lift my spirits. But, with the exception of those few friends, and of course my mother and sisters back home in St. Petersburg, Florida, I figured I was pretty much forgotten.

I was wrong. Law enforcement remembered me.

I LOVE TO PLAY GOLF. Contrary to the popular misconception, at the Camp we were not permitted to play golf. "Doing time ruined my handicap," I used to joke. But after some boring jobs as an inmate, I finally got myself assigned to the inmate work detail on the Air Force base golf course. I became a greenskeeper.

It was a pleasant and a fairly loose assignment. I worked with a good crew. No snitches to tell on you if you took a few shots with a 9-iron, or snuck a cold Budweiser. It certainly beat washing dishes or mowing lawns, even though we began very early in the morning.

I figured that I could easily get through another seven months and start a life with better direction than the one I had come from.

Seven months. Sure.

IT WAS ANOTHER CRISP FRIDAY. I had just finished raking the sand-traps around the Third green. It was only 10:30 in the morning, I had completed my duties for the day and was looking forward not only to a relaxing afternoon, but to a softball tournament over the weekend.

The Third green and the Fourth tee adjoined the stretch of River Road that ran up to the Prison Camp. Looking up to the top of the hill, I could see the Camp. And as a foursome approached the Fourth tee, I noticed an official-looking car turn down the hill in my direction.

I always enjoyed watching the golfers. I especially liked seeing the golfers drive from the Fourth tee. It was a short par 4, only about 295 yards, but it had wide water in front of the green. For months, I had never seen anyone try to carry the water, even with the wind at their backs. To go over the lake, the shot would have to fly at least 240 yards in the air. So the golfers would hit irons left of the water and go for the green in two. Air Force pussies.

"If this was a Marine base," I would joke to my buddies, "we'd see some bigger hitters."

Number 4 was down as far as the inmates were permitted to go along the road when they weren't working. No fences, walls or wire, the "invisible line" was marked by a white out-of-bounds stake. There, you could distinguish the inmate joggers from the others. The inmates would turn around at the marker and run back toward the Camp. While the others continued down River Road through the Air Force base. To cross the line technically made the inmate an escapee.

On weekends, we would stand on the road watching the golfers play the Fourth hole. Doing our best Howard Cosell imitations, we would whisper our make-believe broadcasts, laughing, but mostly wishing that we were playing instead of them.

My mouth watered every time I got near the tee. I swear, given the opportunity, I could drive the green. I even considered going directly to the 4th tee when I was finally released, just to try it.

TODAY WOULD BE a perfect day to attempt it, I thought. A strong breeze was at the golfers' backs. Just as I thought it, a muscular young officer pulled his driver out and took a few practice swings.

The others were going to hit first, but, holy shit, I could see that the big boy was going to go for it. Finally.

"John Bellamy." I was startled by the stern voice behind me calling my name.

"Me…?"

"Could you come with us." It was a command more than a question.

Bob Waters, my work supervisor, was with two determined-looking men, and he smiled weakly as they led me to the official white car I had just seen driving down River Road from the Camp. The moment I saw them, I knew they were Feds.

ALL OF THE inmates on the golf detail loved working for old Bob. A former Army Sergeant, Bob Waters had been disabled in a service-related traffic accident several years ago. Forced to leave the Army, he was employed by the Air Force MWR recreation program, and he had been a fixture on the Maxwell Air Force Base golf course for over a decade. He was tall and lean, and when he smiled, he had an uncanny resemblance to Bill Russell, the Boston Celtics legend.

Now, although close to retirement, Bob seemed constantly

busy...but always at a measured pace. He was quiet and relaxed. More importantly, he was fair, and if you did your job, he would occasionally look the other way. You could sneak in a pair of tennis shoes, or a quarter-pounder with cheese. Ah, the little delights.

Sometimes even a big delight here and there. An inmate or two had been known to make a secret rendezvous with a wife or girlfriend in the bushes beyond the 15th fairway. But such days were coming to an end. The recent changes in the prison population meant stricter supervision.

It had been at least six months since anyone had tried the bushes. He got caught by a patrolling MP, who turned the surprised inmate over to the Camp authorities. That inmate was shipped to a higher-level institution...a real prison with a wall around it. Always remember, things could be worse.

WITH ME IN the backseat of the car with Bob, they drove the short distance to the Camp and parked the vehicle in front of the administration building. Telling me to wait, the two agents got out of the car and went into the Warden's office.

"What's this all about?" I asked Bob.

"Hell, I don't know. They just called the clubhouse and asked me to come over to the Camp. Then we went out and got you."

"Did they say anything at all?" I was quickly trying to recall what I had done recently that might have attracted attention. I had gotten into a groove, not routinely breaking any rules because I did not want to worry about looking over my shoulder. I was going home soon, and things were just fine the way they were. I did recall that I'd received a golf shirt about a month ago from a Major with a 2 handicap...but they wouldn't call the Feds in on that. Damn, I had no idea what was going on, I concluded.

"They asked where you were, that's it," Bob responded. "They didn't have a thing to say after that…not particularly friendly types."

I smiled. Bob was always preaching at everyone to be friendly and to exhibit a positive attitude.

"I thought you'd know what was going on," he added.

"I have absolutely no idea, Bob." I was suddenly nervous…little pricks of fear worked at the back of my neck.

"Well, just sit tight, John…I'll see you on Monday. I'll let you sweep the range." He knew that would cheer me up. At the driving range, I could hit a few balls out behind the cart-house.

Moving slowly, and using both hands to help swing his bad leg through the car door, Bob slid out and went over to his truck. I sat there worried, watching him walk away. Then he stopped and returned to my open window.

"By the way, he knocked it in the drink." He grinned.

"What…?" I said, puzzled.

"The big guy…he hit it in the water."

I was so unnerved by being taken in the car; I'd neglected to follow the action on the 4th tee as we drove off. Bob had not missed it. He never missed a thing.

We looked at each other and laughed. Then he patted my arm affectionately.

"Hang in there, John," he said warmly, and returned to his truck.

As he drove away, I thought to myself that he was as decent a person as I had met since arriving at the Camp. After months of working for him, I still never took his low-key personality for granted. He cared about the guys on his detail. Sometimes he even made you forget that you were in prison.

I reminded myself that it would be good to see him again on Monday. But I would never see Bob Waters again.

Chapter Two

The intimidation used in interrogating a suspect ranges from the subtle to the oppressive. Once a person has been subjected to official questioning, of any sort, he does not want a repeat experience.

I thought all of that was behind me. After so many adventures, I had finally been caught, questioned, tried, convicted and sentenced for a marijuana conspiracy. I had already served most of my sentence, I had come to grips with my past, and I had adjusted myself to the fact that in less than a year, I could begin to rebuild my life. I could put this bad dream behind me and do something productive. I might not have a solid idea about what to do, but I had some money stashed away and I had a positive attitude. No matter what, I was finished with the smuggling business.

Now, here I was again, pressed by a large, square-looking FBI agent in a rumpled, charcoal-gray suit, and his slightly built, tie-less, hip-talking DEA partner. The quarterback, I called the shorter man, since he appeared to be calling the signals.

They had taken me into an empty office in the Camp administration building. I was nervous, but I didn't fail to notice, or remember, that all government office interiors looked and felt disconcertingly alike. No matter where, even here in Montgomery, Alabama, the small offices were interchangeably furnished with formica and inexpensive carpet, their walls covered with plaques of every imaginable size and shape, signifying unheard-of awards and accomplishments. And always, a rather flattering framed photograph of the President, Ronald Reagan.

They bombarded me with question after question, at such a rate I couldn't catch all of it. Their inquiry seemed to relate to activities I was unfamiliar with. Specific events I knew nothing about. By the wording of the questions, however, it was clear that they were already well informed about some major drug deal. Five boats, rendezvousing in the middle of the Caribbean with a mother ship from Columbia off some point called the Mysterioso Bank...

I held up my hands to stop them, saying, "It seems like you are informed enough to know that I had nothing to do with all that..."

The quarterback scrambled. He was loud and crude, and, as if by habit, he scratched his closely cropped dark beard.

"Don't give us that bullshit, Bellamy. We know that you know Stevie Peak and Charles Gregory...that you have done business with them in the past." He scratched his beard again, continuing, "Look, we have photos of you, together with Peak, and Gregory, and James Rasmussen, along with some other pieces of shit..."

He shuffled through his stack of papers, pulled out an 8 by 10 glossy photograph, and threw it on the table in front of me.

"Here's a good one," he gloated. "At Beefeater's, just three months before you came in here."

As I looked at the big smile on my face in the creased photograph, he threw the remaining package of papers at the table. His pass fell short, hitting the edge. The papers fell to the floor and scattered. The FBI guy slowly shook his head and smiled faintly. I began to think that maybe the quieter guy was somewhat more reasonable. I looked directly at him.

"Listen," I explained. "I went to high school with Stevie and Dog. Of course I know those guys, and probably a whole bunch of the other guys you are asking about too…"

I went on, explaining how most of my friends back then, knowing that I was going to jail, took turns taking me out to cheer me up. Sure, I knew them, and yes, I hung out with a lot of them. I even added that, like so many of my old friends, most had long since forgotten about me. And I had not heard from Stevie since coming to prison.

I did not tell them that at one time I was irritated at Stevie for not writing or contacting me. Now, it seemed that it was just as well.

"That's all there is to it, period," I maintained.

I was being completely honest with them. I had never worked with those guys even when I was active. Stevie and Dog were way over my head in the business. I heard that Stevie was bringing in boats every other month, and his team had been well-established long before I got involved.

Over an hour passed, and they seemed to get angrier. The quarterback continued on about some large-scale drug smuggling operation that hauled tons of marijuana on five different vessels to five separate drop-off points…two of which were way up the Mississippi River. He hinted of things that meant absolutely nothing to me except to indicate that he was extremely knowledgeable about it all. It became obvious that the government was probably assisted by a snitch or two at the top. He confirmed that, adding, "And we have informants who place you in a managerial role."

I exploded, "Come on…that is total bullshit, and you know it!"

My mind began racing. What in the hell did they want from me? I received a thirty-eight month sentence in my own case. I could have testified against others back then…on matters that I did in fact know about, and I wouldn't have had to serve one single day. I wouldn't roll over then, and these agents should know that from my file.

Why did they think I would cooperate now...even if I did know anything? And what in the hell did they need from me for this case? They seemed to possess all the information and legitimate testimony they needed...

Wow, to think they would finally bust Stevie. He and his dad were the first smugglers I had ever known. And they were always generous with the folks who grew up in the area, building docks, repairing boats, or helping out financially when families ran into hard times. But I truly knew little about their operation, and absolutely nothing about this particular deal.

Finally, the agents took a break. Leaving me in the tiny room to brood alone, they went out to make a phone call. I sensed that we had reached a point where they had everything they needed and were going to let me return to work. Boy, was I wrong.

They stormed back in, and in ten short minutes, they laid out their case against sixteen individuals, including some guys from Everglades City, Immokolee and Big Pine Key, New Bern, North Carolina, and two sisters from Louisiana. It was impressive.

They seemed to have everybody cold...except perhaps Stevie Peak. And they wanted me to help deliver him. How bad did they want him? They not only wanted me to fill in details about some of his past deals where they possessed only sketchy information, but they wanted me to manufacture testimony for this case. To lie for them if need be.

Evidently, Stevie had been smart in setting up his operation. So smart that only one person could positively link him with any of it.

That was Popeye...Jimmy Rasmussen. Stevie set things up, Popeye carried them out. The government listed Popeye as Stevie's lieutenant. He was the buffer between Stevie and informants. Between Stevie and trouble.

We called him Popeye because he had huge forearms. And because he was a sailor. His uncle grew up with Stevie's dad, and together they started the first charter fishing service out of Pass-a-Grille, down in St. Pete Beach.

Big Steve and Popeye's uncle were the first fishermen to bring pot into the Suncoast. They just sailed over to Mexico, picked it up and brought it back. That was in the '60s, and in broad daylight. It was a sport then. Simply-equipped boats and handshakes. Florida boys just doing their thing. It used to be so...American. Now, it's all Latin and hi-tech, CIA and money laundering. Sinister sophistication and...anti-American.

Man, before cartels, before terrorists, before gangs and organized crime, before guns and violence...even before cell phones... there were just Florida boys. I really thought it was okay back then. Romantic rogues not really hurting anyone. It's all bullshit today. Guns, liars and assholes with attitudes. And the governments, legitimate as well as rogue states, have all the best connections and transport routes.

Big Steve passed away years ago, taking that era with him. It's just as well that he was not alive to discover that his best friend's nephew, Jimmy...Popeye to us, had flipped, and was preparing to betray his son Stevie.

SO THAT WAS IT. They had one rat. And technically Rasmussen's testimony was all they needed. But they reasoned that a seasoned defense attorney, which Stevie would undoubtedly employ, might create some doubt about the case in a jury's mind.

Popeye was looking at thirty years or more in prison, so he

made a deal to testify against Stevie. I guess the government figured that a good defense lawyer could convince many a reasonable man that a witness would say anything to avoid thirty years in jail. Especially if that witness is the only witness against his client.

Popeye was the buffer, so all the evidence would work against him as well as Stevie. It would be easy enough to make it look like he was blaming Stevie for his own crimes. Essentially, what they were afraid of, was that if Popeye, the only witness against Stevie, could be impeached or compromised in front of a jury, Stevie might walk. They did not want to take that chance.

The government knew that it would be hard for a jury to ignore two rats.

It became clear to me. I was supposed to be the second rat. It did not matter that I had no part, nor knowledge, of this deal. The quarterback would provide me with a suitable script. I looked up at them, immobile.

The smaller agent smiled, saying, "I think he needs convincing."

Hit the nail on the head, why don't you, I thought. I had nothing to say. I was paying the price for my own mistakes and I didn't need other people's problems. I was suddenly tired of it all. The scheming, the evasion, the lifestyle, the police…all the bullshit. The constant bullshit. I was relieved to be out of it for good. I just wanted to finish my sentence and go home.

He continued. "We know what you're thinking. Just sit tight, and be home by Christmas."

Bingo. They were reading my mind. I wish I was one of those tough guys who could just say, "Fuck you." Stevie probably would have said, "Fuck you." Instead I just mumbled, trying to act invisible, my words trailing off.

"Sorry, pal," he interrupted. But he was not sorry.

THE BOTTOM LINE WAS DEVASTATING.

Stevie had been a friend of mine since grade school. We had graduated from high school together twenty years ago. When I went down, he felt badly for me, so he continually tried to lift my spirits. Between the time of my arrest and my trial, I was out on bail…for almost a year. Stevie took me fishing. He took me diving. He took me out on the town, and unfortunately, he took me out of town.

Evidently, when we went some places, like the Keys, or Miami, Stevie was also working, setting up this deal. So there I was, unknowingly right smack dab in the middle of it all.

The quarterback stood over me and spelled it out. "We have you placed at several meeting sites, where critical decisions were made. Technically, you have made several overt acts contributing to this conspiracy."

…overt acts, contributing…here it comes, I thought, almost aloud.

"That's right, buddy boy. We have a case against you…a solid case. That places you in a managerial role in this conspiracy. You'll get…say…"

"…at least thirty years." The FBI man finally spoke.

They had finally gotten my undivided attention. I felt like a drowning man. I gasped.

"But you know different…and Popeye will tell you that I had nothing…"

"Tough shit," the small man interrupted, shouting. "Popeye will say what I tell him to say."

The quarterback grinned like he had just thrown for the go-ahead touchdown with ten seconds left in the game.

"Hey, that's…that's against the law," I stammered.

He leaned close to me and laughed in my face. He composed himself enough to whisper, "So what…" Then he laughed again.

I wanted to speak, but he anticipated me. "Fuck you, maggot," he spat. Then he got up slowly, gathered his papers and walked out of the room.

I WAS IN SHOCK. I had heard stories about this kind of thing. There was always someone crying about getting screwed by the government, especially here at the Camp, where there seemed to be an endless stream of whiners and "innocent" men.

Although I was a convict, I still believed in…well, right and wrong. "Truth, justice and the American way." I had not been bitter about my own incarceration. I figured I deserved it. In fact, I thought I had become more enlightened about my purpose in life, and that I would be a better person upon my release.

But this was wrong. Worse, they knew it was dead wrong. Well…the quarterback knew it. The FBI guy seemed more professional. The DEA might pull this kind of move, but not the FBI…

I suddenly realized that he was still in the room with me. The FBI guy had not joined the quarterback in his dramatic exit. I looked at him closely. He was big, clean-cut, and indeed he looked like the Bureau's P.R. version of a professional FBI agent. Hopefully with a bit more honor than the DEA.

I took a deep breath and turned to face him. "I don't know how close you are to this case," I began, "but he knows that I honestly have nothing to do with this. I don't want to give perjured testimony and…"

'Shut up," he barked. "I know all about it. You heard the deal… you testify accordingly…or you'll do another twenty or thirty years inside. And it won't be in a soft, fuzzy-wuzzy place like this Camp, you can bet your ass on that."

"Wait a second…" I stood up. I was frightened.

"Sit down wiseguy. You have fifteen minutes to decide." He walked out abruptly.

Alone in the office, I slumped down hard in the chair, wondering how I had gotten to this depressing point. I couldn't help thinking of Stevie.

IT WAS BACK toward the end of the summer between my junior and senior years in college. I had finished my summer job building fiberglass boats, and I had two weeks off to lie around and prepare for my return to school. I had also earned a few thousand dollars to take with me.

Some of the old high school crowd were planning a sort of cookout reunion up on Belleair Beach. This was back before Sand Key and the north end of Belleair Beach were developed into condominiums and hotels, and we had plenty of room to build a bonfire and get a little crazy without bothering anyone.

It sounded like everyone planned to attend. Most importantly, some of the Serious Sandbar Standers were going to be there.

The Serious Sandbar Standers was a loosely organized club that we'd started early in high school. At beach get-togethers, a handful of us surfers...all guys...would swim out to the farthest sandbar. Once there, we would...just stand there, looking back at the bonfire on the beach, or up at the busy night skies. I remember spotting my first satellite from a sandbar a quarter-mile off the beach down in Ft. DeSoto Park.

Oftentimes we had irritated our frustrated dates, spending an hour, or more, out on the sandbar, talking softly about life, love and our dreams for the future. Immersed in the warm waters of the Gulf of Mexico.

But college and jobs had separated the Serious Sandbar Standers, and its memory passed into high school lore. So news of a reunion after what then seemed like a long period of time was too much to pass up. Of course, during the ensuing years we learned that the practice could be dangerous, that sharks usually glide across the sandbars at night to feed. But, we had all survived many a "stand," and the thought of one more would not be tarnished by good sense.

THE PARTY LIVED up to all expectations, despite the fact that we had all matured...especially the girls. I smile when I think about it now, but then the years between high school and the party made everyone appear more...sophisticated. And more motivated. We all dressed a little different than we used to, and we all talked a little different than we used to...and about different things. Not to mention that we were all finally of legal drinking age. And me, I felt like a grown man, heading into my senior year at Florida State.

And it was bound to happen. Despite the warnings of other skeptical partiers, and over the groans of our dates, four of the old Serious Sandbar Standers embarked on the last, and most fateful, sandbar adventure in our short history.

It began calmly as we inched our way seaward, shuffling our feet to shoo away any stingrays. There was very little current, and the Gulf swells barely raised the level of the surface. The farther we got away from the beach, the clearer the stars appeared.

We no sooner reached the outer bar, when the water splashed nearby. It was probably a ray or a small fish, but it caused nervous concern among our now wiser group. The sandbar seemed farther out than we remembered, and we were up to our necks in the water.

We laughed nervously and half-joked of sharks and amputations. We found ourselves scanning the water's surface instead of watching the shadowed figures on the shore dancing between us and the bonfire. Or gazing at the beautifully active night sky.

The water behind us ripped again, and without a word, two of our group briskly headed for the beach. And I was left alone on the sandbar with Stevie Peak. We convinced ourselves to stay on the bar…not to "chicken out" and rush back to the beach with the others. So we finished our beers and tried to relax in the warm water.

Suddenly, a large shape broke the surface to my left with a loud thump. Out of the corner of my eye I saw it come out of the water, then submerge. It was coming in my direction…and worst of all, it was as big as I was. Stevie saw it at the same time and froze.

"Uh, oh," he managed to croak in a deathly tone of voice.

"Oh, shit," I replied, spinning around to face the threat. I imagined the razor sharp teeth and the bloodthirsty, unblinking eyes of a demon shark.

Fear in the water is a horrible thing. You feel awkward…you really can't freeze. Rather, you kind of dangle, much like a piece of bait. Swaying and bobbing, constantly off balance.

But the shadows in the water also bobbed, and we quickly realized that they were no more streamlined than we were. Sea turtles, or manatee, I thought, as the panic slowly dissolved to free my stricken limbs.

"Holy, moly," Stevie exclaimed, "…floaters."

Two bales of marijuana had floated into my world.

We spent the better part of the next two hours dragging the bales to a spot down the beach away from the party. While Stevie was excited about our catch…he even swam around the area, in vain, searching for more…I was uncomfortable with it.

I wasn't much of a pot smoker. Hell, the first few times I tried it there seemed to be no effect. But I had nothing against people who did smoke. It actually seemed preferable to alcohol in some cases. Nevertheless, the presence of such a large amount…more than I'd ever seen…set off a tiny alarm in my head.

But Stevie was composed and at the same time, surprisingly

knowledgeable. "We'll come back and pick this up later," he said, grinning in the moonlight.

"Do you know where we can get rid of this stuff?" I asked with a whisper.

Stevie just nodded.

"When...?" I asked, feeling a rush of excitement.

"Maybe tomorrow," he responded, still smiling.

It allowed me to return to college with an additional nine thousand dollars in my pocket. Three times what I had earned laboring all summer over the molds of sailboat hulls.

My first experience with the illegal trade. So many, many years ago.

"So, what'll it be?" Having returned to the room, both agents were now standing over me. They were so close I almost felt physically threatened.

I didn't know what to do...what to say. My only thought was...I was screwed...totally. Worse than that, the peace I had managed to build around me over the past year had suddenly crumbled. I felt like a hunted rabbit, trapped and scared, and my mind raced, searching for a solution.

The hunted rabbit, when cornered...my lawyer, I thought. I gotta call my lawyer.

"Can I call my attorney?" I asked timidly, expecting them to be outraged by the suggestion.

"Good idea," they said together.

"Hey, now calm down, John." His voice was steady. I was trying to tell the whole story at once.

"Owen, look I..."

"First things first. I have an idea why you're calling. Now relax, and tell me where you are calling from." His tone remained positive and reassuring.

I took a couple of breaths. "From an office in the Admin building…"

"Now are you alone? If not, who is there with you?"

"No, I'm here with a couple of guys…agents or something…and they want me…well they're trying to drag me into something I don't know anything about."

I saw them listening to my end of the conversation, and while I was positive they knew it was true that I was not involved, I wanted to keep insisting on that in case there was any doubt.

"Okay," he said calmly. "How are you otherwise…everything else okay?"

"Yeah, I guess." I was relaxing a bit.

"Great. Now why don't you let me speak to one of the agents, and then we'll talk in private afterwards, alright?"

"Good idea," I agreed. I turned around and held out the phone. "He wants to speak to one of you."

The quarterback crossed the office, took the phone and sat on the table next to my chair. "What's his name?" he asked, holding his hand over the receiver.

"Owen Singer," I replied. He smirked, then smiled broadly.

He put the phone up to his ear. "Hello Owen, it's Jeff," he said in a very familiar manner.

Then he winked at me and continued, "We're sitting here with your man, and he's in a lot of trouble."

Owen Singer was an experienced criminal lawyer, not that much older than me. A former prosecutor, he now specialized in drug defense cases. Between prosecuting and defending criminals, Owen got to know several officers, agents and investigators. He had a great reputation around the courthouse. He didn't play games with judges or with prosecutors, and he had won several notable trials over the past four or five years.

The most common complaints heard around the Camp were about attorneys. Every inmate had a lawyer story. How they had been screwed and overcharged, and then locked up and forgotten.

My experience was different. I was satisfied with the way Owen had handled my case. He had charged me fairly, but more importantly, he had comforted my mother throughout the ordeal, and he even still occasionally called her.

Owen even encouraged me to call him, collect, every once in a while from the Camp. And he or his secretary would drop me a line from time to time. Last Christmas, he sent me photos of himself on the golf course, shooting me a bird.

Owen fancied himself a good golfer, but he was always too busy to play. On bail, I managed to get him out on the golf course only twice. I told him that I would have won back my whole legal fee if I could have only gotten him out more often.

We became friends, and I trusted his judgment. In my original case, he was able to reasonably predict what happened later. He told me which charges he could beat. He also honestly told me that my conspiracy charge would be difficult to get around.

Owen explained how conspiracy was a nebulous area of the law. How seemingly innocent acts can link some poor soul with the incredible consequences of a greater scheme. He said that most countries don't even recognize the crime of conspiracy, as it is often unfairly applied. But that the United States not only recognized conspiracy, it embraced it as a powerful crime-fighting weapon.

Feeling that I had little chance to beat the conspiracy charge, he negotiated a great deal for me...guaranteed probation, if I would agree to testify against my co-defendants, and to shed some light on where we got the relatively little amount of pot...some three hundred pounds...my co-defendant was caught with. But they were friends. I could not do it, and I think Owen knew it from the outset. So I went to trial. Hey, it wasn't even in my possession.

At my trial, Owen was tremendous. I was acquitted of my other charges. But I was convicted of the conspiracy charge, as Owen had foreseen, thanks mostly to the testimony of Robbie Tannenbaum, one of the "friends" I had protected.

As much as I hated to admit it, the conspiracy law had probably been applied fairly in my case. I did commit most of the alleged acts, although the prosecutor made the whole thing sound so immoral.

Owen Singer was not displeased. He would get irate over petty or questionable prosecutorial tactics. But he maintained that I had received a fair trial, and he accurately predicted my sentence. Afterwards, he did not bullshit me. He suggested that I do my time like a grownup and learn something from the experience.

THE QUARTERBACK WAS on the phone with Owen for close to twenty minutes. He finished and handed me the phone, saying very formally, "Your attorney has requested that he have a privileged conversation with you alone."

He turned to the FBI man and said, "Let's go." Then, he looked at me and snapped, "When you're finished, we'll be waiting next door."

Singer was livid. I was relieved that he could accurately read what was going on. But I never heard him so upset. It only made me more nervous and distracted, and I barely heard what he was saying.

"Look Owen," I pleaded. "Just tell me this. Can they make this shit stick...or are they just sweating me?"

His words were measured. "Jeff Banner, the DEA agent, is a bad one. I've dealt with him before. He's...everything I can't stand in the system."

He went on to explain that this case had already hit the streets and several arrests had been made. They had not picked up Stevie Peak yet and that angered them more. This was a major effort and they were giving the case top priority. The U.S. Attorney himself was heading the prosecution's team.

He was not answering my question. "Owen..." I started.

"I know...I know what you are asking. Here it is. You are in deep shit. If they have what they say they have...hey, Jeff told me that he showed you a lot of what they got..."

"Yeah. They have a shitload...photos, timelines, informants," I moaned. "And they have me together with Stevie in a couple of bad places..." Goddamn Stevie, I thought. I could taste the acid in my stomach.

Owen was silent. I continued slowly. "Owen, you've always been straight with me, man. Just tell me, do they have any chance of hanging this on me?"

"...yes, they do." He could not be any straighter than that.

"I mean a good chance?"

"If they want to pull all that shit, they can make you look real bad, buddy. But hang on, nothing's happening yet...I told Jeff that I'll come up there on Monday morning. They'll hold off until then."

He paused for a second, then said, "I'll get together with you and we'll take it step by step."

"...One more thing," I choked. "They said I'm looking at...at thirty years. Are they just scaring me?"

"The government has enacted strict new sentencing guidelines to combat the increasing drug trade." Owen sounded like a lawyer again. It was reassuring. He continued, "And this case deals with large amounts of illegal drugs...amounts that call for heavy minimum mandatory sentences. I don't have the statute in front of me, but I think the least they're talking about, for the amount of drugs involved...is twenty years."

"Minimum?" I whispered.

"Minimum, John."

I almost dropped the phone. I couldn't speak coherently. "You mean...they can just...?"

"Listen, John...they are bad men chasing a bad man. But look, I'll be up there on Monday. Try not to get too upset over the weekend. Remember this is a process. It's time to use some of that Stoic strength you've been teaching yourself in there...come on."

"You're right," I said. I took a deep breath. Alright, I told myself. I can make it to Monday. One stage at a time.

"It is important," he concluded, "that when you leave that office today, don't be a wiseass. And don't act like you won't be helpful... they could pull your ass out of that Camp tonight and charge you before I get a chance to talk to them...or to you. Just let me get up there and see what I can do."

"I hear you, man...my best manners."

"That's what I want to hear. Okay, I'll see you Monday." His voice had turned very serious.

I stared at the receiver in my hand for a moment. Then I hung up the phone and walked into the adjoining office. The FBI had already left. Jeff Banner, surprisingly, seemed more sympathetic. He told me to return to my duties. He would return on Monday morning...with a tape recorder.

My heart sank.

Chapter Three

We lived in newly-constructed dormitories that resembled two-story apartment buildings, all wrapped around a pleasant, landscaped courtyard. Each of the three buildings was named after a major city in Alabama...Mobile, Montgomery and Birmingham...and collectively housed about 800 guys. I lived in a cubicle in Birmingham's F-wing. There were two inmates in each cubicle. Each had his own locker and bunk...one guy on the top bunk and one on the bottom. New arrivees were assigned to the top bunks, and would move down as the lower bunks were vacated. I had long since moved to the bottom.

My first bunkie was Michael Sanders, a young former businessman from Mobile. Approximately my age, he was well read and intelligent. He had been convicted of fraudulently selling unregistered securities...phony oil and gas leases. He was halfway through his two-year sentence when I arrived. Seemingly well-adjusted, he helped me through my early weeks at the Camp. It was not surprising that Mike and I became good friends. He subscribed to *Golf Digest* and shared it with me.

When he was released, he gave me his address and phone

number...and the bottom bunk. We swore that we would hit the links together someday.

Just as I had gotten used to having a bunkie whose interests were similar to mine, along came Anthony Washington. About a month after Mike went to the halfway house, Terry High-Five roared into my life. That was his street name.

Arrested on a crack charge in Washington D.C., Terry was actually from Tallahassee, Florida. Since I had graduated from Florida State University, also in Tallahassee, we had something in common. That was the only thing.

We barely even had that in common. He was only twenty-three years old, dark black and extremely animated. His Tallahassee was a completely different one than mine had been. Terry summed it up well, quoting, he said, some famous basketball player; "You drank beer on your side of town, and I drank wine on mine." Yeah, nice quote. Same town...worlds apart.

Mike was meticulous, Terry High-Five was a mess. Mike could hit a 9-iron 145 yards, Terry once put his cousin in the hospital with an 8-iron. "Jack muhfuckin' Nicklaus," he recalled with a satisfied grin. I instantly liked this kid...probably because he was non-stop entertainment. He was never distant, like a stranger, and being with him one-on-one was always disarming.

During the months I bunked with him, I never saw Terry High-Five without his headphones on. They were at least around his neck, along with a cheap chain he brought in from the street. When he took a shower, he hung his phones on the hook with his towel. And every night he would go to sleep with the music pounding in his ears.

Once I tried to make him listen to John Prine. In retaliation, he and a couple of his "hip-hop brothers" held me down and forced me to suffer through Public Enemy.

I missed Mike. I would miss Terry more.

DEPRESSED from the afternoon's events, I had retreated to my bunk, where I was recovering.

A voice exploded in my cube. "Yo, Bunkie, get somewhere." My momentary peace was shattered. Terry High-Five was back from work. Terry was assigned to a work detail at the supply warehouse on the Air Force base. He was constantly pilfering strange items and sneaking them back into the Camp.

"My man, I have scored to-day." He tossed a small item on my bunk.

"Damn Terry, that looks like a computer chip." I examined the microchip. "What the hell are you going to do with this?"

"Is it worth somethin'?" He snatched it out of my hand and held it up to the light.

"Sure it is," I said. His enthusiasm for nonsense always made me smile.

"Then I'll wear the muhfucker around my neck." He pulled his chain necklace over his head. Then he sat down on the floor and started looking for ways to attach the microchip to his chain.

"Terry, it's expensive. And it's contraband. Christ, they catch you with that around your neck and they'll ship your butt to Atlanta."

He hesitated for a moment and looked up at me. Then he put his chain back on, reached down and pulled his high-top sneakers out from under the bunk. "Got any tape?" he asked me.

I gave him some tape from my locker. He tore off a piece and taped the chip to the top of one of his shoes. Then he gave me a big smile and announced, "Now I ain't nothin' nice. I'm Computer Man. Plug me in and watch this muhfucker fly." He leaped in the air, stuck out his tongue like Michael Jordan and spun as if to deliver a reverse jam on some imaginary basket.

Vintage Anthony Washington. He found a use for everything he lifted.

Eventually, Terry noticed that I was upset. I told him generally what had happened. He felt badly for me…he actually shut up and sat on the edge of my bunk to listen. However, I could not convince him that I was not guilty of the vast conspiracy looming over me. He had spent too much time in county jails and other lockups before coming to Maxwell, and he had heard too many men profess their innocence.

But guilt or innocence meant nothing to him. His only concern was beating the rap. And making me feel better.

"Can I have yo' dictionary when you leave?" He laughed out loud at his own joke. My dictionary meant as much to him as a cinder block.

I laughed too. "What would you do with my dictionary, man, tape it to your other shoe?"

We laughed. Terry's eyes were wet.

Suddenly I stopped laughing. Something hit me wrong. Terry was uneducated, but not unintelligent. He had recognized something I had not.

"I wonder when I'd have to leave," I said softly, somehow already sensing the answer.

Terry answered the question honestly. "Homeboy, it sound like you be history on Monday."

I remembered Owen Singer had said something about them being able to take me out of the Camp. Of course, if they charged me with Stevie's huge conspiracy, they would hold me somewhere other than a minimum-security camp. Shit, then I would be sentenced to heavy time at some higher-level institution.

"Shit…shit," my voice was low.

"Whassup?" Terry leaned in close.

"I don't know, T. I think you just rang a bell." I sat frozen.

"Are you going to say anything to that dude tomorrow?"

"What dude?"

"Oh, man, that dude…the salt of the muhfuckin' earth," he said, mimicking my voice. "Yo visitor."

"Oh, I forgot...I forgot all about my visit. Shit, I'd better call it off."

NORMAN JANUARY WAS my best friend in the world. The salt of the earth, I always said, when describing him to anyone.

Stormin' Norman was laid back...a gentle soul with wire rimmed "John Lennon" glasses and long sandy hair, usually pulled back in the ponytail of an old hippie. He was my roommate in college, where we met. We took an instant liking to each other and our friendship developed fast. We shared every secret and every adventure for years. People began to view us as a team...Johnand-Norman, NormanandJohn, they would say, as if it were one person they were speaking of.

But we weren't one person. We were two distinctly different individuals, and in that difference lay the strength of the relationship. He was frugal where I was a showboat. He was quiet where I was loud. Actually, the differences in our personalities were dramatic, but somehow the underlying chemistry formed a lasting bond.

We used to bore people with stories about our adventures together...how we started out for Woodstock, but never made it past Atlanta; our failed attempts at importing suede coats from Istanbul; or how I finally talked him into moving to St. Petersburg...each story meaningful to us.

It was only natural that I was the best man at his wedding. And only natural that he was one of the only people who continued to write. He and his wife, Judy, sent me funny cards and pictures all the time.

And tomorrow, bright and early Saturday morning, he would be here again to visit me. I could not call it off. I tried...I called and talked with Judy. But Stormin' was already on the road. He was driving the nine hours up from Florida with another friend, Larry Martin, and they had already departed.

Terry had asked me if I would tell my visitor about what was happening. Of course I would tell Norman...every damn detail. "Wait 'till he hears this shit," I mumbled to myself.

It was Friday night. There was a full moon and I was restless.

THE INMATES WERE PERMITTED to use the phone room until 10:00 pm. The room contained twenty-eight phones. It resembled the phone bank at an airport, except only collect calls could be made from each of these phones. It was from this room that I had earlier phoned Judy.

My anxiety continued to build into the night. Finally, at about 9:30 I decided to return to the phone room and call Owen Singer. I tried his home number and, thankfully, he answered and accepted my call.

Unlike the phones in the administration offices, these phones could be monitored by officers assigned for that purpose. One had to be careful discussing anything of a confidential nature. Owen was well aware of that.

We chatted briefly. Since this afternoon he said he had received additional information about the situation, but we couldn't get into details. Though there was one critical question I needed addressed. "Owen, should I be getting my affairs in order? Will I be here much longer?"

He answered by saying that Monday would prove to be a real showdown. It was his opinion that they thought I would eventually cooperate. And if I basically satisfied them, my situation would not change.

"Man, it doesn't look good," I muttered. Cooperation seemed to be the only sane alternative. Owen didn't say so, but it hung in the air like the aroma from Terry's stale socks.

"I know it looks grim, John, but I promise you that I'll be there with you through every step of the way. We have some things to discuss but let's do that on Monday when we can have some privacy."

One last thing. "Tell me truthfully, what if they are…not satisfied?"

He hesitated. He was thinking. I know he had a lot to say. And I knew that he would fight this to the end. That this kind of unethical behavior appalled him. But while he was fighting them, a contest that appeared more and more desperate, he clearly understood what I was asking him. Should I be ready to move?

After a moment, he said, "Have your bags packed, just in case."

I really didn't need him to tell me. I already knew that if I failed to cooperate, they had the power to make things extremely uncomfortable for me. And the first thing they would do would be to move me. "You gotta get your mind right," I remember them telling Cool Hand Luke in the movie as they punished him. Now, they would ship me to a real prison somewhere to get my mind right.

I walked back from the phone room to the dorm. The moon was still high.

It was a sleepless night. When dawn broke, and we were permitted to leave the dorms, I went for a walk on River Road. Strangely, I was not tired.

I walked down to the river and watched the sun rise over the trees. I was alone in the early morning mist…a thin, knee-high shroud that rose off the surface of the river every morning this time of year. Although the sun would burn away the mist within the hour, its presence at dawn created a temporary dreamlike state.

I moved along in slow motion, as if in a trance, trying to get a grip on a barrage of contrasting emotions. The sudden upheaval in the simple regimented life I was living had me reeling. After spending the whole night awake and feeling sorry for myself, I passed through a curious stage of…feeling betrayed, although I wasn't sure exactly who or what had betrayed me.

But as the sun rose, my emotions began to turn…to anger. I raged at the unfairness of the situation, and at the state of helplessness that overwhelmed me. I was angry at the system, and even more angry at myself.

I took a deep breath…almost springtime.

"Fuck them," I grunted out loud. "Fuck them all."

I walked along the road. The birds ignored my approach and chattered through their breakfasts. I got to the stake…the stake that marked the furthest boundary we could go to. I stopped there and looked down the road as far as I could.

River Road stretched along the riverbank. And although the golf course was still wet with dew, gentle gusts of wind kicked up spirals of dust in front of me, as if beckoning me to follow along the trail.

Out there, I thought, people don't have to worry about this kind of shit. Out there people are waking up and beginning their weekends. Out there.

The solution hit me like a clean breath of air. "Fuck them…I'm outta here."

I had found my alternative. Escape.

Suddenly, I realized I was not alone. Trailing behind me was prison guard Lieutenant Gene Wilson. "Mean Gene" Wilson.

Today was visiting day, and on visiting days Lt. Wilson would often walk the road early in the morning, looking for packages dropped during the night. Sometimes an inmate's wife or friend would leave clothes, food or money to be picked up later by the inmate.

"Good morning, Mr. Bellamy," he said to me.

"Mornin' Lieutenant." His presence sobered me like a slap in the face.

"Out for an early morning walk?" His eyes searched the ground behind me.

"Yes, sir. It's a beautiful morning." I was sure that I had "escape" written all over my face.

He looked me over, probably deciding whether or not to search me. Instead, he asked, "How much weight have you lost?"

"Twenty one pounds, sir." It amused me, momentarily, that I knew exactly how much.

"Well, you look a hell of a lot better than when you first got here." He laughed, then added, "You have a visit today?"

"Yes, later this morning."

He nodded and said, "Have a nice visit." Then he walked on. Without smiling, he glanced back at me as if to say something further. But he didn't speak. He just continued his stroll.

His sudden appearance reminded me that one doesn't just run away. Damn, if I was really going to do this, I needed a plan... before Monday.

I TOOK a shower and waited for them to page me for visitation... which they did almost immediately. Stormin' Norman was waiting for me alone. Larry Martin was not on my visiting list. He had come along to help Norman drive the long hours up from St. Petersburg to Montgomery. Larry was back at the motel room, asleep.

We hugged, and found an empty table in the visiting yard. He looked me over and said, "Man, every time I see you, I can't get over how fantastic you look."

"Yeah, well don't tell me that prison life agrees with me." We laughed…a laughter that had been shared for years.

At that point, I had been over what was happening to me so many times in my mind that I could recite it readily. Norman was stunned…but not as stunned as when I informed him what my solution was going to be.

I told him my plan. Simply, we were permitted to wear our civilian clothes on the weekends. I would put on a jogging suit, with a golf shirt underneath, and run out with the first group of Air Force joggers that came through the Camp and down River Road.

It would have been much safer to escape from my work detail when I was away from the Camp. But I would not work until Monday, and anyway, Monday I was being held out of work for interrogation. It had to be Saturday or Sunday.

I explained to Norman that I needed a little help. I could not carry anything with me, so I would need some extra clothes, and some money. I also told him that assisting me was probably a crime, so he should stay as far away as possible. But, that I was hoping that he'd leave a small bag for me.

As I suggested a location, he interrupted. He leaned in close and said softly, "No. You come down that road, and I'll be there to pick you up, pard. And we'll haul ass."

I couldn't speak. He looked directly into my eyes and smiled. Then he grabbed my shoulders and said, "No argument…that's the way it's going to be."

"I love you, man," I finally said.

We agreed it would be after the Camp's 4:00 pm count, so I would be long gone by the 10:00 pm count. If successful, it would give us a five or six hour head start. We also agreed not to tell Larry. He would stay in the motel room until we came by to pick him up on the way out of town.

I warned Stormin' to be careful on River Road. I advised him not to come up too far towards the Camp…to let me run to him. And to keep a sharp eye out for the heat.

"Just like the old days," he said. "I won't let you down. But let's not wait 'till Sunday…let's do it today."

We agreed. We set the time, and refreshed ourselves on some old hand signals. We also went over a few contingency plans.

"Thanks, man," I said.

"Don't even say it," he replied. "You've been there for me too many times."

As he left the visiting yard, I was praying that we would not need hand signals or contingency plans.

I walked back to the dorm to prepare.

Later, I went over the whole situation in my mind. My conclusion was drawn. I had to go. Besides, even if they catch me, "What are they gonna do," I asked myself out loud, "throw me in jail?"

IT WAS A CLEAR AFTERNOON, and there were several joggers and walkers out on the road. Without stretching, I started down the hill behind a loose group of about six or seven runners. Their easy pace felt good.

As I headed between the river and the lake, I saw Terry High-Five walking up the road, telling war stories to two amused Jamaicans. He was waving his arms, using the exaggerated gestures of a storyteller who was bending the truth.

As I jogged by him, he looked over and smiled. "Yo, Bunkie, you workin' it out," he shouted.

"Hey Computer Man," I called back. "Look under your pillow."

I had to leave everything. After destroying a few personal items like my address book, I'd slipped my dictionary under Terry's pillow. Sooner or later he'd get the message.

I continued on, not sure if he'd even heard me, for his headphones were over his ears, blasting away.

Maxwell was not constructed to prevent escapes. People rarely tried to escape from minimum-security institutions. And there was rarely any staff out on River Road. It looked easy.

I ran down River Road, holding a steady pace just behind the small group of joggers. Eventually, we approached the stake marking the 'invisible line'. I swallowed hard. I quickly glanced around, looking for any indication of trouble. In a few seconds there would be no turning back.

My heart began to pound as we closed on the stake. I began to experience second thoughts, and slowed my pace ever so slightly.

But I was committed, and it was no time to turn back. I had to focus my attention on the task ahead. I put my head down and pumped my arms harder, accelerating as I passed by the tiny white marker.

I exhaled heavily, blowing twice, in an attempt to clear my head. I was now an escapee. Damn, I thought, what have I done?

I didn't even look back, but concentrated on the road ahead. There was no sign of Norman as I continued to run around the perimeter of the golf course. And I was beginning to tire. My heart was still pounding wildly and the runners ahead of me began to pull away.

Norman was using his head, I reasoned…or hoped. He would not want to pull over by the side of the road this close to the Camp.

It surprised me that I was tiring so soon. I was in good shape, and I was used to running almost daily. Perhaps the stress, mixed with the lack of sleep, was taking its toll…but I was laboring.

Up ahead, there were two cars and a small truck parked haphazardly by the river…weekend fishermen. And there was Stormin' Norman, leaning on the back of his car fiddling with a fishing rod. Perfect.

"Just in time," I puffed, slowing down.

"Nice hat…" I was startled by a woman's voice right beside me. Goddamn!

There she was, the girl of my dreams, little Captain joggerette, running alongside me, apparently complimenting my G&S Surfboard hat.

I had run by her at least once or twice a week for the past eighteen months. I would nod, I would smile, and sometimes I would just stare. She had to recognize me from the Camp.

Before I could stop myself, I tugged at the brim of my hat. Some disguise, I thought, although my thoughts were clouded by my fatigue. I had put the damn thing on to alter my looks a bit. Besides, I did not want to leave my favorite hat behind.

I flashed Norman the danger sign…one closed fist…as we passed under his nose. I did not stop running. There was no sense having a witness see me…him…his car…everything.

We continued jogging around the curve of the road. Without looking back, I could hear Norman starting his car behind me.

THE LACK of rest began to nag at my legs. By now, I had lost track of how far I had come. I still had not spoken to her, and it was difficult to think on the run. I figured that I would just slow down and allow her to run on, then double back to Norman before he drove off.

As I slowed my pace down to a walk, a patrolling Military Policeman suddenly appeared from around the bend in the road. He cruised toward me at about 15 miles an hour, looking at the joggers. I froze.

Just as suddenly, she took my hand and walked along with me. "I said, nice hat," she repeated cheerfully.

Exhausted, I looked into her beautiful face. Shaken, I actually said, "Will you marry me?" She was laughing heartily as the MP passed by. If he's any kind of man, I mused, he's looking at her face, not mine. But he breezed by us and continued up the road.

Norman pulled up abruptly beside us. "Come on, partner," he said nervously, looking into his rear view mirror.

I stopped…I didn't know what to say. She squeezed my hand and whispered, "Good luck." I couldn't believe it.

I went to get in the car. Then I turned around and put my hat on her head, pulling it down over her ears. She giggled.

"Thank you," I said, as I stared at her face for one more second. I was overcome.

I really wanted to kiss her. But instead, I hopped into Norman's car. She waved.

I was gone.

Chapter Four

I was on the run. We took the Interstate south out of Montgomery and headed for Panama City, Florida. While it was only a few hours drive, it was a world of difference away, and I could be safe there for a few days. And off the road.

Because of the suddenness of the situation, I was unprepared for the days ahead. I needed to gather together some money, as well as sufficient identification to move around. It was now our plan to rent a condominium on the beach for a week. Larry would stay with me while Norman went home to round up some cash and shop around for a reliable set of phony IDs.

Larry Martin had readily enlisted into the escape enterprise. He was, at first, shocked to see me at the motel when we went to pick him up.

"What in the hell are you doing here?" he shouted in surprise when I rushed through the door.

"Look, we don't have much time," I answered firmly. "I escaped, and I have to get out of town...right now."

Larry sat on the bed and fumbled to make himself a drink. "But..." he started to say.

"Listen, Larry," Norman interrupted, "we'll explain it all later. We gotta go."

Norman briefly told Larry that he had been an accessory to my escape, and that he planned on staying with me until I was safe. He advised Larry to catch a plane home.

Given the opportunity to separate himself from the crime, Larry acted like the suggestion was an insult. He was excited to be part of it and he demanded to go with us. He called us the "Escape Brothers."

I HAD KNOWN Larry Martin for a few years. About ten years ago he had been a driver for Charles "Dog" Gregory, driving pot up from the Keys to Toledo, Ohio.

Larry didn't get wealthy, but he did put together just enough money to open a surf shop on Clearwater Beach, where I met him. It was in a prime location, and it should have been a booming business. But Larry partied when he should have been working. His was not an uncommon story among get-rich-quick players. He was inexperienced, and not responsible enough to realize what was happening. He lost his whole investment.

But the party didn't stop. Now here he was, coming out of the Mini-mart with a 12-pack of Heineken and a bag of ice. I was elated to be free, but Larry's exuberance added to the excitement. One would have thought that he was escaping with me.

I leaned up against the back of the car, while Norman pumped the gas. "I thought it would take some adjustment...but it's easy," I said.

"What's that?" Norman looked up.

"You know...being out...just cruising down the road again."

The car door was open and the music was blaring out. "Listening to tapes for one thing," I continued.

"I thought all you guys had Sony Walkmen in there," Larry interjected, as he walked back toward the cashier.

"Nah, no tapes allowed...only AM-FM headphones," I replied, thinking briefly of Terry.

My attention turned to the music in the car. "Jeez, Stormin', I haven't heard Little Feat for eighteen months."

Larry yelled from the ice machine, "Hey, you think two six-packs will be enough?"

We laughed. "Looks like you'll be in good hands," Norman said, shaking his head.

"Maybe you should take him with you," I joked.

I pushed myself away from the car, and yawned. It was a beautiful sunset. Bands of bright stripes, from blood coral to fiery orange, colored the lumpy outstretched clouds. Beyond the brilliant colors, an eternity of deepwater blue filled the sky. It was still light, but two stars were already visible overhead.

I reflected on the sunrise earlier this morning out on River Road. What a difference...to be free.

I turned to Norman. "Hey Stormin'...thanks again, I mean it."

He grinned. "We did pretty good, didn't we? How'd you like my fishing pole?"

"Ha...where did you come up with that?" I was getting giddy, and I yawned again. I was finally winding down.

"It was in the trunk. The reel is busted." He chuckled at the memory. "I'm glad I didn't have to do any real fishing."

"You never could catch anything...even with a good reel," I joked.

"Yeah...well I caught a big one today," he countered and pointed at me. "The catch of the day."

I grinned and nodded. It was all too good to be true.

We climbed into the car, Larry at the wheel, and me stretched out in the back. Dusk was falling. I grabbed a cold bottle of Heineken and relaxed.

Norman turned around in his seat, and said softly, "Hey, John?"

"Yeah?" I answered, almost dozing off.

"She was beautiful..."

"Yeah, man...I know." She was almost a dream, clouding my sleepy eyes. I could picture the short blonde ringlets surrounding her healthy cameo-like face. Just once I would love to have seen her in uniform.

"Did she know?" he asked.

I reviewed today's adventure on River Road in my mind. How could she not know?

"She knew," I concluded.

I was asleep before my second sip of beer.

P.C. Panama City. Formerly Florida's best kept secret.

"Ain't it great to be alive and in Panama City," was a slogan I had heard several times over the past years. Whenever the action was dying down, the bartender or party host would get up on a table, raise his glass and howl at the top of his lungs, "Ain't it great to be alive and in Panama City." The crowd always responded to this battle cry. They would immediately re-charge, refuel and rally late...into the morning hours.

Up in the Florida panhandle, the beaches at Panama City begin a stretch of the most beautiful, sugar-fine sandy beaches in the world. The gateway to the "Redneck Riviera," running from Florida to Mississippi...where one out of two people claims to be an expert fisherman, and two out of two claim to have gotten high with Kenny Stabler, the legendary pro football quarterback and folk hero.

The multitudes had finally discovered Panama City. In fact, we pulled into town the weekend before "Spring Break" began. Spring Break in Panama City is a madhouse...thousands upon thousands of vacationing students with no place to put them all.

"If you want to get drunk and look at beautiful women, go to

Lauderdale. If you want to get drunk and get laid, go to P.C."... another slogan, which perhaps accounted for the coming hordes.

We were lucky to find a place on the beach. Almost everything was reserved for the coming celebration. Within a week every hotel, every condo, every cottage...every available room of any sort...would be filled. At the same time, every restaurant, gift shop, amusement park, putt-putt golf course and parking lot would be jammed with sweaty, underfed, oversexed partiers.

"Money talks," Larry puffed. But in our case, it was more like good timing. Several new units, previously unreserved, had just opened up. One more day and they too would be gone.

MY FIRST NIGHT out of prison was not the fantasy I had always envisioned. No wine, women or song. Rather, I slept soundly...the dreamless sleep of an exhausted animal of burden.

By habit, I awoke at dawn. Norman slept restlessly. He heard me moving around and got up. Larry slept until noon.

Norman didn't waste any time. He settled us in, and made arrangements to return home that night. "Spring break won't really be in full swing until next weekend," he said. "I should be back by then to get you out of here."

After Larry finally got up, we stocked up on food from the local supermarket, and bought me a couple of T-shirts and shorts from a little surf shop. I enjoyed the shopping...hell, I was like a little kid, trying on everything in the surf shop, and throwing exotic foods into the basket at the food store. Norman and Larry laughed at my enthusiasm. Freedom, believe me, is all about the little things in life.

Back at the condo we reviewed our situation, and the methods and times for making phone calls from the pay phone. Norman was really on top of things. He had it all worked out for us.

"You're my hero," I said.

He bowed graciously, then said seriously, "I called Judy from the store. I didn't say where I was, but she knows generally what I'm up to."

"That's cool," I said, meaning it.

"She also said she loves you…and she's scared."

Larry popped a beer and cracked, "She seems to be the only one scared."

"Maybe we all ought to be a little scared," I remarked. But in my mind, I felt no fear, only relief. Relief from the vice that had, only yesterday, gripped my every thought. But it went beyond that. I was also light-headed over being freed from the constant supervision I had over me at the Camp.

"You'll be okay here awhile…" Norman reassured me, patting my shoulder.

Larry took a long swallow of his cold beer. "Besides," he bellowed, "we can't be taken alive…we're the Escape Brothers."

He handed us each a bottle, and we held them high, crossing them in the air like swords. "The Escape Brothers," we chanted in unison.

"Do you want me to call your mom?" Norman asked.

His car was packed and gassed up. He was ready to leave. We were all set up in the condo for the week, and he had left me a few hundred dollars. Larry had some money too, but these days he never had much…if he could just pay his own bar bill we'd be fine.

"No, it probably wouldn't be a good idea," I answered. "That'll be the first place they stake out. You might call Owen Singer and ask him to call my mother later in the week to say I'm safe…but no details.

Norman nodded. He understood. "Do you want me to call anybody else?"

"No. It's best you don't tell anyone anything. Let me get settled first...and safe."

I thought for a moment, and continued, "Oh, hey...and listen, if they take the time to check who visited me yesterday, your name will come up..."

"You think they might suspect me?" He grimaced slightly.

"Wouldn't you?" I answered honestly. They could be looking to question him already...what a can of worms that would be.

He pondered this new twist for a second, then he shrugged his shoulders, threw his suitcase in the back seat and climbed into his car. He started the engine, lowered his window and stuck his head out.

"Okay, partner, this is it...can you think of anything else?"

I could only imagine how much more difficult this whole thing would have been without his assistance. I'm not sure I could have pulled this off alone. Hell, I should thank him every day I'm free. Instead, I held up my hands and said, "What more can I say, buddy."

"Don't even start. I know what you're thinking," he began. "John, we're pards. And remember Horseshoe Beach...if you hadn't come back for me..."

"Horseshoe Beach," I exclaimed. "That was a long, long time ago, man."

"Yeah, well I have a long, long memory...and...you can't be any happier to see me now than I was to see you then..." He was about to say more, but he realized Larry was listening and hesitated for a moment. Then he concluded, "Got it?"

"Yeah, I got it. K. I. forever," I responded.

"K. I.," he saluted. And he was off.

K. I....THAT was what we named our mutual admiration society. Kids Incorporated. The K. I. bond was established years ago, and formalized on a surfboard off Cocoa Beach. The bond was simple…the kids took care of each other.

We swore that we would be friends forever, and always look out for each other's best interests. There was no ritual involved in the pledge, other than those actions required of one of us, from time to time, to assist the other.

As undefined as this principle might seem to outsiders, its meaning was very clear to Norman and me. It had been tested over the years, and even though we had gone our separate ways after Norman married Judy over six years ago, our loyalty remained steadfast.

And now, that same chivalric vow, trumpeted with bravado by two foolish young men years ago, held together once again during troubled times. Even an avowed pessimist would have to concede, looking at Norman and me, that some bonds don't break.

It made me feel…great to be alive and in Panama City.

PANAMA CITY WAS AS FAR from home as Montgomery was, just in a different direction. In the past, we would occasionally take a road trip to P.C. to get out of town and away from it all. I was not known or expected there…besides, it had been a few years since my last visit.

Still, I had to be careful. I had to keep my attention focused on the mission at hand. Nevertheless, Larry was a professional partier, and I had been cooped up for a year and a half. Adjustments to the plan might have to be made.

LARRY WALKED along with me while I explained to him the dilemma that had forced my decision to escape. He shook his head in disbelief as I recounted the series of events that led me to his motel room.

It was a gorgeous spring day. There had been a little nip in the air last night…the last breath of winter's passing. But this day was warm and sunny.

The sandpipers scurried along the water's edge, running up and down the wet sand, following the flow of the waves. The pelicans were feeding just beyond the breakers, dive-bombing the shallow water in search of their shiny prey.

I stretched in the sun. "Heaven," I sighed. Two days ago, the last thing I had expected to be doing was strolling along the beach, throwing shells into the Gulf of Mexico.

"Shit, John, you look great," Larry said, looking over the change in me.

I had not seen Larry since I went away. I guess the change was dramatic. I was trim, and my body seemed to respond to its sudden freedom on the beach much like a race horse anticipates the starter's gun. My skin bristled in the seabreeze, my legs ready to spring into a run at any second. I felt alive and electric.

I looked at Larry. He was puffy-eyed and bloated, a victim of too many late nights. I chuckled, remembering that same look in my own mirror.

"Larry, you look like shit, man…don't you…"

"Hey, now," he interrupted, "I pay good money to look like this." I suppose if you added up his bar bill and his drug bill he had a point. We laughed…that's exactly what he was referring to. "In fact, let's double back for a cold one," he suggested.

I was just getting started. I pointed ahead and said, "Let's walk up to that point and then go back."

Larry twisted his face in mock horror. "You gotta be crazy. You'd have to carry me back."

We reached a compromise…I would go on ahead while Larry went back to hold down the fort.

So I was alone. And as I walked along the beach, it dawned on me that I would soon be by myself. Norman might have a couple of weeks, at best, with me, but Judy couldn't handle their surf shop alone indefinitely. And anyway, he had his own life to live.

God only knows how long I would have Larry to hang around with. He had a bartending job back home at Clancy's, our regular hangout. He was not due back until Thursday night, and we agreed that he would call in then...to take another week off. "Mr. Responsibility," he called himself.

In any event, sooner or later I would be on my own for good. Now, since I had a week or two to think about it, I decided to take a couple days to recover my balance before making any decisions. I wondered though, whether it would ever be safe enough to return to St. Petersburg...and when.

Over the next two days, I relished my freedom. I ran in the morning, swam in the afternoon, and took long walks under the stars. Oddly enough, now that I was not doing time, I had more time on my hands. Even in a minimum-security institution an inmate's life was somewhat structured. Now without the ordered routine, I was a little lost.

"I got out of there just in time," I told Larry. It was apparent that I had become more institutionalized than I'd realized.

But Larry was bored. Every little thing I love about being free, Larry had long since taken for granted. I remembered the feeling, so I could sympathize with him...but I was amused. And I had to laugh when watching TV with Larry. I thought he would fit in well in the Camp TV room...he'd watch anything.

I tried to persuade him to join me in my routine. He did occasionally, but he never lasted long. On top of all that, Norman had taken the car. Ironically, we responded in different ways. I felt free. Larry felt trapped.

It was past time, though, for me to get out and mix. To Larry's credit he never complained about being housebound. He assumed I was hiding out to be safe from capture. In truth, although I had enjoyed our shopping foray to the supermarket and the occasional 7-11 run, I still felt an odd sense of embarrassment in public.

I recalled that, when I was out on bail, I experienced a similar feeling. It wasn't necessarily the publicity attached to my arrest. It was something I could never really explain...a feeling of dejection and of being lost. Who knows, at the time I figured it was the result of depression. In any event, it inhibited me socially.

Imprisoned, the feeling had simply disappeared. Now its reappearance was disturbing. And I knew it was time for me to get out and deal with this awkwardness before it became crippling.

It was time because I had a specialist with me. The party doctor...Doctor Larry Martin.

It was absolutely incredible to be alone in the bathroom. Not having to share the space with several other guys who were always talking, or singing, or shouting...a ceaseless inmate cacophony. I especially enjoyed not being hurried...being able to take my time as I shaved or brushed my teeth in the cool, quiet little room. And it was ecstasy to be able to walk around the bathroom in my bare feet, not needing shower shoes to protect me against the bacteria that runs rampant in public bath facilities. I never appreciated that luxury until I was deprived of it, and I wiggled my toes gratefully on the soft towel under my feet.

I stood in the middle of the floor. I had been shaving...but the razor hung in my hand and I found myself taking a long look at my reflection in the mirror.

They say that no matter how old a man gets, he can still see some of the boy in the mirror. But that boy did not appear before me. Instead, I saw a man approaching middle-age, with flecks of grey in his hair and a distinct weathering around the eyes...though the age was not unattractive, just a fact of life. In fact, I was in better shape than I was ten years ago, and the clean regimen of Camp life had restored a certain vitality and clarity to my eyes. I grudgingly admitted to myself that my time there had been well spent.

But now what...where do I go from here, I thought. So many dreams and big plans behind me, and an incredibly uncertain future. As I wondered what lay ahead, I stood there in front of the mirror, like an ancient journeyer hypnotized by the full moon...

"Look out ladies." Larry cleared the deck of private thoughts as he barged into the bathroom and snapped me out of my trance.

"A couple of...wild and crazy guys," he mimicked, shoving a beer under my nose. I waved him away.

"How about a blast?" he said, offering his oversized coke vial.

"Let me finish in here, you animal," I laughed.

Larry opened his arms. "Just look at you," he said, "the women will devour you." Then he charged out of my bathroom howling like a hungry wolf.

I smiled at myself in the mirror. This might really be fun.

Chapter Five

It was a spacious, multi-leveled club built atop the sand dunes… undoubtedly a popular destination in Panama City from the looks of its huge parking lot. It was once completely destroyed… knocked flat by Hurricane Camille many years ago. But it rose from its own ruins, like the Phoenix. Now bigger and better, the Spinnaker II served as a beacon for the young and the thirsty.

Inside, it was crowded and smoky, and an unending stream of sweaty couples elbowed by me on their way to and from the dance floor. And it was loud…the kind of loud that would leave your ears ringing long into the next day.

Best of all was the music. Not the deejay that was so prevalent in most of these dance clubs, but a six-piece Cajun powerhouse party band billed as Atchafalaya…named after a swamp.

They stretched from one end of the small stage to the other, each player working a different section of the crowd. They looked like hot-blooded young bayou boys, long-haired and bearded… casually ripping through aggressive, ear-splitting licks on their instruments. They were tight…shit, they were great. Goddamn I missed this, I thought, and I edged closer to the stage.

I smiled as the drummer occasionally threw a drumstick from the stage to the shrieking girls in the crowd. He was different from the rest of his bandmates. He wasn't wearing jeans and a T-shirt. Instead, he had the look of a Los Angeles heavy metal rocker... clean-shaven, with his teased long blond hair and his colorful, heavily studded leather clothes...clearly the darling of the female audience.

He noticed my amusement, grinned at me as he slapped his snare-drum, and with an uncanny accuracy, flipped a drumstick in my direction. I caught the stick, saluted him with it, then gave it to a scantily dressed redhead perched next to me. He leaned back and laughed as the girl hugged me appreciatively. I winked as if to ask, "is that all it takes?" He laughed again, acknowledging my gesture.

Eventually I settled in at the end of the bar and away from the stage while Larry went to make his moves. It was a bit quieter there...like the flight line at a busy airport. But that was preferable to the jackhammer convention on the other side of the room near the stage, where the band had whipped the crowd into a frenzy. Damn.

I was enjoying myself. Women were everywhere. While most had come off the beach wearing bright shorts or sexy sundresses, many had taken the time required to make some sort of fashion statement...adorned in newly purchased outfits and sporting contemporary jewelry. Obviously prepared for Spring Break. It didn't matter to me, I loved them all.

And so many of them. After being confined for so long, it seemed like all the women in the world had descended upon Panama City. And to think that Spring Break had not even officially begun yet. Next week, oh my.

I had made a friend. Her name was Cissy...a tiny, athletic-looking bartender who constantly checked on my progress. I forgot which came first, her friendliness or my tipping well. They soon merged, however, and it wasn't long before she was suggesting which girls I should be dancing with.

"Her," she would point, "she's your type...she looks like real road tang." And we would laugh together.

I looked forward to Cissy passing my end of the bar, with an occasional selection, always laced with her attractive mix of sweetness and vulgarity.

Larry pushed through the crowd and joined me. "Look," he shouted, waving in the direction of the liquor bottles. "They serve your favorite rum. Get rid of that beer...doctor's orders."

I surrendered without a fight, saying "Why not," and I ordered a Mount Gay, mixed with orange juice. Cissy suggested that I try a splash of pineapple juice on top...presto, I found a new drink. She flashed a proud smile.

"Wow," Larry exclaimed. "Who's the little spinner?"

"That's Cissy," I said longingly.

He watched her move along the bar. "I'm in lust," Larry moaned. "Good going, son."

I shook my head. "I got nothing going. She has a boyfriend... some bartender from across the street. He's already been in here twice."

"Maybe so," Larry replied, still staring at her. "But she likes you too."

"How can she not?" I boasted, and we smiled. Larry nodded his head and slapped me on the back, as if to say, "That's the spirit."

I was feeling good. The strange awkwardness I was experiencing earlier had vanished. I bought a round of Tequila for the band, and they officially pronounced me a "swamp rocker."

I felt really free for the first time.

Cissy's boyfriend reappeared and they took a break together. So I went to search for Larry. I found him on the deck out back with a drunken beach angel on his lap. They were trying to sober up.

"Want a blast?" he asked me, holding up his vial.

I didn't want to intrude. "Nah, maybe later," I said, attempting to slip away. Larry stopped me, saying, "Oh yeah, John, this is Betty." They were both drunk.

"Nooo…it's Beverly." She punched him softly and giggled.

"Yeah, thas right, Beverly." He held his hand over his face, embarrassed. We all laughed.

As she laughed, she turned toward me and my eyes were drawn to her chest…strikingly buxom, and barely concealed by her tight, cropped T-shirt. She followed my eyes and smiled knowingly.

I winked at Larry. He responded with the goofy grin of a man about to have a picnic.

THE CLUB WAS BUILT on the beach, with a broad deck overlooking the water. Volleyball nets were set up below the deck bar. In the coming days, the beach behind the Spinnaker II would be blanketed with Hobie Cats, powerboats, and thousands of young nymphs and drunken satyrs.

I walked out to the end of the deck and stared at the moon high over the calm Gulf. I was a bit groggy. Although I was trying to moderate my drinking, my head was still not used to alcohol. I took a few deep breaths of the salty night air. Cissy must have beefed up the drinks, I thought.

Those thoughts were disturbed by loud voices. The beach was already crowded, even at night. Couples were strolling hand in hand, and small groups of revelers were shrieking with laughter along the water's edge.

But the loud voices I heard were arguing heatedly. A couple had come up from the beach onto the deck, obviously angry with each other about something. As they approached where I was standing, I saw the guy slap his girlfriend. She swung her closed fist back at him, and missed. Infuriated, she screamed, "Fuck you," and ran back into the club, while her boyfriend stormed off, talking to himself.

She ran right by me. It was Cissy.

THE CROWD WAS THINNING OUT, and the emptying bar smelled of perspiration and cigarettes as I approached Cissy's station. She was wiping off the bar-top and stacking glasses.

Apparently still upset, she managed a weak smile when I offered to buy her a drink.

"You're sweet," she said, touching my cheek.

I was about to ask her to go somewhere after the bar closed, when Larry and Beverly staggered into me. "Party at our place," Larry loudly pronounced. "And we don't need a cab…Betsy's got a car."

"…Beverly…," she slurred, so softly that only I heard. This one doesn't have long to go, I thought.

"Okay everybody, let's go," Larry commanded. A small group of red-eyed volunteers and band members trailed behind him.

He turned to Cissy, and pointed, "You too, honey."

She blushed and looked at me.

"You want to come…?" I asked, a little surprised by the situation.

Larry and his merry group were already piling out the door and into the parking lot. Cissy thought about it for a second, bit her lip, and replied, "Got any coke?"

COCAINE. Everybody's favorite party. There was a time in my life when it seemed like everyone was doing it.

Over the last fifteen years or so, coke came out of the shadows and became the centerpiece of the modern get-together. At wedding receptions, yacht club galas, political fundraisers, concerts, office parties, football games, fishing trips, or just home on Friday night, cocaine was the special guest.

Ultimately, even the special guest became commonplace. The doctor, the lawyer, the dentist, the County Court Judge, the entertainer and the board chairman were eventually joined by the secretary, the construction worker, the printer, the hairdresser, the cashier and the housewife. Everyone wanted a toot.

Norman was never a blowhound, but Judy loved it. Two years ago, cocaine burned a small hole on the inside of her nose and perforated her septum. Mortified, she stopped cold.

Larry, on the other hand, quit time after time, but always found that life was sweeter, the nights were longer and the girls were easier, with cocaine around. He used to joke that cocaine was not addictive, saying "I'm an authority, I've been doing it for ten years." Now he was thirty-seven years old, and it had been more like fifteen years. The joke was stale.

I could take it or leave it. But coke was always around, so like many, I included it on my social menu. Of course, the stuff was not available in the prison camp. Drugs would have been easy enough to smuggle in, but with surprise urine tests, and the threat of being shipped to a higher-level institution, most inmates passed on the choice, as did I. Over time, our choice became a positive choice, based more on our physical well-being than the threat of disciplinary action.

Up until tonight, I hadn't felt the desire to partake of Larry's sizable stash. I had worked hard on my physical conditioning for too many months. Now, however, I was on my way to a party… maybe it was time for a little break, an exception…it wouldn't hurt. Besides, I was a horse…a stud. Of course, those were Lenny Bias' exact words…his last words.

THE PARTY WAS in full swing. Someone set up a giant boom-box and was playing tapes in the living room. The conversation was lively and loud, everyone talking and laughing at once.

Cissy was friendly, even wonderfully possessive at times, and seemed genuinely interested in me…she was on my arm most of the time. Finally, at her suggestion, we slipped out of the party arena and into an empty bathroom where we could hear each other speak. This was an exciting development, as I had been trying for over an hour to get her alone.

D. and C. was one of Larry's cardinal principles of love…Divide and Conquer. Before anything romantic can happen, one first had to separate one's prey from the crowd.

Cissy made me very comfortable, and didn't ask me too many questions about myself. Mostly she talked about her own life. At times she expressed herself like a child, although she claimed she was twenty eight years old. She was extremely talkative, probably the effects of the cocaine. For a tiny girl, she could really suck it down.

"Do you still have that in your pocket?" she queried, moving in close, her eyes big and blue.

I stared into those eyes, saying nothing as I pulled a small vial of Larry's coke from my pocket. I was mesmerized, and suddenly stimulated by her every action. She parted her lips just a fraction. Impulsively I leaned down and kissed her softly. She opened her mouth, and I could feel the movement of her warm tongue.

She moaned quietly as I slipped my arms around her, and she pressed her hips against me. "Let's do another line and take a walk on the beach," she murmured.

She was enjoying the cocaine…it seemed as if her every statement was prefaced with, "…let's do another line and…" I wasn't about to argue with her. Besides, I was feeling the delicious effects of the drug myself. And she was a doll.

We were into the wee, wee hours, and the moon was setting over the horizon. There was still activity off in the distance... lights were blinking down the beach, a car horn was blowing impatiently, and, perhaps a mile or two away, Roman candles sporadically lit the sky. But the beach behind the condo was deserted.

We walked down to the water's edge and kissed deeply. We looked into each other's eyes in the fading moonlight, and kissed again. This is exactly how I had envisioned freedom to be.

Cissy clung to me as we walked slowly along the beach. She spoke again of her troubles, and how screwed up things were for her. I was tempted to tell her how screwed up my own life was, but I sensed that she was not in a listening mood. She obviously wanted to talk, and I was just as happy to listen.

We strolled along, and she wrapped her arms around me tighter as if to fight off the darkness. I began to imagine her going with me on the road. It sounded like she had nothing to stay in Panama City for. As I thought about it, I warmed to the idea. I looked down at her clutched against me.

"You're very nice, you know," I said. I hadn't held a girl in my arms for so very long.

She closed her eyes and purred, snuggling against my chest. I promised myself to talk to her about it in the morning. What a find, this girl. It always happens when you're not looking for it.

My body ached for her as we moved along in the silence. I wanted to carry her back to my room. Instead, I walked down to the wet sand and into the shallow water, thinking that we might go skinny dipping. As if reading my mind, she kicked off her sandals and followed.

But the water was too cold...much too cold. We looked at each other, and together we shook our heads "no." She giggled, and said, "Let's do another line and build a sand castle."

Oh, no, I almost said aloud. I wanted something else, and it wasn't to play in the sand. I hesitated...and then I lied.

"I left it back at the condo," I said, nervously fingering the vial in my pocket.

Cissy looked back at the condo like it was a million miles away. "I'll race you," she finally said.

THE SLIDING rear doors of the place were wide open, and we staggered back inside. The party was still going strong, the music loudly pumping out through the open doors and across the rolling sand dunes.

As I turned around to slide the doors closed behind me, I noticed that dawn was breaking...why was I feeling guilty?

The soft sensual spell that embraced us on the beach was, in an instant, broken by the frenzied activity inside. Larry and Beverly were in bathing suits. They decided to go swimming an hour ago, but had never gotten past putting on their suits. Now, Beverly was passed out on the couch while Larry was up on the coffee table, giving Atchafalaya's drummer and his girlfriend a windsurfing lesson.

Cissy and I eased our way back to the bathroom. I was about to speak when she flung her arms around me and kissed me. I was overwhelmed and immediately excited.

I moved against her and she hesitated. "Oh, I'm so gross from work...and I've got sand all over me," Cissy complained.

In the same motion we both glanced at the shower, and in the early morning light, I saw her blush again. It was the innocent blush of a nervous girl, and it made her look even more attractive.

I threw her a towel. "Make it nice and hot," she pleaded as I twisted the shower knobs.

We started to undress. She pulled off her shirt and bra in one motion, and when she saw me watching, raised her arms over her head and arched her back, smiling seductively.

I was only half undressed, but I reached for her and kissed her again. She kissed me back, wriggled free and slipped her small skirt and panties down around her ankles. They dropped on her sandy feet.

"Ugh," she laughed. "Let's do another line and then wash each other off."

It was a moment I'd dreamed of for many months. Cissy was deeply tanned and built like a mini-surfer…and the running water accentuated each curve and swell on her smooth body.

She murmured and closed her eyes as I methodically washed each supple limb. Then I slipped my soapy hand between her legs, and she moved into me and opened her unfocused eyes. I rubbed my fingers over her petite patch of soft hair. It was like a fuzzy tennis ball, only warmer.

"Oh…" she sighed breathlessly into my ear.

Cissy took the soap and began to wash me. She never finished, for as she moved her hands between my legs, she lightly caressed me with both hands and moaned, "Oh, my…"

Cissy's excitement seemed to match my own, and we attacked each other's bodies greedily. It was aggressive and perhaps overly physical, as if I was releasing a frustration born of many months confinement. But she responded in kind.

After the shower, she sat naked and soaking wet on the counter top and watched me dry off. I was taking my time with the large towel, prolonging the sexual afterglow. I looked over at her… perched erotically on the marble sink, her nudity enhanced by the sheen of the water on her skin. I suddenly felt compelled to discuss the possibility of her going with me, but I didn't know where to begin.

She saw my mind working, smiled, and wagged her finger at me. "Come here," she ordered.

I slid over to the counter, and she wrapped her legs around me and pulled me close. Forgetting my words, I wanted her again, and leapt at her.

She pushed my shoulders back and held me motionless for a

moment, but gently, so as not to push me away. "Slowly," she whispered, moving her hips in slow motion.

We made love again, barely moving, with me standing and her sitting in a puddle of water on the counter top. She cried out in orgasm. And in my own release, I shed the emotional shackles of the past eighteen months. I was a prisoner no longer.

CISSY EMPTIED the last of my cocaine on a small mirror, and held it out to me. Two pitiful little lines.

I passed. "Go ahead," I said. "I'll get some dry shirts."

We dressed, she kissed me again, and we stepped out of the bathroom hand in hand. I could feel her nails pressed into my hand. She was mine...convincing her to join me when I left might not be so far-fetched. I was determined to bring it up at breakfast.

In the living room we noticed that the music had stopped, and that the party was winding down, as if the morning sun was frightening away the beach vampires.

I chuckled at the scene. A freaked-out girl was frantically searching the condo for her car keys, mumbling to herself, and a musician was shaking the empty ice bags over the sink, hoping to dislodge some hidden cubes. But most of the haggard survivors were staring wordlessly at the door, or the ceiling, as if trying to conjure up enough energy to go home.

Beverly was still in the same position on the couch, passed out. And Larry was complaining that he had finally run out of blow, but that he still had vodka...we only had to wait a few minutes for the ice machine to perform its magic.

Cissy frowned at Larry's broadcast, and looked out into the morning light. "Shit, I gotta go," she said.

"What?...not now, let's..." I stammered, surprised.

"No, Roger's going to be really pissed...it's really late and I have to go home," she insisted.

"Who cares what Roger thinks," I cried, almost shouting. I was puzzled by her concern for that jerk who had slapped her earlier. I grabbed her hand possessively and said, "Come on, let's get some breakfast…I have some things I want to talk about…"

"No, really…" She yanked her hand away and shook her head adamantly. "I really have to go." Then she softened and rubbed her hand down my cheek. "Please understand," she pleaded. "I can't stay."

I didn't want her to leave, but I did not want to bully her and lose her either. I was not sympathetic, but I had no option. "Sure, I understand…will I see you later?"

"I don't know…maybe." She grabbed her purse and hurried toward the door.

"Can I call you later…?" I asked, following her outside. The sun was now bright and I squinted in the light.

"Well, I'm off tonight. But I'm working tomorrow. Why don't you come by the club then."

We reached her car. She turned around and gave me a sisterly hug. She opened her car door, gave me a pinch on the cheek and said, "Bye, bye."

Then Cissy drove away, leaving me there rubbing my cheek, confused.

I STOOD in the parking lot for a few minutes, unwinding in the morning warmth, trying to get a grip on the bewildering turn of events. Damn, one minute Cissy had been so intimate, hanging on my arm and talking openly about deeply personal matters. And so uninhibited. Then…boom, she was gone. What in the world had just happened? I didn't even know if she wanted to see me again.

Oh, hell, I thought. We were all a little high. She probably had a good reason. "What the fuck," I finally said aloud, still completely confused. What I really needed was another blast. But we were out of drugs and it was just as well. Sleep was the much better option.

Inside, Larry was the only one still rocking. The drummer and his girlfriend were searching for their belongings. The remaining stragglers were on their way out, and Larry was glad to see me walk back through the door.

"Hey, hey...your first all-nighter, and you survived. Have a drink." He offered me the vodka bottle.

"No, thanks." The last thing I needed was a drink.

"Have a bump then." He surreptitiously dangled a small baggie from his fingers.

"I thought you said it was all gone...?"

"Just to get rid of the riff-raff," he chirped.

I snapped. "I guess you did...Cissy split when she heard the news." I said it, but I didn't really mean it...Cissy had other problems...she really liked me...Goddamn.

Feeling rejected, I snorted one of the lines Larry laid out. I began to explain that Cissy had things on her mind, when the drummer's girlfriend chimed in. "I'll say she has things on her mind. Her husband's going to be pissed as shit again..."

"Husband...?!" I barked a little too loudly. I was shocked.

"Again...?" Larry choked, pulling a pillow over his face.

"She didn't tell you...?" the girl asked. "Yah, Roger's always on her ass...she loves to party."

I shook my head, my stomach churned.

The drummer joined in my misery, saying, "Roger's not one to talk...the way he gets around."

"Yeah, they'll probably both be wheeling into the driveway at the same time this morning, sliding their wedding rings on," the girl joked.

Everybody laughed long and hard, except me. Instead, I slumped in the chair. Can you believe this shit, I thought. Of course, it explained everything. Feeling foolish, I leaned over to Larry. "Hey buddy," I said. "...Guess I'll have that drink."

The party was over.

LARRY FINALLY WENT UPSTAIRS to take a shower. When he hadn't returned a half hour later, I dragged myself up the short flight of stairs to see if he was still alive.

There he was, passed out on the bed, his hair still wet and a semi-smile on his face. With Larry down, the house was finally quiet.

"Gotta have a nap," I decided, talking to myself. I was high, and drunk...and being alone, the sensation wasn't pleasant. So I staggered off to my room, exhausted.

I had been sleeping for what I thought was only minutes when a crashing noise woke me. I got up, slipped my shorts on, and went to investigate. My head was spinning.

I found Beverly sprawled on the kitchen floor trying to retrieve the ice cubes she had spilled everywhere.

"Oh, hi, Beverly...I thought that...is everything alright?"

She was in complete disarray. Still drunk, she struggled after the ice cubes on her hands and knees. Her hair was tangled and strewn across her face, and her long shapely legs refused to fully catch their balance.

She spun around to respond, and I noticed that she did not have her top on. I looked at her bare breasts. They were beautiful...right out of a magazine. Large, but firm and high...and perfectly formed, with big pink nipples. I was staring...I couldn't help myself.

"See something you like?" she asked. Still on the floor, she had regained her balance somewhat, and caught me staring at her.

"...Oh, I'm sorry, I..." Jesus.

"That's okay, I'm proud of my boobs...do you like them?" she cupped her hands under each of her breasts. Kneeling, she held them up for my inspection.

"You're…uh, they're beautiful, Beverly." I started to stir inside. I looked away.

"I'm a dancer. I love men to look at me…go on. I like to use my body." She was drunk, but she knew her own mind, and as she spoke, rubbing her own breasts, I became wholly aroused.

She saw…her face was only a foot or so from the front of my shorts.

Beverly reached out and touched me softly, still talking. "It gives me a certain power…the only one I have." Okay, I thought it was a succinct self-evaluation.

She continued to stroke me as I shuddered. Then, she slipped my shorts down and pulled me to her. "Feel my power," she whispered as she shook her tangled hair back out of her face, using her free hand to hold it away.

As she rose to one knee, she suddenly slipped on the wet floor and, spinning, hit her head hard on the refrigerator. I reached out for her, but with my shorts around my knees, I too slipped on the ice and crashed next to her, slamming my elbow on the floor.

She lay on the floor, laughing hysterically. Then she propped herself up, looked at me and began laughing again. A little trickle of blood ran from one of her nostrils. She wiped it with her hand, looked at it, and laughed again.

Finally, she said, "Help me to the couch, will ya. I need some sleep."

"You think?" I grimaced, through the pain.

Chapter Six

Larry and I sat together on the back patio, talking lazily, alone in the late afternoon sun. Like most conversationalists on cocaine, we were both talking without really listening to each other.

Everything amused Larry. The only thing he seemed halfway serious about was friendship…how friends seemed to be fleeting, or lacking, in his life. He babbled something about Norman and me…about how he envied our friendship…how he wished he was that close to someone. He came to a resounding conclusion, saying, "I'd rather have that kind of a friend than a faithful woman." He gave me the impression that he thought each was equally scarce.

I wasn't paying a great deal of attention to his philosophy. I was busy talking about myself. I mumbled on about Cissy… how I had been completely fooled. I confessed that even up to the last minute, I thought she might leave Panama City with me.

I laughed sadly. She seemed so…innocent. What a joke…and what an asshole I am.

"Talk about a warped perception," I lamented to no one in particular.

"Perception...?" Larry laughed. "Look at us," he said. "What in the hell are we talking about?"

I was high. I took his kidding seriously and answered in earnest. "True love..." I proclaimed. I said it as if I had stumbled upon some brilliant idea.

Larry laughed again. "Uh, oh, Captain...you're as high as a fucking kite." He was right.

He went into the kitchen and brought out two more beers. "Breakfast is served," he sang, and as he dripped the ice-cold condensation from the bottles on my bare legs, I jumped.

Breakfast...beer and cocaine. It was almost sunset. "We really slept late," I observed.

Larry clinked his beer bottle against mine. "Here's to true love," he toasted with a wink.

I rubbed my eyes and smiled at him. I appreciated his continual good humor.

We sat and watched a dull sunset, drinking beer and letting our conversation ramble. A cool evening breeze had picked up. Larry waved at a group of girls in bikinis on the beach, struggling to put on sweatshirts in the sudden onshore wind.

"Need any help?" he yelled.

They waved back, laughing cheerfully.

"True love, huh...and pass up all that?" he asked, theatrically sweeping his arm in the direction of the still giggling girls.

I opened another beer. "Yep..." is all I said. By now, I had burned away any eloquence I might have had.

"What about last night, stud?" Larry questioned.

"Oh...it was great, I guess, but..." I knew what I wanted to say, but my mind short-circuited and I couldn't find the words. "You know, man," I stammered, "...it's over already."

Larry stood up, beat his chest and grinned. "So tonight, you animal, we ravage and pillage again."

I groaned. The thought of another night like last night made my stomach weak.

"Anyway," he pointed out, "Norman will be back soon to save you."

"Here's to Norman," I said solemnly, rallying, ever so briefly, at the thought.

Larry paused, then observed, "You guys are pretty tight…"

I nodded, "Yeah…" My mind unleashed too many memories to speak about any particular one.

"What about Horseshoe Beach?" he asked. "I heard you two talking about it. What was Horseshoe Beach...in 'Nam or something?"

"Nam?" I laughed. "Nam?" I laughed again. "Shit, Larry, we were never in Vietnam." Wait 'till Norman hears that, I thought.

"No, Horseshoe Beach was…a bad experience for us." That's all I told him.

But my memory focused on a remote beach up in Dixie County.

THE WATERS off Horseshoe Beach are very shallow. Not a likely place to attempt to land a large boat, or haul thousands of pounds of any kind of product ashore. Some local fishermen, however, had a large barge leftover from the lucrative days when purse-seine net fishing was permitted.

Purse-seine nets are enormous and are deployed in a wide arc. The lower part of the net is then tightened, enclosing the fish in a hemisphere large enough to entrap mass amounts of mullet, the intended target in their case.

Unfortunately, this method of fishing not only snagged incredible amounts of mullet, but every other species of marine life, including sea turtles and ocean mammals, unlucky enough to be caught in the giant circle of death. Continued use of these efficient nets eventually caused severe depletions of many species of fish, and high dolphin mortalities. This led to a total ban on the use of purse-seine nets.

Up to the time of the ban, the local fishermen had become extremely successful, not only in catching the large schools of mullet, but in bringing their catch ashore where they could be sold. Hauling up more than their fishing boats could hold, they obtained this massive barge, which could navigate the flats and shallow waters, and upon which they could unload catch after catch, tons of mullet, and transport them to shore. They even cleared their own makeshift channel so they could slide the barge right up to the beach.

The barge itself did not have its own power. It needed a donkey boat to haul it to and from the shore. But it proved to be extremely efficient. Until the barge became obsolete overnight with the strict banning of purse-seine net fishing.

These poor, rural fishing communities nestled along the Big-Bend area of the northwest Florida shoreline came up with an even better use for this gigantic, shallow-draft barge, which was able to haul tons of whatever needed to be transported from the open sea directly to the beach. It was a natural conversion for these Florida boys to make.

NORMAN and I were only minor players in this deal. He was on the beach waiting for the ship to sneak close enough to unload its valuable cargo onto the barge. We were only there to pick up eight bales, a tiny fraction of the expected load coming in, but enough to fill our van. The boys responsible for this shipment would weigh and separate the load on the beach, then transport it in different directions across the Southeast in large trucks and trailers.

I was in the van, nine or ten miles away from the beach, in a rundown backwoods service station, fueling up the vehicle for our run back to Tampa. I was also checking my running lights, brake lights and turn signals to ensure that we wouldn't be pulled over for some minor traffic infraction on the four-hour trip south. All the transportation crews, including me, had walkie-talkies that we monitored for signs of trouble. The radios were silent and all appeared to be calm. In a couple of hours, I would receive a "green light" and I would proceed to the beach area.

The old Shell station, with its three gas pumps and two open bays, had, for years, assisted motorists along this two-lane stretch of county blacktop out in the middle of nowhere. The station's owner, a friendly old-timer who had lived in the area his whole life, worked the station by himself.

As he replaced one of my front headlights, I leaned against the grill of the van and enjoyed his slow drawl while we conversed about the weather. Suddenly, there was a loud crash from inside the station. A large shelf of new tires collapsed, sending the row of tires smashing onto the shelf of tires below it, knocking both shelves and tires to the floor. With the bay doors open, many of the falling tires soon came rolling out of the station in several different directions...one even wobbled across the road and settled in a sandy meadow.

I felt sorry for the old guy, so I helped him retrieve the tires. We brushed the dirt and sand spurs off and rolled them back into the station, then leaned them against the wall. Inside, I saw that the collapsed shelves were broken beyond repair, little pieces of them were scattered across the floor of the garage. I had some time on my hands, so I took most of an hour assisting him in the cleanup. He was huffing and puffing, but he didn't seem any worse for the wear. I hoped to be in his shape at his age, I remember thinking.

Appreciating my time and effort, he gave me a free Dr. Pepper, and refused to charge me for the replacement headlight. He even offered me a discount on any new tires. I enjoyed the cold drink, and told him I'd get back to him on the tires, but I insisted on paying for the light. I remarked that he needed to make a living, especially out there in the middle of nowhere. He cackled through tobacco-stained teeth and told me that there was plenty of action out here in these woods.

I LEFT the station and headed in the direction of the beach. I wanted to be a little closer when I got the green light. That way, I could get in, grab Norman and the bales, and get out before the big trucks and trailers moved in. We could be long gone before they even began the loading process. That certainly would lessen any chance of being caught up in unexpected trouble.

It didn't work out that way. Seconds after I left the gas station a single word came over the radio ... "Scatter."

We had all agreed beforehand that everyone was on their own in the event we had to flee...that's the way it is. People run in every direction...on the boats, in the vehicles, and on foot through the woods. And even though Norman and I had also agreed to this, I couldn't help thinking that he would not be able to rely on anyone out there but me to help him. Without a boat or a car, and not being familiar with the surrounding area, he would surely be rounded up within the hour.

I was scared, but I drove the remaining miles to the beach...at the time it seemed like a hundred. Norman was shaking when I picked him up. "Oh, man...thanks," he said, as I sped away.

"Don't thank me yet," I replied. "The heat will be crawling over this whole area...any minute." We both listened for the sound of a helicopter in the air.

I raced back along the way I had come. We were both silent as I drove. The radio crackled again, "Semis followed in...roadblocks... every direction." And that was the last we heard on the radio.

Perhaps someone became suspicious of the big semi-trailers turning off US 19 toward the sparsely populated beach area. Or maybe they had some other advanced knowledge of the operation.

Either way, we were caught in a shrinking net...as the authorities were throwing a blanket over the whole area. While one or two guys might get lucky, the law would methodically catch most everyone on the beach and on the surrounding roads. That included us. It didn't matter that we were not yet carrying any stuff, it would be easy for them to connect our presence and our out-of-county tags to the busted load.

Easy enough. Conspiracy.

As we approached a big curve in the two-lane road, I slowed the van to a crawl and checked my wristwatch. We had expended way too much time trying to exit the area.

"Stormin', I have a bad feeling about going around that curve," I said as I looked over at him. At some point, whether it was here or farther ahead, we would run into a roadblock.

"Should we pull over into the woods?" he responded. We both knew that would just be postponing the inevitable. There was no place to hide the van, which was registered in Norman's name, in the low-lying scrub. It was way too late for anything like that.

As we crept along the road, trying to decide, I spotted the old Shell station on our right. On an impulse, I pulled in. As I drove the van on the lot, the old guy walked out the bay door, smiled and said, "Did you come back for those tires?"

We stared at each other for a moment. He was still smiling when it hit me. "Is my discount still available?" I finally asked.

"Absolutely. Just wheel her in."

I eased the van into the bay and onto the lift. "Replace as many as you think need replacing," I ordered. "I'm not in any rush."

He cackled. Then I added, "We'll just stay in the van."

Cackling again, he said, "That's probably a good idea."

Then he jacked up the van on the lift, removed both rear tires, lowered the bay doors about halfway, and walked back into the office. He left us high in the air, and while the station doors remained open, we were out of sight.

We spent the rest of the evening, that night, and much of the next day, up on the lift. Lying silently in the back of the van, we heard sirens, cars whizzing by, a chopper overhead and radios crackling. At night, we even saw the passing reflections of blinking blue and red lights against the windows of the vehicle.

When we finally left the station with our new rear tires, Norman was shaking.

"John…everyone just bolted…split. I didn't know what to do…I was…" He looked at the floor. "I think I kinda' freaked." I tried to make light of the situation, but he was inconsolable.

I flexed my bicep at him, and mouthed "Superman." He didn't smile. He shook his head and said, "I still can't believe you came back for me." Then he fell silent. I shut up and continued driving.

"You didn't think I would abandon you, did you, buddy?" I finally said, over an hour later, still driving.

He did not respond. He just shook his head again, still upset.

"Hey K. I., my man." I punched his arm.

Norman finally smiled, and I slapped the back of his head.

It was too close a call for Norman. He decided to retire completely from the smuggling scene that day. I probably should have too.

As Larry dozed in his chaise lounge, my mind raced with the memory. Horseshoe Beach seemed like ancient history now. But its resurrected memory led me to reexamine the subject of friendships.

They certainly had their ups and downs. And that fragile chemistry, that mix of familiarity, loyalty and responsibility is often disturbed by time, distance and diverging interests. So many of my friendships have unraveled over the years, I thought, sadly. It isn't often that a friend remains close. Rarer still are those few people trustworthy enough to have your back.

I smiled, thinking of Norman. NormanandJohn.

Not all friendships though. I had turned my back once too often, and I'd wound up in prison. I shivered at the memory of my stupidity...how I'd assisted Robbie Tannenbaum, my so-called friend, in obtaining a trunk-load of pot...how he was later pulled over...just for speeding. He freaked, and he was searched. To this day, I could still see him on the witness stand pointing his finger at me.

Unfortunately, I was about to let my guard down again, with similar drastic consequences.

My remaining time with Larry Martin was spent in a haze. Much of it consisted of...mostly lost thoughts and abandoned adventures. We began each morning without any real plan, and allowed the day to slip by without accomplishing anything...another run to the liquor store, another late night, perhaps a little blow, and another day gone by.

Larry had assigned himself the role of my protector. In his way, he wanted to be another Norman, but he turned out to be more of a social director. It reinforced his role to himself if he could make me laugh, or get me high, or introduce me to a girl. And me...I just sat back and let him take the wheel. No more jogs on the beach. I didn't even read the newspaper. I was generally numb to everything.

I did, however, remember feeling a little sorry for him...me being the only worthwhile project in his world. Where was he heading with his life, I asked myself. But who was I to judge? Actually, I was glad to have him with me. Being around him reminded me of my old life, before the interference of my incarceration. I was floating along, just like before. "What, me worry?" I seemed to be asking.

But underneath, a small part of me grew restless and disturbed.

IT WAS time again to make a phone call. At a predetermined time, I called an unfamiliar number...presumably a safe phone...it turned out to be Judy's parents' house. I had a bag of quarters with me, prepared for a lengthy conversation. As it happened, though, it was short and sweet...and to the point. Norman would be back sometime Friday afternoon.

Judy's voice was full of love and worry. Damn, she's a standup girl, I thought as I spoke to her. Norman's a lucky guy.

In the back of my mind I feared that I was cursed...Larry would call it blessed...with the Cissys of the world. Those confused Cinderellas of the night, flitting from party to party, seeking love, or drugs, or understanding perhaps. A girl like Judy was not in the cards for me.

The idea provoked a response in me...but I lost my train of thought and reached for another beer.

KNOWING that we would soon leave Panama City, Larry wanted me to remember his performance as...one of the original Escape Brothers. He went about making plans for a legendary farewell party, to commence on Friday, upon Norman's return.

He persuaded most of the band, along with some other musicians he'd met, to perform after hours at our condo. And he convinced Beverly to encourage a carload of her dancer buddies to gather for our "last stand," as he put it.

He then called his work to inform them that he wouldn't be returning until the following week. He was supposedly out of town attending a funeral. He said it, not realizing how close it was to the truth.

Larry's preparations were completed rapidly…except for the coke. We had exhausted his stash and, in his mind, no good party was complete without a healthy supply of the drug. He became anxious about it as he didn't want to let his guests down. And in his desperation, he made a huge mistake…one that would bring the law down on us.

I should have seen it coming, but I was too spaced to recognize the disaster unfolding before my eyes.

LARRY not only called Clancy's about missing work. He also phoned his old compadre, Joey DaSilva.

In Larry's mind, he wishfully perceived Joey and himself as another Norman and John. Both Larry and Joey used to work years ago driving for Dog Gregory, and had weathered many a storm together. Also, Joey was married to Larry's sister, Alice.

Larry wanted Joey to drive up to Panama City and to bring with him a bunch of coke for a "party of historical significance," he said. Joey begged off, saying that he couldn't get away. Larry pressed him, but Joey continued to say no. Larry insisted that it was very important, and thinking of me and the party's success, told Joey he wouldn't take no for an answer.

Sensing Larry's anxiousness, Joey asked what in the hell was so important as to require him to miss work. Larry told him a secret meant for Joey's ears only…that the party was for John Bellamy. Me.

It never should have happened…and I guess it was as much my fault as anyone's. I had agreed to the party…well, I'd never objected to it. More importantly, I had forgotten how precarious my situation was. Hell, my whole attitude was an invitation to trouble.

And it was on its way to Panama City with Joey DaSilva.

It was Friday afternoon. I was stretched out on the couch sipping a poorly made vodka drink, watching *Leave it to Beaver* reruns on the television while Larry scurried around the condo, hanging and taping up hastily prepared decorations.

I felt a little guilty and asked, "Don't you want any help?"

"Naw, just relax…we can handle everything."

Beverly danced by. "Do you want me to freshen your drink? Maybe some more ice?" she asked with a throaty voice and a leer on her face.

I shook my head and smiled awkwardly at her, feeling guilty that I still pictured her spread out on the kitchen floor. We both now shared the knowledge that combining Beverly with ice cubes makes for a dangerous mix.

The drummer, who had become a permanent fixture around the condo, was out on the patio setting up some sound equipment for the musicians to use later that night. He shouted through the open glass doors, "We'll be ready to rock all night."

He and Larry had grown close in a few short days. They were of one mind…unabashed hedonists living on impulse. I kidded that they were long lost twins.

Larry shouted back at him. "This party will not go on all night…"

I raised my head and arched an eyebrow at him…in disbelief. Larry grinned and boldly announced, "…it will go on for days."

I saluted him and put my feet up on the coffee table.

And in walked Norman.

"Honey, I'm home," he called. Looking around the room and

seeing the party decorations, he rubbed his hands in anticipation and said, "And just in time, I see."

He sat down on the couch next to me and put his feet up next to mine. "Well, pard," he said, his voice just above a whisper, "the shit has hit the fan back home. You're in the news again…the *St. Pete Times* ran a nice little article. It's in the car."

I closed my eyes and cooled my forehead with my cold glass.

People were darting around the condo, making preparations. Norman tried to keep his voice low. "Look, maybe we'd better go somewhere and talk. And I have some stuff to give you. But not here."

Larry overheard and chimed in, "Yeah, Norman, take loverboy out of here and get some food in him."

Norman and I decided that we would shower and get ready for the party. Then we would go and have a nice dinner together, alone, where we could discuss things in private. After taking care of business, we would return for Larry's shindig, which by then would be kicking off. "Ah, the last meal for the condemned man," Norman smirked.

It turned out to be our last dinner together for a long time.

Joey DaSilva finally found our condo. Between Larry's obtuse directions and the increasing arrival of Spring Breakers clogging the roads, Joey pulled in much later than expected. Joey had driven up from St. Pete with his friend, Denny Cooper. Larry was overly excited to see them. He threw open his arms and howled, "The cavalry has arrived in the nick of time."

He instructed them to put their bags in his bedroom upstairs and, licking his lips, he ordered them to "break out the goods." Everyone was smiling.

Denny immediately returned to Joey's car to unload, while Joey and Larry embraced and shadowboxed in the doorway, oblivious to everything around them. In the parking lot, Denny nodded to two agents parked across the street in an unmarked car. They nodded back, and got on the radio to call in the reinforcements.

The trap was set. It was as simple as that.

THE PARTY WAS A DECADENT AFFAIR. The condominium was overflowing with people...festively dressed, half-dressed and undressed night-owls, including many new faces and, strangely, several foreign accents. Musicians from various local bands were loosely jamming on the patio, and the surrounding beach was scattered with onlookers and refugees from other parties in the vicinity. There were similar scenes occurring throughout the city, especially along the beach, so no one was expecting trouble.

Larry was in his element, greeting everyone, organizing storage for the extra ice and mixers that began piling up in the kitchen, playing disc jockey on the tape player, and kissing every new girl he met...all the while constantly giving directions to the two bathrooms.

The bathrooms were crowded with small groups of people hoping to find momentary privacy to neck, or do drugs. In fact, those who needed to use one of the bathrooms for its intended purpose usually became impatient and escaped to the beach behind the condo...although someone had the stamina to wait until he could use the upstairs toilet, causing a tall, well-dressed stranger to complain loudly on the stairwell.

Shouting indignantly to Larry, and using a very proper English accent, the gentleman said sharply, "Someone has just had the bad manners to take a crap in the upstairs tooting room."

Larry laughed so hard he choked.

In the back bedroom...my bedroom...Beverly and her voluptuous friends had unpacked skimpy costumes and other accessories for the show they expected to offer later. Some had even brought along raunchy videos to accompany the dance routines they intended to perform.

The party rolled on…all oblivious to the outside world. More and more people came and went with each passing hour, and it appeared that this event would be everything that Larry had hoped it would be…an historical occasion, lasting for several days.

A small army of agents approached the area. Filing swiftly along the beach, and splitting into groups to cordon off possible escape routes, they awaited a signal to advance on our unsuspecting condo.

They did not strike until very late. They waited until the peak of the action, ensuring their targets had returned from the nightclubs and restaurants to join in the fun. They couldn't have chosen a better time. All of the doors were wide open, and the music of the Fabulous Thunderbirds was pounding across the rolling sand dunes. Everyone's reflexes had been dulled by overindulging and by the lateness of the hour. Some were even immobile.

In spite of Larry's drunkenness, he was the first to spot the onrushing agents. He was out back, urinating into a hedge of seagrapes, when six agents stormed by him toward the condo. They missed him in the darkness.

Larry sensed immediately what was happening, but he was too drunk to do anything other than sit down in the sand. Before he could warn anyone, the party was overrun. Shaken, Larry stumbled into the night and slipped down the beach through the sea oats.

They came from every direction, a combined force of over thirty agents, wearing baseball caps and dark blue windbreakers that had POLICE, FBI, DEA and SHERIFF printed on the jackets in bold white letters. Their approach was so swift, no one knew they were under attack until it was over. The band kept rocking, and stopped only when a heavily armed man barged up to the microphone.

Their plan was efficient, and only Larry escaped.

Chapter Seven

Earlier that evening, Norman and I sat by ourselves in Angelo's Steakhouse. Although it was crowded, we managed to find a quiet enough table in the corner. The restaurant was softly lit and the aroma from the kitchen made my mouth water. Norman laughed as I wolfed down the appetizers.

"Haven't you been eating right?" he teased, knowing full well that I hadn't.

I leaned back in my chair, making a conscious effort to slow down and allow this peaceful moment to wrap itself around me. It dawned on me that this was the first time since going to jail that I'd gone out to a decent restaurant for dinner. The last time was the night before I'd reported to the Camp to serve my sentence. Strangely, the sensation this night was eerily similar to that occasion.

I began to enjoy myself…here dining with the guy who cared for me so much, and who had literally saved my bacon. It was early in the evening and the fog in my head was clearing. After my extended binge this week with Larry, it now felt as if I was coming out of a tunnel. And the familiar conversation with Norman made me relax.

Though Norman quickly turned to business. He had been able to gather about thirty-five hundred dollars, which was good enough for the short-term. Better still, he had been successful in acquiring a legitimate birth certificate and a Social Security card.

"Okay, Fast Eddie," he said, flipping a large envelope at me.

"What?"

"Eddie…Edward Wallace Walker…that's your new name."

I opened the envelope. Norman continued, "And here's a bonus…a New Jersey driver's license in your name. It still has more than a year until its expiration. But it will give you time to establish your identity and get a license with your photo."

New Jersey, one of the last states that issued a driver's license without a photo. And even New Jersey was now changing over to the photo ID, and any renewal would require that. At least I could drive, and even get pulled over, because it was a legitimate ID. Later, I could obtain another valid license…one with my photo…as well as some credit cards, using the identification Norman had provided. But for now, I was just another Florida boy with a New Jersey license.

"Do you know where Barney is these days?" I asked. Barney was an elusive figure, a true artist, who created the most incredible IDs.

"No, but I figured you'd want to know…I'll keep looking."

"Is he still making licenses?"

"…so I hear," Norman replied.

I held the documents in my hands and, communing with Norman, I felt relieved. He had really come through for me. Much better than I'd expected in so short a time. Better still, it appeared that no one had yet suspected his role in all this.

Norman leaned forward as if examining me, and his face broke into a wide smile. He shook his head.

"What?" I asked, grinning back. He was clearly judging me.

He waved his hand in dismissal. "Nothing..." he said, still smiling.

"No, come on, what is it?" I pressed.

"Nothing really...it's only that when I left you two here in Panama City...I figured that I'd return to find you working on Larry."

"What do you mean?" I asked, puzzled.

"You know, your fitness and mind improvement thing. You'd be getting Larry in shape...Mr. Bootcamp...early to rise, literature, keeping him sober..." He started laughing.

I put down my fork. He went on. "When I walked in the condo today and saw you all fucked up, camped on your ass in front of *Leave it to Beaver*...I thought for a minute you were Larry." He laughed again at the memory.

I was speechless. I gripped the table to steady myself. Norman had spoken in jest, but it felt as if he'd hit me in the back of the head with a shovel. It sure had the same effect.

"HEY, MAN," Norman chided. "I was just kidding." The strength of my reaction had surprised him...and me too.

"I know, I know." I said unconvincingly. But there was no taking it back.

His offhand comment had, in fact, touched a raw nerve, and it connected several uncomfortable feelings I had about myself. All of a sudden I was upset...and angry. I had forgotten so many important lessons in such a short time. I had become Larry. It was embarrassing. More than that, it was scary how easily it happened.

I tried to confess to Norman how my collapse had happened in a matter of days...without any struggle whatsoever.

He wasn't convinced. "Shit, John...you just got out. A little fun is to be expected."

"Maybe so..." I conceded. Given another circumstance, he

might be right. But I clearly recognized that my week in Panama City had been more than "a little fun." I had fallen into a dangerous, and all too familiar, pattern. A routine I'd probably still be following had Norman not awakened me from my stupor.

His accurate evaluation crushed me, and I didn't care to defend myself. Norman sensed my frustration, and attempted to blow it off and change the subject.

"Okay, okay…so what have you decided to do?" he asked.

I drew a blank. "I guess that's what I'm saying. It's been a week and I haven't done crap. I've been so wasted…I didn't even take the time to think about what I needed to do next…"

"Hey…" Norman grabbed my arm. "Don't worry. We'll figure it out. Let's eat and relax."

But I was adamant. Norman had unknowingly given me an honest look in the mirror, and I wanted to let him know I saw the same things he did. "That's the point, Stormin'. You are right, I was Larry. I was just coasting, day by day. No planning…no thinking…no…"

"You're kinda worked up, aren't you, pard?" Norman interrupted, wanting to calm me down.

"Yeah, I guess." I put my hands over my eyes. I had the feeling that I'd wasted a lot more than a week.

Norman reached across the table, picked up the envelope containing my new IDs and waved it in front of my face. "You are not Larry. Hell, you're not even John anymore." He smiled. "You have a whole new story…and it's yours to write. You get to fill in the blanks any way you want. Go to work, Eddie."

I looked at the envelope as he continued, "You may have to assume this identity for a long time. This is a new day…you start the building process now. And let's not begin by whining."

His short speech made me smile. Drop this now and move on. It was a great way to move past this last week and deal with whatever upcoming challenges I might have to face. "Good idea." I concluded.

Norman returned my smile and gripped my shoulder like a father accepting his prodigal son. We laughed, ignorant of the peril that lay in our path…waiting for our return to the condo.

We took our time finishing our last dinner together. We retold old stories and even read his copy of the *St. Pete Times*, passing sections of the paper back and forth. I shared my Beverly story with him and he consoled me about Cissy, saying, "Ah, you never could pick 'em. I don't even think Eddie's going to be able to change that part." He didn't try to hide his amusement.

We laughed again, and ate dessert.

As we drove back to the party, I found another newspaper on the floor of his car. "The *Tallahassee Democrat*," I said, surprised. "I haven't seen one of these in ages."

"Yeah, I picked it up when I stopped for gas on the way here. Remember when we used to get it every day in the dorm?"

"Bullshit," I countered. "I got it every day. You still got the *Times*."

As freshmen at Florida State, I was of the opinion that since we were living in Tallahassee, we should get the *Tallahassee Democrat*. Norman staunchly maintained that we should get the better paper…The *St. Pete Times*, which had an upstate edition. "Mama's boy," I had said then.

"Mama's boy," I taunted him again. He hit me with the paper.

I casually flipped through the paper while he drove. The sun was low in the sky, and it would soon be showtime at Larry's planned circus. The dinner had mellowed me somewhat and I was in no rush to return right away to the condo.

"Jimmy friggin' Buffett," I suddenly shouted.

"What?"

"I said, Jimmy Buffett…look." I pointed to the paper. "He's playing in Tallahassee tonight."

"Really…?" Norman said excitedly.

JIMMY BUFFETT. The shrimp rocker from Key West, New Orleans, Mississippi, L. A…Lower Alabama, that is, and all points south of the Tropic of Cancer.

Jimmy's rise to stardom evolved alongside our careers. He chronicled the story of the Florida boys…and we embraced him as one of us. When the smuggling game was about romance and adventure, his songs were like a recruiting anthem for every guy who lived along the coast, from Key West to Pensacola…and beyond, to Mississippi, through Louisiana, all the way to Brownsville, Texas.

In the early days, his music spoke directly to us … "Sailing on a midnight boat, there were no questions asked." Or, "Son of a son, load the last ton, one step ahead of the jailor." When Jimmy sang, "I've done a bit of smuggling…I made enough money to buy Miami, but I pissed it away so fast," it was as if he knew the same people we did. And when Jimmy crooned, "I used to rule my world from a payphone," we knew exactly what he meant. Hell, he even named his band the Coral Reefer Band. And at his live shows, he would urge his band, "Let's go Reefers…sing one for the boys working hard to keep us high."

In the late '70s, he appeared in concert at Sarasota's Van Wezel Hall. Norman and I went together. In the lobby before the show, we saw at least fifteen local smugglers, including Stevie and Dog, all wearing Hawaiian shirts, jeans or shorts, and gold chains…like it was a uniform. During the show, when Jimmy dedicated a song to "the guys out there on the sea tonight bringing in a load," we all heard Stevie reply loudly, "There's nothing coming in tonight. We're all here." All within earshot, including the band, laughed heartily.

In those days, it was almost the same in every city. You want to know who's moving product in Cincinnati...go to the Buffett concert there and look in the first ten rows...we used to joke that the authorities could have attended the whole tour and made a fair list of targets. The bitch would have been connecting the dots since it was all so disorganized.

At some later time, Jimmy's songs did not embrace our lifestyles anymore. While some of the boys grumbled, plenty of us understood perfectly. Jimmy was about fun, first of all. When one's excesses included owning a pair of shrimp-skin boots or a sailboat, Jimmy was there to put it to music. But when the excesses became threatening...when the business turned ugly...when the romance was replaced by violence and backstabbing, there was nothing fun left for him to celebrate. He was gone.

There was, however, plenty left for Jimmy Buffett to sing about, and it all centered around his playful attitude about life... and life on and around the saltwater. And Norman and I were part of a whole generation of Margarita drinkers who did not want to be LIKE him...we wanted to BE him.

We even met Jimmy back then...in Coconut Grove. He was there to record a live album at Gusman Hall, in Miami, when Norman and I stumbled into Greg "Fingers" Taylor, the Coral Reefers' irrepressible harmonica player, at the Coconut Grove Hotel. Fingers was entertaining and friendly, and we all took to each other immediately. Over the following years, it was through Fingers that we met Jimmy, his band and his crew.

Norman and I had attended Buffett concerts all over the country and, although we didn't know Jimmy well, we were usually welcome backstage with Fingers...and the zany road crew.

Somehow, everyone we knew in Florida felt like they were part of Jimmy Buffett's entourage. We were no exception.

"Boy, if we were in Tallahassee tonight, you know exactly where we'd be," Norman said excitedly.

"Yeah, that would be..." And then it struck me. "Norman... Tallahassee is only a couple of hours away..."

We looked at each other, our minds contemplating the possibility. Norman weakened first, saying, "You think...what time does it start?"

I looked in the paper. "It says nine o'clock...we might be a little late".

"He never starts on time anyway..." Norman laughed.

We stared ahead as he drove towards the condo. Finally, I said quietly, "Let's go."

"But what about the party...? Norman asked.

"Fuck it," I shot back. I was relieved at the thought of missing it...more relieved than I let on. The misgivings I had expressed to Norman at dinner were still fresh in my mind. The drugs, the booze...more of the same. Hell with it.

However, it did dawn on me that Norman, after being on the road for so long, might prefer to attend Larry's party...especially this particular party. "But if you want to go..." I began.

"Judy would be just as happy if I missed this one," he said, with a surprisingly serious tone. Then, without warning, Norman pulled the car over. "Okay, Eddie, if we're going, you drive."

I jumped eagerly behind the wheel. "It's been awhile," I warned.

"Ah...like riding a bike," he laughed. "Besides, I am so tired of driving all over creation."

We headed east to Tallahassee, the opposite direction the party, and out of harm's way...temporarily.

"Think Larry will be pissed?" Norman asked as I concentrated on the road ahead.

"He won't even miss us. We'll drive back tomorrow and pick him up," I replied. "Hell, the party will still be going…and he'll have weeded out the amateurs by then."

We laughed together at the thought of Larry playing Ringmaster, and settled in for the trek. As I drove, Norman was busy playing tapes and arranging his luggage in the back seat. He played Buffett music to get us in the mood.

I sang along with the Reefers. Jimmy was about forty years old now, I thought…and in a couple of years, we would be there too. Maybe when he's fifty or sixty, Jimmy might circle back and write us a song about the way it used to be…maybe about the last man to quit…the last Florida boy.

The change in events elevated my whole mood. Driving along in the late evening, just Norman and me…and Buffett.

Halfway to Tallahassee, Norman reached over the seat and pulled out a gym bag. "Your survival kit," he said.

He handed me my fake drivers license. "Here, put this in your pocket…Eddie." He smiled.

"Eddie Walker, huh," I said, holding up the small card. "I'm not sure I'll ever get used to using another name."

"Well, maybe not if you're just using it," he said softly as he rummaged through the gym bag searching for something. "But if you earn the name, you might enjoy it."

I laughed. "Earn it…an intriguing, spiritual concept, man." I laughed again.

Norman stopped his search and looked up. "No, I'm serious. Like we talked about at dinner…build your new identity one decision at a time. You wake up one day, and you'll be comfortable being Eddie."

"You really think so?" I asked, suddenly serious.

"Yeah, I do," he answered. "Maybe not all at once…but it'll come to you.

I pondered his theory and turned to him. "You know, Norman, sometimes you…Wha…What's that?" I was startled by the…mop… on Norman's head.

He grinned a silly grin. "Judy sent you a few things…here's a wig."

He removed the dark, shaggy wig and handed it to me. "Go on, John, try it on," he prodded, still grinning.

He held the wheel as I slipped the wig over my hair. I looked in the mirror…quite a drastic change. And, indeed, a humorous touch. "Call me Eddie," I teased. We started laughing.

"Oh yeah," Norman said, coughing with laughter. "Judy sent this too, with love." I glanced over and he held up a gram of cocaine.

"I'll even do one with you." He smiled at my surprised look and snorted two little spoonfuls of the coke. Then he handed it to me. I took the tiny vial and held it up with one hand, examining it through the dangling locks of my new wig.

"Do you really even do this stuff anymore?" I almost laughed.

He had a wicked grin on his face. "With you, pard. For old times' sake."

"Okay, when we get to the concert," I agreed. Then on an impulse, I pitched the vial out the car window.

Norman put both hands on his head…in mild shock.

Instantly regretful, I asked, "Are you pissed?"

He paused. "I'm impressed…Eddie," he replied solemnly.

Chapter Eight

"What did I tell you," Norman boasted.

He was right...we were late for the concert and Jimmy Buffett was still backstage. I bowed in respect. Norman grinned, he didn't want to miss even one song.

The show was a sellout, but we were able to purchase two tickets from one of the many scalpers in the city center's immense parking lot, and we hurried to find our seats.

The crowded arena featured an explosion of tropical colors... brightly printed clothes and banners, worn and waived by jolly would-be pirates and their bawdy wenches. Row upon row of suntanned faces, bleached hair, flowered sombreros and sandaled feet. And still circulating after all these years were several hats with shark fins sticking out the top...all glorifying the sun, sand and sin...in the grand Buffett tradition.

There was an electricity still common to Buffett fans. His Parrotheads flocked to see him, many traveling great distances to partake in a healthy mixture of intensity and frivolity, like the cross between a tent revival and a tailgate party.

Now, most everyone's attention was focused on a comedian onstage. Evidently he was the opening act.

ALTHOUGH BUFFETT occasionally shared the stage with acts of his own caliber, he hardly ever toured with an opening act. The last time I remembered one with him was years ago...in Gainesville, Florida.

The Amazing Rhythm Aces came out first, and while the rowdy crowd enjoyed them, the Aces looked as if they were not satisfied with the sound quality. It sounded fine to us out in front...but onstage they were distracted by whatever problem it was. They allowed it to interfere with their performance, and the show suffered.

One of Jimmy's road crew later told me that it was always a problem having an opener...they constantly bitched about the sound...it was never to their liking. He explained that the intricate sound system was always fine-tuned for the headlining act, and too much re-adjustment would detract from the quality of that act...the act most fans came to see.

Several touring bands struggled with this awkward situation. "Send out the clowns...and check the sound," was a popular refrain of many a hardworking soundman, who would often intentionally distort the quality of the opening act's sound because he was tired of their complaining.

Buffett neatly avoided the entire hassle. Using a creative presentation, he extended his performance to cover the extra time. And if he got tired, he simply took an intermission. His audience understood, and used the time to...readjust their attitudes.

THE COMEDIAN WAS HOLDING his own as an opening act. The sound was booming in the echo of the cavernous hall, but most of his routine was understandable, and hilarious…the guy was pretty good.

He did a short take-off on New York surfers and degenerate Jersey beach life that had Jimmy's fans roaring with approval… especially when he swore to the crowd that he had proof of Jimmy's being born in Brooklyn.

"Don't be fooled," he warned them, "Jimmy first learned his water sports in front of a fire hydrant on Flatbush Avenue."

The loud audience cheered and hooted each irreverent comment.

The comic's set only lasted about twenty-five minutes…brief enough to avoid interfering with Jimmy's show, but long enough to get everyone laughing, and in a good mood.

I wondered if having a comedian was another one of Buffett's ideas. I'd have to ask someone after the show…if we could somehow get backstage.

THEN IT WAS Jimmy's turn. Some old songs…some new songs…all delivered with his engaging stage manner that many of us liked as much as the music. His antics made you smile…alternatively preaching, cajoling and entertaining the crowd without appearing to take himself too seriously. He even thanked us for supporting his lifestyle…treating us like shareholders in the dream he was living.

When he sang "Havana Daydreamin'" he even made a subtle reference to the outlaw lifestyle…like the old days. Norman elbowed me and we screamed our approval. The crowd also roared, for he was also a hero to anyone who had ever smoked any reefer.

And the band…the Reefers. He carried talented players with

him. And although he had changed several musicians over the years, I had never heard the band without a first-class rhythm section, or some tasty island percussionist.

Stalking the far end of the stage was Fingers Taylor, the first member and one of the sole survivors of the original Coral Reefer Band. His physical appearance surprised me…he looked great.

I could remember when he always looked like he was on his last legs…pale, skinny and in need of sleep. Now, he appeared strong and healthy. And he still played, and moved, with passion.

The change in Fingers was incredible. "What prison camp has he been to?" I joked to Norman.

The crowd was loud, and they sang along with several songs. And they bombarded the stage with gifts for the band…silly hats, Frisbees, bras and little packets of god-knows-what kind of drugs.

DURING THE LAST part of the show, I edged my way through the happy mob and headed for the side of the stage. Norman was right behind me, singing the lyrics…loudly and off-key. I put my fingers in my ears, and he laughed, shoving me forward, still singing.

We moved ahead, until we were stopped by security at the barrier.

"Hey…is there any way I could speak to Kenny D?" I asked the well-muscled guard.

Kenny Dunaway was a longtime Buffett roadie and tour fixture. Simply referred to as Kenny D, he was the calm amidst the storm and a self-styled "gentleman amongst the road savages." It was Kenny D to whom everyone seemed to turn during tour crises.

And I turned to Kenny D to get backstage. Even after long periods of time, he would always remember me and treat me well.

"He's busy right now," the young bouncer said.

"I'm a friend…" I began.

"Isn't everybody," he replied sarcastically.

Over his shoulder, I spotted Smurf…Pat Smith. He resembled one of those Smurf characters, and he never answered to Pat…or anything…only Smurf.

"Smurf," I hollered.

He spun around, and vaguely recognizing me, he waved.

"Is Kenny D around?" I shouted.

Smurf came over to the barricade and explained that Kenny was busy at this point of the show…right before its conclusion. It was one of his jobs to escort the band on and off the stage. Finally recalling who I was, he suggested that I wait there, and he would send Kenny D over if he could.

As we waited for Kenny D, Buffett did two encores. The final one ran twenty minutes and included the songs "Margaritaville" and "A Pirate Looks at Forty." No wonder Kenny D was busy, I thought. The place was a madhouse. People were standing on their seats, pushing toward the stage, and literally screaming for more. The temperature in front of the stage was oppressive. I loved it.

The concert finally ended, and I flinched when the house lights came on. As people began to clear the area, I stood next to Norman by the side of the stage, drinking the watered-down beer served at the concession stand…but not complaining. Norman sat on the floor with a silly smile on his face.

After about fifteen minutes, Kenny D walked out. Saying "It's okay" to the security guard, he greeted us and escorted us backstage.

The backstage jungle is as ever-changing as an African waterhole. Some nights are raucous and wild, with the meat-eaters noisily feeding on the rock and roll carcass. While other nights can be quiet and contemplative, with the sound of a single instrument being soulfully played, crying out like a night bird's lament.

It all depends upon an odd mix of circumstances…like the tour schedule, or the varying health and collective moods of the band and crew. And since "backstage" is not a single place…but a labyrinth of dressing rooms, passageways, offices and storage areas…there is enough space to accommodate many different moods at the same time.

Most of the action, however, centered in the main dressing room, where Norman and I milled about, picking at the food trays and drinking at the band's bar.

I was disappointed to hear that Jimmy Buffett and his tour manager had departed immediately after finishing the show. His young daughter had attended, and someone said they saw Jimmy leaving with her riding on his shoulders.

We looked for Fingers. There was a time when I could always find him close to the bar. Kenny D said he thought Fingers was doing some kind of media interview in one of the offices. Norman went to find him and Kenny went back to work while I leaned against the portable bar and surveyed the action.

Some familiar faces hurried about…but most of the crew were busy tearing down the equipment onstage. They were leaving for the next stop on the tour within a few hours…there would be no wild party tonight.

Though hectic, the large dressing room was festive. Well-groomed dudes in flowered Hawaiian shirts and heavy gold jewelry, accompanied by flashy, expensively dressed women in very tight designer clothes, moved casually around the cellar-like chamber. I did not recognize any of them.

Towards the rear, talking excitedly to the roadies, was a small flock of groupies, clustered along a row of guitars lying in their still-opened cases.

And in the middle of the room, the remaining band members

slouched in soft chairs and couches, unwinding and chatting with friends.

Standing alone, slightly apart from the scene, was the comedian who had opened the show. He caught me looking at him and smiled. So I walked over and started up a conversation.

His name was Don Diamond. Approximately my height, he was a little heavier, with close-cropped, dark curly hair and a very prominent ethnic nose. His most striking feature, however, was a pair of extremely penetrating eyes.

His eyes were dark brown, almost as black as his hair, the effect of which was hypnotizing. But they were not threatening...in fact, quite the opposite. Framed by equally dark bushy eyebrows, his eyes expressed considerable emotion and warmth.

Diamond was friendly and outgoing, but a bit...overwhelmed. I had assumed that he was part of the entourage, but he said otherwise. He was on his own tour of small comedy clubs throughout the Southeast, and was added to two Jimmy Buffett concerts...this show and one last night in Orlando. He said something about Buffett's management adding him to the shows at the last minute.

I told him that Norman and I had arrived late, but what we had seen of his act was very funny. He was appreciative of my review and he seemed to welcome my company.

I DIDN'T KNOW MUCH about comedy. I had seen Rodney Dangerfield once in New York and, of course, I loved Johnny Carson, and comics I'd seen in the movies like Steve Martin and Eddie Murphy...but I'd never followed comedians as eagerly as I had musicians.

As I talked with Diamond, he struck me as...not so much funny, as...intelligent and expressive. He seemed bizarre in a way I couldn't exactly say...perhaps he was always searching for a joke instead of making direct communication...but his quick wit made him fun to be around and I immediately related to him. I'd spent so many recent months in a dormitory full of pranksters, always riding each other about something. So I was well-practiced in trading barbs. And it was by habit as much as anything that I sat there with Diamond laughing at every little thing.

He would have made a good bunkie, I concluded. In any event, he appeared to be as entertained by my rude comments and old Coral Reefer tales as I was by his outlandish observations.

I WAS CAUGHT up in the backstage revelry when two uniformed police officers suddenly rushed in. I looked around the room for Norman, and saw him over by the bar searching frantically for me. I turned my back on them and dropped down on one of the couches.

It turned out to be a false alarm. Apparently, someone's purse had been stolen…or more likely, lost or mislaid. Or perhaps they used the excuse to get some autographs. But their presence reminded me of my predicament, and I became wary.

Norman called me over. It was getting late and the action was slowing down. We finished our drinks and decided to check around one more time for Fingers, then leave. We couldn't find him anywhere so we said our farewells and headed for the exit… but not before Kenny D took a short break to give us each a tour T-shirt and a bear hug. Kenny D wasn't aware of my situation. But, had he known, I was confident he would have treated me with the same warmth. What a guy.

I walked out into the empty parking lot feeling lighthearted. Norman was still singing…I think it was "Trying to Reason with the Hurricane Season." Tone deaf.

WE SLEPT late and ordered a room service brunch. It had been way past midnight when we finally limped away from the arena. We were both beat and had decided against driving back to Panama City. Instead we found a room at a nearby Holiday Inn. Norman had his suitcase with him, but I had come unprepared, since all my stuff was back at the condo. I used the toiletries provided by the hotel, and Norman lent me some clean underwear. And…I still had my new tour T-shirt to wear.

We were slow getting started…both of us still tired from the drive over and the night's excitement. Eventually we planned a quick drive through the FSU campus, for old times' sake, before calling Judy and returning to Panama City.

I SAT in the car in front of Bill's Bookstore, across from the university, as Norman used the payphone. We were so late checking out of the room, Norman thought we should stop and call Judy before our tour of the campus. I chuckled to myself, wondering if Smith Hall, our old dorm, still looked like a tenement house.

Watching the students walk leisurely along the sidewalk, I had already counted three Buffett T-shirts exactly like the one I was wearing. All the students looked so young. Has it been that long, I asked myself. I looked at my eyes in the car mirror, searching for some spark of youth. Then, I glanced over at Norman on the phone.

He was white…he ran nervous fingers through his hair and suddenly winced and closed his eyes. Then he hung up the phone and slowly returned to the car, turning his head back and forth, scanning the surrounding area. Something was wrong.

"What's up?" I immediately asked.

He started the car and pulled away quickly. After turning the corner he finally spoke. "They busted the party last night."

"The condo?"

"Yeah...Panama City. Judy got a call in the middle of the night. She thought we were busted too." We would have been.

"Is she alright?" She must have been going crazy.

"Now she is," Norman replied. "...or at least she's a lot better."

"And Larry?" I thought of poor Larry sitting in the county jail.

"Judy doesn't know...I guess they got him too."

"What now?" I asked, trying to concentrate.

"I don't know...I told Judy that we would call her tonight at her folks' house." Norman was upset. He slumped in the car seat and clenched his jaw tightly. I knew that he was worried about Judy. She was obviously beside herself.

I was disturbed, but calm. "Why don't we just go check back into the room and lay low until then."

A GLOOM HUNG over us as we sat around the hotel room. No laughing or joking...so different from the good-natured camaraderie of the preceding days. Although we were presently safe, we were shaken. We took turns staring at the ceiling.

Later that afternoon, we attempted to formulate a plan...to fight off a developing depression. We found a phone and called Skip Shelby, an old friend of ours up in Hilton Head, South Carolina.

Skip was an affluent ex-smuggler from an old South Carolina family. In his younger years, he used to allow shrimp boats full of marijuana to unload on his family's spacious, yet isolated, plantation property.

Ironically, Skip was never caught...for his own crimes. However, he was convicted of a conspiracy, which took place after he had retired, and he served forty months in the Federal Prison Camp at Eglin Air Force Base for something he never did. Good-naturedly, he figured that it somehow all evened out.

Skip agreed to put me up for a while. He could even provide a job at his brother's marina, where I could lie low and work out some better plans. I also knew he figured to take some of my money on the golf course..."Dream on, Skippy boy," I said under my breath, mechanically practicing a slow backswing with an imaginary golf club.

Norman would drive me up, stay with me until Skip could arrange a car for me, then make his way home...all within a week. We would both be relieved to get me out of Florida, and I knew he'd be relieved to finally get home.

Events were racing ahead of me. My life was in turmoil. It had all gone so smoothly up to this point, causing me to drop my guard. Now, I knew I was running...that they hadn't forgotten about me. They had served notice that they were out to recapture me. I was scared...so was Norman.

HAVING MADE A DECISION OF SORTS, we were feeling better. Back at the room, we had time to talk ourselves out of our funk. We even started kidding again.

"We could go back to Montgomery," I suggested. "They won't be looking for me there."

"This next time, let's try a place that's more fun to visit," Norman cracked. Each time he visited me at the Camp, he would complain about how dead Montgomery was.

"Oh great, man. How would you like to visit Marion, Illinois?" I shuddered, thinking about confinement behind the razor wire at the infamous Federal lockdown in Marion.

We laughed nervously.

The day dragged on. We napped and watched the television absentmindedly. Daydreaming, I thought about eventually escaping to Toronto...I knew a great girl there. I was considering the possibility as I drifted off to sleep.

I WOKE with a start and looked over at Norman in the next bed. He was still sleeping. And snoring…loudly. I was amused…when did he start snoring like that? Christ, at that volume, they would hassle him to death in the Camp dormitories.

I was restless and it was still early, so I went down to the restaurant to find something to eat. I let Norman continue his nap. He still seemed uptight from his earlier phone conversation with Judy.

"Hey…over here," a voice called to me as I walked into the coffee shop. It was Don Diamond, the comedian. I joined him happily.

I ordered some food and ate hungrily as we took turns teasing the waitress. She giggled self-consciously, but kept returning for more good-natured abuse.

Eventually, he turned to me, somewhat embarrassed, and said, "You know, I don't remember…or you never told me, your name."

I had purposely not used my name backstage. I hesitated and said, "Oh…it's…Eddie Walker."

"Eddie? Weren't they all calling you John last night…?" He got me.

"I…oh…that's a nickname…" I stammered. I was in no condition to go through this. Then I added, "I thought you didn't remember."

He ignored my question and answered his own. "Oh yeah, of course…Johnny Walker, the Scotch."

Johnny Walker, Owen Singer's favorite whiskey. Man, this guy was quick.

"…exactly," I agreed. You can call me John…or Eddie." I must have sounded ridiculous. I needed to get better at this…fast.

As we talked, he told me more of his plans. He was traveling by himself, beginning a tour of Florida comedy clubs…Coconuts Comedy Clubs.

"Coconuts," I exclaimed, my mouth full of grouper sandwich. "They have one of them in St. Pete, where I…used to live."

"Yeah, that's the one," he replied. "They have clubs all over the State…Jacksonville, Merritt Island, Miami, Key West…" He went on, obviously enjoying my company.

Diamond said that the best part about the upcoming tour was the Showtime cable TV special they were shooting at Coconuts' Key West club. He was scheduled to perform on the show, and he was excited.

"Do you have any more big concerts coming up?" I asked.

"Nothing definite," he answered. "They pop up from time to time." He explained that more and more concerts were using comedians because they were less expensive than a musical opener, but more importantly, because comedians had no sound requirements…only one microphone. Plus, a good comic put people in the audience in a fun mood, ready to enjoy the music.

"Yeah, you certainly did that last night," I agreed. He smiled appreciatively.

But Diamond emphasized that big concerts were not his favorite thing to do, because the thick sound in most large halls muffled too many words, making some of his act indecipherable. And, in an arena, everyone sat so far away from the stage that much of the intimacy needed for successful comedy was lost. He added, though, that a concert like Buffett's was tremendous exposure…and he never turned them down.

"Have you ever been to a real comedy club?" he then asked.

"Only once, years ago," I answered, relating my one Rodney Dangerfield experience. But the passage of time had blurred many of the specifics. "No" would have been the better answer.

"That's where you really see a comedian at his best," Diamond stressed. "It's important to a comic's timing that you hear every sound and see every expression."

Picturing a small club in my mind, I laughed and said that I could never be a comic myself…on any stage…up there all alone, trying to make people laugh. "No offense," I said sincerely, "but comedians…seem kind of strange."

"What do you mean, strange?" he asked, pretending to pick his nose. I laughed.

"Anyway," he continued, "you struck me as someone who could handle it easily."

I laughed again, still picturing it in my mind. Absolutely no way.

Then he surprised me by asking, "What do you do for a living?"

The conversation turned…suddenly getting difficult. "I'm…a writer."

"Really?" he said, surprised. I surprised myself, too, with that comment.

"What, you mean books?"

"Ah…no." I was struggling…what a jerk. "I used to work for a newspaper. But now, I'm…kicking around, trying to put together material…for a book." Where was I coming up with all of this ridiculous shit?

I'm digging myself in deeper, I thought. I was uncomfortable lying. And I had a lifetime of it ahead of me. It was depressing.

"Ever write any comedy?" he questioned.

"Comedy…?"

"You know…jokes?"

"No." I was already nervous enough. I wanted to change the subject. I finished my sandwich. He was lost in thought for a minute…calculating something.

"Listen…I've got a few weeks ahead of me in Florida. I'm all by myself and…well, would you like to come along?" he asked unexpectedly.

"…and do what?" I responded, knowing the idea was out of the question. The day after tomorrow, I'd be playing golf with Skip in Hilton Head.

"Well, you could…hey, wait a minute…I don't want to kiss you," he bellowed, loud enough for everyone in the bar to hear.

That particular thought never crossed my mind...I'd only asked the question for conversation. I laughed awkwardly and looked around the room. He had attracted attention with his booming voice. I turned red and, noticing, he laughed too.

"No, no..." he continued, laughing. "I don't know, you could write some bits with me and stuff, and...show me around," he explained. After a pause, he added, "I'd enjoy the company."

I closed my eyes in an effort to quiet him down. He threw up his hands in exasperation, still laughing. What a damn nice guy, I thought. It was a wild idea, and I was oddly interested, but circumstances were forcing me in another direction. And hell...I couldn't even be honest with him about who I really was. No, once your life gets fucked up, it stays fucked up, I silently concluded.

"Thanks, man," I said. "I mean it. But I'm heading up north tomorrow."

"I can dig it," he said. "Well...I'm pulling out tonight myself." He thought for a second, then said, "Hope to see you down the line."

I shook his hand. "Break a leg...and I'll be watching for you on Showtime."

We finished our meal and parted ways. I returned to the room, wondering just what I was going to do with myself.

IT WAS time to call Judy. We hustled out of the hotel and drove slowly across town, searching for an isolated payphone. Within minutes, Norman pulled the car into a 7-11, down to the end of the parking lot, and we went to the phone together.

Judy answered on the first ring. She had evidently received some more information...and listening to Norman talk to her, I could tell that she had calmed down a great deal.

"She's a solid lady," I whispered into Norman's free ear.

Norman turned to me and laughed. "Larry got away," he chuckled. "He called Judy today."

"What...?" he said into the phone. Turning to me again, he repeated Judy's words. "...and Larry says he has only ten dollars, no shoes...and no blow."

We laughed. "It's funny he even mentioned the shoes," I cracked.

Judy overheard my comment and I could hear her laughing... that distinctive laugh of hers...over the phone.

Loud voices disturbed me from the other end of the parking lot. Norman put his finger in his ear and hunched over to hear better. I turned around. Three black jokers were shouting at a car pulling into the store. I couldn't catch exactly what they were yelling...and although I heard at least three distinct "motherfuckers," their tone did not strike me as particularly belligerent.

I hadn't heard that kind of loud jiving since leaving the Camp. It reminded me of Terry High-Five and his buddies. I smiled. I had grown accustomed to brothers bad-mouthing the world. But that guy in the car is probably scared shitless, I thought.

One of them turned and caught me standing with my hands on my hips and a smile on my face. He flashed a toothy smile and saluted me with his fist. I nodded in return, thinking of how time in jail had changed my perspective. Two years ago, I would have either been annoyed, or nervous about a possible confrontation. Rave on, fellas...what the hell.

Norman tapped my shoulder to attract my attention. "Judy wants to say hello," he said, obviously feeling better. "I'm going to get some chips or something...and a brew. Want one?" he asked.

I nodded and took the phone.

I HAD KNOWN Judy for a long time. I had actually met her before Norman had.

I remember it clearly. It was one of those Tuesday nights, and I had just finished playing softball down the beach at Egan Field, near Blind Pass. It was a ritual that after the game, the team would head to the Golden Phoenix, a local Chinese restaurant, for appetizers and a few drinks at their friendly bar. It also gave us ballplayers the opportunity to persuade Ginger, the dazzling bartender, to finally go out with one of us. Up to that point, she never had.

As the team filed in and occupied nearly every seat around the horseshoe-shaped bar, I noticed a lovely new face sitting in a booth across from the cash register. She and Ginger were engaged in an animated discussion.

When Ginger served me my first beer, I asked her the identity of the fair-haired maiden in the booth.

"Oh, that's Judy Oliver," she replied offhandedly. "A friend of mine."

After the softball team had consumed their fill and moved along, I purposely stayed behind to talk with Ginger and her friend.

Judy turned out to be a special person. She was casual, humorous and direct…and honest. I remember being extremely impressed. But I never had the chance to follow up on that first meeting with Judy, because Ginger noticed our warm conversation, and my obvious captivation, and, as women will sometimes do when they are removed from the center of attention, she began to flirt with me.

And as fate would have it, I wound up accepting Ginger's invitation to go have a drink, as Judy slipped away. Again…chasing the Gingers of the world.

But my short relationship with Ginger brought Norman and Judy together some days later. And for them, it was love at first sight.

After she and Norman began seeing each other, Judy and I became even closer. And my opinion of her never diminished. She was originally from Indiana, and had moved to Florida with her parents when she was very young. I always kidded her about her farm girl roots, but what I truly thought was that she had "horse-sense"...good judgment and intelligence. Not to mention that body...what was that story about the farmer's daughter?

By the time of their wedding, I counted Judy as one of my closer friends. And after I went to prison, she stayed in close touch and encouraged Norman to visit me as often as possible.

I loved her in a very healthy way...and I appreciated her attention.

JUDY DIDN'T WANT to just say hello, though, she wanted a serious conversation...

"Johnny...I want to ask you a big favor," she began. She was the only person in my whole life to always call me Johnny.

"Anything, darlin'."

"Would you please send Norman back home tomorrow...," she asked. I could hear her holding back tears. I was silent.

She said that strange people were calling the house asking for him...and the longer this went on, the more chance he could get himself into trouble. She also made a good point...that Norman hadn't bargained for this in his life the way so many other people had with their precarious lifestyles. I knew she was referring to me.

She began to cry.

"Judy..." I said.

"Don't hate me, Johnny," she sobbed. "I know how much we owe you...money, and..." She couldn't continue.

Judy was correct...enough was enough, especially under the circumstances. I did not know what to do...I didn't even have a car. But I said, "He'll be home tonight."

"Are you sure you don't hate me, Johnny...I..."

"Damn, Judy, I love you guys..." I hesitated, searching for something else to say.

"And...I agree that it's better for him to get his ass home."

She continued to cry. Then she caught herself and said, "Johnny...don't tell Norman that I..."

"Hey," I said forcefully, "I understand...leave it to me, okay?"

"...okay...I'm sorry."

"And don't say that...there's nothing to be sorry about."

She calmed down. "Are you going to be alright?" she asked weakly.

"You bet, darlin'...and thanks for the wig. It's really me."

Judy was silent, so I added, "And if I arrive on your doorstep one dark night, disguised in drag...do you know what else I'll want?"

"What," she asked more cheerfully.

"Your famous tuna casserole." We had a long-standing joke about her tuna casserole. She swore she made the world's best... and I always avoided eating it...something from my childhood years. It was a corny thing for me to say, but it was a point of closeness only we shared.

"Oh, Johnny..." She started crying again.

Norman tapped my shoulder. I looked around and he handed me a beer.

"Okay, baby," I said loud enough for him to hear, "enough phone sex."

He smiled and choked on his beer.

As Norman grabbed the phone to say a quick goodbye, I reflected once more on our friendship. There was nothing left to explore. He had come through for me...and now it was time for me to give something back.

He hung up and turned around to find me sitting on the curb, slowly sipping my beer. He sat down next to me, put his elbows on his knees, and sighed deeply, as if reading my mind.

We were both silent. Although it was a cool clear night, we could hear thunder rumbling in the distance. It would pour before the night was over.

Norman spoke first. "Well, they didn't get Larry."

"They will, man," I said softly, still staring off into the distant sky.

"You really think so...?" Norman asked, surprised.

I turned toward him, put my hand on his shoulder, and said evenly, "Norman...it's time for you to go home."

He wanted to speak, but I stopped him. "Listen to me, man." I didn't know where to begin. "Larry's a good guy...but he's a fuck-up. They'll catch him quickly, if they haven't already got him."

"So...?" Norman tried to stand up. I held him down.

"Just listen to me for a minute." He looked at his shoes as I continued. "And after they get him, he may not be strong enough to...hold out." I searched for the right words. "Even if he doesn't rat on you, he could just as easily screw up and unintentionally implicate you."

He nodded in understanding. I took another sip of my beer.

Measuring my words, I said, "Look, man, you have to go home. If they call your house, you should be there...not out on the run with me."

"That makes sense," he agreed. "So after we..."

"No, man," I interrupted, "tonight."

"John...you have no clothes, no car..." he protested.

"I've got money in my pocket, solid identification, a great head start, and..." I paused, "...a very good friend." I held out my hands and laughed, "What more can a fugitive want in life?"

He didn't smile. "Let me take you to Skip's anyway. We could leave tonight...and it would make me feel better."

"No," I said, unbending.

"At least let me stay the night...take you to the mall and find some clothes. Shit...I'd feel guilty..."

"Guilty...?" I exclaimed. "My main man Stormin'...you've already gone above and beyond..."

"You'll need a ride to the airport..."

"You go tonight, Norman," I insisted. "I'll take care of everything else...I'll take a cab, a bus...but you go tonight."

He hung his head. It was decided.

"I can take you back to the room, can't I?" he asked meekly.

"Hell, yeah...I'm going to steal all your underwear and socks."

He finally laughed. It began as a chuckle, then grew.

"You're lucky you're such a skinny shit," I said, "or I'd be taking all your clothes."

He kept laughing. I pretended not to notice the mixed emotions in his laughter, and quipped, "Laugh if you want, shithead...I'm serious."

But I wasn't serious. I was sorry that Norman was leaving. I hadn't had enough time with him. And who knows when I'd ever see him again.

I TOOK his baggiest T-shirt and put it on. It was still tight on me. I handed him the Buffett T-shirt that Kenny D had given me.

"Here, give this to Judy," I said.

He smiled and took the shirt. "Seems like you're always giving your clothes away to women." I chuckled at the memory of my G&S hat on River Road. I wish I had that hat back now.

We stared at each other. It was getting late...I had so much to say, but no time left. "Look, man, it won't be a good idea for me to call...at least not for awhile," I said haltingly.

"I know..." he answered. "But I'll be checking in with Skip from time to time..." This was difficult for both of us.

Damn, I was not ready to be alone yet, but I couldn't stall any longer. Norman had to get on the road. It was at least five hours to St. Petersburg.

I steadied myself and reached for his hand. "Norman…thanks," I choked.

He pushed my hand away and hugged me…hard. "Good luck, pard," he replied, barely audible.

It was pouring rain as he wheeled out of the parking lot. Under the streetlight, he looked back once and waved. I just stood there watching him drive away. For the first time in years, I actually felt like crying.

"Mount Gay and orange juice…with a splash of pineapple," I told the bartender.

"Sorry, we don't carry Mount Gay. How about Bacardi?" she replied tonelessly. She was tall and lanky…and bored.

"Fine," I said. I was in no mood to cheer her up. I was only back in the hotel bar because I didn't feel like spending any more time in the room. I didn't want to think about being alone, or about the future…or about anything. This lonely joint was the perfect place to wash away my misery.

"How about an injection of love lava, honey," Don Diamond suddenly boomed at the startled girl.

His unexpected appearance immediately livened up the atmosphere in the near-empty bar. He sat down on the barstool next to mine, and said, "Why the long face, Hemingway?"

I ignored his sarcasm, and said, "I thought you were leaving tonight."

"I am," he hollered, still eyeing the timid bartender. She had retreated warily away from us.

"Kinda' late, isn't it?" I asked, amused at the girl's reaction.

"I only have to drive to Jacksonville. They tell me it's just a couple of hours." He smiled at me.

Then he turned and growled at the bartender. "How about an Australian kiss?"

"What's that?" she asked timidly, still at the other end of the bar.

"Same as a French kiss, only down under," he cracked.

She finally smiled.

"She loves me...I can tell," Diamond joked, elbowing me.

I WAS STILL NURSING my first drink, when Diamond ordered his third. He was jovial and boisterous, and he finally had the bartender, Gloria, laughing and hanging out at our end of the bar. He made me feel better too...with his continued barrage of one-liners.

Gloria bought his drink. He ordered her to pour herself a shot, and they toasted. I studied him...I couldn't determine whether he was older or younger than me.

Then I looked at his glass. "Jacksonville's not that close," I warned him.

He twirled his ice cubes with his finger, licked it mischievously and said, "Maybe Gloria will drive me..."

She slapped his wet hand, and he turned his barstool toward me. "How about you?" he said. "You're soberer than me...or Gloria."

Looking into his eyes, I could see that he was halfway serious. I played along. "You mean this afternoon's offer is still open?" I responded with a laugh.

He didn't blink. "You bet your ass."

I decided on the spur of the moment. "What the hell..."

Chapter Nine

"Thank you very much, ladies and gentlemen...you've been a super crowd."

Don Diamond was talking to his audience, having finished what he would refer to as "another great show by the Double D."

It had been that...a great show. It didn't take me long to understand why he preferred working a smaller, cleaner-sounding room. Every sound effect and every vocal inflection he made added to his inventive routine. And the cozy crowd was seated so close to the tiny stage that their reaction to his material was emphasized by the stage lights...all adding to the intimate living-room type atmosphere.

Diamond was much funnier than I had originally estimated. Of course, I knew he was naturally quick-witted and humorous. But on the stage, he was transformed into another animal altogether... he was intense, a comedic wizard talking in many tongues, rapidly shifting from identity to identity, and easily employing dramatic mood swings to enhance each character he assumed. After viewing his act for two weeks now, I was extremely impressed.

I sat at the bar in the back of the room...happily, because he relentlessly harassed those close to the stage. In fact, while his act consisted of pre-planned routines, a good portion of his time was taken working off the audience's reaction and personality.

For me there was an unexpected bonus. At the Buffett concert in Tallahassee, I was a bit intimidated by the possibility of trouble in the large crowd. And when the arena lights came on at the conclusion of the show, I found myself looking over my shoulder, unconsciously searching out avenues of escape.

But in the small, dimly lit comedy club, I experienced a wonderful sense of anonymity. A comfortable feeling of being lost, out of the way and on the move...all at the same time.

I mentioned this sensation to Diamond, and while intuition told me that I had touched upon a sensitive area, he made no reply...he just shook his head and shrugged. I couldn't put my finger on it, but something in the way he shrugged made me wonder if there was more to it. Or he might have been toying with me as he sometimes enjoyed doing.

Diamond joined me at the bar and ordered a ginger ale. During my short time with him, I noticed that he had a peculiar drinking pattern. Most nights he would only have one or two...and usually no alcohol at all. But once in a while he would drink heavily, as if to exorcise some unknown demon.

He was not an obnoxious drunk. Actually, he was non-stop charming. But when he was in that inebriated condition, he needed company badly...he wanted an audience. I came to the conclusion that these occasional escapades were meant to repel an undefined loneliness that surfaced every so often. It was sad, though somewhat eerie.

My original intention was to drive Diamond to Jacksonville, then go on to Skip's from there. But it wasn't long before I became comfortable with the safe feeling that grew around me. And since the club paid for our room, and Diamond enjoyed having me aboard, I remained. He would introduce me as his manager and co-writer. That got me employee discounts on food, drinks or an occasional extra room.

After putting Skip off for days, I finally called to inform him that I wouldn't be traveling to South Carolina anytime soon. He was disappointed...he had been looking forward to a summer of golf. He understood, however, and left the invitation open.

My call to Skip was timely made, for he had been in contact with Norman, and he was able to bring me up to date on what was happening at home. Norman wanted me to know that Larry had, indeed, been picked up by the law...in Panama City as I had predicted. In addition, I was distressed to learn that government agents had spoken to Norman twice already, and that he was definitely suspected of assisting me to escape. Norman told Skip to assure me that he was fine, that they had only questioned him, but I cursed myself anyway.

That news prompted me to call Owen Singer. Surprisingly, he was not judgmental of my actions. Owen even laughed when he told me that Jeff Banner, the DEA agent, had called, furious about losing me. I could hear in Owen's voice that he thought it served Banner right.

Owen also said that my mother was frantic with worry, but that my sisters were elated...my little sister had even wanted to throw a party. And he confirmed that Larry was under pressure to talk about my escape.

He explained that it was early yet, but as far as he could determine, the government had no witnesses, or any other evidence regarding my escape...except perhaps Larry. And Larry had told them nothing to this point.

"You can bet they'll be turning up the heat on Larry to deliver someone," Owen said.

I asked him how much heat they could realistically apply. Owen replied that Larry was looking to do time, as an accessory to my escape, and for some related cocaine charges they had pinned on him from the Panama City bust. In other words, considerable pressure could be brought to bear. Now we'd see what Larry was made of. It wasn't comforting, and I worried for Norman and Judy.

I COMBED through my new suitcase, searching for a pen and the notebook that had become my new address book. After spending two hours in a local mall, shopping for clothes, toiletries and other odds and ends, I had everything jumbled together…a result of poor packing.

"How can a writer not have a pen and paper at his command?" Diamond complained.

Out of nowhere, he had decided that it was time for me to begin comedy writing. My attempts up to this point were lame, consisting mostly of making notes of his suggestions…"Let's do a bit about diseases…" he would begin to say as I scribbled. And then he would race ahead, too fast for me to follow. But he would run a small tape recorder anyway, so I was rather useless.

Now, he explained that he wanted me to carry a notepad in order to jot down ideas that popped into my mind. He said that most of his extensive routines were developed through the tape machine…that the rapid flow of comedy could never be captured by a pen and paper. Nevertheless, he insisted that the material was usually born on a handwritten note, hastily written at the spur of the moment and shoved into a pocket for later review.

He gave me my first assignment. I was to sit in the audience and concentrate on only one thing…hecklers.

THE HECKLER. Wherever there was comedy, there was the ever present heckler. Unchecked, he could disrupt the flow of even the most talented of entertainers. It was critical to the success of one's act to either work the heckler into one's routine or, failing that, to immediately eliminate the problem.

Most heckling was innocent...people merely into the mood created by the figure onstage. Most people considered themselves funny, and once the comedian provoked laughter, it sometimes naturally followed that people would attempt to join with their own good-natured additions to the joke.

These people could usually be dissuaded gracefully...in fact, most comedians hoped for some mild heckling. It created a humorous tension, and gave them the opportunity to work the audience creatively, or embarrass the offender to the amusement of the rest of the crowd.

Although the serious heckler was an infrequent visitor to comedy clubs, when present he could be a major problem. All by himself, a loudmouth could destroy the show. According to Diamond, there was only one-way to deal with him...using the put-down.

He said every comic should be armed with a series of put-downs to deal with the inevitable know-it-all drunk that finds his way to every comedy club. An effective put-down re-establishes command of the room, and keeps people laughing at the same time. The best put-down will even get an audience to rally to the comic's defense, shouting down the boring offender.

Diamond wanted me to begin focusing on the serious heckler...the asshole.

"This is basic to comedy," he explained. "You naturally exhibit many of the fundamental skills anyway...so concentrate on coming up with some killer one-liners."

I was...flattered. And it wouldn't be long before I was given my first opportunity.

THAT NIGHT I brought my small notebook to the club. I sat away from the bar, over at an empty booth, feeling detached and a little excited at the same time. I studied the show, hoping for inspiration.

The emcee did five minutes of announcements, introductions and Polish jokes. Mildly funny...but standard stuff.

The feature act was a comic from Philadelphia, who would share several dates with Diamond on the Coconuts tour. He was relatively creative, but his show revolved around well-used themes...TV ads, those diarrhea and feminine hygiene commercials, and take-offs on blind dates and growing up in Philly.

It was a thin Thursday night crowd. Although small, they were involved, and they hurled several comments toward the stage. The comic handled the situation masterfully, and even caused more laughs with his make-believe horrified looks directed at those speaking out.

Near the end of his set, though, a large woman seated at the table in front of my booth started getting loud. She was obviously drunk, and she began to shout offensive remarks at the comic.

Try as he did, he was unable to control the woman, and the crowd then became amused at his ineptitude. His act collapsed in failure, and as he left the stage, I heard the woman order another round of drinks.

I studied her as she began to irritate me...and although I could think of many crude insults, I was unable to convert any of it to usable humor. This task might be over my head, I thought.

Diamond was the headliner, and the final act of the evening. He began very fast and loud, not allowing any hecklers the opportunity to intervene. He had the audience immediately laughing. Once, the woman tried to shout something at him, but the noise of the laughter drowned her out.

Though Diamond recognized her attempt, he chose to ignore her presence altogether. Defeated, she went to the bathroom.

She did not return to her seat for at least fifteen minutes, and by then Diamond was rolling. He was halfway through his New York surfer routine...the one he used at the Buffett concert...and the room was under his spell.

The big woman would be quiet no longer. She loudly interrupted Diamond with an incoherent question.

"Yes, gorgeous, you wanted something?" Diamond snapped. Looking at her...her dumpy appearance...the people laughed.

She mumbled something and swallowed her drink. Sensing a shift in the atmosphere, perhaps an upcoming battle, Diamond adeptly slipped out of his routine, and went to conversation with the audience. The transition was slick, so that when the woman began again, Diamond was ready for her, and the show did not appear sidetracked.

"I don't get it...," she bellowed.

I expected a devastating retort, but Diamond encouraged her questions. "Tell me, gorgeous," he replied, "what's so hard to figure out?"

There were snickers in the room. But they soon turned into uproarious laughter as the woman launched into a series of questions, her speech so slurred that no one could understand her. Instead of cutting her off, Diamond wore her out. He neatly translated each question, substituting his own version, and the audience would howl at his intentionally outrageous translations.

"What, gorgeous...you say you're not wearing any underwear?"

"...how many tattoos?"

"...stuck up where?"

I was laughing out loud. So was the woman's friend, who was sitting with her.

Finally, tired of the abuse, she melted back into the crowd, and Diamond, having won the exchange, began another routine.

Midway through a funny, but philosophical bit about going to a funeral, she started up again. This time, Diamond was disturbed, as she had interrupted at a critical point in one of his favorite bits. He glared at her, and she stopped, putting her hand playfully over her mouth.

He began again, and she yelled again. Her caustic voice snapped my senses, and was the catalyst for my initiation into the comedy world. As the barmaid stood by my table with a drink for Diamond, I hastily wrote a few words on my pad. I peeled it from the notebook and sent it to the stage with his drink.

There was a silence in the room as Diamond sipped his drink. He casually read my note and smiled. Then he calmly continued, and was able to complete his act…almost. The woman jabbered something again, intentionally trying to disturb him. By now, she thought she was funny.

Diamond stopped, and said sarcastically, "Lady, would you please close your legs…there's an echo in the room!"

The room exploded with laughter. He'd hit a homerun with that comment, and he nodded slightly to me, acknowledging my contribution.

The people turned on the woman, shouting derisively, "Close your legs," every time she attempted to talk thereafter. It was hilarious, and Diamond finished his show to a standing ovation.

"CONGRATULATIONS," he said genuinely.

I beamed…I was proud of myself. But I was also aware of my meager contribution. "Damn…it took me all night to think of that line," I said honestly.

"A lot of comics can't think of a knockout line like that all year," he replied seriously.

"Does that mean I can take the rest of the year off?" I joked.

He laughed loudly and I was pleased. I enjoyed making this talented comedian laugh.

"This calls for a drink," he said, calling the bartender.

I reached for my drink and hoisted my glass. "Well, I broke my comedy cherry," I said cheerfully.

"Oh, no...you just copped a feel," he stated with some authority. "You break your cherry when you get on stage."

"That'll never happen, man," I replied, shuddering at the thought.

Chapter Ten

The weeks passed. First Jacksonville, then Orlando, then Daytona and St. Augustine…now, we were midway through our week in Merritt Island. I continued to relax inside the safe cocoon of the little comedy clubs we visited.

Every night was entertaining. The new comedians on each bill, the club owners, the bartenders, the waitresses and the varying audiences…all the unusual and frenetic personalities I was exposed to…descended upon me in an unending assault on my funny bone. I discovered that the comedy scene was a stimulating world of lovable lunatics.

In Merritt Island, we were put up in a condominium. It was a pleasant change from our usual hotel room. We each had more privacy, and I learned another important thing about Diamond. He was a fabulous cook…he said *chef.*

He used the condo's kitchen to prepare a succulent leg of lamb, with grilled vegetables and other trimmings, which he served with great fanfare.

"My compliments to the chef," I chided. Chef, of course.

"Just another great show by the Double D," he replied, as if I shouldn't be surprised.

Perhaps I shouldn't have been surprised. But everything about him surprised me. His life was a curious paradox.

Onstage, he opened himself to his audience, exposing his emotional roots. Offstage, while he was merry, he was also guarded and aloof. During his show, he spoke about men and women as if he had had considerable experience with love, and the delicate give and take struggle that makes a relationship work. But after the show, his tastes leaned toward easy women...comedy groupies, which I learned were almost as numerous as band groupies...and in the larger cities, he might even find a prostitute for companionship.

Diamond treated me as a confidant, informing me of the peculiarities of the other comics or club owners we ran across, and graciously sharing with me the tricks of the trade.

However, he never discussed himself...his past, his hopes, nothing...except, of course, his work. It was only in his work that he gave clues to his complex personality. And what one couldn't learn about him when he was onstage, he would not offer later.

Once, in Orlando, he went on another "bender," as he called it. He kept me up all night, drinking and talking in riddles. In an attempt to get closer, I tried to ask him some personal questions about his background.

"Look," he said pointedly, "you jumped in my car with no clothes, a pocketful of money and a name that half the time you don't respond to..." He suddenly changed from being serious, to being amused. He laughed, and said, "...and a wig."

Having said it, he laughed uncontrollably at the thought. And I joined him...my story suddenly seemed so ludicrous. We laughed and laughed.

"...and you're asking me questions?" he said through his tears of laughter. My sides began to hurt.

"Okay, okay..." I choked, holding up my hands, imploring the comedy gods to release us.

We calmed, our laughter turning into rosy merriment. I looked at him over an empty glass, and said, with resignation, "My real name is John...I guess you already figured that much out."

"I use many names too," he winked as he whispered in a hoarse conspiratorial voice. "But call me Diamond," he added.

"And I'm not really a writer," I admitted.

He laughed again. "No shit." He probably had that figured out long ago.

"As for the rest, um..." I stuttered, searching for a suitable starting point to my story.

"No..." he interrupted, "that's enough for one night."

He put his arm around my neck. "Thank you," he said softly, and walked to the ice machine with the empty bucket.

THE NEXT DAY was a day off, and Diamond allowed me to select the afternoon's activities. I took him to a driving range.

He couldn't even swing a golf club correctly, let alone make proper contact with the ball. He shanked it off the toe of the club, he whacked it with the heel and he sculled it with the bottom edge of the iron...all the while muttering obscenities. I chuckled...the sweet spot in the center of the club remained unscathed.

Diamond was definitely not a golfer. It didn't matter, though, for he preferred nursing his mammoth hangover, watching me hit shot after perfect shot.

Feeling my game coming back, I hit balls until my hands were too tender to continue. Then I quit reluctantly...only to find Diamond stretched out on a gallery bench, scribbling furiously in his notebook.

"Something new?" I questioned.

"Yeah..." was all he said.

It was ladies' night at the spacious Merritt Island club, and after the show we ended up with a house full of Coconuts' employees… and ladies, of course. Having the condo instead of a hotel room allowed us to expand our guest capacity considerably, and we had a full-fledged party on our hands.

Everyone was chattering about comedy. And I found it most humorous to watch the comedians work harder at impressing each other than at impressing the ladies. I chuckled, thinking of the many musicians I knew. They would not misplace their energy like that. Man, comedians are their own breed.

It was odd that everyone paid me enormous respect, and every so often, a witty remark was directed my way, as if to gain my approval. I suspected Diamond had something to do with their patronizing me. Diamond admitted it later, when our paths crossed at the icemaker. Opening the freezer door, he confessed, "Ah…I told them that you co-wrote some of my material."

I was speechless. "Hey, you gotta' have some credits in this business," he argued, still grinning.

"But I can't…" I finally stammered.

"Fake it 'till you make it," he suggested, and he rejoined the party.

The ubiquitous cocaine appeared. I laughed out loud at the paltry amount being passed around. It even looked funny…a yellow color. I thought that Larry would have been appalled at its questionable quality…and even more distressed at the rapidly disappearing quantity.

I skipped the drugs, as did Diamond…his reasons differed from mine. It was his theory that the more the girls had, the longer they would stay around. Cissy would have loved him, I thought.

Thinking about Larry and Cissy and Panama City reminded me that I should call soon for an update on the state of affairs at home. I almost lapsed into a sinking spell, but I pushed those disturbing thoughts from my mind...as I noticed a ladies' night refugee separated from the group. I pounced, and followed her into the hallway.

HAVING MANEUVERED the dark-eyed girl upstairs, we kicked off our shoes and sat on my bed, talking about show business. Diamond's gall had no limits. He had "confidentially" told her that I currently wrote for *Saturday Night Live*, and she was overly impressed.

Seeing her close, I realized that she was young. She lit a cigarette and balanced an ashtray on her knee. Then she shook her hair back...as if attempting to portray some degree of sophistication.

Her name was Lauren and she worked at a bank. She said she was twenty-two, although she looked even younger. Apparently, she attended ladies' night at Coconuts every week. "From a woman's point of view..." she said, comedy clubs were preferable to the regular "meat-market" bars. There was no pressure, and they were more fun.

She let me in on a little secret. "Women want to laugh more than anything else," she leaned forward and confided. I was amused that she presumed to speak for all womankind...at twenty-two years old.

As she leaned forward to speak, she lost her balance on the soft mattress. "Oops," she cried, trying not to spill the ashtray. She was unsuccessful, and she fell clumsily across my lap, scattering the ashes on the bed and on herself.

Embarrassed, she let herself go limp, and flashed a disarming smile at me. She looked so very young...

I ran my hand down the side of her face and wiped away the ashes. She closed her eyes. I wish I knew a few good jokes.

I lightly touched her forehead, then her nose, and then each of her soft eyebrows. She responded by slightly rolling her head and she smiled again. I gently pressed my finger against her lips and she kissed it softly.

I let my hand run down her exposed neck, and ever-so-slowly toward her open neckline, just under her shirt.

"Do you have any toot up here?" she asked, her eyes still closed.

"I don't think so," I answered, knowing that all the drugs were downstairs.

She opened her eyes. "Do you mind if we party for awhile first?" she asked sweetly.

Of course I did. "Of course I don't," I said.

As we walked downstairs, I noticed that she had taken her purse…and her shoes. She wasn't returning…at least not to this room.

"So much for the woman's point of view," I said under my breath, silently mocking her.

I knew that, given a few hours of cocaine and inane conversation, I could probably persuade her to join me. But as I watched her sit herself on the floor by the coffee table, just the thought of the effort it would require exhausted me.

I had one more drink and slipped upstairs to get some sleep… alone. I pulled the covers up to my chin, and comfortable with my decision, I slept soundly. I was undisturbed.

"You were making a statement," Diamond said at breakfast the next morning.

"No, I was just tired," I answered.

"You were tired alright…but of what?" he immediately responded.

I conceded with a grin, and returned to the tasty omelet he had prepared.

Diamond smiled victoriously, then said, "If you could answer that question, it would be the beginning of a great comedy routine."

I thought about what he said, then replied, "I don't know where to start...I guess I ..."

"Well, don't tell me...where's your fucking notepad?"

A flashy redhead straggled out from Diamond's bedroom. I recognized her from last night's party. Wouldn't you know he'd grab the trashiest looking one. He started to say something, but I cut him off...

"I know...great show, Double D."

He winked, but I waved him away. I wanted something else in my life, and I had an inner fear that I would wind up like...like him.

He walked over to me. "I can tell you'll not be satisfied with anything less than a queen." He was following my thoughts.

"I'm beginning to believe they don't exist," I groaned. My shallow experiences with women were defeating.

"Oh, but they do," he sang.

I glanced at the redhead in the kitchen and then back at him. He saw the doubt in my eyes.

"Take heart, sweet prince," he stated theatrically, "for yonder in Ft. Myers, our next stop, lies the fairest lady in the land...and she will inspire you."

"Nice, huh?" I brightened.

LISA KENNEDY MANAGED COCONUTS' Ft. Myers operation. She had been an actress, between projects, when she took over the fledgling enterprise. Diamond maintained that it was Lisa's vivacious and intelligent presence that made her Ft. Myers club one of Coconuts' most successful franchises.

"You'll love her," Diamond said matter-of-factly. "I'm not after that type of woman anymore," he said further, disregarding the redhead's glare, and opening himself up a bit.

I just looked at him without commenting. He smiled. "She's in the major leagues," he said with a wink.

Diamond went on to say that those few men who were not intimidated by a strong-willed, glamorous woman, wanted Lisa for their own…forever. And all other men lusted after her from afar.

The touring comedians worshipped her, and looked forward to working Ft. Myers because, above all, Lisa was a fabulous hostess, and they were all treated thoughtfully by this exceptional young woman.

I was following his hypnotic descriptions closely. I was more than intrigued. He looked at me and stopped abruptly.

"You'll appreciate her, and she'll give you hope that, perhaps, there's another one out there like her…but you can't have her," he advised. "Nobody can…except her husband."

"Husband?" He snapped the spell and I dismissed the idea. I wasn't after anyone's wife.

Diamond smirked and continued, "But you'll love her."

I left the breakfast table and stretched out on the couch, out of his view. I closed my eyes, thinking that sometimes Diamond could be so much more insightful than funny. Anyway, it would make next week's trip to Ft. Myers more interesting.

Diamond walked across the room and stood over me.

"My friend," he said, "I can see clearly, you're tired of the Little Leaguers."

Amen.

Chapter Eleven

An emergency arose in the aftermath of our party. The club's emcee was a casualty. Nothing serious…hell, nothing that would even slow down a veteran trouper like Diamond. But the emcee decided to call in sick at the last minute. And that sonofabitchcocksucker Diamond volunteered me to fill the malingerer's shoes. The club, of course, was delighted to have a man with my so-called credentials step in. Goddamn Diamond.

"Absolutely not…no!" I snapped with the finality of an unsympathetic loan officer.

I had enough on my mind already. I had phoned Skip earlier that afternoon, and he brought me up to date on Norman's situation. Although things hadn't changed much, Skip reported that Larry had finally been released on bail, and that Norman was not comfortable with his behavior. Larry was distant…scared and acting strange.

Also, Skip said that Norman wanted me to call him directly, over the weekend, at Judy's parents' house. It must be important for him to want to risk a telephone call. I was upset, it nagged at me, and I didn't need this further aggravation from Diamond.

Although even without the extra worry, I would never have wanted to go onstage anyway. Never.

Diamond promised that I would not have to tell any jokes. I only had to be congenial, make announcements and introduce each act as they came to the stage. He was so supportive and anxious for me to "get my feet wet" that I was tempted to tell him the truth…as to why it wouldn't be such a good idea for me to step out under the lights.

Instead, I skirted the issue. "Man, I just can't," I pleaded. "I wish I could explain all my reasons…"

I kept forgetting how intelligent Diamond was…more than that, how intuitive he could be. And as he looked into my eyes, he must have seen something more than stage fright, and he backed off.

An hour or so later, as we sat around the living room watching the maid finish up her cleaning, Diamond began a long, rambling commentary about comedy.

He traced the history of stage comedy, from court jesters, through clowns, and vaudeville, down to the modern-day standup comic. His perspective was interesting and his occasional anecdotes kept me laughing. But he was serious when he stressed the importance of humor as an educational tool.

He emphasized its value, in or out of the classroom, and he maintained that humor was critical to learning. In his opinion, for the lecturer to ignore humor in his presentation would result in the lecture, in turn, being ignored.

Diamond was standing…preaching, and he was on a roll. As she left, the housekeeper looked at us as if trying to decide whether or not we were dangerous. Diamond often had that effect on people.

Humor was woven into the fabric of our everyday lives, he claimed, disregarding the maid's exit. And during hard times, it could be the single most thing to pull us through.

How true. I thought of my time at the Camp, and remembered

how humor seemed to be the common denominator to every inmate's peace of mind.

Diamond had me following his reasoning and nodding in agreement…he was quite eloquent. Even as I laughed, however, he still gave me the impression of being a troubled soul. He was complicated and secretive…but entirely captivating when he wanted to be. I listened enthusiastically.

He went on. He complimented my wit, and he recognized my affinity for a good laugh. He said that what he did for a living… naked stage comedy, comedy for comedy's sake…might be more difficult to deliver than the everyday exchanges I was used to. He asserted, however, that it was all grounded in the same thing, and it was only a small step from one to the other...from being a funny man to being a comic.

As he spoke, I couldn't believe that he was stone-cold sober. He usually saved this kind of contemplative journey for one of his benders.

Virtually everyone has humor inside them, he insisted. And while people enjoy laughing and joking, most of them lack the confidence to stand on the stage and tell jokes. Even the heckler could broadcast his supposed humor while remaining relatively anonymous in the dark room. Yes, while everyone loved comedy, he concluded, most are quite content to remain comfortably hidden in the crowd.

"You're exactly right," I agreed. "That's me."

"Sure, it's you," Diamond said. "…and most everyone else, even professional comics…me too."

"I don't follow…" I said, suddenly confused.

"That's why clowns paint their faces, why comics change their identities…they allow their alter-egos to go onstage for them."

"Yeah…" I understood that point.

"You see, our real selves remain as anonymous as the heckler in the back of the room…even more so."

"I don't know," I was still confused. "You are *you* up there on the stage," I argued.

"Am I…?" He grinned devilishly.

Now I really couldn't say for sure. "What are you trying to get at?" I asked

"Being self-conscious…you know, the fear of delivering comedy," he replied.

"You've totally lost me," I decided.

Diamond stood up again and placed himself directly in front of me. "Tell me something funny," he commanded. I just looked at him. "Go ahead," he insisted.

His presence immediately before me intimidated me momentarily, and I couldn't think of anything to say, funny or otherwise. He turned around and faced away from me. "Okay," he said, "tell me something funny."

I looked at his back and laughed. "Your ass is getting big," I said truthfully.

"Good enough," he said, turning back around. "See, it's easier when I'm not confronting you, isn't it?"

He was right again. I could clearly feel the difference.

Diamond was not finished. He sent me to another room, and made me tell a joke through the closed door. It was easy, and fun… I told two. We both laughed at the game we were playing.

"You see," he summed it up. "The trick is to remain unseen…to show your audience something, or someone, else…while you remain on the other side of the door."

"And you…?" I asked.

"They don't see me, they see the Double D," he said, artfully rhyming the "me" with the "D." "Clowns paint their faces, and wear funny personality-altering clothes. Me, and most standup comics…we do the same thing, we get in character, in our heads, our minds."

I hesitated. "I keep thinking there's a point to this exercise," I said cautiously.

He pulled me into the bathroom and faced me towards the mirror, staring at myself. "Take a good look," he instructed, leaving me alone for a moment.

He returned. He put the wig on my head. Then, he put a pair of sunglasses over my eyes. I looked in the mirror. It wasn't Ronald McDonald, but it wasn't John Bellamy either.

"LADIES AND GENTLEMEN, please welcome Eddie Walker," the voice over the loudspeaker announced, as I stepped onstage to mild applause.

I must have been crazy to agree to this, I thought, as I stepped up to the mic. But I had to admit it wasn't so bad...I felt armored in my ridiculous disguise. The employees, who had already seen me without it, were tittering with laughter at the sight of me, and it added to the silly atmosphere already in the room.

Diamond had told the staff that I was famous among a small group of New York writers for wearing different disguises on television. And that, if they closely examined some old reruns of *Saturday Night Live,* they might be able to pick me out in some of the scenes. He was an outrageous liar, but it added to my credibility, as he knew it would.

My duties were easy enough. I announced upcoming events and introduced the evening's entertainment. A table full of girls on the front row giggled and sent a drink to the stage for me. I looked toward the rear of the room, and saw Diamond silently applauding, as if to say "so far, so good."

It was a big night for the mild hecklers, but thankfully, they waited for the real comedians to begin. I left the stage untouched. It was also one of those nights where all the comics tested new material on the crowd...

First up was the Philadelphia comic who had worked with Diamond in Jacksonville. He had developed a whole new routine about life after death. It was an unusual bit, and Diamond, who would not normally pay much attention to the other acts, listened studiously...nodding affirmatively, and even applauding during certain parts.

The new material was a real departure from his usual standard stuff. He was clearly moving to a better, more original level, and he earned a strong applause, especially from Diamond.

I took the stage to introduce the next act, an unscheduled hometown comedian, who had recently returned from Los Angeles, where he had just completed his first major California appearances.

His name was James Humphries, and he was a lawyer who suddenly chose to quit his practice and take to the road. I expected him, as a former attorney, to be classy and philosophically oriented like Diamond. Instead, his act was profane, and he was half-drunk and overly loud. But he was so blatantly crude that he had me laughing. Maybe it was just the shock value.

Diamond followed with a series of quick-hitting jokes. He informed the crowd that he was scheduled to perform on television soon, and requested them to listen to each joke, and then yell out "yes" or "no," advising him which jokes were keepers. It was extremely effective, and funny. The audience enjoyed taking part, and they didn't need much encouragement to join in the revelry.

Diamond threw in a couple new golf jokes...about the game's frustration...ending with his observation, "...the best two balls I hit all day was when I stepped on the rake in the sand trap."

His eyes found mine across the room and he winked. I hooted out my approval, along with the rest of the audience.

The night's heckling did not severely disrupt any of the show. Though there was this one big drinker, all the way in the back, who got progressively more troublesome as the night wore on. Diamond's sharp tongue kept him in line. However, when I returned to the stage to wrap things up, he shouted something offensive at me from the shadows in the rear of the room.

In the spirit of the evening, I bravely tried out a new line myself. I thanked everyone for coming, and thanked the loudmouth particularly, for proving once again my theory that…

"…comedy is like a horse. The brains are in the front, and the asshole is in the back," I concluded, pointing toward him.

Everyone laughed, including the heckler, but none more than Diamond, who had expected me to run off the stage as soon as I could.

After the show, he eased over to me at the bar. "I'm proud of you, Eddie Walker," he said with warmth and respect in his voice.

"HEAD DOWN…EASY BACKSWING," I was telling myself on every shot.

I returned to the driving range every free day. It was meditative, and in the discipline of striking the ball, I could relax and think at the same time.

Sometimes Diamond would accompany me, but mostly I'd go alone. Either way, I found my shooting eye sharpen. Bang, bang, bang…three straight, right at the stick.

"The Master of Disaster has returned," I announced, with raised arms, to an imaginary army of fans. That was a title I had earned many times over, in the past. Now, if only there was a good golf course, and a worthwhile wager…

I PHONED NORMAN AS REQUESTED. It was good to hear his voice. He seemed resigned to the fact that things were going to get worse before they got better. And, because of the heat on him, he would call Skip's only in the event of an emergency. This would be our last contact for a while.

Norman said that his lawyer had assured him that without

Larry's testimony, the government had no case against him...and that it wasn't a slam-dunk case to prove even with Larry's assistance. He was calm, even jocular, and he said he was ready for the approaching battle of nerves.

"I guess Larry could still fuck me," Norman reflected, "but I just can't see him doing it."

Norman was confident in his assessment of Larry's character, but I wasn't so sure. A friend of mine, with a much stronger backbone and a lot less to lose, had turned on me. And even after all this time, I still suffered the scars of his treachery.

Saying nothing, I simmered with the memory. Norman broke the momentary silence. "...anyway, pard, I wouldn't have done it any other way," he assured me. God love him.

More than that, Norman was still looking out for me. The real reason he wanted to speak with me, he said, was to give me the current rundown on Barney.

"He's in Ft. Lauderdale," Norman advised, giving me his telephone number.

"Is that why you wanted me to call...?" I was relieved. "Listen, man, forget me and take care of yourself," I ordered. "We'll get together when this is all over."

He laughed. "You still need me, pard." he said.

"You can't help me if you're in jail, pard," I mimicked.

For some reason, we both broke out laughing. "Jesus," I told him, "what a couple of assholes we are."

He signed off, "K. I."

Barnard St. John. To anyone in need of illicit identification documents, he was simply Barney. At one point, he wanted everyone to call him Pimpin', a self-appointed nickname. But no one ever did. He was too refined. He walked around like the president of Nigeria, always dressed in conservative, tailored, Savile Row suits, and he spoke English like a professor and Swahili like a native. He was the only person I knew who actually attended the Ali-Foreman fight, the Rumble in the Jungle, in Zaire. Pimpin' earned his Masters degree studying the Underground Railroad, and he now had a unique clientele. I was amazed at his ability to avoid trouble over the many years he had been in business. Perhaps that was because he never dabbled in passports or other federal documentation...only state and local stuff.

Barney also had a network that could run a check on my present set of IDs. It was critical to verify my Eddie Walker birth certificate as authentic, and, if not, to obtain something better from him. I also wanted another drivers license, with my photograph on it, just in case. I had always heard that the majority of people who've been busted using fake IDs were nailed because of some problem with their drivers license. Altered or counterfeit driver's licenses were much easier to spot...clerks and bouncers were even proficient at it.

Barney's specialty, and his personal favorite, was the phony driver's license. According to him, he had never had one uncovered. That was because he was able to provide a license from an actual licensing machine.

A non-governmental agency is prohibited from buying a drivers license machine in the United States. However, a foreign company or government can. Barney went through the labor of establishing a business in Africa where he had a network of friends and associates. His legitimate African company purchased drivers license machines, which, once in Barney's hands, he promptly smuggled back into the United States.

His operation could produce licenses from Virginia, Maryland, Pennsylvania, and, I think, some other states. And he used his enormous supply of telephone directories from that region to ensure that he had authentic addresses to match each last name he licensed. Barney was thorough.

I called and made an appointment to see him before we went to

Ft. Myers. It was only a few hours drive, and Barney made sure I was back in Merritt Island, license in hand, by nightfall.

He was a very strange guy, but he was a pro. And a Florida boy.

"I'll miss the condo," I said to Diamond as we packed the car.

"Well, in Ft. Myers, the hotel rooms are on the water. And then, the week after, we'll be in another condo in St. Petersburg."

I hadn't yet informed Diamond that I wasn't accompanying him to St. Pete. My plan was to meet him again the following week, in Key West, for the television show.

Our weeks together on the road had drawn us closer as friends. And I was positive that he had suspected, by now, that I had some sort of problem. But I was still reluctant to share the specifics of my situation with anyone. Anyway, he never asked. With the passage of time, however, I would soon have to come up with something to tell him.

I was sure tempted to go to St. Petersburg, to my mother's house. Although my mother wasn't aware of it, I had stashed some money in her kitchen wall. But I was afraid that they were watching my mother and sisters closely, and the money I had with me was holding out nicely.

No need to risk a visit to mom just yet. I had paid Barney five hundred dollars for his services, but I still had over two thousand dollars left, and the comfort of knowing that my identifying documents were solid.

I would eventually have to consider finding a job. While I could never picture myself as a comedian, Diamond hinted that there were other ways to earn "comedy bucks." He was not specific, though...I think he held out hopes that I could be successful on the stage...me and my disguise.

He had a way of making the improbable happen, though, so I didn't dispel the notion. I tagged along.

Traveling leisurely across the state to Ft. Myers, Diamond explained Lisa Kennedy's operation. Her husband, Paul, was her partner, but she was the driving force behind the business. He was a journeyman comic, and toured frequently, so it was up to Lisa to make the club go. And that she did. Her place was beautiful and well run. And she included many little extras for the touring comedians.

"She'll have us to dinner, and arrange boating and fishing," Diamond predicted. "She might even be able to get you a set of clubs to play some golf."

"That's reason enough to love her," I joked.

He said that Paul was relatively funny, and a nice guy, but everyone wondered how he managed to attract Lisa.

"I used to know 'Wheels' in New York," he said wistfully. "She could have had any man she wanted..." The way he said it made me suspect there was more to the story.

"Why do you call her 'Wheels'?"

"You'll find out..." he teased.

Chapter Twelve

I was thunderstruck. Lisa Kennedy was absolutely beautiful, and vibrant, and...everything. She had long, full-bodied, very dark hair, which framed her stunning green eyes. Her fair skin glowed, and had that look...the supple unblemished sheen of movie stars. Her judicious use of makeup made it appear professionally applied. And she had the kind of frame, and bearing, that made even the most casual clothes look tailored and expensive.

She was younger than I'd expected. From Diamond's descriptions of her, I'd envisioned a more experienced...businesswoman. But Lisa was a young lady in her late thirties, possessing all the dynamic charm and style of a much older woman.

I understood immediately why Diamond had called her Wheels. Beneath her moderately short skirt and boyishly thin hips, was the best pair of legs I had ever seen.

It wasn't merely her magnificent physical appearance that made Lisa Kennedy special. It was more her manner. When she smiled, she made you feel that she was smiling for you alone. And when she spoke, she was not distracted, her eyes were not dancing around the room like a politician's. No, her full attention was directed to whom she spoke, and she listened eagerly.

Lisa also had that dangerous quality...whereby doing her a service...anything to attract her attention...made you feel wonderful. Historically, that kind of woman had the power to make a man lose his judgment...leave his family, commit crimes...worse than that, even engage in acts of treason. Hell, I was ready to stand in line to do any of those things.

Diamond was not lacking in his assessment of Lisa Kennedy... she was something.

"Tunnel vision," he chuckled, back at the hotel room.

"Huh...?"

"That's what men get around a woman like that," he answered. "Tunnel vision."

Again, he was keenly observant. She was all I had seen for the first hour I was there.

The only factor that afforded you any control was that, in her uniqueness, she exuded a certain unattainability. You couldn't imagine her belonging to you. One could only hope to share a few moments with her...up there on her pedestal.

"Damn, Paul must give thanks to the heavens every night," I said, feeling more than a touch of envy.

"Ah...he's probably tired of fucking her by now," Diamond replied in a cynical tone.

"Yeah, right..." I returned his sarcasm. Sometimes it was impossible to tell whether he was joking or not.

"I mean it," he said with a smirk. "He'll be in St. Louis next week, probably humping some pie-faced waitress."

I almost challenged him. But I heard such a sharp edge in his voice...and maybe he was still egging me on. I decided to let it go.

Our first show in Ft. Myers was packed...even the seats at the back bar were filled.

Paul Kennedy opened the show. It was to be his last night in town before heading north on a short tour through the Midwest. He was personable, and mildly amusing...that's all. In fact, his mediocre presence made me feel strangely embarrassed...for him.

During some of his slower segments, I would sneak a peek at Lisa, standing in her hostess position by the door. Each time, she would be laughing and applauding, thoroughly enjoying Paul's performance.

I leaned over to Diamond and remarked, "He must be great in bed, or...a multi-millionaire."

Diamond just smiled. Some of his earlier bitterness had faded.

I watched Paul onstage and made another assessment, "No... he's neither."

Throughout the remainder of the show, I continued to wonder what the attraction was...what Lisa found so vital in him.

Near the close of the show, all of the comedians returned to the stage to take part in group improvisation. "Improv" is a very creative presentation, in which the comics instantaneously come up with off-the-cuff lines, characters and situations. To my surprise, Lisa was invited to the stage during this part of the show.

She was sharp, and at home onstage. She was also much funnier than her husband.

I had not yet seen Diamond do improv. He was superb...brilliant. His timing was so precise, I wondered how long he could sustain it. I was on my feet applauding him.

After the show, Lisa and Paul invited us all back to their house for a late-night breakfast. It was quite a chore to feed the large group of hungry entertainers. I noticed, though, that while we all positioned ourselves to assist Lisa in her tasks, Diamond did not lift a finger to help.

Lisa seemed to thrive on being the center of attention, and while she and Diamond were obviously old friends, he refused to accommodate her in that way. Even during the critical cooking stages, he sat casually at the kitchen table drinking apple juice.

Nevertheless, she appeared happy to see him again.

"Diamond speaks very highly of you," Lisa said, as I helped her wash the dishes.

I enjoyed her company. We had been discussing my relationship with Diamond. I had briefly outlined our meeting backstage at the Buffett concert, and how we'd been traveling together since.

"He's a loner," she stated, nodding toward Diamond. "And it's unusual to see him enchanted by someone."

I wanted to tell her that enchanted was what I was…by her. Diamond was not enchanted with me, he was…

"I think I'm his experiment," I corrected her.

She had an honest laugh, and touched my arm. I melted.

"Have you known him long?" I asked.

"For a few years at least," she answered, counting the years in her head.

I waited for additional information, but it didn't come. I pressed on, "You seem to know him pretty well…"

"Yeah," she said, looking back at him briefly. He had moved to the living room and was talking to Paul. She continued. "He married my roommate, and he used to take me along with the two of them when they went out. I got to know him well during that time."

I hesitated, wondering whether to continue on this line. I couldn't help it. "Is he…still married?" I asked, feeling guilty for prying.

"No." She said nothing else.

All evening, Lisa had been straight-forward. Maybe a bit

rehearsed or affected, but never evasive. Now, I wanted to know more about Diamond, and I trusted her to either answer me or stop me, whichever she considered appropriate.

"May I ask, what happened?"

Lisa thought for a second, then answered, "She was a very successful model. Gorgeous and fun...they made a great couple."

Her face turned sad at the memory, and again I was moved by her caring expression.

"Gorgeous" was the perfect word, I thought. It was also one of Diamond's words.

"Anyway," she continued, "Diamond caught Vicki in bed with her photographer, and..." she shrugged. The look on her face told the rest of the story.

I gazed into her eyes, lost for the moment...then suddenly caught myself. Unnerved, I looked back at Paul. She masterfully removed any discomfort in the situation by calling out to Diamond and Paul, asking if they cared for anything more.

I THOUGHT I had discovered an important key to Diamond's misery, and debated whether or not to probe that area further. But, since he had not questioned me about myself, I intended to let him address it, or not, as he pleased.

Surprisingly, as Diamond gave me a quick tour of the club the next afternoon, he remarked, in passing, that Lisa had been his ex-wife's best friend. While that wasn't much information, for Diamond that was like striking the mother lode. I nodded, pretending to take the information in stride.

Diamond walked me around the premises of the small club, showing me the bar, the patio and the main showroom. Along the wall approaching the showroom, several rows of photographs hung in a semi-orderly fashion. They were all comedians...well-known stars mixed with the lesser-known and the unknown stars of tomorrow.

"Notice anything unusual?" Diamond asked.

I looked around. Most of the comedy clubs we had passed through displayed a similar décor...photos of various comedians covered the walls. I was surprised, though, at the vast number of comics who were out there performing.

"There's so many..." I said, pointing to the rows of framed pictures.

He smiled. "That too," he said. He turned my shoulders towards the montage of smiling faces, and asked, "Don't you find it strange that, out of all these photographs, there are no pictures of women here?"

I searched the walls for a female face. There were none. There were several excellent female comics on tour throughout the country, and I had seen many of their photos on the walls of other clubs.

In Orlando, a comedienne named Lucy Valentine shared the bill with Diamond. She was wacky, and a favorite of the Orlando audiences. She also provided a dynamite photo for each club to hang on the wall, and I remembered its distinctive heart shape hanging next to the bar in Merritt Island.

"Lucy Valentine will be happy, when she plays here, to find another club in need of her photo," I laughed.

"Lucy Valentine won't be playing here," Diamond corrected me. He turned towards me.

"Lisa seldom, if ever, books women into her club."

I was astounded. "Really...why?"

"Lisa is the star here," Diamond stated simply.

"But the barmaids...?" I began

"They're not onstage, and she dresses them in those fruity outfits."

I laughed. "Surely she can't feel any competition."

Diamond shrugged and put his hands in his pockets.

What an odd twist. Lisa certainly loved to be in control of a man's world. With the possible exception of Diamond, she had everyone at her beck and call...even me. But she never ordered anyone about, and she rarely even requested a favor. She was always friendly and outgoing. It was just fun to be around her, and it was a pleasure to do things for her.

It was also obvious that even Diamond had a soft spot in his heart for Lisa Kennedy. They constantly huddled together and teased each other. And they would occasionally hold hands, in a friendly manner, during casual conversations.

Evidently, her husband was aware of their close relationship. When he left for his tour, he walked out to his car with Lisa and Diamond, and said ceremoniously, "I leave her in your care," as he placed her hand in Diamond's.

Regardless of that, I felt that Lisa didn't need watching over. She was in control, a queen in her realm. And it was very clear that she wouldn't be dallying with any of her subjects.

I stared idly at the photographs, confused by this unusual woman. I suddenly became uncomfortable at how easily I followed her along.

"Are you looking for Diamond's photo?" Lisa said brightly.

She had come into the room from her office and found Diamond and me standing in front of the photo wall. We were both surprised, and we quickly turned around together.

"His picture is in the office," she said, "in a special place of honor."

"Wouldn't it be better over by the cash register?" Diamond quipped.

We all laughed as she hooked her arms through each of ours and walked us over to the bar. The club was closed, and the afternoon sun was peeking through the cracks in the heavy curtains, casting magical streaks of light across the unlit room.

Lisa guided us to barstools at the end of a long, dark mahogany bar. Then, she slipped under the service counter to play bartender. Slicing fresh pineapple and coconut, Lisa prepared massive pina coladas, made with dark rum, in the blender.

She raised her glass. "Here's to the last one," she offered.

"And to the next one," Diamond responded. He winked at me.

"Hear, hear," I added. They looked at each other, and laughed. I was perplexed.

Seeing my discomfort, Lisa took my hand. "You're supposed to say, 'and to the one I'll never have'," she gently advised. "It's an old toast we used to recite."

After the drinks, Lisa brought us back into her office. She had a quarterly report spread out on the desk. She was excited about the growth of her club, and was gesturing emotionally to Diamond about small facts reflected in the report.

I looked closely at her. Her jeans were well-worn, and both of her knees were poking through. The soft, form-fitting denim was relatively tight, and enhanced the shape of her exceptional legs.

She wore a brand-new black T-shirt, with something French splashed across the front in hot pink letters. The bottom of the shirt was pulled up and tied in a knot around her tiny waist. She was confident and poised. It was beyond me how this girl could be sensitive to competition…any competition.

"What do you think?" Diamond asked. They were both looking at me, waiting for an answer.

Lost in my study of Lisa, I had completely blocked out their conversation. Evidently, they had asked me a question.

I blinked. "I'm sorry…I wasn't listening," I managed to say.

Diamond smiled, and mouthed "tunnel vision" at me. Then he grabbed the back of my neck. "Look at this," he said, pointing to a paper on Lisa's desk.

Lisa had outlined the costs of opening another comedy club.

She had already discussed the idea with the Coconuts main office and had received a tentative go-ahead.

It was surprisingly inexpensive, especially if the club was located in a pre-existing hotel lounge as she planned. She suggested that Diamond might also be interested in having a club of his own somewhere.

Lisa was aware of Diamond's heavy road schedule, but she had instantly recognized his relationship with me. She considered Diamond and me a good team...with Diamond on the move and me at the helm...much like her operation with her much-touring husband. It was her opinion that a club for us, at such a low cost, would be a natural.

Diamond was controlled, but both Lisa and I could see that he was enthused.

"Would you consider living in New York...Long Island...for awhile?" he asked me in an offhand manner, barely concealing his enthusiasm.

This sudden development could be the answer to a prayer, I thought silently. I too was charged with excitement. To do this fairly though, I would have to tell Diamond everything. But, damn right, I'd love to do it...it was indeed the answer I'd been seeking.

"See that look on my boy's face," Diamond said to Lisa, nudging her. "I can tell he's already planning on checking out Long Island's golf courses."

"We have to sit down and talk, man," I said plaintively.

"Don't try to negotiate with a Jew...I'll cut your heart out," Diamond joked.

"No, it's got nothing to do with business..." I started.

"Oh, I see, you want to go on the road with me...you don't want to stay home and tend the club." He was animated and happy. Lisa was smiling at me.

"No, it's..."

He interrupted again, saying, "...well, yes or no?"

We should talk, I thought, my mind racing. But what the hell, he could always change his mind later when he heard what he was getting into. It was a sweet offer. The whole thing would probably cost us less than five thousand dollars apiece. I had that much… much more…at my mother's house. There were so many things to ponder…

I looked over at him. He didn't say anything, but his brown-black eyes were piercing…"yes or no," they were asking.

"Okay…yes," I said hopefully. Having said it out loud, I would be more than disappointed if it didn't work out.

We gathered around Lisa's desk and pored over the figures. At that moment I had the feeling of a great weight being lifted from my shoulders.

I was convinced Diamond wouldn't care less about my past, or my escape. I might have some trouble getting to my money soon, but I could more than likely make a deal with Skip in the meantime. I would call South Carolina as soon as I had a heart-to-heart talk with Diamond.

DIAMOND PUT his arm around Lisa's shoulders and asked, "Hey, Wheels, can you get my boy some golf clubs to use?"

"Sure," she answered, ignoring the nickname. "Paul has a fine set of Callaways in the garage." She turned to me and asked, "When would you like to play?"

"Anytime," I beamed.

Lisa looked at her calendar, then said, "I'm free all day Saturday…let's go."

"Do you play?" I was shocked.

"Sure." She shook her head back, put her hands on her hips and stuck out her chin.

"Don't act so surprised."

Surprised? The only other woman I knew who played golf seriously was my mother.

We looked at each other and laughed. She was suddenly back in my good graces. In fact, it was love again. But looking into her eyes I could see that while she enjoyed my company, to her I was merely another man under her spell.

I was happily spellbound though, and I was looking forward to finally playing golf.

Chapter Thirteen

"Christ almighty, did Buffett's people know?" Diamond asked.

I had just finished the tale of my adventures to date, including my troubled past, my recent escape and the subsequent close call in Panama City.

"No," I answered honestly. "They don't know me very well. They probably didn't even know that I'd gone to jail…I only see them once, maybe twice a year, if that."

Diamond slowly shook his head, and whistled in disbelief. "And I thought I had problems," he added.

"So maybe…having me as your partner is not such a good idea, huh?" I was disappointed.

"Probably not," he agreed. "But the time for me is now…or never." He rubbed his chin with his open hand, then said decisively, "Let's do it anyway."

I jumped up and hugged him. "You can always swear that you never knew," I said, still selling the deal.

"Yeah," he mumbled to no one in particular, "I can swear I never knew a lot of things."

HAVING DIGESTED MY INNERMOST SECRET, Diamond began to make plans, scribbling his calculations into one of his notebooks. Looking over his shoulder, I saw the outline of a new comedy routine sketched on the preceding page. It was a bit about young couples wrestling with the decision of whether or not to have children.

"Where do you come up with these unusual slants on life?" I chuckled, pointing at his outline.

He looked up at me, and without hesitation, he put his pen down and announced that it was time for him to tell me something...something he rarely shared with anyone else.

I prepared myself for some juicy story about his life. Instead, he sought to let me into the inner sanctum of his genius...his writing.

"I'm not doing this simply because you confessed your sins to me," Diamond said with great intensity.

I smiled, as if I knew different.

My attitude brought a grimace to his face. He maintained that he wasn't opening up to me because I had. Nor was it just because I was about to become his partner. Diamond insisted that I wouldn't need such knowledge to handle a club. No, I was to be enlightened because, in his words, I was "...a natural, with the comedy gene."

In his opinion, I had taken every opportunity he had provided and had achieved more than either of us had expected.

"I have...are you sure?" I joked. I still refused to be serious.

He finally laughed, and said, "Maybe it's just your attitude...I don't know...I haven't figured it out yet. But you have something."

Diamond also believed that my troubles, along with my change in identity, had delivered me unexpectedly to what he called the "land of inside-out." And this could be, he was certain, a catalyst to extremely creative writing.

"Bury yourself in Eddie Walker," he preached, "and you'll be able to travel artistically to places you would never go as John Bellamy."

Each comic has his own method for writing, he continued, but his own formula was simple.

"Make yourself a third party…a witness…to every important emotional event in John Bellamy's life," he commanded.

Diamond explained that the most emotional experiences I could recall would bring out the deepest responses from within. Reflecting upon what he suggested, it dawned on me that some of the most emotional times in my life had been unhappy ones. And I told him that.

"Yes, yes…" he said with a satisfied smile. "You're going to be a great student," he added, poking my chest.

There is an old axiom in comedy, he said, that "…comedy is pain, plus distance." He argued that even my saddest experiences could be made funny if they were not viewed through my eyes. Rather, he said again, "Let them be seen by a third party…someone without the emotional attachment."

I concentrated hard, but he could see that I did not fully understand.

"Look," he said, "you know my bit about going to a funeral?"

"Of course…it's one of my favorites."

"Do you think it's funny?" he asked.

"Sure." I reflected on the bit…the drunk uncle, the grand-mothers running in the rain, the irreverent little kids thinking they were going to the circus because of some relative's misguided explanation of what a funeral was all about … "Yeah, it's very funny."

"Well, that is about my father's funeral," he said solemnly.

"Wow," I whispered. He had struck close to home. My father had also passed away when I was in my early teens. I was close to him, and the memory of the event was still vivid in my mind.

"I don't think I could find humor in my dad's funeral," I confessed honestly.

"I understand," he said quietly. "Not enough distance for you yet. In my case, it really helped me deal with it." I nodded at his explanation, and he continued.

"But the point of it is…that if I looked at the event, not through my own eyes, but through the eyes of a bystander, I would see all the funny little things that happened…and come up with a sensitive and personal bit of humor." Diamond smiled and said, "I think my dad would have appreciated it."

He insisted that any material developed this way could be extremely thought-provoking as well as funny. But more importantly, the writer could avoid the standard, well-worn gags used by other comedy writers.

He had a great point. His material was all very funny, yet rich in originality.

He asked me to forget my father's death, and to concentrate instead on something else…perhaps something I had come to terms with. I was still unsure of what he wanted.

"How about the death of your first pet," he suggested.

I thought back to my childhood years, and remembered my cat. It had been squashed by a passing car, and my older cousin had prepared an elaborate funeral procession and celebration. He forced us to dress up and parade around the yard…to a hole he had dug in a corner of the back garden.

When I was a child, it was tragic. But in later years, from a distance, my whole family laughed uproariously at the absurd event, blown out of proportion by my crazy cousin. And Diamond was right, it made a funny, yet human, story.

"Of course, there weren't that many deaths around me," I joked. "I'd quickly run out of material."

Diamond laughed. "What are most people interested in?"

"Sex," I suggested, half kidding.

"Yeah, well…I was thinking of relationships," he said. "Any pain there, wiseass?"

He really touched a raw nerve with that question, and I

launched into a story. I told Diamond how, after six months in prison, my girlfriend at the time had stopped visiting, and had also discontinued her letters. She became evasive, and made more and more excuses about her flighty behavior. Worse than all that, I found out that she was going out with one of the guys who'd testified against me at my trial.

At the time, I was devastated. But during the ensuing months, I heard so many stories from other inmates about their unfaithful mates, and their incredible excuses, that it all became amazingly humorous…including my own experience.

There were many times that I would be in the phone room, talking to Norman, or to my mother, and I would overhear other inmates screaming at their wives, or pleading with their girlfriends, and I found myself laughing at the ridiculous melodrama and paying more attention to their conversations than my own.

"See," Diamond said excitedly, "as a witness to those situations…rather than a participant, you were laughing…laughing even while those poor guys were suffering."

"You are absolutely right," I agreed, feeling enlightened.

Using Diamond's formula, the ideas began pouring out of hidden parts of my brain. Events in my life that, at the time seemed personally overwhelming, but now I could relate to the humor I had previously overlooked. The passage of time had put me in the position of an observer.

I spouted out potential topics, "…the first time a girl told me she was pregnant…the time my car was stolen, and I went through a runaround trying to recover it…my kidney stone…hell, my own arrest and subsequent court appearances…"

All of these experiences seemed devastating at the time. But, in retrospect, they could be made humorous and personal.

"Hey, slow down," Diamond laughed. "Pain is the best way to start. But it's okay to remember the good times too…falling in love…the first time you went to the ballpark…anything that was emotional, that hit you hard."

Diamond paused, took a deep breath, then looked me in the eyes. "Just remember," he concluded, "humor is the spoonful of sugar that lets you drink life's bitter espresso."

I stood up, as fired-up as a sinner who has just found Jesus. "I need to find a bigger notebook," I cracked.

As we drove to the club for the show, I was sky-high. I now had a plan, a purpose and a future. I was on the inside track of an interesting business. I was…happy.

Before leaving for the club, I snuck a phone call to Skip Shelby in South Carolina, and he had assured me that we could work something out on the money I needed. But he wanted to speak to me in person. That would be easy enough…Diamond and I could stop in Hilton Head on our way north.

Sometimes life has a way of working out, I thought. Then again, sometimes life has a way of fooling you.

A VENTRILOQUIST from Denver had the crowd laughing, as we sat with Lisa at the bar. It was the ultimate in alter-ego humor, I concluded. The ventriloquist was the straight man hiding behind his wooden dummy, who told the jokes. I mentioned the thought to Diamond.

"You're a star pupil…you get an A-plus," he replied with a grin.

We relaxed in the warm glow of our recently made decision. We each ordered a shot of expensive cognac and mapped out plans for the future. Lisa was delighted to hear that Diamond was going to appear on the Showtime TV special.

"Oh wonderful," she squealed. "Maybe I can drive over. Is it going to be in Miami?"

"No, this time it's in sunny Key West," Diamond replied. "But you're still welcome to come down." Yes, please come, I almost blurted out.

Lisa was silent. It appeared that she was trying to decide

whether or not she could attend. As it happened, something else was on her mind.

After at least a full minute of silence, she took Diamond's hand, and said with sorrow in her voice, "You know, Vicki is down there."

He was startled. "In Key West?"

"Yes...she and Sandro are there for three more weeks, on a shoot for some bathing suit line."

Diamond was visibly upset. He sat motionless for a few minutes, and then went to the bathroom. I turned to Lisa, "I take it that Sandro is the photographer?"

She nodded yes, still looking at the bathroom door.

"Is he going to be alright?" I asked, looking at the door myself.

"Sure. This happened one time before. It was a big blowup, but everyone suffered through it."

"Maybe we won't even run into her," I reasoned. No sense looking for trouble.

"No...more than likely, she'll see the ads for the show and go." Lisa held her head in her hands, and said, "Sometimes Vicki can be a real bitch."

"Maybe Diamond can trash her from the stage," I said, laughing at the suggestion.

"Maybe...I hope one day he can. But he has a true weakness...a real vulnerability...for that girl," she lamented.

Lisa suddenly looked worried. The story was obviously much deeper than I had perceived.

Diamond returned to his barstool and ordered a vodka martini. He was sullen.

But Lisa was effervescent, and clearly skilled at brightening the mood of any man around her. She assaulted his senses with her charm. I was dizzy just from being in her vicinity as she unloaded...all of her guns at once. No one, not even Diamond, could resist her astonishing personality.

Diamond's face finally broke into a broad smile. And before he went to the stage, he kissed her on the forehead and pinched her chin. But I was a wreck.

Once onstage and away from Lisa's magnetic powers, Diamond's concentration dissolved. For the first time since I'd met him, his show lacked confidence. He was distracted, his timing was off, and the whole thing was dismal.

Later he remained moody and distant, and he was unresponsive to any of my attempts to make light of the situation or to cheer him up. So I left him alone.

The rest of the week was similarly shaky. Diamond's shows, while better, were lifeless, and he walked around in a trance. Without discussing it among ourselves, we all stayed out of his way. I suppose we were waiting for him to get a grip on himself.

I spent the time puzzled by Lisa, and worrying about Diamond.

Chapter Fourteen

Saturday morning finally arrived, and Lisa picked me up at the hotel, ready for golf. She was a vision. She wore a collarless, fire-engine red golf shirt tucked into snug white shorts. It was my first close-up, full-length view of her magnificent legs…I knew I was going to be distracted all day.

She had on low-cut, shoe-top white socks, and expensive Footjoy saddle-shoe golf shoes. To top off her matching red and white ensemble was, oddly, a hand-me-down Chicago Cubs baseball hat. It was the perfect touch, and I was off balance as we proceeded to the first hole.

Although I was steady off the tee, my short game was erratic. It improved as we played, and as I got more familiar with the feel of Paul's clubs. Lisa was well-schooled in the game. She wasn't a big hitter, but she was deadly accurate…and she didn't dawdle. She was a player.

She said that her father had been a golf pro. She had no brothers, and her father had dragged Lisa and her sister out on the golf course before she was eight years old. Lisa continued to follow golf because her sister had finished college on a golf scholarship and was now a touring professional.

Even more telling of her interest in golf was revealed when she said, "Daddy always said that you could tell a lot about a man on the golf course."

Lisa proved a lively companion. She would even gamble with me on the shorter holes. Better yet, she was mindful of golf etiquette…for some reason, that always made playing golf much more enjoyable for me.

"You certainly are an enigma," Lisa said to me as we waited for a slower group in front of us to finish putting.

"How so?" I was checking the wind direction for my approach shot to the green.

"Let me see…well, for one, you're the only person to ever walk into a comedy club not bragging about his past successes."

"Maybe I've had no past successes," I deadpanned.

"Hardly likely, Mr. Walker. If Don Diamond thinks you're special, then you are."

I looked over at her. She was studying me. I tried not to smile, but I couldn't stop myself. I knew that Diamond hadn't repeated those fables about *Saturday Night Live,* and all that other bullshit… not to Lisa. God knows what he'd come up with. But I was happy that she was interested.

"Yes, the mysterious golfer," she said, laughing.

Her laugh was infectious and I couldn't resist joining in.

"Tell you what," she said, "ten dollars says you don't hit the green."

It was an easy 7-iron to the green. I would bet that I could punch the ball in close to the stick, let alone land it on the relatively wide-open green. This must be some sort of a test, I thought.

"You're on," I said, as the golfers ahead of us walked off the green.

I addressed the ball, and took a practice swing. Then I peeked over at Lisa leaning against the golf cart. As she saw me look up, she licked her golf ball in one long slow motion. My concentration evaporated and I pushed my golf ball into the right sand-trap.

It was the first overtly sexual action she had ever exhibited in my presence. I knew immediately that that was the test. I might be enigmatic, a mystery man…but a man nonetheless…to be channeled or manipulated, as she had obviously controlled every man she's ever met. The queen's loyal subject…nothing new. She found out everything she needed to know about me with that one pathetic shot.

THE THREESOME AHEAD OF us was holding us up on every hole with their slow play. Once, when we ran into them on the tee, I suggested that it might be better for us to play through. Instead, they promised to speed it up.

Finally, two holes later, Lisa approached the three men to ask them to permit us to play through. I couldn't make out exactly what she said, but I heard them all laughing with her. And again, I had the feeling that her speech and mannerisms were somewhat exaggerated, for maximum effect.

She thoroughly enjoyed being in command, and her power was almost scary. But I loved propping my feet up on the cart and letting her drive me past the three drooling golfers.

As we played, she talked about her past experiences as an actress. She also detailed the pleasures of running her own business.

"Do you get much time to play golf?" I asked.

She didn't answer. Instead, she blasted a ball out of a tough lie in the sand-trap to within three feet of the stick. "Does that answer your question?" she boasted, barely concealing a smile.

We laughed together, then she said honestly, "Actually, that was lucky. I don't play that much anymore. I don't like too much sun on my skin."

Up to this point, I listened to her, but could offer nothing specific about my own life. Finally, she said, "Diamond says you're extremely talented, and intelligent."

I grinned. Maybe he had, in fact, told her some outrageous tale about me. "He's lying, whatever he said," I replied.

She chuckled. "I don't think so…he doesn't lie to me." She tapped my chest with her finger, for emphasis. "And there's something about you that's…different."

We finally came up the 18th fairway toward the clubhouse. Lisa hit a long iron shot that fell just short of the green, and then she came over and stood by me as I prepared for my next shot.

Standing over the ball with a 7-iron in my hand, I realized that it was much the same shot, angle and distance, I had missed earlier when she had bet me. I looked up at her but her face showed no expression.

"Do you recognize this shot?" I asked her.

"Vaguely," she deadpanned. She finally chuckled. She had seen it too.

"Watch this…I won't be nice this time." Using a full backswing, I coolly knocked the ball high in the air, with a slight draw, and dropped it on the green. And with one bounce, it rolled to within eight feet of the pin. I bowed pretentiously in her direction. She clapped her hands, and then started for the golf cart. As I walked up beside her, she stopped.

"That other shot, before…did you hit it into the sand-trap on purpose…to be nice?" she asked, a little too seriously.

"I'll never tell," I sang.

Lisa kept staring into my eyes, thinking perhaps that they would betray the answer. Had she looked at my knees, she might have seen them buckling.

As we walked up to the green, she picked up her golf ball and put it in her pocket.

"You're not playing it out?" I asked, surprised.

"I'll watch you," she replied evenly.

I stood behind the ball and looked down towards the hole. It was a challenging putt of about eight feet, down a gentle slope.

"I'll bet you a hundred dollars you don't make it," Lisa suddenly said, smiling broadly.

I shot her an amused look. I already owed her about twenty dollars from our small bets out on the course...nuisance money. Here's a decent bet, I thought, looking back at the hole. I noticed that closer to the cup, there was a tricky break away from me. The ball would run downhill and then drop a little to the right before going into the hole. I wondered if she thought that I hadn't seen it.

It was a tough putt. My putting had been spotty all day…some holes good, some bad. And even though I had been going to the driving range on occasion during the last few weeks, I had not practiced any putting at all, so I felt very rusty.

I was not at all confident that I could make it. But I enjoyed a big bet on the final hole…this woman was really a sport. To add some glamour, and to show the little girl I wasn't scared, I said, "Make it two hundred." That might quiet her down a bit, I thought. My confidence swelled.

"Make it five hundred," she immediately responded.

I backed away from the ball and stared surprisingly at her. She returned my stare. Not maliciously…rather, in a way of womanly challenge, and still with a beautiful smile on her face.

"Okay," I said. I would have fun whether I made it or not.

I paced around the green, surveying the shot. It was more difficult than I'd first estimated. Damn, I should have demanded two-to-one odds. When I finally thought I had the line figured out, I stood over the ball again.

"Grab the flag, please," I asked, requesting her to pull the pin out of the hole.

Lisa stepped slowly across the green, pulled out the flagstick, and straddled the hole…placing one beautiful leg on each side of the cup. Then, she tossed the flag aside, and put her hands on her hips.

"Go ahead…and don't be nice this time," she instructed, in a flagrant and provocative breach of etiquette.

I almost dropped my putter.

I was suddenly flustered. Did she truly suspect I had purposely muffed the earlier shot, toying with her…that she hadn't really distracted me. Who knows. While I was baffled, I was certain that this had nothing to do with the money we were betting...this was a power thing. But, whatever her motive, there was no confusion about the fact that her gauntlet had been thrown...at me.

The putt was difficult enough without any distractions. And, of course, this distraction was severe. I had been sneaking glimpses of her legs all afternoon. Watching them stiffen as she drove the ball, or flex as she climbed out of the bunker. Now she wanted me to have a good look, and I couldn't help myself.

They were extraordinary…perfectly defined, as if shaped by a sculptor. With tapered ankles, strong calves, sharp knees and thin, curvy muscular thighs. Long and smooth, no cuts, scratches or bruises…just the healthy legs of a sexy female animal. And they were spread, astride the target, her feet apart.

I searched her eyes again. They had changed. She had been watching me assess the situation, and she now appeared more confident that whatever her questions were, they were answered. And she was right…I was no different. But it didn't matter, no man…no great money-putters I knew…could overcome this sudden obstacle. Putting was ninety percent confidence and concentration…and my concentration was not on the golf shot. My fuses were overloading…I was weak.

Lisa saw it clearly in my eyes, and that's all she wanted to know. She had won, I said to myself, and went to kick the ball toward her in a gentlemanly act of concession.

"Do you want to call it off?" she asked graciously. But her eyes resembled the steely eyes of an unconquered leopard. And it felt almost as if I'd been slapped.

I remembered that I had beseeched the heavens for a worthwhile wager…and here it was. This was golf, I thought, and I was a free man with a putter in his hands. What the hell, I'd give it a roll.

My loins ached as I stood over the ball. The only way I was going to block out the distraction was to borrow a page from Diamond's book…conquer it, and her, with contempt.

I took one last look at the hole, and attacked. Okay, this weird woman wanted me to make a feeble, embarrassing attempt, I told myself. Fuck her, I'd do better than that…I'd roll the goddamn thing right between her plastic legs…grrr.

I struck the ball with authority, and watched it roll towards her. It skittered down the hill and, at the last second, it snaked to the right. But not to the right of the hole. Rather, it plunked right in the cup…dead center.

I raised my arms. The Master of Disaster had drained the sweetest putt of his notorious life.

Lisa stood motionless as I walked across the green. For me, it was over. I let go of the intensity and the aggression…the hostility I had talked myself into in order to block out the distraction and make the putt. Now, I was high on my success and ready for a cold beer. It was fun.

But it meant something different to Lisa, and I could see the first weakness in her armor of superiority. Her face was flushed as I stood before her, and her lower lip was slightly quivering.

I put my finger under her chin and turned her lips up to meet mine. The thrill of victory…

She kissed me back.

"It wasn't for the money," I whispered.

"I know," she replied in a shaky voice.

We kissed again. Damn, I love golf.

Chapter Fifteen

"Hey, come on...get up." I shook Diamond's outstretched body.

It was time to get ready for the show, and he was still asleep. Actually, he wasn't really sleeping. He had passed out, with his clothes and his shoes still on.

Diamond slowly rolled over, groaned and stared up at me. He was disheveled...all of his clothes were completely wrinkled... from top to bottom, and his eyes were swollen and bloodshot.

He finally struggled to sit up. Then he groaned again and rubbed his temples with his fingertips. His hair was as tangled as his clothes. Clearing his throat, he asked, "How was your golf game?"

"Fine." But my excitement was dulled by my concern for him. He looked terrible. Jesus, what a mess.

"Man, what have you been doing?" I asked him.

He scratched his head. "I don't know...sleeping and drinking... but not in that order." He made a half-hearted attempt to laugh.

"Damn, let's get you in the shower."

I dragged Diamond to the bathroom and turned on the shower.

He labored to free himself of his wrinkled and twisted clothes, and wound up stumbling into the shower with his socks on.

It was Saturday night, our last night in Ft. Myers. On Sunday, Diamond would head up to St. Petersburg. I had originally planned to go to the Keys, and await Diamond's arrival...and do some leisurely fishing and diving. But Lisa Kennedy's attitude toward me had changed considerably after our round of golf. She had even kissed me again when she dropped me back at the hotel. She had kissed me...and let it linger.

I was now considering spending a few more days in Ft. Myers. It all depended upon what happened at the club tonight. Hell, I knew what was going to happen...I felt like the U. S. Open champion.

When it was my turn to shower, I couldn't keep my mind from wandering over Lisa's body, and I became excited about the impending possibilities.

In prison, a man can go for months, or years, without the opportunity to seriously put his hands on a woman. In fact, of the many deprivations one suffers there, the lack of physical female companionship is, arguably, the hardest to bear.

Before I went to the Camp, I had been advised by friends, and other veterans of doing time, that I would adjust to it. And I suppose it was true enough...to a point.

My daily prison routine had not permitted me to linger on the fact that I was to remain celibate for awhile. But I think it subconsciously affected me, and every inmate, to some degree. It made some guys cold and spiteful, and destined to forever look upon women as sex objects and nothing more. Ironically, it made other inmates more romantic and overly idealistic...almost unrealistic...about what to expect from the future loves of their life.

I could never calculate how many men would bear permanent

scars from such an unnatural existence. My own experience suggests to me that any damage would be short-lived, and that most would move on to relatively normal lives.

Besides, many situations have long affected men in a similar manner. For example, long naval voyages…or for that matter, any kind of military service…have separated men from normality for centuries…for millennia.

I suppose we in jail also considered ourselves soldiers of a sort. And we suffered our fate with the same dignity that fellow celibates had shown through the ages…that is, with no dignity whatsoever. Just the absurd contradictory frustration of masturbatory macho men.

I laughed at the humor, born in prison, that dealt with this sensitive area. I laughed again at the thought of the extremes my fellow inmates had gone through to rendezvous with female companions.

It would make a classic comedy routine. And maybe I'd be the one to write it…

"Hey," Diamond shouted, interrupting my thoughts. "You're not in jail anymore…you don't need to spend an hour in the shower whacking off."

I chuckled at his uncanny ability to virtually read my mind. I stuck my head through the shower curtain, dripping water on the floor.

"Whacking off…?" I wiped the water from my eyes. "Whacking off…?" I repeated. "Can't you come up with anything better than whacking off?"

He laughed, obviously feeling better. "You've had a lot more experience than me…" he began.

"Okay, how about…choking the chicken," I offered.

"Battering the bishop…" he countered.

"Spanking the frank…"

And we went on, each suggestion either more vulgar, or more descriptive, than the last.

"I think you're onto something, son," he said.

"Well, you asked for something deeply emotional," I joked.

We laughed so hard I had to sit down in the bathtub.

WE WALKED into the comedy club. Lisa was there to greet us at the door. Dressed in a tight, shimmering emerald green, Asian-type outfit, slit high up on the left side, she appeared to be more than her normal beautiful self. She had taken on a slinky, decadent, sensual attitude that immediately aroused my senses.

Lisa hugged Diamond. I kissed her fragrant hand, as she gazed into my eyes and tapped her teeth together once…as if taking an imaginary bite out of me. Then she smiled playfully and walked us both to the bar. I wanted to beg her, then and there, to take me home with her.

Diamond continued drinking. Apparently, he was still upset. His moods shifted dramatically from one minute to the next. First loud, then silent…then aggressive, and finally, passively remote. He wandered off to await his turn onstage.

"Come with me," Lisa said as she tugged my sleeve. I grabbed my drink and followed her.

She flipped on the lights in her office, and walked me over to her desk. In the middle of the desk was a small silver tray, upon which five one-hundred dollar bills were neatly spread…fanned out like a five card poker hand.

"Your prize money," she announced with a stunning smile.

I looked at the money, and then into her cheerful eyes. "You look a lot different without your Cubs hat on," I joked.

Her smile broadened, and she gestured toward the money.

"I don't want your money," I said softly.

"I insist. You won it fair and square," she replied, her perfect face directly below mine.

"It wasn't all that fair..." I said, cocking my head in a mock attempt to scold her for her antics on the golf course.

She grinned like a petulant little girl. Then she looked at the floor, feigning shyness.

I gently tilted her head up and gazed into her eyes again. Cautiously, as if taking a gamble, I moved in slowly to kiss her. She did not back away, so I kissed her on the lips.

Lisa did not move, nor did she complain. But she did not kiss me back. She continued to look into my eyes, as if she was searching for something.

"You know, I couldn't make that putt right now," I said, smiling.

She did not smile as she spoke, "...I'm not so sure about that."

I took her statement as a compliment, and felt a surge of confidence. I moved closer. Again, she did not retreat, so I bent to kiss her once more. Her eyes were open.

"Kiss me back," I ordered, as I wrapped my arms around her.

She did, suddenly and passionately. Lisa whimpered as she pressed against me and smothered my face and neck with hungry kisses. I was momentarily overwhelmed by her aroused response, and I staggered back into her desk. She continued to press against me in her passion.

"Lisa, you are beautiful..." I began.

"Don't say anything..." she panted, and pressed her mouth to mine.

I ran my hands down the length of her body, until my hand slipped from the cool of her silk dress to the warmth of the skin on her exposed leg.

As she moved, the tight dress slid over her hip and I reached around to bare skin behind her...she was wearing nothing underneath.

I recovered my balance, and pulled her leg up, almost around me, and pushed my hips against hers.

"Yes," she whispered.

She reached for my belt buckle as I slipped the bottom of her dress over her hips. Holding it there, I could see that she had shaved herself completely. My God…

The surprise served to arouse me further, and I dropped her dress to help her with my own clothes.

There was a sudden knock, and a voice calling Lisa's name through the wooden door. She bit my neck in not-so-gentle frustration and eased herself away from me. Straightening her clothes, she answered the door.

"Just tell them a personal check will be fine…but get a driver's license number," Lisa instructed one of her bartenders. "…Oh, and bring me a bottle of champagne, please," she gracefully added.

I SPRAWLED across a large comfortable office chair. Lisa sat on the arm, and poured two glasses of Perrier Jouet.

"That was close," she laughed. I was still breathing hard.

We clinked our glasses, and sipped the bubbly champagne. She kissed my cheek, and I nuzzled her neck. But the interruption had altered the mood. Lisa sensed my disappointment, and mussed my hair. "Oh, poor baby…" she said with a pout. I almost smiled.

She laughed. "After the show, and after you drop Diamond back at your room, why don't you come by the house…"

I perked up. I wiggled my eyebrows in anticipation, and she giggled. "And…I don't know how to say this…so I just will," she said with some hesitation, "Could you maybe stop and get some… some condoms?"

She had spoken so softly. "Condoms?" I asked, not quite hearing what she said.

"Oh, God, I'm not accusing…I don't want to offend," she stuttered. "Look…I'm not used to this…"

I pressed my finger against her lips to silence her. "Of course I will," I said soothingly.

"I'll wear swim fins if you want me to," I added.

"Thank you," she said, and looked away embarrassed.

We finished our champagne. She jotted down simple directions, and her telephone number…just in case I got lost…and we returned to the bar for Diamond's set.

"Oh, and please," she demanded, "don't breathe a word of this to Diamond. He's not in a very understanding mood, and I…well, you know…"

"I promise," I said. And she could sense that I meant it.

———

Diamond's show was horrible. His worst all week. Evidently, he continued to drink. Not that drinking, by itself, ever hurt his act… I'd seen him kill an audience with laughter in the middle of a bender. But this time the heavy drinking added to his indifferent attitude onstage. And he quit twenty minutes early.

The emcee hastily returned to the stage in an attempt to fill some of the time. And some last minute improv by the ventriloquist saved the night. It would be a relief to put him to bed, I thought, and then gallop off to Lisa's house.

After the show, Lisa walked us to the car and helped me pour Diamond into the back seat. She squeezed my hand deceptively as she bid us goodnight. I looked back at her in the mirror as we drove away. She was waving. What a luscious woman.

"I don't know what I'd do without you," Diamond mumbled.

"You'd run out of ice, that's what," I joked.

I tried to remain light and talkative, to keep his spirits up. He leaned over the front seat. "You're exactly right," he agreed, laughing. But as we pulled into the hotel parking lot, Diamond sat in the back seat of the car sobbing.

———

Diamond was wracked with emotional pain as I took him to the room and put him to bed. He was a mess, and my heart ached for him. It shook me to see him so upset, and I sat silently with him for a while, hoping that sleep would ease his mind.

"Can I ask you a favor?" he said between sobs.

"Anything, Double D."

"Please stay with me…talk to me…don't let me go over the edge…" He was pleading.

Two hours passed. My own emotions were overtaxed…between thoughts of Lisa waiting for me in her silky dress, and the presence of Diamond's intense pain. I couldn't focus my attention completely on Diamond because of the fantasy of Lisa's longing lingering in my mind. Nor could I concentrate on her while my friend was in such anguish.

I found her note in my pocket. It was now apparent that I could not leave the hotel anytime soon.

"My man," I said to Diamond, "I have to make a quick phone call…and I'll get some more ice."

He glanced at the hotel room phone on the night table. I followed his eyes, and said, "No, this call has to be made from outside." He was distracted, and didn't seem to focus.

Lisa's phone rang and rang. I tried her number four times, and no one answered…and no answering machine. "She's probably asleep by now," I said out loud to myself. "Shit."

I refilled the ice bucket and returned to my vigil.

The night passed slowly. Diamond gave me no trouble as I paced the floor impatiently, and stared at the walls. And stared at the television. And stared at the clock…tick…tick…tick, tock.

I SLEPT FITFULLY...ON and off. When I finally awoke, Diamond presented a bag of fresh donuts, and he immediately called room service to request that hot tea be sent to the room.

"No coffee, right?" he said as he winked...a gesture to assure me that most of the crisis had passed.

"Right." At least his memory was intact. I had stopped drinking coffee my second month at the Camp.

I was still tired, and my mind was frazzled from the fraughtful night...filled with nightmares and sudden waking moments.

"How are you feeling?" I asked him. He looked so much better. He was freshly shaved and wearing clean clothes...a marked difference.

"Better...I guess," he answered as he turned away.

I watched him as he packed his bags. I could sense that there was something building inside him. I had the ominous feeling of being in the calm of a hurricane's eye...and that all hell was about to break loose.

I had seen men at the Camp going calmly along in their routines day after day. And then suddenly, out of nowhere, something would cause them to fly off the handle and do crazy things. This occurred more frequently with those inmates who internalized their problems.

"You want to talk about anything?" I offered.

He continued packing as I waited for a response. Finally he looked up at me, but said nothing.

"Man, sometimes it's better to talk these things out," I added, hoping to draw him out of his shell.

He stared at me for a moment, as if deciding whether or not to talk. Then, he resumed packing.

"Fine," I said with an irritated edge to my voice. I snatched my toothbrush and headed for the sink. Since he seemed to have pulled himself together, I became consumed with thoughts of Lisa Kennedy, and I was angry at Diamond for his untimely interference.

As I stomped toward the bathroom, Diamond grabbed my arm. "Hey…" he said hesitantly. I looked at him sharply, saying nothing.

"Thanks...I just…" He attempted to say something.

"Come on man, what is it?" I demanded. I was edgy. And hell, I had told him everything about myself.

He hung his head and spoke very softly. "I can't believe Vicki's still with him. I thought…I thought it would be over by now."

I put my hand on his shoulder and looked down at him, sitting on the edge of the bed. This brilliant philosopher-comic had been reduced to a pathetic figure by the oldest of tragedies, the loss of his woman. His defenses…the cynicism, the contempt, and his wonderful ability to find humor everywhere…had completely deserted him.

I didn't know what to say. "We'll get through it, man," I finally assured him.

He sighed, and nodded.

"THERE'S NOTHING TO TALK ABOUT," Lisa said angrily. She shoved the five hundred dollars into my pocket with such force that it tore the corner of my shirt pocket.

"Look, Lisa…" I was pleading. I followed her around the bar.

"I don't want to hear it," she snapped. "You could have called, you…you didn't have to leave me waiting."

"Jeez, I tried. I swear…" I grabbed her shoulders. "This was an emergency."

"Okay." She calmed, but only a fraction. There was still a thick wall between us.

"Lisa, you're the most wonderful…" I began.

"Is that how you treat someone so wonderful…to humiliate them?" she fired back, suddenly angry again.

Diamond had been on the phone to his agent in New York, and I expected him to come out of Lisa's office at any moment.

"Lisa, talk to me. Diamond will be back any second..."

"And you don't want him to see you begging," she taunted, shaking her head in disgust. "Just like a man."

I was incredulous. "You're the one who didn't want me to say anything to him..."

"And you don't need to say anything now," she concluded. This conversation was going nowhere.

Lisa was furious about being stood up. Furious that anything, even Diamond's problems, would prevent me from rushing to her bed. "He's a big boy," she had shouted. "He doesn't need a sitter."

Damn, I felt a hell of a lot worse about it than she did. I was the one really suffering, and knowing that, the absurdity of her charges made me smile. Seeing my smile, she thought I was mocking her, and she refused to be reasonable thereafter.

It got worse. The angrier she got, the more frustrated I became at my inability to communicate with her. It was so silly, I was laughing. And my laughing, of course, enraged her. Lisa thought I was playing games with her. She, the consummate game-player, was accusing me...

I realized that it was hopeless to continue explaining.

I spun her around, and handed the money back to her. She was momentarily stunned...flushed and breathing hard. Small bands of perspiration dotted her forehead, and little red stripes of sunburn stood out on each of her cheeks, under her clear green eyes. God, she was delicious.

"I don't want your money," I growled, reaching for her in a heat of my own.

She pushed me back with surprising strength. Then she stuffed the money back in my pocket, tearing my shirt further.

"Take it, you bastard. You won it," she hissed. "And that's all you won."

I was stunned by her treatment. I wanted to shout that I was going to spend the whole five hundred on condoms. Instead I dropped my hands in defeat as she stormed out of the room.

I SAT IN THE CAR, waiting for Diamond. After twenty minutes, he strolled out, taking his time as he made his way to the car.

"Where have you been?" I demanded, my temper still lingering.

He looked at me, surprised. "Just going over my bookings with my agent," he explained, eyeing me closely. "Everything okay?"

"Just fine," I snapped. The frustration of losing my chance with Lisa was gnawing at me…and part of me blamed him.

"Let's get something to eat…we need to talk," Diamond said forcefully.

WE ATE A LONG LUNCH. It began in silence, but eventually we started to converse…around the edges at first, skirting anything of importance…just mealtime pleasantries. We were both a little weary.

Finally Diamond talked briefly about his ex-wife, and about his inability to deal realistically with the collapse of what he thought was a good relationship. He was not entirely coherent about the details of his marriage. And there were several questions I wanted to ask. But my own nerves were frayed, and I was unable to generate enough energy to cross-examine him further.

I assured Diamond that I truly cared about him, and suggested that we just ride it out as best we could…until that day when he could de-personalize the whole thing, and write his best comedy routine yet.

He smiled weakly at my suggestion and agreed that it was the best way to deal with it…day by day. He told me how happy he was to be my friend, and his partner-to-be.

He began to discuss our decision to open a comedy club, but I gently cut him off. I informed him that it was more important for him to focus on the upcoming TV show…only a week and a half away.

I stressed the importance of getting his act together, and I was honest with him about the series of bad performances he had given. He accepted my criticism thoughtfully and with some gratitude. We both vowed to approach the future with a whole new attitude. I sensed he was relieved…I was too.

I was tempted, as a diversion, to tell him about Lisa, but I decided to limit it to just telling him that I had won five hundred dollars from her on the golf course. I omitted all the personal information. He was amused, but his attention was still focused on the days ahead.

"Now I have something else on my mind," he said with some hesitation.

"Go ahead and spit it out."

He ran his hand through his hair. "Would you consider going to St. Pete with me?" he asked, knowing it was a delicate question.

Diamond explained that my presence was more helpful than I could imagine…that just talking to me would relieve a great deal of pressure…and that he thought my being with him this coming week would be critical to the success of the TV show.

"That's an incredible amount for me to admit," he laughed. "But with your help, I know I can handle it," he concluded.

He described the roomy, two-bedroom condominium we would be housed in, and he promised to cook several mouthwatering delights. I could lie low, work out, and make a few phone calls, he said. Moreover, he felt that the time had come for me to be put on a modest salary. I was moved. We had truly become a team. He added, however, that, "You can buy the liquor from your winnings."

"You got a deal," I said.

"You'll come?" he asked, his voice buoyant.

"Yeah, I'll come," I answered with great trepidation. "But I have to be very careful."

Having come to a general understanding about our present and future plans, we both purged ourselves of our poisoned feelings. The familiar comedic exchanges re-appeared in our conversation. It was like sweet medicine, and we laughed, unburdened, for the first time in days.

I assumed that I had a much better understanding of Diamond's agony. It wouldn't be long before I would find that I still had much to learn. And while I didn't kid myself…Key West was going to be dicey…for the meantime we were road brothers again.

I BOUGHT lunch with one of the bills still crumpled in my torn shirt pocket. Diamond looked at the large bill and laughed. "She's some woman, huh?" he said, carefully gauging my reaction.

"I suppose," I said in general agreement. But I pondered Lisa Kennedy further as I waited for the cashier to make change.

When Lisa was in control, she was marvelous. But she also had a defensive, even spiteful, underside. She was polished, but perhaps a little too rehearsed…though, admittedly, I was enamored with the show she put on. I was still confused by her…and maybe it was sour grapes, but in my mind, I summed her up as…disappointing.

"What do you think she sees in Paul?" Diamond asked honestly.

That was a question no one but Lisa could ever answer. But I gave my theory. "Paul probably sank a fifty foot putt," I said, almost as a private joke to myself.

Chapter Sixteen

I drove down the steep slope of the Sunshine Skyway and peered ahead in the distance to St. Petersburg. It was a remarkably clear day, and the bright sun was high in the sky. From the top of the bridge, we enjoyed seemingly unlimited visibility and a breathtaking panorama.

"Wow, what a beautiful bridge," Diamond exclaimed.

I identified with the bridges that spanned the mouth of Tampa Bay. When I was in high school, there had been only a single span across the miles of water. A thin ribbon of concrete, appearing even more fragile as it dramatically climbed over the busy shipping lanes in the middle of the bay.

At that time, the Sunshine Skyway was unique, easily the tallest structure within hundreds of miles. Alone in the sky, the bridge took on a semi-religious spirit. We would drive out on the bridge late at night, just to stop at the top, in a sort of awe, or respectful worship, which included the rite of spitting from its uppermost reaches.

Later, as the Suncoast grew, another identical span was

constructed parallel to the original bridge. One serviced the northbound traffic, and the other…southbound. The two structures, climbing into the sky, lost any religious significance the first bridge, by itself, might have had. Instead, together they proclaimed the prowess of engineers, and man's triumph over nature.

Maybe it was because we had also grown older, but we never braved the increasingly heavy traffic for one of our visits to the top of the newer bridge. Sure, we'd drive over to Sarasota, and points south. But we never again stopped to worship.

Then, in the spring of 1980, a huge tanker struck the bridge in the middle of a vicious storm, knocking down the southbound lanes of the newer span. Several vehicles, including a crowded Greyhound bus, drove off the broken bridge…just like driving off the end of a giant diving board.

Of course, that left only the original bridge for traffic. It had withstood the collision, and it subsequently held together under the strain of double duty long enough for the State to build a newer, even bigger, bridge.

The newer Sunshine Skyway towered over the old structures, which had once seemed so tall. And as I drove over the new monster, I had the distinct feeling that the original bridge was resting, after a life of remarkable service, alongside his shiny new grandson.

I could also feel the proud old veteran laughing at the heavy traffic, the overdevelopment of the area, and the increased strain on the daily lives of the Suncoast residents…as evidenced by the amount of steel and concrete that strangled the neck of once fertile Tampa Bay.

I felt a kinship toward the proud old bridge. They could build ten other bridges across the spectacular ship channel, I thought, and never equal the magic supplied in the early days by that one span, standing alone, seemingly above the clouds.

THE SIGHTS AND THE SOUNDS, but most of all, the familiar smells of the area...a combination of sea and asphalt, of fish and humidity... flooded my senses, and made me happy with my decision to accompany Diamond here. Momentarily happy.

Wearing my wig and sunglasses, we drove up the beaches, searching for our condo. I recognized the village-like shopping areas, the marquees on Gulf Boulevard...even the people sitting on the porch of the Suncoast Surf Shop. I used to honk at Joe, the owner, each time I passed. Now, of course, I barely glanced as we drove by.

Although it was good to be home after so long, for the first time since hooking up with Diamond, I felt like a genuine fugitive...tense, and keenly alert. I longed to join in the celebration of life on the beaches, but I knew that, for me, danger lurked almost everywhere. I had grown up here, I was acquainted with so many people, and I could easily be recognized. I hunched defensively behind the wheel, and kept a sharp eye on my speed.

We finally reached the condo, a ground-floor apartment, and I settled in, hoping for a week of relaxation. Truthfully, after being barraged by second thoughts, I was a bit overwhelmed and ready to leave.

DIAMOND CAME HOME from his first show in St. Pete, with a cocky grin on his face. I was watching television.

I jumped up from the couch. "How did it go?" I asked anxiously, needing to know immediately.

He held up his hands, and smirked, "Just another great show by the Double D."

I slapped his hands...a double high five. I was more than relieved.

He had more interesting news. Hassled that evening by another drunk woman, he had taken the opportunity to use my "close your legs" line again. "The crowd went wild," Diamond proudly reported.

This inspired me. I decided, then and there, that I would spend my time trying to craft an extended comedy routine. I switched off the television...I was determined that my week here would not be wasted.

Even Diamond felt the creative electricity in the air, and opened his own notebook.

I WAS DYING to call Norman, my mother, my sisters...somebody. I donned my wig and glasses, and walked across the street to the payphone. I called the safest person I could think of...Owen Singer, at his law office.

"Good God, how are you?" Owen asked, purposely not using my name.

"I'm doing well," I replied, warmed by the friendly tone in Singer's voice. "What have I missed?"

"Well, they finally picked up Stevie Peak two weeks ago. They caught him on a boat, in the Bahamas, of all places. And they are holding him without bail."

"How...?' I could barely contain my surprise.

"They say a friend of his tipped off the government," he said, as a distinct warning to me also.

"And the trial...?"

"It won't be for months...maybe not even this year," Owen replied.

Owen said that each side was gearing up for a long and contentious trial. I knew immediately that it was definitely not the time for me to be in the area.

I sensed Owen was itching to ask me where I was, but he knew better. I also knew that, if he figured out that I was in town, he would be disappointed in my unbelievable lack of judgment.

I wanted to know the status of the Norman and Larry situation, but I didn't want to say anything specific over the phone... just in case.

"I want to ask so much," I hinted, hoping that he'd catch on.

He did immediately. "Still no change on other fronts," he responded. "But, there will be soon...it's now or never for some people."

He was letting me know, clearly, that Larry was more than likely going to fold. Norman's future looked bleak.

"Hey...take care of you-know-who," I pleaded.

"He has another attorney handling him," Owen replied, "But have him call me if you'd like."

I wanted to see Norman and Judy, but it was out of the question...for their sakes as well as my own. It was so frustrating to be home...and unable to contact anyone. I had to continually remind myself to be disciplined.

I SAW it happen again in a vivid dream...

He was Hispanic...Mexican I think. He didn't move well, but he had a good right hand. And fierce determination. The younger fighter, however, slipped away again and again, using the incredible movement and quickness that had won him a gold medal at the Olympic Games.

The kid peppered the slower man from long distance, and finally, when he sensed his opponent's fatigue, he stepped inside with several hard shots. The fight was stopped.

The kid later went on to become champion of the world, presumably leaving the beaten man to a loser's obscurity. But it didn't happen that way.

The beaten fighter was from St. Petersburg. He had been fighting locally at a relatively advanced age for a boxer. But he had gone undefeated through many widely-publicized regional bouts. More than that, he was a hero to the Bay area kids, and everyone who knew him bore witness to the decent and productive life the man was living.

So the whole city was excited when he was chosen to fight the well-known former Olympian in a nationally televised event, to be held in Virginia. Not that anyone expected him to win it, but everyone agreed that he deserved the chance, along with the notoriety and the financial rewards.

He entered the ring strong and confident, wearing his trademark beard, and distinctive tattoos on his shoulders and upper torso…

The tattoos were easily recognized by a Colorado Corrections Officer, casually watching the contest at his home in Golden, Colorado. He quickly got on the telephone, and sought assistance to apprehend the tattooed fighter, still in the ring…fighting on television.

The gallant slugger, admired by so many, was actually an escapee from a Colorado prison. He had let his guard down, and was knocked out by more than the flashy punches of a future champion.

I awoke in a cold sweat. Shaken and paranoid, I abandoned my bed and retreated to the kitchen for a glass of milk. It was time to get up anyway, I reasoned, rubbing my eyes.

I looked around for Diamond, but couldn't find him. Then I remembered that he'd mentioned something earlier about having a meeting with Bob, the founder of Coconuts, who lived nearby on the beaches.

Feeling the sticky fingers of sweat around my neck, I escaped to a cold shower.

I HOPPED out of the shower, feeling better. I hurried, drying myself with a large towel. I wanted to see that boy again.

A ten year-old kid lived in the condo unit next door. I had been covertly watching him in the backyard for the past two days. Sometimes he would be playing catch with his friends, and sometimes he'd be out there by himself, throwing the ball up in the air. Wouldn't you know his name was John.

He was thin, but solid, and big for his age. At first, I thought he was twelve, or older. I was drawn out into the yard by his youthful energy…and radiant health.

I had informed him that my name was Eddie. And for the first time, curiously, it troubled me to lie about my name.

"Okay, Eddie baby," the kid said in a wiseass sort of way, "let's see whatcha got." He threw me a baseball glove, followed by a blazing fastball which hurt my hand.

He was cocky, but well-mannered. And he had a developed sense of humor. John was definitely one of those special kids with the whole world open to him. Being around him, even for a short time, made me feel…optimistic.

It's funny how something can unexpectedly affect you. It was just a kid, doing his thing in the backyard. But I had a strong feeling that I would trade everything to be like him. Or better still, to have one just like him.

I STEPPED QUICKLY out of the bathroom. Perhaps he would be playing out back.

"Oh my God…!" a female voice shrieked.

Assuming I was alone, I'd swaggered into the living room stark naked. In my haste, I had surprised, and shocked, the housekeeper.

"Shit…sorry," I said, struggling to wrap the towel around me.

"You scared the…Oh, God…John, is that you?" She put her hands over her mouth.

She had recognized me. Modestly covered by my towel, I crossed the room and pulled her hand down.

"Karen?" I asked, knowing full well it was her.

Shit, it had taken me only two days to get discovered.

KAREN VANZANT originally burst upon the scene nine or ten years ago. A skinny beach bunny, then nineteen years old, with almost white-blond hair and large, pale blue eyes, she was one in a succession of popular barmaids who'd worked at the now-closed, but still legendary, Quarterdeck Lounge on Treasure Island.

I had known her on and off through the years. At one time, I had even dated her roommate. Like so many of the other flighty young girls who worked the beach bars, she and her roommate were tons of fun and always ready to rock 'n' roll.

But Karen tired of the day-to-day...or more appropriately, the night-to-night...existence of bar life. She began to attend the local Junior College on a part-time basis. And, some years later, she finally finished her degree at the University of South Florida in Tampa. All the while working as a bartender, and talking of big dreams and a life of adventure.

After graduating, she sought some sort of professional work, but found that there were no jobs available that would come close to matching the money she could make working in a bar.

Disillusioned and tired of the lounges, she began her own house cleaning service.

One night, while I was over at her apartment on Sunset Beach, watching TV with her roommate, Karen proposed an idea of expanding her business. I was on a roll at the time, and I fronted her three thousand dollars to get her started.

It was, in part, out of respect and some admiration for the road she had chosen. At least, that's what I maintained. But, to be truthful, for the most part it was probably done in some vague hope that I might impress her. She was a foxy thing.

Anyway, while I never got around to getting a date with her, I did get a pen-pal in prison. Every two or three months, I would faithfully receive a card, or a letter, from Karen. It was more than a pleasant surprise. And for that alone, I did come to truly respect her.

AFTER SHE HAD RECOVERED from the shock of seeing me again, I apprised her of what had happened to me at the Camp, and of the reasons for my escape. "So, what in the hell are you doing back here?" she asked disapprovingly…coming directly to the point. I had forgotten that she had such a husky voice…letters could never convey that.

"It's a long story," I answered, not yet ready to inform her of my plans with Diamond.

She looked at me through large glasses. I never remembered her wearing glasses. She noticed the quizzical look in my eyes, and mistook it for discomfort.

"John, you know I won't say anything to anyone…" she began.

I interrupted. "When did you start wearing glasses?"

She laughed and shook her head. "Boy, you haven't changed," she said. Then she added, "I've always had poor eyesight…but I either wore contacts, or stayed blind." She laughed again.

I laughed too. "They look good," I lied. The lie was apparent.

"Well," she said with a shrug, "now that I'm an old broad, I don't care so much."

I examined her closely. She looked great. Granted, she was not the young rocker I had known for years. Her hair, while still blonde, was darker, and she had little laugh lines at the corners of her eyes. But she had filled out nicely. And she had the same striking face…not the common cheerleader button-nose, but a longer, European-type nose…and with those high cheekbones, she was extremely exotic-looking,

But her moneymaker was a gleaming friendly smile. Those perfect white shiny teeth had emptied many a pocket, and filled a cistern full of tip jars. Karen had the type of beauty that would last for many, many years…if she would only lose those glasses.

"So, what are you…twenty-five now?" I guessed.

"Twenty-nine, John…and in a week, I'll be thirty," she groaned with regret.

I laughed again. "Why the long face? I bet a lot of twenty-year-olds would love to look the way you do now…at twenty-nine…or thirty," I frowned, and added, "Thirty…wow."

"Don't mess with me," she warned, playfully digging her fingernails into my arm.

I became serious. "Karen, it would really screw me up if you told anyone about me being here…"

"Now, John, I already told you…"

As she spoke, Diamond exploded through the front door. "Eddie…" he called out, not seeing us.

"Eddie?" Karen questioned. Diamond turned at the sound of her voice.

"Oh, I'm sorry," he said with a smile.

We all looked at each other awkwardly. I couldn't think,

"Ah…I told him my name was Eddie," I finally fumbled.

Diamond recognized the futility of the situation. "It's alright," he said, turning to Karen. "I know everything."

"Don…" I tried to stop him.

"Too late, I've already confessed. So, young lady, if you turn him in, you must expose me as well."

Karen laughed, and said, "You don't need my help. You look like the type who exposes himself regularly."

I choked with laughter as Diamond twisted his face, pretending to be highly offended. Then, with the gaping leer of a schoolyard pervert, he burst out laughing.

Karen cheerfully introduced herself, laughing with us.

"My God, a beautiful maid with a sense of humor…I believe it's the next Mrs. Diamond," he loudly announced. "Tell me, you don't also happen to be an expert in oral sex, do you?"

I closed my eyes in embarrassment, but Karen punched his shoulder, still laughing.

"No…oh well, I thought for a minute I had found the perfect woman," Diamond joked.

I DRESSED and returned to the living room to find Diamond and Karen in an animated conversation, filled with laughter. He continued to assault her with jokes, and she loved it.

As she prepared to leave, Diamond invited her and her friends to be his guests at Coconuts. But before she left, he turned somber. He took her by the arm and flexed his expressive brow.

"Look, you wouldn't say anything to anyone about Johnboy here, would you?" he asked very clearly. "I have big plans for him."

"You mean Eddie?" Karen replied with a laugh, refusing to be serious. "No, he's the one who got me started in my illustrious career."

Diamond smiled contentedly. He bowed and said gallantly, "I was wrong about you. You couldn't possibly be the next Mrs. Diamond…you have too much class."

She smiled and kissed his cheek. Then, she hugged me again. Promising that she would check in with me the following day, Karen was out the door in a wink. I stared after her.

"Don't worry…that one won't say anything," Diamond said, his voice totally confident.

Karen and Diamond had certainly hit it off well. And it started me thinking about the possibility of getting them together again. I guessed that someone like Karen might be the perfect remedy for Diamond and his problems.

I SAT IN THE LAUNDROMAT, waiting for the clothes to dry. I was lost in thought, inventing schemes to put Karen and Diamond together in a comfortable setting. My mind raced ahead…maybe she could even go with us to Key West. Yeah, on Diamond's arm, he would look confident, imposing even.

"Freeze!" a loud voice screamed at me.

I looked up to see a uniformed policeman pointing his service revolver at me. I unconsciously straightened my wig with one hand.

"I said don't move," the officer commanded.

A second officer charged into the empty laundromat. "Well, we got him," he scowled at someone outside.

My heart pounded. Deep-seated fears, and memories of my original arrest, surfaced in an overwhelming nausea. I was trapped. How? Who…Karen?

An elderly woman entered the building. She removed her garish sunglasses and squinted her eyes at me from beneath an oversized straw hat. "No, officer, that's not the one," she said with certainty.

"Are you sure?' the first policeman asked, slowly holstering his pistol.

"I told you, he was my height," she scolded the two young policemen.

I looked down at the tiny woman, and half-smiled.

"You said that he ran in here," the officer corrected her. He turned to me and asked, "Did you see anyone come through here?"

I looked around and shrugged, still too shaken to speak. Without saying anything to me, the old woman wheeled around and briskly walked out, followed by the second policeman. The other man stood with his hands on his hips, and eyed me closely. Finally, he said in an extremely sincere manner, "We're very sorry, sir." And he left.

My hands wouldn't stop shaking. I realized what an error I had made by returning home. Goddamn Diamond. I had to be more careful. And we had to get out of town before I became a nervous wreck.

Chapter Seventeen

Karen appeared the very next day with a surprise...fresh hog snapper filets. Pleased, Diamond sprang into action in the kitchen.

This time, Karen wasn't dressed in her "maid clothes," as she called them. Instead she wore a low-scooped sleeveless shirt and a pair of rainbow-colored shorts made of lightweight parachute material. Her long blond hair caught the shiny sun, and with her sunglasses pushed up on her head, she looked more like the beach girl I remembered.

She rolled into the parking lot in a yellow Jeep Cherokee, with windsurfing racks on the top and a bicycle lashed to the hinged rear-end. She bounced through the front door, asking for a beer. I let Diamond fetch it for her.

I wouldn't let Karen leave. I persuaded her to stay for dinner, knowing that Diamond's cooking would bowl her over. She accepted, as I silently applauded myself.

Dinner was excellent. Artichokes, hogfish sautéed with some special citrus sauce concocted by Diamond, and some wine... Pouilly Fuisse, courtesy of that rich golfer, The Master of Disaster.

Karen was suitably impressed with Diamond's culinary skills, but I raved on anyway.

Later, as Diamond prepared to leave for the club, I suggested that Karen go see the show. She declined, saying that she would perhaps attend over the weekend.

"I have to get up early tomorrow…and besides, I've got to clean up this kitchen," she said.

"Hell, just leave it for the maid," I joked. She glared at me, and I started cleaning up without her help.

Diamond came out of the bedroom and jumped up on the huge, almost six by six, coffee table. Using the table as a stage, he practiced a new routine about late-night parties…those after hours affairs held by people not yet ready to go home at closing time.

It was very funny, and disturbingly familiar…especially the segment about the young girl who worked in a bank, who purported to speak for all womankind. Diamond was a wonder, and his characterizations were a scream.

We applauded as he stood on the table. He spread his arms. "Thank you, ladies and germs," he said. "I'm trying that one out tonight." He winked at me and added, "Why don't you slip on your wig and come down to the club tonight to see it?"

"I'll pass," I said nervously, still gun-shy from my visit to the laundromat. "Besides, I've already lived it."

"Ah, yes…I remember," he laughed knowingly.

With a wave, Diamond was out the door. It suddenly felt as if a crowd of people had made a mass exodus from the room…his presence, when he was on, had that much impact.

I returned to the kitchen chores in the quiet aftermath. Karen joined me, ordering me to sit at the counter while she took over the cleaning duties. I protested, but she laughed.

"I can do it quicker by myself," she argued, "without you in the way."

As she cleaned, we reminisced about the old days on the beaches, recalling where our paths had inevitably crossed at some of the more memorable events that had occurred over the years. We each had particular memories.

"Remember the Seafood Festival, where we…" she would say, or "…the hurricane party at Captain Hank's…" I would suddenly remember.

Our varying recollections, of landmark concerts and of giant sandcastles…or even of questionable acquaintances…served to soften the mood. Sensing this, I seized the opportunity to talk about Diamond. But she stopped me.

"You aren't, by chance, trying to set me up with your friend, are you?"

"Well, not exactly," I replied. "But there are worse guys, you know."

"Oh, John, I appreciate it, but you have to know that this isn't a good time for me…"

I laughed. "Not a good time for what?" I asked.

"Men." she said with a sigh. I was silent.

She went on to tell me that her luck with men over the years had not been good. At first she spoke reluctantly. But the more she discussed it, the more therapeutic it apparently became. Years of frustrating experiences spilled out.

Disregarding her inhibitions, she explained how, ever since her early bartending days, she somehow wound up with bums for boyfriends. Unmotivated types that she herself had to support. Then, she fell for a married man…a doctor. She said that at first he was great for her ego. But that after about a year, she began feeling used…tasting a certain humiliation. The whole thing ended badly.

Finally, some months ago, she had gotten engaged to a very nice guy. "Remember, I wrote to you about that one," she said.

"Yeah, that's right…what happened?" I recalled her letter. They had even set a date for the wedding.

"Well…" she thought for a moment. "…who knows," she concluded with disgust.

I saw tears in her eyes. I walked around the corner and put my arm around her shoulders.

"He called me a whore," she sniffed.

"Hey," I teased, "at least you're not on the run from people trying to throw you in jail for thirty years."

She smiled a pathetic little smile, her eyes still wet.

"So much for matchmaking," I sighed. She smiled wider, and finally laughed at that comment.

"What I need is a couple of friends," she said with a sad conviction in her voice.

"Darlin', isn't that what I've always been?" I replied innocently.

"Who knows what you've always been," she answered without smiling. But she gave me a big hug.

"HE'S A FUNNY GUY, THOUGH," Karen admitted.

"...a real genius," I added.

"That little thing he did about the late-night party...you acted like it was a real event," she stated.

I told her about the party in Merritt Island, and how I had passed up little Lauren, the bank teller. It was refreshing to talk honestly with Karen, as a friend. So I left nothing out of the story.

Karen was amused. "That certainly doesn't sound like the John Bellamy I used to know," she teased.

I tried to defend myself, but she pointed out several instances that she had witnessed in the past...where I never passed up the chance at a girl, or a good time.

"Maybe I'm getting old," I joked.

She grinned. "I guess I'm not the one to be challenging anyone about their past."

She held out her hand as a peace offering, and I shook it. "But you were disgraceful," she said, immediately breaking the truce.

I SPENT the next few days exercising heavily. And writing a comedy routine. I started with prison humor, but it just didn't click. I think I was inhibited by the unresolved nature of my plight. "Too soon," Diamond remarked.

Next, I attempted to spoof my warped reflections on love and communication. I tapped a well of funny emotions with that topic. I filled my notebook with ideas, and even tried five minutes on the tape recorder…it didn't go down well. Something was missing…I felt like I was really over my head.

Diamond occasionally listened in and offered terrific suggestions. "You have great ideas there." he often said, frequently reminding me not to instruct the audience that something's funny…but to make the material itself funny, and let the audience buy into it. Again, I was clearly over my head, but I got progressively more excited with each positive comment he offered.

"It's a process, but your instincts are really good," he stated. "Keep at it."

Karen continually made herself available to run errands for us. She even came by and prepared dinner for us at the condo. After the meal, Diamond opened his big mouth again. He mentioned my new material, and she pestered me until I was forced to show it to her.

Reluctantly, I opened my notebook. "No," Diamond shouted. "Get up on the table and do it right."

As I stepped up on the coffee table, he fetched my wig and handed it to me. "Come on, Eddie," he said with a smile. "Just do some of the finished portions."

As he and Karen sat on the couch laughing at my appearance, I started into my routine about how men and women listen differently…"How true," Karen immediately interrupted.

Diamond laughed, "See, the audience is buying in already."

"Shut up, you guys," I interjected. "I'm already lost."

Diamond rolled off his chair, laughing. Karen put her hands over her mouth. "Tough crowd," Diamond said, "but we're with you. Go ahead…continue."

As I began again, talking about a couple listening to the same phrase, but hearing completely different things, Diamond halted me again.

"You are not giving a lecture here, or reading a research paper."

I shook my head. "See, it's just not ready yet. Let me work on it some more."

Diamond stood up and said, "The material is actually solid…it doesn't need much more work. Let me show you."

He snatched the wig off my head and pushed me off the table. Then, putting the wig on his own head, he jumped up on the table with my notebook. He reviewed it for a few seconds then launched into a bit about a couple spending the evening together at home… both with entirely different expectations. He stopped abruptly.

"Wait," he said, "Let's not make this some anonymous couple, let's make it every couple." He rubbed his chin and continued, "Let's make it Adam and Eve."

Using my very same material, he was brilliantly funny. His body took on each of the characters as they spoke. When Eve asked a relaxing Adam, "what are you thinking?" Diamond twirled his hair like a girl and pursed his lips, assuming the feminine role in a comedic way. As Adam, he became a bored Joe Six-pack, completely out of touch with his wife. And even when he acted out the bits that I thought were too poorly written, too schmaltzy…too sensitive, the effect was outrageous. Karen was squealing.

"This material is fine…actually you have a great piece here," Diamond said as he hopped from the table. But it was his little additions to the material, and mostly, his experienced delivery, that made all the difference.

"Let's work on this together…I have some ideas to give it more impact," he offered, as he scanned the remaining pages of my notebook.

"You're kidding..." I replied. Watching him work, I couldn't wait to provide him with more ammunition.

Diamond turned to Karen. "I'm going to make him a star," he proclaimed, as he divulged our plans for a future comedy club. I couldn't stop him as he went into detail.

I stiffened. "Karen, please don't tell a soul..."

She put her hand over my mouth and frowned at my distrust. And later, when Diamond had gone to work, she took my hand and peered over the top of her glasses.

"John," she said, "When I desperately needed a change in my life, you thought enough of me to give me the money to get me started. I'll always remember that. And, if nothing else, I would never repay your faith in me by...betraying you."

She was very sincere...and eloquent. Certainly unlike any maid I had ever known...or for that matter, most people.

I nodded, feeling guilty about my mixed reasons for giving her money...not to mention that I had passed out a lot of money in those days.

I STRETCHED out on the couch. It was growing late. Karen sat in a large chair across from me, with her feet on the coffee table.

"You know," she said thoughtfully, "your comedy thing is really deep."

"Yeah," I agreed. "That's Diamond's influence."

"I can tell that you've experienced a lot of what you wrote... haven't you?"

"That's the deal," I confessed.

"Yeah, I was laughing," she continued, "but if you think about it, some of it was uncomfortable, even sad." She was getting the point.

I explained Diamond's theory of being a witness to your own life...and his vision of traveling through the "land of inside-out." "It's pretty effective," I instructed.

Karen nodded in understanding. "But you touch on such sensitive areas," she exclaimed. "You have always been a funny guy…but I never knew you to be so vulnerable."

I laughed. "That's not me, that's Eddie Walker…looking back at my life."

She stared out the window for a moment, then turned to me. "I think I like Eddie Walker," she purred.

DIAMOND CAME HOME LATE. Much later than I expected. Karen was asleep on the couch, and I, inspired by their reaction to my writing efforts, had remained awake writing at the dining room table.

He staggered into the room, incensed, noisy and drunk. Karen awoke immediately.

"So you're still here," Diamond barked at her in an irritated tone.

Her eyes flashed…first in fear, then in anger. She jumped up and put on her shoes. Without a word, she reached for her car keys.

"Wait a minute, please," I said to her softly, as Diamond straggled back to his bedroom.

I followed him to the rear of the apartment. "Before I ask you what happened, why don't you go apologize to Karen," I snapped.

He hung his head. "I'm sorry," he said sincerely. He pushed himself up and plodded to the living room. Karen was at the front door.

"Stop or I'll shoot," Diamond shouted, making an attempt at being humorous.

I could see the hurt in Karen's eyes as she looked at Diamond.

"Please, I'm sorry," Diamond said, his voice breaking. "I hate myself."

He started to say more, then he stopped himself, marched into the living room and jumped up on the coffee table. He was onstage again, and he looked at us if we were an audience of a thousand.

"Men and women are two different tribes…" he stated to the imaginary crowd. "Two tribes constantly at war with each other."

Karen and I looked at each other uneasily. He continued, his speech slurred.

"We are as different as fire and water…and we can never really become one. Someone…always…either gets burned, or all wet." He paused, and laughed at himself.

"And there is no forgiveness between a man and a woman…not really. They can reach an accommodation…" He was unsteady, and he began to ramble. "A woman just cannot be rational…but I guess a man…"

He couldn't finish. Tears were running down his face.

I ran to the table and reached for his arm. "What happened?" I asked.

He attempted to focus…I realized that it was going to be another long night.

He drew a deep breath and steadied himself. "She got married yesterday," he said in disbelieving horror.

"Vicki got married…how do you know that?'

He choked. "Tonight…my agent…" He didn't finish the sentence.

I helped him down from the table and he slumped on the couch.

"Is there anything I can do?" Karen asked. Her voice was thick with honest sympathy…Diamond's earlier rudeness already forgiven.

"Maybe you better get going. Don't you have to work tomorrow?" I asked.

"My girls can handle it," she replied with a voice of authority. The confidence in her voice caught my attention…impressive.

But there was nothing for Karen to do. I had the feeling that this time I was going to have to be forceful…to demand that he face up to all this…to count his blessings and put this shit behind him. I had to convince Diamond that…things could be worse.

Karen waved at Diamond, and kissed me on the cheek. "I'll look in on you tomorrow…and pick up the other laundry." She had volunteered to finish the remaining laundry after learning of my laundromat experience. I shuddered at the mention of it.

"Thanks, Karen…you know, he's really a good guy."

"I know that," she said, very seriously.

"See you tomorrow." I opened the door for her.

"Be gentle with him, I know exactly how he's feeling," sniffling as she said it.

I TOOK his drink away from him, emptied it into the sink and returned to sit across from him.

"Let's talk," I said firmly.

"I threw it all away," he mumbled.

"Man, stop blaming yourself, these things happen every day."

"No…you don't understand," he said louder.

"Shit, Diamond, listen. Forget that bitch…it happens." I stopped…it was easy for me to say.

"She's not really a bitch…" he started to say.

"Okay…so forget that whore," I responded, trying to be funny.

"No, no…it was me," he blurted out.

"What…?"

"Me…I cheated first," he sobbed.

I looked into his troubled eyes. He continued. "It meant nothing. I don't even know why I did it. Vicki was hurt…I tried to make it up to her, but things were never the same…" He attempted to carry on, but I put my hand on his shoulder and stopped him.

His confessions were a revelation, and I was momentarily silenced. But I composed myself and tried to reach out to him. "That's a heavy burden you're carrying, man," I said, putting my arm around him. "But maybe it wasn't meant to be…I mean, maybe you were dissatisfied…"

"No, we had a good thing," he argued.

Trying to help, I foolishly asked, "Then why did you do it?"

He exploded. "Goddammit, I guess because I'm a fucking asshole."

We sat without speaking for a few minutes. Finally, he asked, "How about a drink?"

"No, man," I sighed, "no drinks tonight. We talk, we sleep, we cry…but we do not drink."

He looked at me harshly, then laughed softly. "Good idea," he whispered. He slowly raised himself to his feet and stumbled back to his bedroom.

I followed him to make sure everything was alright. As he slipped beneath the covers, I reached for the light switch and turned out the lights.

"John," he said in the darkness.

"Yeah?"

"You're a good man," he said clearly.

"Thanks."

"No, I mean it…you don't deserve what's happening to you. I hope you can work everything out." He was speaking very softly, and I had to move closer to hear him.

I sat down on the edge of his bed. "Man, I'll just settle for our plans working out."

"You have talent…take care of it. And take good care of ole Eddie for me," he spoke louder, his eyes wide open in the dark room.

"Don't you worry, I'll surprise you. And Eddie will make you proud," I assured him. I stood up. "Goodnight, man," I said softly.

"Yeah." He closed his eyes.

I WAS NOT SLEEPY. So I sat on the couch, examining the figures Diamond had written in his notebook. He had everything about the comedy operation estimated...right down to the last phone call. Evidently, his meeting with Coconuts had been successful.

It was a simple deal, with little chance of my being exposed to trouble. What I hadn't realized was the large amount of money we could earn if we paid attention to it. Diamond's projections were conservative, but unexpectedly high. I was pleasantly surprised...

"And it's legal," I chuckled.

At the bottom of the page, I noticed that he had us listed as fifty-fifty partners. We hadn't discussed that, but I somehow expected him to take more of a percentage. Seeing that, I became even more determined to live up to his faith in me. I would guide him through these troubled times, I vowed, and together we would realize our dream.

More than that, I would get Diamond ready to knock them out on television. Yeah, knock them out. I would be the trainer and we would focus on Key West.

"Key West, Key West," I chanted aloud, psyching myself up. Float like a butterfly...

I'd figure out a game plan to deal with Diamond's ex-wife. Maybe I'd meet her and keep her away...if I could just get us past Key West, I thought, it would be clear sailing from there.

Racing with adrenaline, I dropped the business figures and reached for my own notebook...suddenly compelled to review my own material. Alone in the quiet apartment, I re-wrote complete sections of my comedy routine, tailoring it to fit Diamond's edgy persona. After watching him perform it on the coffee table, I could really "see" what needed to be done. In a frenzy of inspiration, I ripped out the weak spots and strengthened the material considerably. I was a madman, full of emotion and truly creative.

Three hours later, I re-read the final product. I was finally satisfied...it was really a step up from where I'd started. I couldn't wait to show Diamond. It was "good stuff," as he would say. Yeah, he's going to be blown away.

Diamond might just be right…I could get good at this.

I was also tired. I finally fell asleep on the couch. The last thing I remembered thinking was that Diamond was going to be proud of me. Yes, in the morning we would get a bag of donuts and I would hop up on the coffee table and entertain him with my version of life and love…and he'd see himself in my work…and would indeed be proud.

Chapter Eighteen

"Wake up," a voice was crying. I pulled the pillow over my head...I wasn't ready to get up. Come on, I need more sleep.

"For God's sake, John, please get up."

It was Karen, shaking me roughly. I groaned and rolled over. But my brain had begun to work, and something in her voice... something severe...grabbed my attention.

I sprang to my feet. The law, I thought. "Karen, what...?" I asked, instantly awake.

She dragged me down the hall towards the bathroom. When we reached the door, she stopped and motioned for me to go in. I looked at her, trying to understand her panic. I was about to speak when she pushed me through the door.

Diamond lay naked on the floor. And as soon as I saw him, I knew that he was dead.

"Man, what have you done," I whispered, as I dropped to one knee.

With the exception of an occasional funeral in the past, I had never seen a dead body. And never in this state. But I knew he was gone. His body was pale and lifeless, and discolored all along the underside…almost bruised looking, as if his blood had settled there.

Nevertheless, I felt compelled to make certain I had lost him, and I reached for his wrist. Diamond's body was cool, and rigid. There was no pulse.

I was numb. I could not speak…or even think. Like a robot, I went to his room, took the top sheet from his bed, and returned to the bathroom to cover him. He was my friend, and I didn't want him so…exposed.

I sat down on the floor next to him. Thankfully, he was turned away from me. I was determined not to look at his face in death.

Karen put her hand on my shoulder. She gently squeezed me, and said, "We have to do something."

"Yeah, I know," I replied without moving.

I looked into her eyes. "I'm sorry," she said softly, squeezing my shoulder again.

With Karen's help, I got to my feet. I walked around trying to clear my head of the paralysis threatening to seize it at any moment.

"John, let's get your things together," she said from across the room.

"Just give me another minute…" I was lost.

"No, come on…right now," she said more firmly.

I didn't argue with her, and robotically moved into action. She walked with me around the apartment, helping me gather the scattered pieces of my existence. In a fog, I packed everything and moved it all out by the front door. I looked at my possessions…a suitcase and a carry bag. I wasn't a wealthy man.

I wandered into the kitchen, and reached in the refrigerator for a beer. There was no beer left. Karen followed me and stood silently as I searched for something…anything…to drink. I found a bottle of bourbon and poured some into a small glass. Noticing Karen, I held it out for her…without speaking. She nodded and took the drink. I reached for another glass and poured a larger one for myself.

She finally spoke. "Do you have any place you can go?"

"I don't know what to do…shit, Karen. I shouldn't even be in town." It dawned on me that I was in big trouble. More than that, all of my future plans…gone, suddenly evaporated.

In a feeling of desperation, my mind quickly ran through my limited options. "Maybe I can crash at Greenbean's," I said, thinking aloud and scratching my head with both hands.

"John, look…take my car up to my house for now. I'll call the police and clean up here…and meet you there later."

"Are you sure?" I asked. "Maybe I should just…"

"We'll talk about it later," she interrupted, taking my glass. "Get going."

Karen wrote her address on a scrap of paper, and handed it to me along with her keys. "Please…" she ordered.

Resigned, I walked to the door and picked up my bags. Everything was moving in slow motion.

"Hold it," Karen shouted. She stepped over and slapped me in the face. Not viciously…just hard enough to get my attention.

"John, wake up. You need your wits about you."

Her stern warning was enough to shake me out of my daze. "You're right," I said crisply, my mind snapping into focus.

"Just let me see him one more time," I added, realizing that I would be unable to pay my respects to him again.

I rushed past her without waiting for an answer.

KNEELING by Diamond on the floor, I drew back the sheet and turned him so I could see his face. I braced myself for a shock, but his face was serene, as if in a deep sleep…with his eyes peacefully closed.

"I'm so sorry, Double D," I said, breathing uneasily.

Underneath his body, clutched in his hand, was my wig. It puzzled me that he had it, but I reluctantly retrieved it. Then, I put my hand on Diamond's forehead for a moment of silence. This can't be happening.

Replacing the sheet over his body, I went into Diamond's bedroom, thinking that he might have left a note for me. On the floor, just under the bed, was a large prescription bottle…empty. It was Darvon, issued in the name of Vicki Diamond. There was no other message.

I limped out the door, carrying my bags. "Love kills," I muttered angrily.

KAREN'S HOUSE was easy enough to find, even in my misery. A short, twenty-minute hop up to Indian Rocks Beach, her little cottage was only three blocks off Gulf Boulevard, nestled into a sleepy beach community.

Still in a trance, I fumbled with her large key ring, searching for the proper door key. I found it on the third attempt and let myself inside.

I was immediately struck by the quality of Karen's furnishings. The dining room set, the living room area, the few art pieces on the wall…even the rich tile on the kitchen floor…were not only tastefully selected, but it was all expensive looking.

What a beautiful place, I thought, as I took a quick look around. Although it was compact…with two bedrooms and a small porch…it was renovated and clean. I chuckled, thinking of Karen cleaning her own house after a full day's work.

This cottage was so different from the crowded messy apartment she shared with a roommate in the old days. The rent here must be high, I concluded, especially if it included these furnishings.

For a moment I pictured Diamond cooking in her tiny, but well-equipped kitchen. And then I remembered again that he was gone…forever. I surrendered to the harsh realization and collapsed on Karen's sofa.

My plans for a creative endeavor were crushed along with all the rest of my hopes for the future. Even more tragic was Diamond's irreversible course of action.

Suicide. The ultimate act of desperation.

A SURPRISING NUMBER of people have contemplated suicide, either casually or seriously, at one time or another. Discouraged by fear, guilt, embarrassment, confusion, physical pain or mental anguish, or even a lack of direction, many of us have looked over the ledge of life and wondered if the short trip to the other side might provide an escape.

I still had clouded memories of methodically loading a .38 and pointing it, with conviction, at my own head. At that time I was positive that the impact of my arrest had destroyed any possibility of achieving my life's expectations. And facing an extremely long prison sentence, I despaired.

While it can be argued, in retrospect, that such notions were absurd, in that ever-so-brief moment I was convinced that my only option lay in that dull-grey blunt-tipped bullet coiled in the chamber of the gun. Maybe I was attempting to have a talk with myself, using the dance of death for effect. I can't exactly say now. But the memory of the event is stirred at unusual moments.

What makes one take the final step? Out of everything, what do all suicide victims have in common…what do they all share besides death?

It would have to be the total abandonment of hope. To stand on the edge, to look down the barrel, to open the prescription bottle...with no hope in the heart...can lead to the loneliest of all forms of dying.

I WAS DISTURBED by the noise of a car pulling into the driveway of Karen's house. I jumped up and ran to the bathroom.

Peeking through the blinds, I saw Karen hop out of the passenger side of a van. It was driven by a fresh-faced girl with dark curly hair, wearing a bikini top and big baggy shorts.

Without turning off the engine, the driver jumped out and helped Karen unload two boxes from the van. Then she stepped back into the van and backed it out of the driveway.

The van was a relatively new, powder blue Chevy. And as it pulled away, I saw, painted on the side of the van in scarlet letters, two words... "Maybe Tomorrow."

Maybe Tomorrow. How prophetic. That phrase expressed my present state. Hell, it summed up the story of my life. It would even make an appropriate epitaph...carved into my gravestone, using the same script that was painted on the van.

The van disappeared around the corner, and I stared after it, my mouth open.

"JOHN, WHERE ARE YOU?" Karen asked.

I walked out and helped her with the two light boxes of cleaning supplies. Then she sighed and flopped down on the sofa, exhausted. Her face was drawn and expressionless. I brought a beer over to her and sat on the floor at the foot of the sofa next to her fallen body. She ignored the beer and rubbed her eyes.

We sat in silence, taking advantage of the peaceful moment. I looked at her as she stared off into space. Then she caught me watching her and she gave me a weak smile.

"How did it go?" I asked.

"It was a scene," she said with a sigh. "The beach police had to call the County. An hour ago there must have been a hundred people there."

"Everything okay?" I was emotionally drained also.

"I think so. They asked a bunch of stupid questions," she said, sitting up.

Karen looked at me. Her eyes were large...and troubled. "You know," she said with a tremble, "it's so sad."

Suddenly, out of nowhere, the enormity of what had happened struck me hard. I put my head down on my arm to hide my face. I tried to speak...but I couldn't find any words.

From deep inside a hidden passion surfaced in a fountain of tears. I couldn't move. I was paralyzed by months of anxieties... and now, the uncertainties that lay ahead seemed insurmountable. On top of everything else, I felt terribly guilty. Guilty that I was the closest person to Diamond at the time, and I did not perceive the depth of his pain. Nor could I predict the horrible consequences.

"Where was I...what was I thinking about?" I pleaded aloud. Guilty...guilty.

Karen stood by without responding to my cries. She made tea, put on some soft music, and rested her hand on the back of my head. Between fits of despair, I noticed that she too had tears in her eyes. It was a sad afternoon.

"Let's take a walk," Karen suggested, after the sun had set and we'd run out of tears.

We walked the three blocks to Gulf Boulevard and crossed over to the beach. It was a quiet evening. Even the Gulf was calm and flat…the tiny waves barely lapping the wet sand. We strolled in silence.

The first evening stars appeared in the sky. I stopped at the water's edge and gazed up at them. "How many wishes can I have?" I asked, counting the rapidly appearing night-lights.

"None," Karen answered wistfully. "I've used them all up…from this very spot."

I was moved by the subtle power of such a heartfelt response and put my arm around her. "I'm sure you missed one or two," I said, trying to remain positive.

She almost smiled and said, "Yeah…I'd like to think that there was still some magic left up there."

The sky became more and more alive by the minute. In the cool offshore breeze I felt myself regaining my composure. I looked over at Karen. She had borne the heaviest part of the day's burden, and still had not complained.

I kissed the top of her head, and spoke softly in her ear. "Thank you," I whispered.

She patted my hand, still around her shoulders. Then she looked up at me. There were tears in her eyes again.

"Are you sure you're okay?" I asked.

She bit her lip and nodded. "Yeah, I'm fine." Then she thought for a moment, and added, "You know, John, I…I've been there before."

"A close friend?" I asked.

Karen took a deep breath, and turned to face me. "No…myself. I was…very close." She shuddered.

I was sympathetic, and I wanted to confess that I truly understood her emotions. But it was something I could never fully explain in fear of appearing weak. But she looked up at me searching for meaning, and the look in her eyes demanded some sort of response. So I made a bold attempt at being honest with her.

"Yeah, I can dig it," I said with a manly tone. Then I looked skyward and added, "Me too."

"Why, John Bellamy," she said, almost cheerfully, pushing me back a step. "A tough guy like you making an admission like that…?"

I grinned sheepishly. I had nothing more to say about it.

"But it's not John Bellamy, is it?" she chided. "It's my other friend…Eddie Walker."

Embarrassed, I frowned. "Oh, come on…"

"That's okay," she stopped me. Then she gave me a warm hug. "Why don't we order a pizza," she suggested.

KAREN WAS a bit more animated as she set her table with plates and linen napkins. I watched her as she reached for a bottle of Chianti, stored in a cupboard over the refrigerator. She was so different from the simple carefree kid she once was…with her bikinis and her headphones, bopping down the beach on her bicycle.

Now, she was complicated and…mature. Sometime in the last three or four years, she had become a woman. And now, a needed friend. I would miss her, and I told her so.

"What are you going to do?" she asked.

I told her about Skip Shelby in Hilton Head, South Carolina. I explained how my original plan had been to go there and work at his brother's marina…before I had run into Diamond.

"I guess I'll go there and figure things out," I said.

"What about your writing?" she asked, concerned.

"I can't really have a club now…not without Diamond." I had a sinking feeling as I was again reminded that all my big plans would be buried along with him.

"I'm not asking about your club," she insisted. "But your writing was coming along. What about that?"

To me they were all the same, the jokes, the club, the writing,

Diamond...all the same. I wasn't going to be a comedian, or some kind of a writer...at least not without Diamond. I shrugged.

"Anyway," she persisted, "you should think about some outlet for it."

Some dreams die hard, I thought. And it was time for me to be realistic.

The pizza arrived, and we ate. Actually, Karen ate. I gobbled down my food, barely chewing the large bites.

The Chianti made me sleepy and I was more than thankful when Karen directed me to her guest bedroom, which looked more like a small office, with a pull-out bed.

I didn't sleep. I stared at the ceiling, reliving my days with Don Diamond...knowing that they would haunt me forever.

I WAS UP EARLY, ready to plan my exit from town. I called the airport, then thought better about using a local facility. Orlando was only about a two and a half hour drive. I figured that it might be safer to hire one of those Disney World shuttle services to take me there. And catch a flight from that airport, or a bus from somewhere over there.

I was tempted to call one of my sisters...or even Norman. But Norman was already in enough trouble, and I was positive my family would be even more difficult to approach during this time. No matter how desperate I was feeling, it wasn't worth the risk to any of them. Besides, I wasn't thinking very clearly...it was too easy to make mistakes now.

Better to get out of the area and bury myself somewhere... soon. I only hoped that I would still be welcome at Skip's place.

ALTHOUGH KAREN'S Jeep was parked outside, I was aware that I was alone in the house. But I was comfortable with my solitude...I had so much to think about.

I found a note on the refrigerator door. It was from Karen, informing me that she would be home before noon. She had also left her car keys on the kitchen counter for me to use.

I found yet another note saying that the refrigerator held fresh egg-salad, and requesting that I make myself at home until she returned.

I laughed at her little yellow notes. Another note person, I chuckled. I was even more amused at her tiny little writing. She could write at least ten words in the space of my four. I remembered her midget writing from the letters she used to send to me at the Camp. It probably comes from writing so many itty-bitty notes, I concluded, as if I had solved some great mystery.

I decided to wait for Karen to return before venturing out to call South Carolina. I grabbed the newspaper from the dining room table and stretched out on the sofa.

On the front page of the B section, there was an article about the suicide of comedian Don Diamond. While it was prominently featured, it offered only sketchy personal information. I was surprised to learn that he was survived by a brother and a sister, and by his mother and stepfather. It was also interesting to learn that Diamond had had small parts in three movies, none of which I'd seen.

I searched for further clues surrounding his death. But the article mentioned nothing other than stating that it was reported he had been despondent as of late.

I burned at that remark. They could never know. Hell, I never knew, God help me.

Karen returned a little after eleven…driving the blue van. She was smartly dressed in a cotton dress, and she was carrying a briefcase.

"What's in the briefcase, more cleaning supplies?" I joked.

She laughed. It was refreshing to hear her laugh again. The fatigue was gone from her face. She kicked off her sandals and sat on the floor. Then she pointed to the newspaper.

"Have you seen the article?" she asked.

"Yeah," I frowned.

"It didn't say much," she commented.

"No, but I found out more information in two paragraphs than I could pry out of him in two months."

Karen instinctively tidied up, folding the paper and picking up my used glass.

I laughed. "Still working, huh?"

She smiled and said, "It's become a habit, I'm afraid."

She breezed by me and carried the glass into the kitchen. I watched the dress swish around her hips. "You're not exactly dressed for house cleaning," I remarked.

"John, I don't clean too many houses anymore." She shook her head. "In fact," she added, feigning a snooty tone of voice, "I've just come from a meeting with my accountant."

"Well, la-di-da," I chimed. "And are we rich?"

She glanced over her shoulder and smiled. "I wish," she stated. "No, at the end of every month, I'm close to broke just paying for all this."

I was amazed. "You mean, all this stuff is yours…?"

"Yeah," she said, not with pride, but with a sigh. "The house too."

"You own this beach house…?"

She laughed heartily at my unabashed amazement.

I continued, shaking my head. "I've been gone too long."

"I got this house long before you went to jail," she said with another laugh.

"You're kidding," I said, almost shouting.

"You never did stay in touch with me after Marsha moved away," she said, referring to her old roommate...my girlfriend during those days.

"Sure I did," I protested, not really remembering.

She flashed her prizewinning smile. "With our different schedules, we were lucky if we ran into each other once a year."

Karen explained how her business had grown considerably. She employed over 12 girls to clean houses, offices and time-sharing condominium units. She had even invested in a carpet cleaning system.

She said that she still occasionally cleaned some places herself when things got backed up. Especially for her longtime clients... like Bob at Coconuts Comedy Club.

I was still surprised. "Are you sure you're the same wild barmaid who ran her beach cruiser into my new Corvette?"

She covered her eyes, embarrassed by the memory. "That was my favorite bike too," she said, peeking through her fingers.

I stared at her. Some of us actually do grow up.

Karen looked around the room. "It can be a real hassle..." she started.

I cut her off. "Man, you should be proud."

She looked at the floor, and said, "Thanks."

"You know what I like best?" I said, pointing outside. "Your van."

"I have two of those vans," she said, more assuredly.

"Damn, Karen...a tycoon."

"My dad helped me get the second one...that one outside."

I was bewildered. "I saw one of them yesterday...when you came home..."

"That was the other one," she proudly explained.

"...with the same writing on its side?" I asked, still confused.

"Sure, that's the name of my company," she said, trying to follow my thoughts.

"Maybe Tomorrow?"

"Yeah…Maybe Tomorrow Maid Service," she said self-consciously. "When I started out, I was always a little behind…I guess it just stuck."

My motto…my epitaph…there's a laugh in there somewhere. Oh, Double D, I thought, if only you could have lived to record this small irony in your list of jokes…

Chapter Nineteen

It was Tuesday morning...departure day. I was nervous but relieved to be finally leaving. It felt almost as if I was escaping all over again.

I had phoned Skip and he was anxiously awaiting my arrival. He even offered to pick me up in Savannah or Beaufort if I had to take a bus, which was actually the easiest way to get there from Orlando. I was relieved, for I was afraid things in Hilton Head might have changed.

Karen and I had stayed up very late...commiserating. Neither of us had slept well, but it was worth it, for we talked of simpler times and of long lost friends. We also promised to stay in touch with each other.

"Would you consider visiting me once things settle down a bit?" I had asked her.

She seemed pleased that I had asked. "I'd love to, John," she replied. As an afterthought, she added, "I haven't taken a vacation in so long."

And later, before going to bed, she kissed me warmly on the lips. Twice.

KAREN TOOK the morning off to help me prepare for my trip. After a light breakfast, I thumbed through the phone book while she went out to grab the morning paper in her front yard.

As I jotted down the numbers for the available shuttle services to Orlando, Karen spread the paper before me.

"Check this out," she said, her voice cracking.

ST. PETERSBURG MAN PLEADS GUILTY TO COMPLEX DRUG TRAFFICKING CHARGES.

The article reported Monday's scene at the Federal Courthouse in Tampa, where Stevie Peak had pleaded guilty to the several charges brought against him. It gave a brief history of Stevie's complicated operation, detailing the efforts made by law enforcement officials to break the ring and apprehend the participants. The agents had named it "Operation Mullet Fever" and said they had originally expected a long and arduous trial.

My heart stopped when I saw a short section referring to the alleged co-conspirators. Among the listed names, was mine...

"John Bellamy recently escaped from a Federal minimum security prison camp. He is currently a fugitive believed to be somewhere in Central or North Florida."

Karen was reading over my shoulder, and said, "You know, they should have run your picture."

I looked up sharply. I wasn't amused.

"I never did tell you how great you look these days," she added.

She smiled, and put her hand on my arm. I wasn't paying attention. I was shocked. Where did they get that information, I wondered. How did they draw that wild conclusion as to my whereabouts?

Wild conclusion...shit, it was pretty damn accurate. On top of all that, there was something fishy about how quickly Stevie's plea was heard. It sure smells like a deal, I thought.

I took a few breaths. Goddamn it all. Stevie pleaded guilty to the goddamn charges. They didn't even need my fucking testimony to nail him. I could have agreed to the damn deal and not suffered any of this. And now the government was quoted as vowing to hunt me down. I closed the phonebook with a thump. Things had definitely changed.

IT TOOK Karen the remainder of the morning and early afternoon to doctor her schedule, contact her responsible supervisors and arrange for a few days off. Her efficient manner bolstered my confidence somewhat. But the cold clamp of fear hampered my every movement.

"We'll leave before rush hour, and drive until we're out of Florida," she calmly stated, looking at her watch.

"Karen," I said, "you're a great fucking girl..." Gibberish...I could taste the desperation in my own words.

"What a nice thing to say," she replied sarcastically, trying to make me smile. But I was too tense.

She cheerfully packed a small bag, and we planned our route of escape. It was simple...

We drove her Cherokee north on I-75 to Ocala, switched to U.S. 41 taking us to I-10. Then we crossed over to I-95, picking it up south of Jacksonville. In a little over four and a half hours, we were in Georgia.

Karen drove the whole distance. And while we were aware of each other's presence, we had little to say over the monotonous drone of the Jeep's engine. My mind wandered...I recalled another trip.

THE MONOTONOUS DRONE of the ancient Aerocommander's engines sang an endless lullaby. I looked at my watch through heavy eyelids…we had been in the air for over seven and a half hours.

Lee saw me checking the time, and broke the silence. "Anytime now, son," he informed me.

Lee…I only knew his first name…reminded me of my father. Or, how my father might have appeared had he lived. He had white hair, a tanned, heavily lined face, and experienced eyes… always covered by his aviator's sunglasses. He was constantly alert, and he gripped the controls with forceful hands and strong arms.

Lee was a former U. S. Marine Corps fighter pilot, but had spent the past twenty years flying small planes around the Caribbean.

I had been informed earlier that the pilot was a former combat ace, but I'd expected an intense Vietnam-era jet jockey. Not an older, easygoing, chain-smoking veteran of the war against Japan. But Lee knew his craft, and I was immediately comfortable with him in the cockpit.

Why I was aboard was a long story. I didn't know anything about planes…or flying…except that the drinks were free in First Class. But we all agreed that I would be the one to accompany Lee, because I was trustworthy. I suppose I should have been flattered.

"You can be the ax-man," Lee joked. I didn't get it.

He handed me a large, short-handled wood-chopping ax, and instructed me to stow it next to my seat. Naturally, I was concerned.

Halfway across the endless water, I waved the ax, humorously letting him know that I was prepared to do my part…whatever the hell it could be.

Lee laughed, and said, "We won't need it until the return trip home…and hopefully not at all."

I didn't smile. And the engines continued their steady drone…

There were no more islands below us. Only water…hour upon hour of blue water. And a relentless sun hammering my eyes.

Then, out of nowhere, the northern coast of Colombia appeared on the horizon.

HIGH ABOVE A BEAUTIFUL burst of pink flamingos, we crossed the coastline, but continued flying, adjusting our course twice as Lee apparently searched for landmarks. I was lost.

Finally, Lee said, "There it is," as he banked sharply and pointed below.

I looked over, and saw hill after hill of jungle growth, with the sea in the distance, back from where we had come. But I saw nothing resembling a landing strip. Then, as the plane came around, straightened out and descended, I spotted the brown target. It was not remarkable. A little strip cut out of lush green growth. A straight dirt-grass road…a little wider than a standard road. Like a few narrow par-5's strung together.

"How in the hell did you find that?" I shouted over the engine noise.

"See that sharp cliff?" Lee replied, pointing to the right. "And see that village…?" He pointed in the opposite direction. "It's easy if you know what to look for."

I spotted the prominent cliff easily, but as I twisted my neck to find the village, Lee dropped the aircraft into a steep descent and I lost my bearings.

We soared low over the treetops and touched down in the middle of the strip. I exhaled…I must have been holding my breath…as we brought the plane around and taxied up the road to a stand of trees.

Beneath the trees were three trucks and a group of worn-looking men. Ragged and dark-skinned, they stood slowly. Instinctively, I reached for the ax. Lee caught my movement, and laughed.

"Not yet, son…these are friendlies," he said.

He spun the plane in a tight circle, revved the engines, then cut them off. I unhooked my seatbelt, and stretched my arms and legs as I sat. My ears were humming.

Lee gave his instrument panel a quick look, then popped out of his seat. He walked back down the tiny aisle and opened the rear door.

A happy Columbian, dressed in a faded Polo shirt, new blue jeans and a white straw cowboy hat, greeted Lee with a broad smile. And his small group of men immediately began to work on the plane.

A truck, full of 55 gallon drums, backed up to the plane, and as one group of men refueled the aircraft using a crude pump, another group began loading bales of marijuana into the cabin.

The seats of the cabin had been removed before leaving Florida, allowing more room for several hundred pounds of pot. The bales were compressed and wrapped with plastic and spongy burlap…with the corners heavily duct-taped. And they were all numbered according to their respective weights.

Without resting, Lee supervised the loading and packing of the bales. He wanted them strapped in the cabin as close to the cockpit as possible, with the weight close to the wing. He maintained that the plane would fly better that way. No one contradicted him.

Lee also insisted that I check-off each bale as it was loaded. Everything appeared to be in order. The ragtag bunch of Indian-looking helpers were efficient in their work. Before the last bales were strapped aboard, I climbed into the cockpit and watched the action through the windows of the plane.

The ground crew filled the wing tanks, and the main fuel tank first. And then they filled a large bladder that Lee had rigged in the cabin…connected to the main tank, so that we could fly directly back to Florida without making a dangerous stop for fuel.

Lee explained that in the old days, one could fly to the Caicos Islands to refuel…for a five thousand dollar fee. But now, those airports were under surveillance, and the only safe way to make the journey was to fly nonstop.

So extra fuel had to be aboard. Lee sought to avoid the cumbersome extra fuel tanks that were the telltale sign of a smuggling plane. Instead, he had devised the bladder system…a rubber tank used on boats, and purchased at most marine supply stores, that would fold up for storage, or disposal, when emptied.

Satisfied with the loading and refueling process, Lee began to preflight the aircraft. The Colombian group leader followed Lee as he checked the engines, the wing sumps, and the undercarriage with a practiced eye. They conversed in Spanish. Both of them laughed and exchanged curses. Finally they hugged…and Lee saluted the crew. The crew smiled toothy grins and waved at him.

Finishing the check of the plane, Lee crawled into the cockpit. It took some effort to crawl over the bales and the fuel bladder, and work his way into his seat.

He buckled his belt, and turned to me. "Got your ax?" he asked with a grin.

Puzzled, I held up my weapon.

He nodded in approval and explained to me that if we had to ditch the plane in the water, we wouldn't be able to climb over the bales and out through the cabin door. He told me that it was my job to take the ax and smash the side window in the cockpit so that we could escape before the plane sank. My stomach churned.

Lee turned over the first engine. He smiled as it instantly jumped to life. Then he hit the second switch. It labored and was slow to start, but it also finally came alive, as I fingered the ax in my sweaty hands.

"Are you ready?' he asked.

I gave him the thumbs up, and he nodded again. He patted my knee in a friendly gesture, and opened the throttles. We moved forward slowly.

We taxied out, all the way to the end of the road. The trucks were already leaving the area. Only the group leader stood by the strip, waving his cowboy hat...a romantic scene as he stood on a tiny mound of grass waving in long, exaggerated sweeps of the hat.

We started sluggishly. I could feel that the plane was heavy with fuel and cargo as we lumbered down the uneven surface. It took the full length of the runway to get her off the ground. Lee winked at me as he eased the fat plane over the trees and into the clear blue sky.

With our airspeed climbing rapidly, we managed to gain altitude as Lee carefully monitored the many gauges on the panel before him. He leveled the plane off at five thousand feet, then reduced the power setting to maintain our altitude, yet conserve our fuel. As he trimmed the aircraft for a comfortable flight, Lee said, "Right now, the fuel is our most valuable cargo."

As I looked at the darkening water below, I wasn't about to argue with him. We were a long way from home.

The engines settled into their familiar drone. But I was a little too nervous to sleep. The sun set, painting the western sky a glorious red. I glanced over at Lee...his face had a seasoned, weathered look, the result of a thousand sunsets in faraway places.

I was uneasy as the darkness settled around us. The water was black below us, and the vast array of stars seemed to swallow us up. I was happy to have the company aboard, and I struck up a conversation with Lee in the calming red glow of the instrument lights.

I asked about his years in the air, and his travels throughout the islands. I also confessed that I had been unnerved by the swarthy, hard-looking Colombians attending to our plane.

He laughed and told me that those men were very simple people...that they had always been hospitable, and honest with him. He went on to say that he never worked with gangsters...or guns...or cocaine.

His was an easy creed, and he insisted that too much had been made about the whole state of affairs concerning drugs. He believed that the country's real problems were rooted elsewhere.

He was comfortable with his work, and with the freedom life had blessed him with. In fact, he argued that the only time he felt dirty or guilty about his life was the short time he had worked for the shadowy figures who were sanctioned by our government to work the Central American arms trade. Sophisticated weaponry, mountains of cocaine, great bundles of cash…all under the guise of National Security. It made him sick, he said.

"If the public only knew…," he mumbled. "Ah…don't get me started."

I asked him if he thought it strange for a smuggler to struggle with such conflicting morality issues.

"Not really," he replied. "Think about it."

THE SOUND of our dying starboard engine alarmed even Lee. Without warning, it shut down in a wisp of smoke. Suddenly, the heavily loaded plane began to pitch…and drop.

"Can we go on one engine?" I asked nervously.

"Normally we could…but not with this load," he said, as he nosed the plane into a shallow dive to keep the airspeed up.

Lee checked the fuel gauges and attempted to restart the failed engine. It coughed and sputtered, but it wouldn't turn over. The plane slowly fell closer to the black water below. My eyes were glued to the altimeter, dropping close to 300 feet each minute.

Lee tried again to restart the engine. This time it struggled for a moment, then caught. Lee eased the plane out of its dive and attempted to gain back some altitude. We had dropped below 3,500 feet.

"Do you know what's wrong?" I asked, fighting an unfamiliar panic.

"I think it's the fuel," Lee announced, still busy at the controls.

"Are we already out of gas…?" I asked loudly. I was shocked.

He glanced quickly at me as if to calm me. "No…probably

water, or insecticide, in the fuel. Or maybe some obstruction in the line…"

As soon as we regained our cruising altitude, it happened again…the starboard engine quit. This time, Lee immediately hit the fuel selector valves, drawing fuel to the dead engine from a different tank. The engine restarted with a loud pop.

He calmly explained how he had been feeding fuel to the engines from fuel tanks located in each wing…one for each engine. He preferred to use up that fuel first, to take the weight out of the wings before switching to the main tank. Evidently, something was wrong with the fuel in the starboard wing tank, he said.

"Is everything okay with the fuel in the main tank?" I asked excitedly.

He grinned, as if I had asked the right question. "Seems to be," he answered, matter-of-factly.

"Well, then stay on that tank," I suggested.

"It won't be enough to get us home," he replied through gritted teeth.

Lee explained that he would have to nurse the plane along, drawing as much fuel as he could from the wing tanks…and then as the engine faltered, switching back to the good fuel in the main tank. Back and forth, until all the fuel in the wing tank was eventually consumed.

But then, he also warned that the whole labor would waste precious fuel re-climbing and falling, varying our speed, and running the other engine hard. It was a serious problem, he stated honestly. And it was complicated by the fact that we could not land at some island airport for assistance. Not with close to one thousand pounds of high-quality marijuana strapped aboard.

"I'll be busy tonight," he said, shaking his head.

THE GOOD ENGINE FAILED FIRST, its wing tank depleted. Lee switched to the main tank and restarted it with ease, as we began picking up navigation signals from Port-au-Prince.

"We're nearing the Windward Passage," he informed me.

Then the starboard engine shut down without a sputter. The wing tanks were now exhausted. Lee had done a good job using every bit of gas in each of them. Now, the remainder of the trip would have to be flown using the main tank…along with the bladder hookup.

I looked over my shoulder at the bladder. It was soft and flabby…much of its gas had been used.

Switching the starboard engine to the main tank, Lee attempted to restart it. It wouldn't turn. Again, we went into a shallow dive. This time, the engine failed to respond to Lee's attempts…even with the good fuel. I could feel us falling rapidly. The remaining engine whined, protesting the demands put upon it by the pilot.

Lee made several more attempts to restart the engine. But it would not cooperate. "Shit," I mumbled under my breath. I swallowed hard as the altimeter dropped below 1,000 feet. The ocean below us was blacker than the night…and approaching fast.

"Look, we only have a couple of minutes," Lee suddenly advised. "Pull the life raft up between the seats…and strap that emergency kit and fresh water cask to the raft pack."

I could hear the controlled alarm in Lee's voice, and I was scared as we dropped below 500 feet. But I managed to do as he ordered.

"Okay, now it's easier to take the window out before we hit the water," he said evenly.

"Get ready with the ax."

I shook as I tightly gripped the ax. Lee turned the plane away from our course heading to gain an optimum wind direction for ditching the aircraft. I readied the ax.

He looked down at the sea…now directly below us. "It doesn't look too rough," he coolly observed. I was frantic…he was totally under control.

Then, as if in answer to a prayer, the starboard engine fired to life. I could instantly feel the extra muscle in the plane as Lee climbed away from the immense blackness below.

We were silent as we slowly regained altitude. First 1,000 feet, then 2,500 feet, then 3,500 feet. I relaxed…just a little…when our altitude again reached 5,000 feet.

"That was close," I said in the dim light.

"It's not over," Lee replied soberly. "God knows how much fuel we used going up and down."

And on we flew.

I LOOKED AGAIN at the fuel bladder. It was emptied…like a giant baggie with the air sucked out of it. Lee saw my worried look. "And people say smuggling is an easy life," he remarked.

Then he checked his charts…we were in the Bahamas.

"Okay, time to ditch all of our charts and papers reflecting where we've been," he commanded.

We quickly gathered all of the maps, charts and weather reports that had directed our journey south of the Bahamas. I commented that it amused me that we were throwing away the paper evidence of our travels, even with the stark evidence aboard…all that pot.

"Just do as I say," he ordered.

I shoved the papers through the side window. The wind ripped them out of my hands and scattered them into the night. Then I glanced back at the bales jammed together in the cabin. Lee looked over and smiled, "The little things can be important too," he said.

I nodded. Who knows how little time we would eventually have to clear everything out.

After using the navigation signals to find our location on the charts, Lee plotted a course up the island chain to West End, where he expected to cross over the Gulfstream to the coast of Florida.

The fuel gauges were dangerously low. "We can forget the rendezvous," Lee said as he tapped the gauges with his fingers.

We had originally planned to land at a pre-arranged location many miles west of Ft. Lauderdale. The rest of our team should already be there, nervously waiting with some pickup trucks.

"We'll just have to try for Bennett Air Park," he decided.

He said that the people at the park knew him and his airplane. And that there was a good chance we could slip in with the normal traffic without arousing suspicion. If we made it at all.

As we neared Lucaya, Lee banked the aircraft and headed west…toward Florida. Then he brought the plane down on the deck, only 100 feet above the water, to stay under the Miami center's radar.

After some time in the darkness, I was surprised to see the city lights ahead of us, looming larger and larger. As we approached land, Lee pulled the plane up sharply and leveled off at about 500 feet. I looked over at him, almost asking for an explanation.

"Don't want to hit a condo," he chuckled, as we crossed the coast and headed inland.

He tapped the fuel gauges again. "Shit…shit…shit," he said too loudly. They all indicated empty…empty…empty.

Lee was in familiar airspace, and he maintained a heading directly for the Air Park.

Without looking at me, he said, "We may have an unwanted reception committee if we've been followed, or if we've been caught acting suspiciously on radar."

At that point I didn't care about the police. I stared at the red fuel lights, blinking their warning. Dead empty. Lee followed the direction of my eyes and grimaced. "If we lose power," he advised, "we'll either aim for a field, or put her down in the inland waterway.

I held up my ax, letting him know that I was still on the job.

He laughed. "You're alright, kid," he said.

We closed on the little airfield as Lee adjusted his course for the final approach. He lowered the landing gears and flaps at the last moment…to get maximum glide. I heard the tires squeal as we hit the hard runway. I had the ax in my lap.

As we taxied down to the end of the flight line, the port-side engine died…the good engine. Lee and I looked at each other in silence, both realizing how lucky we had been.

He pulled the weathered Aerocommander into the line and shut it down as if we were just another local flight in from Palm Beach. Then we drew the curtains closed and locked the plane.

I headed for the payphone and called a number I had memorized…to be used in case of emergencies. Within an hour, the plane would be unloaded and we would all be on our way.

There was no reason for Lee to wait around. He had completed his job. He walked over to the payphone and handed me the keys to the plane.

"And here…take this…a souvenir," he added with a big smile, handing me the ax.

I thanked him and shook his hand. Then, without looking back, Lee walked off into the night.

"I'm tired," Karen said, snapping me out of my daydream.

"We must be pretty close…where are we?" I asked, sitting up straight and looking around for a highway sign.

"Savannah is just ahead," she quickly announced.

"Savannah...hell, we're less than an hour away..." I was trying to remember the distances.

"John, why don't we stay here tonight, and drive up to Hilton Head tomorrow afternoon?" There was the slightest edge of urgency in her voice.

"Sure, Karen...is there anything wrong?" I thought that she perhaps wanted me to catch another ride from here.

But she assured me that nothing was wrong. She merely wanted to take advantage of the forced vacation...stay in a nice hotel, have a quiet dinner, and do some shopping along Savannah's famous waterfront in the morning.

I accepted her explanation, although I suspected there was more to it than she was letting on.

Chapter Twenty

"This is perfect," Karen exclaimed joyfully. I laughed at her as she jumped up and down on the bed.

The hotel room was a spacious semi-suite with two queen-size beds, a sitting area, and a refrigerated mini-bar. The air conditioning in the room was a little too cold, adding to the secluded cave-like atmosphere that made us both feel so comfortable.

I pulled back the curtains to view the city below. Night had fallen and the city was alive with lights. I was not familiar with Savannah so I was unable to distinguish any of her landmarks. But the overall feel of the city was charming...and extremely refreshing. I was happy to have slipped out of Florida so effortlessly.

We took turns using the large bathroom, and at Karen's request, I prepared myself for a night on the town. "First dinner, then to a club or something...the whole deal," she had demanded.

"What's the occasion?" I laughed.

"This isn't much of a vacation," she replied, "but it's the only one I've had in two years."

"Well, hot damn, let's do it," I joked.

"Well, hot damn, let's," she echoed.

I MADE myself a drink as I waited for Karen to put on the finishing touches. I was feeling so much better…this was a marvelous idea. A night out in Georgia.

Karen came out of the bathroom and asked me to make her a drink.

"My pleasure," I answered as I turned around to greet her.

"Damn, Karen…" I choked as I looked at her.

She was beautiful…but more than that. She was sexy. But even more than that. Karen was only casually dressed in an airy, brightly patterned summer dress. It was backless and shoulderless, with its top provocatively fastened around her neck. She smiled and turned around slowly.

Her movements were not those of a girl who brandished her beauty as a weapon. Rather, they suggested a woman who oozes a barely controlled sex appeal…naturally naughty. The kind of woman who doesn't grab your attention with her physical beauty. Yes, she had that…but it was something else. Maybe it was just that appealing wholesome smile that also said, "Spank me, I've been a bad girl."

"Damn, Karen," I said again.

"Is that all you can say?" she giggled merrily.

"I've…I've been missing something all this time," I stammered truthfully. "Please forgive me."

"Well, you've had a lot on your mind," she laughed, feigning patience.

"Right now, I can't think of a thing that was bothering me," I said gallantly. "You are an enchantress."

"And you are a bullshitter…but thank you," she replied, kissing my cheek. Then, with a laugh, she immediately wiped her lipstick from my face, saying, "It takes longer and longer to get ready."

I held her at arm's length and took a good long look at her… and I growled.

We laughed and left the room arm-in-arm.

DINNER WAS A WONDERFUL CHORE. After choosing the restaurant herself, Karen inspected every dish, every item on the wine list... and, after sampling a wide selection of appetizers, she wound up playing with the rest of her food.

But she enjoyed herself. She joked with the waiter, laughed with the diners at the adjoining tables, and even barged into the kitchen to chat with the chef. After weeks of avoiding attention to myself, I was now part of the show, although the real spotlight was on Karen. I couldn't stop laughing. It was so out of character.

"Am I making a spectacle of myself?" she asked as we paid the bill.

"Of course, my dear," I replied, faking the role of the embarrassed escort.

"Good," she concluded, laughing again.

"DO WE DARE?" Karen whispered, showing genuine concern in her voice.

"I don't know," I said softly. "For some reason, I want to."

A few blocks from the restaurant, we'd stumbled across a comedy club. The sight of the club's entrance froze me, and confronted with its flickering marquee, I yearned to go inside.

"You know, I think Diamond would want us to go in," I said, perhaps rationalizing my desire to see the show.

Karen squeezed my hand and said, "Let's go in."

We approached the doorman and requested two tickets...there was only a short wait until the next show.

"Sure," the doorman said, accepting my money. But before putting the money away, he glanced at Karen and asked for her ID.

We roared as she proudly handed her drivers license to him. The beefy doorman dutifully examined the license, then he smiled and returned it to her, saying, "You're entitled to a free drink... Happy birthday."

"Birthday...?" I almost shouted. I had forgotten that her thirtieth was near. "Wow, your thirtieth birthday..."

She nodded and sighed.

"So that's what this was all about. Why didn't you say so?" I asked excitedly.

Karen shrugged. "I don't know," she moaned. Her voice was suddenly sad, as if she had been reminded of bad news.

Noticing her change in attitude, I immediately became loud and boisterous, obnoxiously demanding a birthday cake from the confused doorman. Karen laughed at my antics and hugged me as I continued to yell at the doorman from a distance.

"Is that your wife?" the comedian inquired of me. The audience snickered, thankful that it wasn't one of them being picked on.

I knew that we had taken a table too close to the stage. But Karen had chosen the seats, not wanting to miss a thing.

I laughed a nervous laugh...and ignored his question, hoping that he would move on to someone else.

"Oh," he continued, "was that a trick question?" He walked over to the table, carrying his microphone.

"Oh, shit," I muttered.

He was young, black and very thin. But he was handsome and articulate, and he worked the predominately white crowd well.

He leaned over the table, and pretending I was deaf, he mimicked a phony sign-language as he said slowly, "Is...this... your...wife?" The laughter of the audience grew louder.

"Ahhh...no," I finally responded.

"Ahhh...no," he echoed my answer. Then he turned to the

crowd and quipped, "He sounds like he's not sure." There was another burst of laughter.

Embarrassed, I put my hand over my face.

Then, he turned on Karen. "So, honey, is this your main squeeze?"

Karen giggled, but didn't answer. The comic, still waiting for an answer, turned again to the amused audience, and said, "I think I'm going too fast for this table…"

Karen shook her head, and blurted out, "He's a friend…"

He spun around and sat in the empty seat next to her. He asked for her name. Karen told him while he kept a straight face.

"I see…a friend," he said seriously. "Well now, Karen, what does a friend get?"

"What do you mean?" she questioned. I knew what he meant, and I wanted to hide.

"Karen," he whispered in a loud stage whisper, as if they were having a private conversation, "Do you two do the dirty deed?"

"You mean…?" Karen stuttered.

"I mean, do you ever give him a little mud for his turtle?" He was two inches from her face with the microphone.

The audience howled as Karen turned red.

The comic stood up and yelled, pretending to be shocked. "Look at her," he screamed, "That means she did it." The audience cheered.

"Karen," he continued, unrelenting, "Tell me, was he any good?"

She burst out laughing. "Go away," she cried.

The comic grinned, and said graciously, "You've been a good sport." He called for the waitress and told her to bring us a round of drinks, but he added, "put it on their tab." The audience loved it.

He started back to the stage…then he hesitated, and spun around. "Hey, Karen," he said from across the room. "Are you really noisy in bed?"

The audience exploded with laughter, and applauded the smiling comedian as he returned to the stage.

While I loved being back in the comedy club, each laugh brought some sadness with it. It dawned on me that I'd never been in a club without Diamond. I wasn't quite ready for the experience, and I vowed not to return to another comedy club until I'd resolved my conflicting emotions.

A gentle rain was falling as we walked out of the club. We hailed a taxi.

"The Hyatt Regency," I directed the cabbie.

"Take the long way, please," Karen added, "and show me the shopping area."

The cabbie turned around in his seat. He pointed to our hotel, just up the street, and said crossly, "There is no long way, lady... and you're right in the middle of the shopping area."

"Then go real slow," I snapped.

Karen giggled, as he slammed the accelerator.

We paid the dour driver and headed for the hotel lounge in search of a nightcap. But the lounge was dead...we didn't even go inside.

"Let's go upstairs so I can take off these shoes,' Karen suggested.

"Yeah, we can hit the mini-bar," I agreed.

"Hey, birthday girl," I yelled from my knees.

I was kneeling in front of the mini-bar, pushing the small bottles of liquor around in a frenzied search for champagne.

"There's no bubbly in here," I said, disappointed.

"It's probably just as well," she replied with a laugh. "My head is spinning already."

"There's always room service..." I sprang to my feet, turned down the overly loud room stereo, and skipped over to the phone. As I reached for the receiver, Karen stopped my hand with hers.

"How about a cold beer instead?" she suggested.

"Only a beer...I can't let that happen." I picked up the phone again.

She stopped me again. "Please, John."

"Okay, a cold beer it is," I complied, walking back to the tiny refrigerator.

I used the bottle opener to remove the cap. Then I placed the cold beer bottle on a small tray. Hanging a hand towel over my arm like a waiter, I marched over to the bed where she sat taking off her shoes.

"Your drink, madam," I said, formally. She giggled, and held her glass as I poured the beer.

"Did you have a good time tonight?" I asked.

"It was wonderful," she replied sincerely. "Thank you."

Her eyes sparkled as she listened to the soft music in the room.

"Oh, I love that song," she said. "Could you turn it up a little?"

I twisted the knob on the stereo. A powerful voice was soaring, "If you don't know me by now..."

Karen closed her eyes as she listened.

"Hey darlin', how about a birthday dance," I suggested, putting down my beer.

I took her hand and led her to the middle of the room. She laughed as she followed. "It must be Eddie Walker, the romantic," she joked.

I held her in my arms as we moved slowly and soulfully...we were shoeless on the soft carpet...the stirring music filled the room. And we danced.

I held her tighter, and she responded by putting both of her arms around my neck. Then, she looked up into my eyes.

"Happy birthday, baby," I said softly. There were tears in her big blue eyes.

I leaned down and gently kissed each of her eyes. She smiled through the tears. I moved to kiss her lips. She saw it coming and lifted her lips up to meet mine. Stretching her arms around my neck in a passionate embrace, Karen opened her mouth and stopped dancing.

When I recovered from her response, a different song was playing. We tried to continue dancing to the slow rhythm, but the effect of our touching bodies wouldn't permit it.

I ran my hand down her bare back. She shivered to the touch, and pressed harder against me. We surrendered to the passion of the moment…and melted together on the bed.

As I turned to remove my shirt, I was suddenly inhibited by Karen's apparent vulnerability…and by the possibility that I was taking advantage of her. I caught my breath and held her away from me.

"Karen," I said reluctantly.

She opened her eyes. She was still very excited…her body was moving slowly…and rhythmically.

"Are you sure it's alright…" I whispered. "We've both had a few drinks."

"Oh, John," she sighed as she yanked my shirt over my head, "just do it."

THE MORNING LIGHT…THAT harbinger of regret, which so often heralds a change of heart…poured through the large window of the suite. I winced, angry at myself for not having remembered to draw the dark curtains before going to sleep. Then, I smiled…last night my attention was focused on something else.

Karen was still asleep in my arms, her bare back pressed against me. Her breathing was even and her body was warm. And her skin was soft…incredibly so.

My mind retraced her lithesome curves, her moans of delight, and her eager cooperation. Without thinking, I stroked her shoulders and arms. She sighed, and snuggled further into me. I hugged her gently…I did not want to wake her and have it all suddenly come to an end.

It had been a night to cherish. After the months of imprisonment, followed by the running and all the worrying and deception…and the last minute flight from Florida, Karen's body sheltered me from the unending turbulence, and she made me momentarily forget the obstacles that lay ahead. In fact, her quiet strength had actually encouraged me, unwittingly, to carry on. Exhausted, yet refreshed…is that possible?

I gently slipped out of bed and tiptoed over to close the curtains. I looked out the window at an ominous line of black clouds…a light rain was still falling. And as I fluffed through the billowing drapes in search of the pull-cord, Karen's sleepy voice called out, "Don't close them…"

I turned around, the cord in my hand, and smiled. "Don't you want it darker?" I asked.

"No…I want to look at you," she purred. Then, she beckoned me with her hand to return to bed.

The room was chilly, and when I slid back under the covers, her body felt like a velvet heater. I shivered as I wrapped my arms around her waist and buried my head into her neck.

We had loved, and talked, into the wee hours. Karen had been caring and aggressive, and both tender and deliberately arousing. Everything had been perfect…well, almost perfect.

In our late night conversations, she had again brought up the fact that I had given her money to get her business off the ground. And again, she seemed so grateful for my faith in her…at a time when so few people had…and how special it made her feel. For some reason, it nagged at me that a potential point of insincerity had arisen…although I was also a bit amused at my discomfort over such a trivial item.

It wasn't that I had actually been insincere…I guess I had had some faith in her. It just wasn't as deliberate, or as thought-out on my part, as she seemed to believe. It was something that felt right at the time…just something I did.

"Hey," Karen whispered, interrupting my thoughts and rolling over to face me. "Your mind seems to be working overtime."

I laughed. "Good morning," I said.

"Good morning to you," she sang. Then she added in a throaty voice, "I'm hungry."

I looked at her. Her hair cascaded over her shoulders and spilled across the pillow. And her eyes sparkled…that look.

Perhaps to ruin an unexpected euphoria, we can sometimes ask the dumbest questions…and for some reason, I did. My motive was a good one…it was important to me to be honest with her. But I blundered ahead without thinking it through.

"Karen…?" I began.

"Yes," she answered, her still sweet breath warm against my chest. She opened her eyes.

"I…I've always had respect for you." Christ…my words sounded so stiff and imprecise.

"So…" she responded, a little more interested. I could feel her body stiffen, ever so slightly, along with my words.

"Ah…never mind," I said. I was creating an unneeded tension. Something like this could just as easily upset the fragile nature of our blossoming interest in each other. Just let it go.

She raised herself on one elbow. "John, did I do something wrong?"

Now she was getting the wrong idea…I was committed to barge ahead. And I did so reluctantly.

"Karen, about your business…what would you say if I told you that part of the reason I gave you money…well, that it just seemed cool at the time." "Hell," I quipped, "it might even have been some subconscious attempt at getting you into bed…"

Shit, bad timing on the intended joke…I had couched it in the worst possible terms. And as soon as I said it, I wanted to take it back. It hadn't come out as lighthearted as I'd wanted…and I hadn't thought that such a stupid question might actually hurt her feelings until after the words were spoken.

But her response was just the opposite. She sighed openly, and her body relaxed. "Oh, at this point, who cares," she said. Then, she giggled and added, "I guess it worked."

With that response, she rolled over on top of me and pinned my arms.

"Hey," I said, surprised. "I thought you were hungry."

"I am," she replied in her husky voice.

Chapter Twenty-One

It poured rain...sheets of water with deafening thunder and spectacular bolts of lightning...driven by heavy gusts of wind. Small craft warnings were flying all along the coastal areas.

We did no shopping in Savannah...and no sightseeing. Because of the miserable weather, we were even tempted to stay another night at the Hyatt. But I phoned Skip and he urged me to get up to Hilton Head. "We need to talk...get up here," as he put it.

I could tell by the tone of his voice that something was happening and I became wary. Immediately sensing my defensiveness, Skip assured me that all was well...danger was not lying in ambush. Rather, opportunity was knocking, he said, and I could hear the rush of excitement in his voice.

What was supposed to have been a short drive, of less than an hour, turned into a two-hour ordeal because of the conditions. I was disappointed that I could not experience the often talked-about beauty of the Carolina lowlands. Instead, I had to keep both hands on the wheel and my attention on the barely visible road ahead.

The only moments that my concentration wasn't directed

toward the highway, it was on Karen, sitting next to me. She wasn't deliberately trying to distract me as we drove through the storm, but it couldn't be helped.

At one point, during a particularly heavy deluge, I pulled the Jeep over to the side of the road, and impulsively, I kissed her. Listening to the rain drumming on the roof of the car, we almost leaped into the back seat. But the fear of being hit by another blinded vehicle brought us to our senses. We laughed and swore to try it again in better weather, as I pulled back on the wet road.

We arrived in Hilton Head late in the afternoon. I got soaked attempting to use a payphone, but I eventually contacted Skip, who met us in front of a convenience store and guided us to his house.

SKIP LIVED IN A LUXURIOUS TWO-STORY, four bedroom townhouse. It had a large fireplace, a Jacuzzi and a well-lit three-car garage. And while he occupied the master bedroom, the guest bedroom suite he directed us to was private, roomy and had its own spacious bathroom. Best of all on a day like today, it was dry.

"I'll be right back," he said as he stepped out of the room.

In an intentionally less than subtle statement, Karen tossed her suitcase on the floor of the room...next to my bags. I smiled.

"I'm wearing a T-shirt tonight," she said with a grin. "I was freezing last night."

"The honeymoon's over already," I joked, as I sat on the edge of the bed to remove my wet shoes.

Karen jumped into my lap, and knocked me back on the bed. "It's either the T-shirt or the glasses," she challenged.

"Okay, wear the T-shirt," I ordered.

"You bastard," she said playfully, rolling me off the bed.

There was a knock on the bedroom door. "Hey, can I come in?" It was Skip. He entered the room and stood over me with an arm full of fresh towels and a smile on his face. "I can't believe you're finally here," he said sincerely. "It's been a long time."

Skip Shelby was tall…at least six-five, and thin. But his slight frame belied an amazing physical strength, and he pulled me to my feet and hugged me with the brace of a weightlifter. I examined his long forearms and thick wrists.

"How are you hitting them?" I asked.

"Long and straight, baby," he replied with his thick Southern accent, and a wicked grin.

"We'll see, big boy," I answered with total confidence. Then I turned to Karen and said, "This will be like having a second income," referring to all the money I planned to win from Skip on the golf course.

We all laughed as I re-introduced Karen and Skip to each other. I didn't think their brief introduction in the driving rain had been sufficient.

"Man, I'm sorry I'm late…" I began.

Skip laughed. "Yeah, over two months late."

"Well, I was sidetracked…"

Skip looked over at Karen and cracked, "Sidetracked?...I'd say it looks more like you were derailed."

Karen put her arms around me and hugged me possessively. "Poor baby, he's had some rough times," she said with a semi-sarcastic maternal whimper. "But he's recovering."

She kissed my cheek.

Skip was still smiling. "Well, you're here now," he said. "And not a moment too soon."

"What's up…?" I questioned.

"A whole lot…we'll talk later. For now, let's get you guys settled in."

Then he tapped our bags with his toe. "You two didn't bring very much gear…" he observed.

"Karen can't stay," I replied, with a trace of sadness in my voice.

"Really…" Skip said, surprised, as he turned to her. "How long will you be here?"

"Just a day or two," she answered. "I'll have to call home soon to find out just how long I can be away."

"What a bummer…" he said. His voice rang with genuine disappointment, causing Karen and me to embrace…wordlessly agreeing with him.

We spent the next day recovering from our journey. The storm had passed, it was bright and sunny, and Skip gave us a brief tour of the area, which included a stop at his brother's marina for a quick look.

A quick look was all I needed. The marina was full of extravagantly expensive yachts…many bearing names from distant ports-of-call on their broad transoms.

"Very nice…" I said excitedly, drooling at a schooner-rigged Irwin beauty with a raised afterdeck that must have been over sixty feet long. "What's my job?"

He waved his arm, as if waving away my question, and said, "I have something special in mind." Then he grinned as if he knew something I didn't.

On the way home, he drove us through Harbor Town, which took us, naturally, by that beautiful golf course. My mouth watered when I saw the superb condition in which the immaculate turf was maintained.

Karen laughed at the expression on my face. "My God, I wish he would look at me like that," she joked.

Her comment hit Skip in the funny-bone and he burst out laughing. "He won't be smiling when he has to play it," he remarked, catching his breath.

Since Karen would have to return to Florida soon, Skip and I agreed to delay our first golf match to allow me to spend my time with her.

But I wasn't allowed much time with her before she was called home.

WE STOOD on the screened-in patio, alone in the afternoon sun.

"I'm sorry…I have to go," Karen explained. She was close to tears.

It appeared that Catherine, the girl whom Karen had left in charge of business, was to fly to Michigan for some family emergency. Her father had been hospitalized, and Catherine's family was gathering in support.

I couldn't help thinking that such emergencies were normal in life. And I was uncomfortable with the realization that I could never respond to a similar emergency if it ever arose in my own family. The thought was made even more depressing by the sense of great loss Karen's planned departure made me feel.

"I'll come back soon, I promise," she assured me. She put her arms around me, but it only made me feel worse.

"I understand," I said. And, in fact, I did understand. I was also a little confused at the depth of my feelings for her, and I knew that it was going to be an emotional parting.

We stared at each other awkwardly…each of us at a loss for words. Or perhaps, we each had a lot to say. We just couldn't bring ourselves to speak the words.

Finally, I took her hands. "I'll miss you," I said weakly.

"I know…me too," she replied, as she looked down at the ground.

Skip suddenly appeared on the porch with a bottle of chilled white wine. "Oh, sorry," he said. "Am I interrupting?"

"No," we said together…loudly. We laughed at the tension in our combined voices.

We each took a glass from Skip and stood silently as he slowly poured the sparkling liquid. Then, Karen explained to Skip that she planned to depart for Florida early in the morning.

"That's too bad," he said, touching her shoulder.

She thanked Skip for helping me, and asked him to take good care of me. Skip put his arm around her and told her not to worry. He winked at me as he promised Karen that he would keep me busy. And he added that he wouldn't even allow me to mope around the morning she left.

"We'll go out and hit a few balls on my secret range," he said with a conspiratorial smile…a smile that suggested something further.

Karen seemed satisfied and poured herself another glass of wine.

"Oh yeah," Skip added as an afterthought, "Tonight I'm having a little get-together. I guess we'll make it a going-away party."

"A party?" I blurted, suddenly alarmed.

"Don't worry, everything's cool," he said, putting his arm calmly around my neck. "Just a couple of people I want you to meet."

I glanced at Karen, but she was relaxed. It seemed that I was the only nervous one, and I shrugged with resignation.

And later, when Skip went upstairs to shower and ready himself for the party, Karen and I made love…slowly, yet desperately…and without words.

ALTHOUGH I WASN'T in the mood for a party, this particular affair was casual and low-key. There were only three other couples invited, and Skip was the only busy person trying hard to entertain his date, a newly discovered tourist girl, while at the same time playing host in an attempt to make everyone else comfortable.

I had not expected to know anyone at the party. But a pair of eyes followed me as I came into the room, and at the moment I realized I was being observed, the unmistakable freckled face of an old friend broke into a broad smile.

"R. V…." I almost shouted.

Russell Vlasic…or R. V., the Pickle Man, slid across the room and shook my hand. It had been several years since I'd seen him.

He was short and round, and always impeccably dressed. His manicured hands glittered with gold rings and gold bracelets…to match his gold watch and gold neck chains. The life of any party, this jolly renegade had virtually disappeared three or four years ago. After working his illegal trade for so many years with Skip, Stevie Peak and other smugglers, he had decided that it was time to retire.

R. V.…the name did not stem from his initials as many people thought. Rather, he picked up the nickname for his singular ability to safely move large amounts of marijuana over long distances, usually in his collection of oversized RV motorhomes.

There could be no big deals without a competent transportation guy. In his day, R. V. could procure eighteen-wheel semis, cargo vans and pickup trucks to transport contraband from the offload sites to their prescribed destinations. And he was the first to use dumptrucks, each having the capacity to carry over seven thousand pounds on bad roads. He had theorized, correctly, that a dumptruck was never out of place, or suspicious looking, on any country back-road.

But his pride and joy were those motorhomes. Rebuilt with reinforced, substantial rear axles for heavy loads, and outfitted with tourist stickers from the Grand Canyon, Yellowstone National Park, or a recent bass fishing tournament, these vehicles blended in anywhere.

R. V.…the transportation king.

"The last time I heard, you were in San Diego," I said, still surprised to see him.

"Yeah…I'm in New Orleans now," he replied with a twinkle in his eye.

"So what are you doing here?" I asked. His presence in Hilton Head struck me as odd.

"Partying..." he chuckled evasively.

"Who's the fox?" he asked, changing the subject and nodding toward Karen. She was in the kitchen assisting Skip with the food.

"Easy, big fellow...she's mine." Mine, I thought...until tomorrow. My heart ached.

"You fugitives have all the fun," he joked.

"You heard, huh?" But I didn't laugh. I was growing tired of hotel rooms and disguises, and of constantly looking over my shoulder. "It gets to you," I finally admitted.

"Shit, John, most likely, we'll all be joining you soon," he said gravely.

"What do you mean...?"

"Stevie Peak has made a deal," he stated.

"A deal...?" I said, shocked.

"That's right...he was looking at a zillion years in jail..."

"What's he telling them?" I interrupted again.

"Nobody knows for sure...but for that kind of deal you have to give up everything...everybody. A lot of us are nervous," he said softly.

"Holy shit," I sighed. Stevie knew so much about so many people.

"Damn, John, you don't have to worry...you're a small fry. And you never scammed with him," he responded.

But I was not comforted by R. V.'s assurances. I had a bad feeling about how everything was developing. The net was being drawn. Friend was turning against friend. Everyone was vulnerable. No one was going to have an easy time escaping from their past.

Strangely, my thoughts turned to Stormin' Norman. I couldn't shake the feeling that I had dragged him back into the murky world of danger and deception. He could also become a casualty... and it would be my fault.

I WANTED to kiss her boldly and move her body wildly, but I wound up holding Karen tenderly in the darkness. My mind raced. I was saddened by her pending departure, and troubled by R. V.'s strange appearance. More disturbing was my sudden realization that even Skip's attitude was bewildering.

He had always been so cavalier about everything. But as I lay in Karen's arms and reviewed the past two days, I recognized that Skip was overly excited, and…constantly in motion. Something's up, I concluded. Something was definitely happening…

I looked over at Karen. And even though the room was dark, I could see that her eyes were open. I smiled and kissed her. "If you don't come back to see me, I'm going to come after you," I said, trying to dismiss the other distractions.

She smiled…a forlorn grimace.

"Hey, come on," I whispered, wrapping my arms around her.

She hugged me back. "I'm sorry," she said in a shaky voice.

"What a mess, huh?" I offered.

"I always seem to fall for the guys with some sort of problem," she said with a sigh.

"I certainly fit that bill," I replied with a chuckle.

She stared at the ceiling. "Damn, John…a beach bum, a musician, a weirdo, a married man…shit, I think there's something wrong with me."

Although I was generally aware of Karen's past, I experienced a flash of jealousy in response to her lament. But it vanished as rapidly as it appeared, and I attempted to cover it with humor.

"Don't I rank in the top ten?" I joked.

"Top ten?" she laughed. "Let's see…an escaped convict traveling under an assumed name, with no idea of what to do next… hmmm…we'll put you at number one."

The uneasiness returned. "Do I really remind you of those other guys?" I asked plaintively.

Karen pulled back abruptly and said sternly, "Don't be like that, John. I have to be able to talk openly to someone...please."

I hastily placed my finger over her mouth, silencing her. "You're right...I'm sorry."

She bit my finger and smiled. I continued, "It's just that this is all so new to me," I explained, being equally candid to her.

"What's so new to you?" she asked, still smiling.

I thought for a moment, and said, "...Caring."

It must have been the right answer because she rolled into me and kissed me deeply, wedging her leg between mine. She giggled as I pulled off her T-shirt and threw it across the room.

"Oh, darling," she growled in her earthy voice, "you have something going for you that no one can match."

My manly pride swelled. "What's that...?"

"A beautiful alter-ego," she said with reverence as she slid down beneath the covers.

Good ole Eddie Walker, I thought, congratulating myself.

THE EARLY MORNING sun had barely risen, when Skip loaded a large duffel bag full of golf balls into his car.

"Are you guys really going to hit all of those?" Karen asked, her voice still sleepy.

"As many as we can," Skip replied with a grunt as he lifted two sets of clubs into the trunk.

"Who picks them all up?" she questioned. I too wanted to know the answer to that question. There must have been several hundred golf balls in the enormous nylon bag.

"These are old range balls...we'll be leaving most of them there," he said with a laugh.

Suddenly silent, Karen nodded her head. I walked over and put my arms around her as Skip thoughtfully slipped away.

"Are you going to be alright?" I asked.

She nodded again. "I guess I'd better be going," she said softly.

We looked at each other. I wanted to say so much to her...I struggled against the rising sadness. I remembered my parting with Norman, and the moment I realized that I had lost Diamond. But, in Karen's eyes I saw an even greater sorrow, and I knew that when she left, I would suffer an emptiness of unbearable weight.

"God, Karen..." I stammered. I couldn't find the words.

"I ought to get out of here before I start to cry," she said. But there were already tears in her eyes.

"I'll call you tonight," I promised.

"Please do...I'll be waiting," she said immediately.

With that, she reluctantly climbed into her Jeep and started the engine. I leaned into the car window. "How about one more kiss, darlin'." I said, trying to be lighthearted.

She responded with a tiny smile. "John...I..."

She acted as if she had something to say. But the words wouldn't surface. Instead, she looked up at me with sad eyes, and I kissed her on the forehead.

She took a deep breath and swallowed hard. Then she spoke softly, "Take care of yourself."

"You too, baby."

And she drove away. I watched her Jeep go down the street until it turned out of sight. There was a lump in my throat. I waved, but she had already disappeared.

I could have done better. I had much more to say to her.

Chapter Twenty-Two

The already miserable day positioned itself to take a turn for the worse. Skip wedged a cooler into his cramped car, and ordered me to climb in.

"Man, look at all this stuff," I complained. "Where are we going, to California?"

He laughed. "Patience, my friend…it takes a couple of hours to get there."

"To the golf course?" I shouted in surprise. "We must have passed fifteen of them yesterday, not five miles away."

"This is a very special place, you'll see," he said with a hushed reverence in his voice. "It's part of the reason I wanted you to come here." Something's up, a little voice inside me whispered.

I was not in the mood for a long drive. I had hoped for a little time alone. Also, I wanted a chance to phone Owen Singer for an update.

"We could get there a lot quicker if we took 'Rocket'," he said, referring to his baby, the black Porsche Carrera sitting in his garage, ready for blastoff. "But with all this gear, we're stuck with

'The Beast'." I chuckled at his use of the nicknames...each possession had its own personality.

I inspected the huge, four-door Buick. It was a few years old, but Skip kept it in immaculate condition. I knew it would be a comfortable drive. I also realized that Skip was trying hard to be a friend, so there was no sense in complaining.

I apologized for my impatience, offering in explanation the fact that Karen had just pulled away.

He slapped my leg and said, "Yeah, I feel for you, buddy...she seemed really special."

I nodded...I just loved the slow roll of his Southern accent. But I silently cursed myself for not expressing my true feelings to Karen before she left. When I finally do figure out exactly what I'm feeling, the words won't have the same impact over the telephone.

Skip grinned appreciatively and wheeled the long sedan out of his driveway. "I hope today will brighten your spirits a little," he said as we drove away.

But it wouldn't be long before the roller-coaster day began playing with my emotions.

"THEY ARRESTED NORMAN YESTERDAY," Owen Singer said over the telephone.

My premonition the night before had nagged at me, and I took the opportunity of a pit stop to call Owen's office.

"Oh, no...is he alright?" I asked, barely audible.

I looked from the phone booth over to Skip standing by The Beast. He had completed gassing up the car and was in the process of cheerfully putting ice in his cooler.

But my attention was focused on the conversation. Owen explained that Norman was still represented by another attorney. But he said it appeared that the lawyer was handling the matter competently. Norman had been bailed out immediately and he was now home. Owen also informed me that Norman had called him as soon as he was released.

"Damn, what did he say?" I exclaimed.

"He told me to tell you, K. I....whatever that is," Owen replied. "He said you would know what it meant."

I laughed. Norman was still hanging tough.

"What do they have against him...Larry's testimony?"

"Larry split," Owen answered. "And no one knows where he is."

Owen said he couldn't speculate as to whether or not Larry was somewhere in government custody...or just gone...and he couldn't think of any other evidence the government might have against Norman. He did know that the prosecutor was trying to trace Norman's whereabouts the night of the party in Panama City.

Poor Norman, I thought. And poor Diamond. Now, I also worried about Karen...I shouldn't drag her any further into this shit. It was probably for the best that she had gone, I rationalized. And it occurred to me that it might even be wise not to call her for awhile.

But the thought of not speaking to Karen made me dizzy. Not now, I thought...that would be too much.

WE TUCKED the news of Norman into a neutral place for the remainder of the trip, and chatted idly as we drove. Heading north, we skirted large bodies of water, crossed shallow rivers, and penetrated serene marshlands on the way to Skip's mysterious destination. And even though I was gloomy, the spectacular surroundings caught my attention. Indeed, the diversion was therapeutic and I relaxed as Skip pointed out the landmarks.

While the beach areas had reminded me of Florida, the wetlands had a special character. The fields and the forests were thick with wildlife...especially birds. The birds were swooping, fishing, socializing and preening during every minute of the drive.

To my surprise and enjoyment, Skip was able to identify a variety of the birds we disturbed with our loud passing. He also entertained me with stories of Francis Marion, the Revolutionary War hero…the great Swamp Fox. He was openly proud of his South Carolinian heritage.

"You're just a big redneck, aren't you," I joked at one point.

"Damn straight," he replied, accentuating his drawl. "But even you Yankees can appreciate this…"

"Yankee?...I'm a Florida boy." I argued.

"Same fucking difference," he spat. We both laughed.

Eventually we crossed over to Edisto Island and headed through a heavily wooded area. Finally the pavement ended and Skip took a series of winding back-roads until we came clear of the forest into an open area that fronted deep blue water.

WE HIT BALL AFTER BALL. Some back towards the trees, and some out into the water. We obviously weren't there to play golf.

As we mindlessly repeated the process of hitting the endless supply of golf balls with different clubs, Skip painted a worded portrait of the development he dreamed of building on the property. His descriptions were vivid…the wooded neighborhoods, the ambitious plans for a marina…I could actually picture his long-range vision. It was an exciting prospect.

"Is this your family's plantation?" I asked.

"That's right," he answered.

Then he continued to explain how he wanted the project laid out…where the golf course would run, and most importantly, where he was planning to build his own house.

"Right where we're standing," he said with an enthused certainty.

My eyes swept the miles of lush property. His enthusiasm was infectious. "Out of all this beautiful land, why here?" I asked.

"Because...this is 'The Spot'."

THE SPOT HAD BEEN a legend among smugglers for over a hundred years. Skip's grandfather's grandfather, Confederate Colonel Jasper Benton Shelby, first developed The Spot during the Civil War to circumvent the Union blockade of Charleston Harbor. He discovered the deep-water channel, large enough to accommodate sizable ships laden with smuggled goods and necessities, that ran up to the very spot upon which we stood. During high tide, even oceangoing vessels could dock alongside the shoreline for speedy and convenient unloading.

Later, in the 1920s and '30s, Skip's grandfather used The Spot to smuggle bootleg liquor into the United States. And Skip still remembered many of the adventures that the venerable old rumrunner recounted to Skip as a little boy.

So it could be argued that Skip was only following a family tradition when he opened The Spot to boats carrying bales of marijuana. And even though Skip was eventually convicted and imprisoned for some unrelated charges, The Spot had never been discovered by law enforcement agents of any age. It remained a natural deep-water port of entry for the next forbidden product.

"BECAUSE OF THE PROPERTY'S HISTORY," Skip was expounding, "I think I'll call my development 'Felonwood Estates'."

We laughed heartily, and opened the cooler. We each grabbed a root beer and settled on a large mound facing the water. A steady breeze blew in from the bay. We sat for a moment and scanned the horizon, as I rubbed my sore hands.

"Okay," Skip said as he turned to me and rubbed his own hands in anticipation, "down to business."

He pointed down the dirt road to a cluster of huge overhanging trees, magically dripping with Spanish moss.

"In three weeks time, under those trees and out of sight, some trucks and motorhomes will be parked..."

"R. V.," I said excitedly, putting it all together.

"That's right, his trucks," Skip said, with a nod of his head.

"Shit...don't tell me you're doing a deal..." I said, instinctively hushing my voice.

Skip grinned like a buccaneer, and went on to explain that in approximately three weeks, a shrimpboat carrying in excess of sixty thousand pounds of marijuana would arrive with the new moon...at The Spot. He said that he had assembled a team of veteran smugglers to swiftly carry out a well-planned operation.

He maintained that this deal would be the last big deal of the era...before everyone involved scattered in the face of Stevie Peak's cooperation with the government. And it meant big money...huge money...for everyone.

"Hell, R. V. doesn't need the money," I argued.

"Everyone needs the money," he countered.

"What about you, man...you can't need the money," I pressed him.

"Everybody needs this kind of money," he maintained steadfastly.

It was perhaps left unsaid that when Stevie Peak was finished talking, and people had to run, to incur large legal bills and property confiscations, or even serve prison sentences, they would all need plenty of money.

I smiled. "You're a fucking maniac," I said with a laugh...it was a compliment.

He laughed with me. "This is true," he agreed.

I walked down to the water's edge. "You're serious," I said, still reeling from the shock.

"...as a heart attack," he replied without blinking.

Skip fidgeted with nervous excitement as he laid out his elaborate scheme. With the exception of a few details, his general plan was effective and well thought-out. He had obviously taken his time in setting up this deal, and I couldn't help but be interested. Skip had never had a deal go bad...ever. Not one.

"What kind of big-ass boat are you bringing in? That's a big load for a shrimpboat," I exclaimed.

He laughed to himself, seemingly entertaining some private joke. "Ruby is providing the boat and captain," he announced, as if that name alone answered the question.

Ruby...short for Rubio...which is Spanish for 'Blondie'. I had never met him, but I had heard the name for years. Rubio was a Florida boy...a conch, born and raised in Key West...but he could speak Spanish and he supposedly had great connections in South America. It seemed that virtually everyone I knew in the business, at one time or another, had run across his name.

I pondered this deal...Rubio with the boat, R. V. with the transportation, Skip with the unloading site and crew. Shit, and all three of them with great markets. Skip had indeed assembled a top-notch group...an all-star team.

"This won't be some derelict boat, but a real working shrimper," Skip was saying. "You know those boats Ruby uses... one of those 78-foot Texas steelhulls."

"Damn...there could be more than sixty thousand pounds aboard one of those."

"Maybe so..." he said with a sly smile.

Skip confided that Rubio had personally been into The Spot before, twice, years ago. And that he was using one of his old reliable captains to bring this boat in.

He spoke of Rubio warmly, and with great respect. His words teased me, promising adventure and excitement. As I listened to him, I looked out across the water…and I could almost see the huge shrimper sailing up the estuary.

Skip must have been envisioning the same scene in his mind… that of a fully laden shrimpboat sailing toward us. Because he laughed, and said, almost as an observation, "You know how Ruby likes those freezer boats…"

He was referring to the fact that freezer shrimpboats, as opposed to ice boats, sat the same way on the water whether they were loaded or not. There were no telltale signs of a super heavy load…like a boat sitting or riding funny on the sea.

I truly appreciated the professionalism involved. "Where do I fit in?" I inquired.

Skip offered me several different levels of participation. He said he preferred that I supervised the unloading process, and perhaps ride with one of the motor homes. He said he would pay me $300,000 to show up, along with a piece of the action of each of the expected twenty offloaders.

"What do you mean?" I asked, confused by his rapid arithmetic.

He stated that he had earmarked a dollar per pound for each of the offloading team. I remarked that sixty thousand dollars was healthy for one night's work as a bale thrower.

"Exactly," he responded. "With your help, we can get a super crew at fifty thousand per man." He laughed and said, "It's as good as done already."

"So…?" I said, puzzled.

"So, the additional ten thousand, per man, would go to the supervisor…you." He smiled as he saw my mind computing the figures, and added, "John, you know it's a critical job…we want the best at each post."

"Shit…" Ten thousand, times twenty guys, was an additional $200,000 for me. More if the load was larger.

"And…" Skip continued, "you can take it all in product, sell it with mine, and even after a cut for me, you could almost double that…"

"With a little patience..." I added.

"Not much patience," Skip laughed again. "R. V.'s got the whole load sold already. You just need to get it on the trucks."

I scratched my head. I had never before been involved in a scam of this magnitude. Seeing my hesitation, Skip offered me the opportunity to act merely as an off-loader. He would pay me seventy thousand for the night..

"Or better still," Skip suggested, "I need a loyal man on the insurance boat."

"Insurance boat...?"

Skip explained that he always sent a small boat out to meet the laden shrimper when it came in from the open sea. The small boat communicated last minute instructions and assisted with directions to The Spot.

More importantly, it unloaded approximately 3,500 pounds of the load to be sent to a predetermined location on an adjoining island...miles away from The Spot. Skip informed me that, in the event of a bust, that smaller amount...over 700,000 dollars worth...would escape confiscation and be available to help with bail, legal fees, and support money for those who might go down. It was admirable, but Skip had always been known for taking care of his people.

He suggested that I stay with him, play golf, help him plan the remaining details, and if I would rather not supervise the offloading and moving of the product, I could take charge of the small boat's efforts. "I need a man on that boat I can trust... someone who won't run off with the goods in case it all goes bad," he added. "John, we all trust you."

And, if the scam was successful, half the insurance load would be mine.

I was speechless. Every level of involvement was tempting.

"So shoot," he chirped, opening himself up to any more questions I might have.

SKIP HAD answers to every question. Some of them were merely forged from common sense and experience. For example, he explained that half of the load would be loaded into a semi-truck and shipped directly from The Spot to Atlanta.

"That night?" I asked.

"No...at first light the next morning," he answered, maintaining that a big truck would appear less suspicious in that area during the daytime.

He added that the other half of the load would be transported by dumptrucks and motorhomes to a farm about forty miles away. There, it would be broken down into smaller shipments destined for places like Ohio and New England.

Some of his other answers were extremely creative. When I asked if the nearby small-town motel where he expected to house the crew of more than twenty five off-loaders and lookouts prior to the ship's arrival, would be suspicious, he laughed and pulled a brand new baseball hat out of his car.

"Everyone gets one of these to wear,' he chuckled.

"Hats...?"

"And jerseys." Skip went on to explain that they would roll into the cozy motel posed as a traveling softball team. They would carry uniforms, and bats and balls. And a few of them might even play catch in the parking lot. It was a reasonable explanation for a gathering of strong young men, sprinkled with a few Latinos.

"What's the 'S' stand for?" I asked, pointing to the letter embroidered in old English script on the front of the cap.

"Please..." he waved me away, laughing.

"Jesus...Smugglers...you can't be serious," I laughed.

Skip just grinned.

I POPPED ANOTHER ROOT BEER. "How much time do I have?"

"Think about it for a few days," he advised, adding that the shrimpboat was presently in Key West. It would take the vessel approximately six days to sail to Santa Marta, and another nine or ten days to reach South Carolina. And all before the new moon.

"Add a few days for loading and other bullshit..." His voice trailed off.

"When does she leave Key West?" I asked, my voice quivering.

"Maybe tonight," he replied, almost whispering, "Maybe tonight."

Almost as a reflex, we both turned and looked out towards the open sea.

WE DROVE BACK to Hilton Head at a leisurely pace, and talked for the entire length of the trip. It was a philosophical, and a self-reflective, conversation. Skip was intelligent and articulate, and I appreciated the pirate's spirit in him.

I reminded him that, up to this point, my involvement in smuggling had been sporadic, and interspersed with legitimate enterprises...some more successful than others. And while I myself had never experienced the dark side of the trade...the violence and the victimization...I had grown uneasy about the reports detailing many of these related excesses.

I laughed guiltily. "Shit, man...it's hard to believe some of the latest stuff I've been reading."

Skip argued that he was comfortable with the morality of smuggling...that he reserved the right to smoke pot, or snort cocaine, or do anything else to his body without government interference. Furthermore, he believed that smugglers were the last bastion of the free enterprise system. And that our country had been founded upon the effort of smugglers and blockade runners.

I wasn't about to argue the ethics of drugs with him. I was more concerned about the reality of the public sentiment against drugs, and that outcry's effect upon the future of the business.

"Ah...the outcry is manufactured," he asserted.

"By who?" I asked.

"By the government...by the press." Skip was convinced that all the bad publicity surrounding crack-cocaine, which in his words was "truly nasty stuff," was causing everyone to lose their heads.

"Maybe so," I conceded. But I told him that I couldn't help noticing that at the previous night's party, he hadn't done any coke. And that I hadn't seen him smoke a single doobie since I had arrived at Hilton Head. I stressed that my observation meant something, for my memories of him over the years always included a joint in his mouth.

"Well," he grinned sheepishly, "my time in jail, and on parole, cleaned my act up."

"You're not on parole anymore," I stated.

"There's nothing wrong with staying healthy," he argued.

"That's what I mean...the decision to clean up had nothing to do with the press or the government..."

"That's right, it had something to do with keeping the johnson hard," he said with a smirk.

We both laughed at that remark, and he continued. "I see what you're saying," he said, still laughing. "Indeed, the times they are a-changing. But it should still be our own choice."

"In any event," I reflected, "right or wrong, the politics of it has made smuggling so much more difficult...it's created heavy prison sentences, and has all but closed out the small operator. Only real hard men will be doing it in the future."

We both agreed that organized crime had taken over more and more control of the business...that the government's increased efforts in surveillance and interdiction had just about driven the free enterprisers out of the trade. And we concluded that nowadays the business was dirty and dangerous on both sides of the law. The smuggling days, as we knew them, were coming to a close.

Accepting this as a reality, I argued that we should perhaps be searching for other paths of life…dreaming other dreams…not trying to fit in one more deal. And expressing my thoughts out loud, I realized that, for several months now, I had already begun the process of dreaming about a different way of life.

But Skip shook me. "That talk may be fine for me, John, but what about you. They fucked you good…you don't really have much choice." Raising his voice, he argued, "I figure that you have a little money put aside somewhere, but where are you going to make a living…working at Burger King somewhere under some alias?" He was preaching.

"Look at me, my friend," he continued. "I am your future."

He had touched upon a sore spot with me. "Goddamn it, they did fuck me," I fumed.

"You're goddamn right…now fuck them back," he shouted.

I smiled at him. He smiled back, and added, "…and make a few bucks in the process."

He was a diehard rebel.

I WAS NOT uncomfortable with Skip's plan, nor with the morality of the scheme. The participants were all solid, standup guys. But I was uncomfortable with changing my direction in life. Months ago I had put aside any thought of further illegal activity…I had dismissed it even as a possibility. My jail sentence had certainly gotten my attention, and I concentrated on assuming a much different lifestyle upon my release.

But Skip was also correct in his assertion that all my good intentions were now crushed by the government's unethical behavior, and that my future options were severely limited because of that. At this point, I owed no allegiance to anyone but myself. And, of course, the money was outrageous.

There was also my family to consider. And now there was Karen.

I SAT on a worn barstool nursing a watered-down rum and coke. And instead of analyzing the question of whether or not to join Skip's team, my mind sought to compose what I wanted to say to Karen on the telephone later tonight.

After all my adventures, and at the most troubled and unbalanced point in my life, somehow, out of thin air, I was involved in the beginnings of a genuine relationship. With someone who had a promising and enriching life in progress. And…she was gone.

I glanced at my watch. By this time, Karen was almost back in St. Petersburg.

I did feel a little foolish being consumed by all this, and how it interfered with my ability to concentrate on other important issues. I had long since dismissed all that love-conquers-all bullshit as a fable. Nevertheless, her presence in my life was undeniable, and she tugged at my thoughts like a hooked tarpon on a light line.

I was fully aware that I would have to resolve my feelings for Karen before my mind was clear enough to make a rational decision about my participation in Skip's deal.

I checked the time again. Skip had been outside on the pay-phone for over forty minutes. I tapped my fingers on the bar…I was ready to go. At the same time, I was not ready to climb back into The Beast. Damn, we were still over an hour away from Hilton Head.

I looked again at my watch, shaking my head as I thought of the combined hours we had spent on the pay-phones of the world…

I flinched as Skip tapped my shoulder. "Okay," he said. "Let's get going."

For the remaining hour of our drive, my mind played an awkward game with itself...between talking to Skip about business and piecing together my intended conversation with Karen.

I realized that I had allowed her to get away without better expressing my feelings, and there was nothing I could do, or say to her over the telephone that I couldn't have better expressed in person. Face to face, it sounds meaningful...over the phone, desperate.

I cursed myself for my caution. I had her in my hands and I blew it. Yes, I would call her...and yes, hopefully she would come back to visit, but I had allowed the natural moment to escape. And now I was suffering.

Curiously, rather than wallowing in my bad judgment, I rallied. I vowed to myself, then and there, not to permit life to push me around any longer. Instead, in the future, I would push back in an attempt to control my own destiny. It was laughable to think, in my crazy situation, that I had much control, but I was adamant that I would exert as much control as possible in those few areas of life left open to me.

A wave of confidence surged through me. Although I had been somewhat timid since escaping from the Camp, I knew that I had also discovered a few valuable things about myself, and that I should act to preserve the best of them.

"I'm a survivor" was a common catch-phrase used by many of my friends. By Norman, by Skip...hell, even by my mother. But as we pulled into Hilton Head, I knew that I would never be satisfied being a survivor. I did not want merely to survive. I wanted to prevail...

I STRUGGLED WITH THE WORDS. What can I say, I silently asked myself. What can I say to Karen over the phone that could express my feelings and to convey my determination. And how could I explain that it was a mistake to be apart, and even more of a mistake to blame it on fate or circumstances.

"Blah, blah, blah," I muttered. What a load of horseshit. I needed to do better.

As we drove up Skip's street, I labored with my intended speech. I checked the time again. In an hour or so, I would call her…

Skip broke my concentration with his casually delivered inquiry. "Isn't that Karen's Jeep in the driveway?"

I looked up. Startled, I gasped. "Holy shit…" Then I leaned across Skip and blew the car horn…several long blasts.

We eased The Beast into the driveway next to the Jeep. I jumped out of the car and raced toward the front door. Karen came around the side of the townhouse in a bathing suit and called my name as she ran towards me.

"Oh, God, honey," I cried, as she dropped the towel and ran into my arms. "I didn't want you to leave."

"I know, baby." she whispered.

So much for pre-planned speeches.

Chapter Twenty-Three

"Plants are green, so is money," she stated with a certainty uncommon to other nine-year-olds. In an ironic way, her words stuck with me far beyond childhood.

I was eleven years old when my father's job took us to Washington D. C. In those three years away from Florida, we lived in the suburbs, a happy family in a picturesque, split-level house built on a gentle hill in Springfield, Virginia. My mother's hobby of gardening kept the house alive with the smell of fresh gladiolus and roses, and made our backyard a haven for hummingbirds and praying mantis.

I look back on those days as a very settled part of my childhood. As the country raced to keep up with its booming population of schoolchildren, a world of new housing developments, shopping centers, little-leagues and neighborhood schools bloomed across America. Our dads commuted to work, and our families were cocooned within a soft network of family and friends.

My best friend was Richie Peoples, a goofy little kid with huge glasses who lived across the street from me. He was a good four inches shorter than any of our other friends, and he made a contented bench-warmer for the Safeway Pirates, our struggling little-league team.

Richie was obsessed with animals, "zoology," he would say. His enthusiasm for all creatures past and present spilled over onto my active imagination as we explored the surrounding wooded area. Through my daily romps with Richie Peoples, I learned the difference between mammals and reptiles, between beetles and arachnids.

As eleven year-old boys, we discussed the many species of animals we encountered as we followed the creeks to the streams, to the river, to the reservoir, near our neighborhood. We compared countless numbers of bugs…the head, thorax and abdomen…we collected pollywogs and turned them into frogs, and we displayed the occasional snake to frightened kids as evidence of our fearlessness, carefully avoiding the copperheads that slithered through the damp weeds.

We identified birds and bullfrogs that looked remarkably like the pictures in our wildlife books, and we searched for signs of long-extinct dinosaurs, of which we had memorized each name and era from the plastic models that littered our bedrooms.

IT WAS CHRISTMASTIME AGAIN, and the school holidays had unexpectedly begun two days early as a sudden snowstorm closed the schools across Fairfax County. Warmly bundled-up, Richie and I tramped through a woodland covered with freshly fallen snow, leaving our footsteps along the pristine pathways and half-frozen creeks.

We were in a deep conversation about our lack of funds for the upcoming holidays and what we could possibly do to make some money fast. Of course, lawn mowing and other seasonal activities were ruled out.

"Well, I guess it's back to shoveling driveways," Richie glumly concluded.

"Aw, shit," I responded, using a word I had only recently picked up from my cigarette-smoking cousin.

"Yeah, shit," Richie answered. We both giggled at our taboo-tickling exchange.

I was about to point out that Richie was never very proficient at shoveling snow, and that the money we would earn was hardly worth the pain, when we were interrupted by a puny voice behind us saying, "Plants are green, so is money."

We wheeled around to find Richie's little nine year-old sister, Grace, standing with her hands set defiantly on her hips. Grace was a tiny, doll-like figure who often followed her brother around. We were constantly ditching her and we almost never permitted her to accompany us into "our forest."

At eleven, I wasn't into girls yet, but Richie once told me that Grace had a crush on me. I thought it was extremely weird, but I liked seeing her in the stands at our little-league games, especially those nights when I went three-for-four.

"Aw, sh…" I stifled myself with my hand.

"What are you doing here?" Richie demanded in the condescending voice of a big brother.

Grace ignored the question and continued. "Plants can make you money."

"What are you talking about?" he asked with his face screwed-up into a frown.

"You guys," she said with a feigned disgust. I felt chastened for some reason and remained quiet as she spoke. "You guys always look at the animals. You see the hummingbirds but not the flowers, the frogs but not the lilies."

"So?" I finally said, quietly.

"So, you need money but can't see the money trees."

Richie and I laughed together. We had both exhausted these paths over the past two years and we would have definitely noticed any trees sprouting money.

"C'mon, let's go," Richie said to me, waving his hand at her in dismissal.

"Wait a minute," she squeaked, still defiant.

"John," she spoke directly to me. "Like a farmer or a florist, we can make plenty of money from the plants." I noticed that suddenly "we" became a larger entity.

"Like how?" I asked, humoring her.

"It's Christmastime," she answered brightly.

"Oh, I get it. We sell Christmas trees." I rolled my eyes.

"Noooo, look at this holly," she instructed. "And that mistletoe," she added with a blush, pointing forty feet up in a bare, leafless tree.

Richie and I looked at each other. It did make sense. But would it really pay? "How much could we really make?" I asked honestly.

"I bet a lot more than shoveling snow," she answered, almost like a brat, her hands still ground into her hips.

Her testy little face made me laugh. "Okay," I relented, "what do WE do?" I asked, stressing the "we."

She went right into action, directing us to cut some holly, "…get as much as you can with the red berries," and to clip a clump of mistletoe, "…a healthy-looking bunch," she ordered.

It seemed like an easy task, but it wasn't. Our hands were sliced and pricked as we wrestled with the flexible holly branches using our small pocket knives, and the mistletoe was positioned in a difficult and dangerous location, way up and out on the thinnest branches of the tall trees.

We nevertheless managed to gather what she wanted. Richie complained, "What are we going to do with this?" It was a small harvest.

"Sell it," she answered immediately.

"This little bit?"

"Well, let's get some wagons and some blankets to bundle more up in," she suggested.

"Wait a minute," I said. "We'll need some saws and heavier gloves too," I groaned.

Suddenly, shoveling snow seemed more realistic. "How do you know this junk will sell, anyway?"

"Okay then, let's try it out before we do any more work," she pleaded, knowing that she was losing our attention.

We took what we had gathered and approached the house on the end of the street, nearest to the woods. Selecting a few choice pieces of lush, green, red-berried holly and a generous sprig of mistletoe, Grace ordered Richie to wait at the curb with the goods while she and I rang the doorbell with the samples.

Grace reached up and rang the doorbell. After a moment we heard someone inside come to the door. Grace slipped her petite, mittened hand into mine and held up the holly with her free hand. I quickly wiped my nose as a friendly but mildly surprised woman answered the door.

Grace wasted no time with any softening sales talk, going directly into her pitch, "Would you like any fresh Christmas holly or mistletoe, Ma'am?"

"Well hello kids," the woman answered. Then, without a moment's hesitation, she launched into bargaining with Grace. Fanning out the holly as she held it up, the woman exclaimed, "Oh, it's beautiful."

The kind lady bought everything Grace handed her, and most of the holly Richie was holding at the curb. I was astonished when she handed Grace fifteen dollars.

"It's just perfect," the woman gushed. "Where did you get such lovely holly?"

I turned around and was about to point to the path, from

where only a fifty yard walk would take her to a patch of holly trees, when Grace interrupted, "Way, way back in the woods. It's real snowy and slushy, yuck." I just stood there with my mouth open, holding up my wet, torn gloves.

The woman rambled on about a spectacular holiday centerpiece she hoped to create and asked us if we could find some more holly of the same quality. Grace looked at me for the answer, and the woman's eyes followed her.

"Um, sure," I stumbled.

We made arrangements to see her the next morning. Thanking us profusely, the woman gave us each some chocolate-chip cookies and gently closed the door. Richie ran down the driveway, cheering and waving his bloodied hands. I stood on the bottom step of the lady's front porch as Grace handed me the money and asked, "Well?"

I looked at the money and smiled, saying, "The plants are green, and so is the money."

Standing on the top step, Grace raised up on her tiptoes and kissed me on the lips. It was my first kiss. I didn't dislike it.

We returned to the woods with saws and with my little red wagon, which I thought I'd outgrown. We also brought sheets in which to bundle the prickly holly. Our plants couldn't sell fast enough. On one block, strangely enough, a woman even gave us one-hundred dollars not to sell to anyone else on her street...the Christmas spirit.

We made hundreds of dollars between us in the ten days before Christmas. And in those days, hundreds of dollars was like thousands of dollars today.

For little kids, we were suddenly swimming in money. We hid most of it in the secret corners of our bedrooms, knowing that our parents would demand that we put it into a savings account or something. Ultimately, though, they found out, and although they were indeed proud of our ingenuity and success, we couldn't help noticing that they were also worried. My dad was particularly annoyed that I spent over forty dollars in the gumball machine fishing for prizes like decoder rings and rubber animals.

And the very next year, my last year in Virginia before moving back to Florida, our little team hit the woods again in anticipation of Christmas. This time, we took and filled advance orders, more than doubling our previous year's take. Though this time our parents were ready, and all of it went into savings bonds...well, almost all of it.

Little Grace Peoples was a cool kid. I distinctly remember her running over to my family car as we pulled out of the driveway, moving back to Florida to live. She had a tear in her eye, but she smiled as she handed me a fragile aloe plant through the window of the car, saying, "Remember, if you need some money, think green."

As it happens when you are young and move away to another city, you lose touch with your childhood friends. And I never heard from Richie or Grace again. But I picture her living on a plantation with a lucky farmer, or, more likely, maybe she's running with a man like Rubio...

SEVERAL YEARS LATER, the memory of Grace surfaced in an unusual way. I was three years out of college, trying to round up enough money to keep a failing music equipment business from going under. Norman and I had tried everything...unsuccessfully. The banks had turned us down, the loan companies ignored us, and our friends were not in the position to bail us out. Exhausted and defeated, we chose to get drunk and accept the fact that we were unemployed.

I was sprawled out on the couch and Norman was lying face-up on the floor when the local television news announced that city authorities were in the process of destroying several thousand pounds of seized marijuana. In a live-camera report, the newscaster was at the city dump as uniformed officials threw bales and bales of the stuff on a huge bonfire.

We laughed at the pillar of smoke that wafted out over the conservative city…particularly smoky because of the moist green substance being burned. It was hilarious.

As the television camera zoomed in for a closer look, Norman sighed, "Look at all that lovely green going up in smoke. Damn, it's like burning money."

Suddenly, the image of little Grace appeared in my mind, reminding me about the money trees, and I bolted upright.

"Goddamn, Norman, if we could get our hands on some of that, our money problems would be over."

"Yeah," Norman said dreamily.

At that stage in our lives, we were unfamiliar with smuggling pot. All that would come later. Stating the obvious, Norman rolled over to his elbows and said, "We don't know anywhere to get what we would need." Then he laughed. "And hell, even if we did, we don't have any money to buy it. We might as well go to the dump and pick up the droppings."

We laughed together at the thought of us sneaking over to the dump, with all the newsmen and armed police there.

But as the hour grew late, and our situation seemed hopeless, we did just that…just to look around. I'll never know why we decided on that course of action, or just exactly what happened, but we hopped in my car with a big box of plastic trash bags from the garage and drove to the dump to check it out. Can you believe it?

It was three a.m. when we slowly approached the front entrance to the dump. The rusted wire gate was wide open and no one was around, so we eased the car through. It was incredible. We could easily make out a small column of smoke some two-hundred yards away, where the bonfire had been. And there was an unarmed, un-uniformed guard asleep in a folding chair just beyond the gate. When we noticed him, we backed the car outside the gate and walked the short distance to the smoldering pile.

We approached the smoky mound, which was covered with ashes, and kicked the surface. My God, immediately underneath the black top layer were clumps and clumps of green, gooey buds of marijuana. We looked at each other in disbelief, and with a bold disregard for our own safety, brought on perhaps by the lingering unreality of it all, we returned to the car, past the sleeping guard, and retrieved the large garbage bags.

Norman and I had come to the dump on a whim, and we were unprepared for what we'd discovered. We had only brought fifteen of the heavy plastic bags with us...all the garbage bags in the box... and no utensils at all. We used sticks to rake off the top layers and search for usable stuff, filling all fifteen bags with the best of the many piles within a half-hour.

The trunk and the back seat of my car were stuffed with bags of pot, each loosely packed and overflowing over the seats and onto the floor of the car.

"Damn, Stormin', we coulda filled fifty bags." It was like a pile of gold.

As we drove away, Norman suggested that we go and get some more bags and grab even more of the marijuana. We looked back. The guard still hadn't moved a muscle.

"He musta been inhaling the night air," Norman joked.

We never did return to the scene of the crime. And when we sobered up and examined our load in my garage, seeing the high quality of the pot in the bright light...after culling out the relatively undamaged portions, we had twelve bags full of shaggy loose buds that resembled rooster tails...we knew that our financial problems were over.

Getting rid of such good product was even easier than acquiring it. It was gone within three days, and we were set. We didn't bother bailing out our failing business. We had found something better. I think Grace would have been proud of us.

SKIP WAS SHAKING the money tree at me again, and I could see little Grace Peoples' face in my dreams as I pondered my decision. I was as mixed up as my life, but I would give him my answer immediately.

Chapter Twenty-Four

I stood on the beach watching the last vestiges of the sunset disappear from the sky. Like an Islamic pilgrim greeting the advent of Ramadan, I fixed upon the crescent sliver of the new moon. It was going to be a clear calm night. But it would also be dark and quiet. A smuggler's night.

My eyes scanned the horizon, looking for signs of traffic on the water. And even though I was nowhere near the action, I tensed at the thought of the boys nervously waiting at The Spot.

"It's perfect," Karen said, interrupting my solitude. She had come up behind me and slipped her arms around my waist.

"Do you really think so…?" I proudly replied.

Karen was back at the house reviewing my latest and final attempt at detailing my legal situation. I had spent days in front of her typewriter laboring over each word.

Actually, until this latest effort, the more I tried to express myself, the more frustrated I became. As I would lay out my story, I would become increasingly outraged and unable to complete it.

Finally, Karen suggested that I follow the advice given to me by Don Diamond…to write my account from the vantage point of a third party...an unemotional witness to the events that had turned my life upside-down.

"It's time to be Eddie Walker again," she had offered with a tiny smile, "and write about John Bellamy's struggle."

And it worked. By writing about my problems as if they were someone else's, I was able to complete the short essay without clouding it with overemotional sentiments. The finished product was a moving, yet succinct account of the government's unfair attempts to illegally manipulate me. I identified the agents, repeated the threats and otherwise told the story exactly as it happened, without outbursts of emotion..

I had enjoyed the task, and the longer I pounded the typewriter keys, the better I got at it. It began as a process of "hunt and peck," but my proficiency with the keyboard increased dramatically as I continued. I dusted off the primitive typing skills I had learned in junior high school and whacked away with the fervor of an investigative reporter.

I REACHED FOR KAREN, and sighed. "Tonight's the night," I said softly, looking back across the water.

In deference to Skip, I hadn't disclosed any details of the smuggling plan to Karen. I had only informed her that I was offered the opportunity to participate in the scam, and that I had to make a decision of whether or not to participate.

Maybe I had been away from it all for too long. My instincts were dulled...I couldn't find the required jazz for the action, and my faith in the overall need to carry it out wavered. Perhaps I was just not comfortable being a smuggler anymore...whatever. But when we pulled into Skip's driveway and I saw that Karen had come back to be with me, the answer was made simple.

Looking back on it now, I can see that I was a man at the crossroads. I know that I recognized Karen as a path to the future, while

Skip represented the life I had led before the purgatory of my confinement. And while the decision was made at the spur of the moment, and I may never fully understand my motives in declining Skip's offer, it felt consistent with the journey I was undertaking. And it was a surprisingly easy decision to make.

THE CLICHÉS DEALING with taking the bull by the horns, or taking a stand in life, could fill an encyclopedia. I guess my father summed it up best when he would say, "God helps those who help themselves." Keeping that in mind, I gathered together my luggage and my girl, and returned to the lion's den. I wanted one good effort to be made at righting the wrong done to me before I vanished into the fugitive world forever.

"You're asking for too much," Skip had warned.

"You're probably right," I conceded, "but it feels right." Maybe it was a feeble response, but I was as comfortable with it as with any decision I'd made along the way.

Skip accepted my decision sadly and embraced me as a brother...brothers going in different directions. We didn't need to say "good luck" to each other...it was in the embrace.

Having rejected Skip's attractive offer, I then left Hilton Head before becoming linked with yet another conspiracy. But now, as I walked along the beach across from Karen's house, I had second thoughts about my decision. And watching the ever-darkening sky, I actually longed to be in the middle of the action, instead of chasing windmills hundreds of miles away.

UPON RETURNING TO ST. Petersburg, I was full of renewed energy and resolve. I immediately phoned Owen Singer to inquire about a lenient resolution of the whole affair.

I was crushed by his response. Owen explained to me that under the new Sentencing Guidelines, I would be sentenced to serve more time for my escape than for my original charge. Furthermore, the sentencing judge would be bound by those Guidelines no matter how sympathetic he might be to my plight.

"You gotta be kidding," I yelled. Christ, I had been exceedingly naïve to believe that reality would conform to my sense of justice. All I could babble was, "...that's not fair." Skip was right to be skeptical.

Owen agreed that it was not only inequitable, but that the new sentencing policy failed to make good sense, and that it had alienated many of the federal district judges. Worse than that, the U. S. Supreme Court had upheld the Guidelines as constitutionally sound, and the Court's ruling had ended the debate over the legality of mandatory guidelines. In the process, the High Court had also cut short the burgeoning rebellion against the Guidelines by a considerable number of experienced Federal trial judges.

Owen's fancy legal-speak meant this...It was now the established law of the land, and it held me in its iron grip.

"Is there any way around such a long sentence...even if I turned myself in?" I desperately asked him.

"Only if the prosecutor would agree not to charge you...or not to pursue prosecution," Owen had answered. Owen hadn't changed. He still answered each question precisely...and came straight to the point.

"Any chance of that...?" I asked, already knowing the answer.

"Come on, John..." Owen pleaded. He too knew that unless I would agree to become an informant, there was absolutely no way that the prosecutor would ignore my escape. Especially not during the anti-drug climate that existed these days. Worse...they now had my escape as a legitimate charge to hold over my head as an additional tool to coerce my cooperation.

Extremely angry, I kicked the phone booth, and in my blind

rage, I screamed that I was going to make a bold statement before I disappeared.

Unnerved by my outburst, Owen pleaded with me not to do anything rash. By the knotted tone in his voice, I was sure he had visions of me up on some tower with a rifle. I laughed and assured him that a reckless statement was not what I had in mind. And at that moment I hatched an equally ridiculous plan.

Fine. I would leave forever. I would righteously assume the Eddie Walker identity permanently. I had the funds, the IDs and a clear conscience. I would figure out a way to get into my mother's house in her neighborhood down near the Junior College, retrieve most of my money, and enter a forced exile with the knowledge that I had tried to do the right thing.

But before I slipped away, I intended to write a scathing article about the injustice of my situation. I was determined to deliver it to the press in the form of an "expose"...my open letter to the world. My farewell.

Karen gave me one of her knockout smiles. "You're an eternal optimist," she said lovingly.

"What...you don't like the idea?" I replied defensively.

"No...it's not that," she quickly interjected. "It's just that I probably would have given up the fight long ago."

But I still had some fight left in me.

ONLY NOW, after the article had been completed, I had already abandoned the idea that it would fall on anything but deaf ears. As I held Karen in the still evening, I was again swamped by the feeling that I had been incredibly naïve to expect otherwise.

"Honey, I mean it," Karen repeated, "your article is fabulous. You practically wrote it for them."

"I thought you were the one who wanted to give up the fight..." I said absently, still looking at the horizon.

"Yeah, maybe…but this is stirring," she said seriously. "Reading it really pisses me off."

I ignored her encouragement and closed my eyes. Listening to the tireless waves slapping the shoreline, I hugged her closely and said, "I have the feeling that I should be at The Spot right now unloading my millions…"

Karen held me away from her and looked into my eyes as nightfall crept over us. "I didn't want to say it before…but I think Eddie made the right decision."

"Damn, Karen, why didn't you tell me this before…when I asked you?"

I had purposely solicited her opinion at Skip's house. Then, she only shrugged, avoiding any answer. Since then, I constantly wrestled with the choice I had made. Knowing that she agreed with me would have made me much more comfortable…it might have even felt like a commitment of some kind.

She shrugged again, and stated frankly, "It had to be your own decision." Then she flashed a guilty smile and added, "Besides, I suppose a part of me wanted you to do it…"

She still had the ability to surprise me with comments like that, and it completely cured me of my somber mood. "Oh yeah," I growled, "Which part…?"

Karen wrapped her arms around my neck and whispered, "… the bad part."

We fell to the sand, and with the urgency of star-crossed lovers, we tumbled to the water's edge. And while that little stretch of beach did not have the history of The Spot on Edisto Island, it would forever-after be remembered in my mind as "The Other Spot."

And the new moon hung a lopsided smile in the twilight.

Chapter Twenty-Five

In a depressing series of events, the newspaper not only rejected my article, but they convinced me that they were not interested in running any pieces whatsoever dealing with issues raised by drug cases. Especially those challenging the methods utilized by law enforcement officials to battle the drug menace.

The only positive thing that occurred was a brief conversation, at a clandestine meeting, with the paper's Features Editor, who happened to be an acquaintance of my older sister's.

The editor praised my effort and encouraged me to keep writing. But he insisted that the newspaper was not the proper forum for what I hoped to achieve. He explained that from time to time, certain issues became highly politicized, and that newspapers were generally reluctant to confront a wall of public opinion about those particular issues unless they contained human rights issues that couldn't be ignored.

As an example, he reminded me of the time when drunken driving emerged as one of those topics. Drunken drivers were not only criminals… "deservedly so," he added…but political criminals as well, because of the public sentiment that was brought to bear against them. Now, he argued, drugs had become the new political crime...and, as in drunken driving cases, the press wasn't about to enter the ring to fight on behalf of a drug offender. Not on the basis of a one-sided claim in any event.

He conceded that he was "appalled" by what had happened to me. He also maintained that his far greater concern was the erosion of our basic liberties from an ever-growing police power over law-abiding citizens...all under the guise of drug prevention.

"Drunk driving yesterday, the drug problem today...who knows, tomorrow it may be under the banner of something like National Security that permits the government to further intrude into our lives," he stated. "It's something I'll certainly keep my eye on."

But he concluded that, at present, tempers were too hot for rational discussion, and that there was nothing he could do to help me. He finally suggested that I send my "report" to my Congressman. I laughed, but he was serious.

I REFLECTED BITTERLY on the whole state of affairs. And poor Karen had to bear the brunt of my verbal attacks of frustration. She listened patiently as I ranted over the telephone to Owen.

Owen, God bless him, agreed with me, but from a more scholarly perspective. And, as always, I was entertained, and calmed, when he launched into his lawyerly way of dissecting things. Man, he was good.

He argued that all during his youth, and all through his formative years, the champions of social change and of the individual's struggle against an oppressive system had been the free press and the federal judiciary. Together they had withstood a whirlwind of public opinion on a variety of important issues. And regardless of the intense fire they had received from every direction, they had remained at the forefront of truth and justice…the ultimate check and balance on all matters concerning right and wrong.

Now, Owen railed, seemingly from his soapbox, all of a sudden these two traditional beacons of hope and humanity had been humbled, emasculated and, in effect, silenced. Their respective missions had been superseded by political finger-pointing and hysteria. The courts were handcuffed by restrictive "guidelines" imposed by politicians in place of judicial discretion, and the once relentless press softened by homogenized news focused on sensationalism or upon ratings and awards. Go, Owen, go.

I cheered him on. "Oh, how the mighty have fallen," I boomed.

But Owen was serious, and started up again. "If mandatory guidelines had existed during the Civil Rights movement…" he stopped himself. After a brief moment of silence, he softly conceded, "John, I don't know where to take your grievance."

As entertaining as he was, he spelled out the reality of my situation. As noble as my intentions might have been in returning home to fight, I summed it up to Karen, "I'm screwed, honey." I said meekly. "I tried. I don't want to run, but I have to."

And run I would, after two important rendezvous.

FOR THE FIRST time in my life, a set of rented golf clubs felt good in my hands. They were balanced and relatively new. And they were undamaged, which was something unusual for rental clubs.

I hit the ball well, but the distraction of looking across the range, the clubhouse and the parking lot caused me to miss-hit several shots. Adding to the distraction was the wig I was wearing. For the first time since Diamond's death, I had put it on. And even though Karen had trimmed its length somewhat, its presence interfered with my swing. But it didn't really matter…I wasn't there to play golf.

I reminded myself that this day would be the last time I would have to use rented or borrowed golf clubs. Karen and I had devised a scheme to get into my mother's house…to clean it, of course… and to snatch my own clubs and my stashed money in the process. More importantly, it would allow me to have a heart-to-heart talk with my mother, and to plan with her a future of deception and disguise. That would be the final item on my agenda before departing.

First, I went directly to where Owen Singer had suggested that I meet him. It was the perfect meeting spot and I was comfortable because I had been to this range often in the past. Hell, I used to play the adjoining golf course four or five times a year.

I checked the time…it was eleven o'clock. Owen had set the meeting for ten, but he had also warned me that he would likely be running late. For even though it was Saturday, he had a heavy schedule nonetheless. Instructing me not to worry, Owen promised that he would get there no later than noon.

"Just keep hitting them," he had advised with a laugh. Again, he sounded so philosophical when he spoke the words…just keep hitting them.

Owen insisted that he planned to go to the driving range anyway. That he desperately needed the practice, as he was scheduled to play in a charity golf tournament the following week.

The tournament was an annual event in which prominent local citizens, such as bankers, businessmen, judges and doctors, mixed with athletes, actors and other celebrities to play golf…all calculated to raise money to assist the Pinellas County's association for mentally challenged children.

It was also a social event, which was widely publicized and heavily sponsored. And while I had never before played in the tournament myself, I had attended as a spectator on a couple of occasions. I had participated in the charity raffles, and had even purchased an overpriced visor knowing that the proceeds went to the hardworking association.

It was my intention to meet with Owen and give him a copy of my paper outlining what had happened to me…hoping that it would one day help me to explain things in the event that tempers ever cooled, the law changed, or heaven forbid, I was ever re-captured. As much to get it off my chest as anything.

But my primary motive was just to see him again, to thank him for his continued concern, to leave him a small retainer for his time, and to inform him of my possible plans. And, I guess, to seek any further advice.

I only had a few more things to do before visiting my mother. Karen also had to make arrangements to take some time off. Against my better judgment, but to my heart's delight, she had decided to travel with me to wherever I intended to go…and to help me get settled. She was attempting to arrange for at least two, but hopefully three weeks away from her work.

As to where I could go…I had a couple of choices. I still had some reliable friends in Santa Fe, New Mexico…and there were several refuges to be had in the islands. But, neither of those alternatives seemed to be anything other than temporary solutions, destined eventually to betrayal or disappointment.

We were leaning toward Santa Fe…for a couple of months to set things up, and then Canada for the ultimate destination. Canada conjured up feelings of a new start. Someplace foreign, but local…far enough away, but close enough to home.

"Dammit, I won't win any tournaments like that," the voice next to me grumbled to himself, snapping me out of my private spell.

I looked around for Owen, but he still had not appeared. Then I looked over at the frustrated golfer. He was an elderly gentleman, but he was trim and fairly well-muscled. He had taken a long time to warm up before hitting his first ball. Then, instead of beginning with a smaller club, he had gone directly to his driver.

He hit several more shots, all rather long and with an exaggerated draw. Then he hooked another one and cursed mildly again. He turned to me and asked, "Is my head steady?"

There was nothing familiar to me about the man until he turned around and looked directly into my eyes. His glare stopped me in my tracks. It was Judge Morningstar.

JUDGE ARTHUR P. Morningstar was probably close to sixty years old. But he was very youthful and possessed with great charm and a sort of noble bearing. When I first saw him at my own pre-trial hearings, I thought that he had been cast in his role by a film director.

He was handsome and erect, with a bold shock of bushy white hair. He was also extremely confident, in total command of his courtroom. And while his thundering voice cowered defendants, attorneys and spectators alike, he always proceeded impartially and considerately.

Owen Singer had been ecstatic that we had drawn him as our judge in the case. "He won't be any easier," Owen had remarked, "but he has no axes to grind...he'll be fair."

And while Morningstar ultimately sentenced me to prison, he acknowledged my family's presence in the courtroom and spoke the dreaded words in a firm and consoling manner.

It had been reported that he was an avid golfer. And I vaguely remembered having heard that he lived here at Bardmoor Country Club. So, it wouldn't be surprising to learn that he too had planned to play in the charity golf tournament.

"Well," he asked with an impatient edge to his voice, "is my head steady?"

"Yes, sir," I stuttered. "But you're rushing your backswing..."

He proceeded to hit a few more balls, concentrating on using an easy deliberate backswing. He hit three beautiful shots, and then topped one.

"Keep your head down, Judge," I commanded. "You're peeking."

He looked into my eyes for a moment. "Head down…right," he answered, hitting three more fairly lengthy drives. He smiled and continued.

His shots were strong, but he complained again at the tendency of the shots to unexpectedly hook. I studied his movements…the mechanics of his swing were solid…

"Maybe you're too close to the ball," I suggested. "Try setting up just a little farther away."

And he did…and it worked…and he beamed at the excellent result.

"Are you playing in the tournament?" I asked.

"You bet, son," he snapped. "And thanks to you, I might not embarrass myself." Then he grinned, and added, "As a matter of fact, I might scare a few people…"

I laughed at the old man's competitive spirit, and remarked, "It sounds like you might have someone specific in mind…"

He cracked a sly smile and clucked, "Could be…"

MORNINGSTAR CLEANED his club head and rearranged the clubs in his golf bag. Without looking up, he asked, "Do you know me?"

"No, sir," I answered, a little too quickly.

"But you called me Judge…"

Damn, he doesn't miss much. I threw up my hands and admitted, "Well, I know you are a judge."

Morningstar did not press the issue. He pulled out his putter and began walking toward the practice putting green. "Would you like to join me?" he asked.

I glanced at the parking lot, and said, "Uh…no…I'm waiting for someone."

He obviously noticed my nervousness, and glanced at me for a moment. But whatever he was thinking, he decided to let it pass. He smiled and offered to buy me a beer at the clubhouse later, in payment for the short golf lesson.

"Sure, thank you," I said, knowing that I would not accept.

As he strolled off the driving range, I noticed that I was left on the tee alone. I turned back, and impulsively, I called after him.

"Hey, Judge, do you have a minute?"

He turned around and waited for me to catch up to him. "Listen, your honor," I said, "there is a way you can repay me for the lesson…"

He eyed me cautiously. "How…?" he asked without expression.

I reached into my golf bag and pulled out a copy of the paper I had planned to give to Owen. I handed it to Morningstar politely but firmly, and said, "Take fifteen minutes of your time and read this…"

WE SAT on a bench in the open air. I watched him closely as he read, trying to decipher his emotions.

He clamped his jaw at times, he smiled at times, and finally, he shook his head and looked over at me.

He finished and handed the manuscript back to me.

"Keep it," I said, pushing his hand away.

He continued to eye me as he tucked it under his arm.

"Well, what do you think?" I asked, my voice cracking.

"I'm trying to place you," he finally said.

I pulled off my cap, and then slowly removed my wig. "Does that help…?"

"Not really…" he said without blinking. "But I do remember your case. And naturally, I have been informed of your escape."

"Judge, did you wonder why I escaped with so little time left to serve?"

"I was told that you hoped to avoid prosecution for an even greater conspiracy charge..." he responded immediately. He was clearly not intimidated.

"Well, you've just read my version," I said, standing up. "Do you think it's total crap?"

Morningstar smiled without answering.

"Do you have any comments at all about it, sir?" I asked, pointing to the paper.

"Hmmm, wherever you go, you should consider writing. It's well done," he offered. But, this time he did not smile, and I couldn't tell whether or not he was serious.

"I see..." I responded, the taste of disgust in my mouth. I grabbed my golf bag. I needed to leave before he could get to a telephone and call the Federal Marshal.

"Mr. Bellamy," he said, his voice rising. He motioned for me to sit back down.

"Yeah...?" I snapped, sitting on the edge of the bench like a recalcitrant child.

"As I recall, I sentenced you for your participation in a marijuana conspiracy...he began.

"That's right..."

"Some three hundred pounds in the trunk of your co-defendant's car, is that right?" he continued.

"Respectfully, sir...what difference does it make?" I argued lamely.

"Being caught with that amount, I can only guess that it was not your first time dealing in drugs." He was staring intensely at me.

"It was my first conviction, Judge," I protested loudly. Drugs... hell...it was grass.

"You know what I mean, Mr. Bellamy," he persisted. He was experienced enough to suspect the history of my illegal activities.

I did not have a reply. I was flustered. "So...?" I managed to say.

"So...you're a drug trafficker," he concluded.

"Correction, your honor, I WAS a drug trafficker," I stressed. "Serving time for my crime." I was nervous and tongue-tied. I was also upset, and strangely, I felt tears of frustration welling up in my eyes.

I stuttered, not knowing what to say. "I…shit, Judge, I want to be something else. I want…" I couldn't finish.

"Just what did you expect?" he asked. But there was no sympathy in his voice, and his arms were folded impassively across his chest.

"Oh, the hell with it," I shouted indignantly, springing to my feet. "Using that logic, we can agree that this isn't the first time a federal agent has coerced manufactured testimony from some poor soul like me." Then I added, "Under oath, probably in your courtroom too."

He blanched, as if I'd insulted him personally. He unfolded his arms, but I continued, "Judge, if you turn a blind eye to it, you're condoning it…you're actually part of it."

He started to speak, but I cut him off. "Funny thing is, I'll be long gone, and it will continue to happen."

"Why did you come back here?" he inquired, standing up with me.

"To put myself on the line…damn, I could have been somewhere else. But hell, I'm proud of myself…at least I tried…" I picked up my golf bag and glared at him…I was angry.

I shook my head in disgust. "I was an idiot to come back," I added.

I stepped away. "You know, Judge," I said coolly, biting off each word, "What happened to me is bullshit, and you all should be ashamed of yourselves."

I spun around and hurried toward the parking lot before he could follow. At the bottom of the steps, I turned around and shouted sarcastically, "Good luck in the tournament. Remember, keep your head down."

Yeah, and keep your friggin' eyes closed too, I thought.

With that, I stormed off to the car.

AS I SPED from the parking lot, I spotted Owen Singer arriving. I honked and pulled up next to him.

"Hey, where are you going?" he shouted.

"Gotta go, man...can you believe that I just ran into Judge Morningstar?" I replied.

"Sweet Jesus," Owen exclaimed. "Did he recognize you?"

"Hell, yes...I gave him one of these," I answered, handing Owen a copy of my essay through his car window.

"Did you tell him that I was coming here to meet you?" Owen asked.

"No, I didn't want to get you in any trouble..." I said, truthfully. I did not know the law as to what a lawyer could or couldn't do for a fugitive client.

I looked over my shoulder and said, "Look, man, I gotta get out of here. Can I call you later?"

"Call me at home tonight," he answered, already flipping through the paper I had given to him.

Without waving, I accelerated the car through the winding lanes of the quiet golfing community, exited the club and headed for Karen's house on the beaches.

The sooner I stopped wasting time, I thought bitterly, the better.

KAREN SAT on my lap as I related to her the tale of my confrontation with Morningstar. She slipped a glass of wine into my trembling hand.

"Well, everybody agrees on one thing," she laughed. "You should become a writer."

I gulped the wine without responding to her wisecracks.

"Eddie Walker, the Canadian novelist," she said, as if trying out the title.

"Of course, talk shows would be out of the question," she continued. "You'd have to be one of those writers who's a recluse. Like a Salinger."

I wasn't paying attention to her teasing. I leaned back and closed my eyes. But Karen squirmed in my lap and laughed again.

"You know something," she said, as if contemplating a scientific experiment, "I've never dated a writer before..."

I couldn't stop myself from laughing at that remark. It began as a chuckle, then grew.

I looked into her eyes, also wet with laughter. I wanted to say "I love you" but instead I studied the clear line of her jaw in silence.

"You know, baby, I think I'll write about you," I finally threatened.

"And what would you call it?"

I laughed again, trying to conjure up a suitable title. "How about...*Maid to Order?*"

She laughed with me. "Can't you come up with anything more romantic?" she protested.

"Okay," I said in a deep voice, "How about *The Maid Who Stayed?*"

She hit the top of my head with her glass in mock outrage, and pouted, "That's not the kind of romance I had in mind..."

Ignoring her objections, I launched into the opening of my would-be book...

"It was a dark and stormy night," I recited with the affected voice of a Shakespearean actor.

"Oh." Karen giggled, pretending to be enraptured. "And what happened?"

"I got the maid drunk on her birthday..."

Karen squealed and elbowed me in the ribs. "It didn't take you long to get to the climax," she choked.

"It certainly didn't," I agreed suggestively, raising my eyebrows.

She squealed again and accidentally knocked my wineglass against me, spilling the wine on my shirt. She tried to jump up to get a towel, but I held her tightly in my arms.

Karen didn't struggle. Instead she wrapped her arms around my neck and locked her eyes to mine. "Oh, John," she cried, suddenly sad. "What are we going to do?"

Such a desperate sound…the bottom of my heart almost fell out. But I fought the urge to despair. Holding her face in my hands, I hushed her.

"We're going to be strong, that's what," I answered steadfastly.

And as quickly as she had lapsed into sadness, Karen regained her composure. "I love you," she said with the authority of a pledge.

And then she kissed me…and I believed her.

Chapter Twenty-Six

"You went over and actually spoke with him?" I asked, incredulous that Owen had actually confronted the judge about my situation.

"Yeah," Owen repeated. "He was sitting on the bench… evidently right where you left him." He laughed and added, "I think he was as spooked as you were."

"Damn, what did he say?" I was excited. The phone receiver nearly dropped from my hand.

"Well, he was guarded," Owen replied. Then he too became excited. "I'll tell you, John, I could see that he was moved by the whole thing…"

"Really…?

"And, of course, he wants you to surrender yourself…"

"Turn myself in?" I pondered aloud. "Well, hell, maybe he would go pretty easy on me…"

"John, he wouldn't be the sentencing judge on this case," Owen warned, his voice suddenly stern.

"Why…?"

Owen explained to me that my escape offense took place in the

Middle District of Alabama, and that a federal judge there would preside over my case. And that, in any event, my sentence would be controlled by the unyielding sentencing guidelines. I went limp. I wasn't about to voluntarily accept another four or five years in jail.

"John, I really think that we got Morningstar's attention today…for whatever that's worth," Owen said, as if talking to himself.

Owen paused for a second, as if thinking, but I was speechless. He continued, suggesting that if I felt safe, I should stick around and lie low, and let him explore the situation a little further. "I have a couple of ideas," he said.

"Okay," I agreed, still depressed. "I can do that."

"Hey," Owen bellowed over the phone, "are you ready for some good news?"

My spirits soared as Owen informed me that they dropped the charges against Stormin' Norman. The prosecution could not gather sufficient evidence to convict him. And on top of that, Norman's lawyer had convinced them that Norman was not even in Panama City on the night in question. He had produced a ticket stub, kept as a souvenir, along with a Jimmy Buffett T-shirt, indicating that Norman was in Tallahassee that night at a Jimmy Buffett concert. I howled.

"What about Larry's testimony?" I asked, still concerned.

"Larry Martin refused to testify. It's over," Owen explained, adding that, unfortunately, Larry could count on doing time himself.

"Well, I'll be damned," I said, almost whispering.

I was proud of Larry…he had held together. And I was relieved and happy for Norman and Judy…and for myself, as the pangs of guilt melted away.

I LOOKED for Karen in the darkness. She was sleeping peacefully, her head buried in the pillow. Her breathing was deep and rhythmic, like the ocean. I thought of Stormin' Norman, and of the surprising way he had snored in our room after the Buffett concert. It was so unlike Karen's hypnotic breathing, I chuckled silently.

I realized that I had come a long way since running down River Road, and my mind rapidly flashed pictures of my run to freedom. I was wide awake.

I slipped out of the bed and crossed into the kitchen. I opened the refrigerator and fumbled with a carton of milk. Standing in the middle of the kitchen floor, I drank the remaining milk and flipped the empty carton into the trash bag.

On the kitchen counter, I noticed a copy of the paper I'd given to Owen, and to Morningstar. I picked it up and read it, imagining that I was the judge reading it for the first time.

While the piece effectively captured my legal dilemma, I couldn't help noticing that it centered itself completely upon that narrow part of my adventure. It did not touch the passion and the excitement of the journey itself. Of course, it was not meant to, for its purpose was to enlighten the reader about my reasons for escaping.

As I stood in the kitchen, however, it occurred to me that a better story lay in the subsequent happenings...my many episodes along the trail. Since I was going to be cooped up for a while, waiting for word from Owen before I could flee, I thought it would be a good time to outline my story while the memories were still fresh in my head.

I turned on all the lights in the living room and grabbed a notebook. I would start at the beginning, and instead of being Eddie Walker accounting for John Bellamy, I would be a wiser John Bellamy and chronicle my discovery of Eddie Walker.

I WAS ENCOURAGED at how quickly the tale unfolded in my mind, and I laughed as I recounted the various characters and situations I'd encountered along the way. But I found myself racing ahead of the natural flow of events. To put it all on paper, I would have to take my time. Not just a few weeks of intensity, but many months of disciplined labor.

In the past, I would have been overwhelmed at the mere thought of a project of this magnitude. But oddly, for the first time in my life, I was thrilled by the prospect, and I was also happily puzzled by the strange sense of elation I experienced as I scribbled away in the late hours of the night.

"Honey, what's going on?" Karen asked in a drowsy voice.

"Did I wake you up, darlin'?" I replied with a smile, putting down my pencil.

I couldn't help but be amused. She was not yet fully awake. She rubbed her eyes and staggered into me like a sleepy little girl.

I held up six pages of typewritten material for her to see. She found her glasses on the table and squinted as she reached for the first page. Then, she smiled as she read it.

"God, John, this is really good," she said loudly. "it's…entertaining."

"I have a long way to go," I sighed. "But…I don't know…it might be a worthwhile thing to do."

Karen sat on my lap and hugged me. She stared at me for a moment, and said, "You know, don't get offended…but it's still hard to believe it's you writing all this stuff."

I laughed. "Exactly. I've always been the man of a thousand distractions."

"I can't wait to find out how it ends," she said softly, kissing my cheek.

I understood her longing. This story was my story.

Chapter Twenty-Seven

There were two reasons why my case attracted further examination from Judge Morningstar. First, he learned of other grumbling about Jeff Banner, the DEA agent. It seemed that even a judge was not immune to the courthouse whispers regarding Banner's methods.

And while I had argued, when shouting at the judge, that Banner was more than likely involved in other misbehavior, I was surprised that it would ever be taken seriously. Owen was not, for it served to prove an old theory that he had about the rotten apple. According to Owen, if that sort of thing was routine for Banner, Owen had such faith in the system that it was only natural that sooner or later the bad apple would begin to stink. I had no such faith.

In any event, those negative reports gave credence to my claims, and led Morningstar to consider the fact that I might just be telling the truth. But it was more than that alone that prompted the judge to act. It was Owen's opinion that the true catalyst of Morningstar's ire was the second agent involved in my interrogation...the FBI guy.

I remembered the FBI agent distinctly from that day at the Camp. Initially, I was comforted by his appearance...his demeanor of fairness and professionalism. But I also remembered in the end being completely flabbergasted by his belligerent support of Banner's tactics.

As it turned out, the FBI agent's name was Charles Hall. He was the son of a noted legal scholar and author of jurisprudence who had practiced law with Judge Morningstar before Morningstar was appointed to the Federal bench.

The judge had known Charles Hall since he was a child, and after the father had passed away, Morningstar continued to follow the boy's career with great interest. Hall had achieved a distinguished early record. In fact, he had developed into a courageous agent who'd received numerous awards and commendations at a fairly young age.

Of all his varied assignments, it was his assignment to duty in the drug arena that had chipped away at his otherwise exemplary reputation. And Morningstar, who had considerable respect and affection for Hall, was disheartened by the lad's possible participation in such overzealous and underhanded tactics as those alleged in my case. Owen was sure that when Hall's name began to surface along with Banner's, it was too much for the old man to ignore.

I couldn't believe any of it, but Owen maintained that this was why he became a lawyer, and why he had so much faith in the system. While others could argue on Hall's behalf that the punishment of drug offenders was a justifiable motive for the agent's actions, it did not matter to an old-line jurist like Morningstar, who believed, as Owen did when he was a prosecutor, that there were no shortcuts to justice.

Although Owen said that the judge would never go so far as to agree with my essay's assessment of the "War on Drugs" being waged in a hopelessly unwise and misdirected manner...actually, in my essay, I referred to it as a "Domestic Vietnam"...Owen felt strongly that the judge did agree with my contention that the unbridled power of the police leads to egregious excesses affecting huge numbers of citizens in subtle ways...making victims of innocent people and, unfortunately, compromising and corrupting decent people in the process...like agent Hall.

Owen related to me that Judge Morningstar had shown concern about the fight against drugs for some time...not that he had any sympathy for drug offenders...for his record clearly indicated that he handed out heavier than average sentences for those convicted of drug crimes.

On the other hand, Morningstar had spoken before the Bar Association about his disturbing perception that law enforcement had begun to justify any means whatsoever in fighting drugs. And he contended that if any means, including unlawful methods, were permitted to fight the drug war, then why shouldn't they be permitted to combat other areas of crime, which could be equally or more offensive and harmful than some drug crimes...such as political corruption, or Morningstar's personal pet peeve, the illegal dumping of toxic materials into the environment...an act Morningstar considered infinitely more horrible than any non-violent drug crime.

The judge argued that following such reasoning could result in a rapid deterioration of the Bill of Rights, and the complete destruction of our system of justice. All because of someone's personal sensitivity about which crimes were most despicable. It followed that since all crimes were particularly offensive to someone, perhaps there should be no rights at all. Morningstar was frightened at how easy that step was to make...the step which disposes of Constitutional safeguards and replaces vigorous prosecution with witch-hunting.

Damn, I was impressed with the reasoning. And even more impressed with Owen's articulation of those ideas to me in a way I could understand. But it still seemed a little over-the-top to me, and I confessed to Owen that all those legalisms seemed to dwarf my little case.

Owen laughed, and had a confession of his own. "You're correct, legalisms don't win cases. But the application of these principles to the prosecution of Stevie Peak can strike fear in the heart of the U. S. Attorney." He laughed again, "That's where you really lucked out."

He said that the U. S. Attorney, deeply involved in the prosecution of Stevie Peak's massive smuggling organization, would fear his office being linked with Banner's dirty tactics. If prosecutorial misconduct could be proven, the case could collapse and everyone, including Stevie, might walk. On top of that, it was Owen's guess that since Stevie Peak was supplying the prosecution with accurate information as to who was really involved in his operation, my name would not be listed anywhere on their chart of conspiracy members…further proof that my story was true.

Even if the prosecution had suspected or tolerated Banner's case-cracking techniques before, they were now distancing themselves from him…and from me…and they were adamantly denying any knowledge of the affair. I had definitely become a liability to them overnight, and they did not strongly protest Morningstar's intervention in the matter.

Owen was tickled. "I'm sure Jeff Banner never dreamed in his wildest dreams that you would break out of jail and confront a federal judge with the case," he said, holding his sides.

"Well, hell, neither did I," I responded, not yet amused. I was still not exactly sure what was happening.

Owen continued laughing. "Amen," he said, slowly shaking his head in astonishment.

WITH SOME RELUCTANCE, a federal judge in Alabama reviewed the situation at Morningstar's request. And the U. S. Attorney's office was more or less directed to fashion an equitable resolution…or show cause why its pending prosecution was not tainted by misbehavior.

When I questioned why the judges needed to request anything from the U. S. Attorney, Owen instructed me that, silly as it seemed, the real power was held by the prosecution. My fate was officially in their hands, not in the hands of the Court...for my sentence under the new Sentencing Guidelines was not determined by a judge's discretion, but strictly by what charge the U. S. Attorney decided to file against me.

Owen reminded me of his earlier explanation of the Guidelines...of how the sentencing judge was bound by unyielding rules applicable to each crime. And how in my case, an escape charge brought with it a mandatory sentence of considerable jail time, regardless of what the sentencing judge might feel about the circumstances.

The trick here, Owen reiterated, was to coerce the prosecution not to file any charges, or to file some lesser charge that did not demand as severe a penalty. That this matter could not legally be resolved by the judges alone infuriated Owen. He decried the absurdity of the prosecution administering "justice" while the judges acted merely as rubber stamps.

As for myself, I was just a pawn...from the beginning...and looking back on it now, I confess that all of it was over my head.

As a result of the judicial arm-twisting, a deal was ultimately offered to me. It was simple enough...I surrender myself back to the Camp, plead guilty to the lesser charge of obstruction of justice, and serve an additional four month sentence on top of the remaining months left on my original sentence. I would be permitted to serve my time there at Maxwell without being shipped to another institution.

I was angry that I had to plead guilty to anything. And the last goddamn thing I was guilty of was obstructing justice. But Owen cautioned that they refused to completely ignore my escape…that the prosecution convincingly argued that I could have successfully challenged governmental wrongdoing without having to escape… and that, most importantly, it was a "take it or leave it" proposition.

I took it…

I COULDN'T HELP WONDERING about Arthur Morningstar, and his willingness to get involved in my case even as he continued to hand down heavier than average penalties to drug offenders. There seemed to be a great many contradictions in his personality, and several questions left unanswered about the whole affair.

It was only later that I discovered that Morningstar had once been a law clerk for the renowned Supreme Court Justice and libertarian Hugo Black. As it was explained to me, Justice Black had expressed strong opinions about the law's responsibility to the public. And during his tenure on the High Court, he had continually stressed the importance of the court's mission to provide fair access to justice…in order that a citizen might redress any wrong done to him. Acknowledging Morningstar's background, Owen speculated that his actions in my case were not as contradictory as I suggested. He merely allowed me to redress the wrong done to me.

I myself knew little about Hugo Black. And while I was not properly versed in these high-minded legal principles…I couldn't really be sure what it all meant. While I was happy about the fact that I did not have to run away to obtain…or avoid…justice, I was not convinced that a universal message could be drawn from my limited set of circumstances. Only a string of unlikely events had brought me to this point. Even then, I could see that I was far from the irresistible force of the aggrieved citizen…and although Judge

Morningstar had remained true to his convictions, he was far from the immovable object of righteousness.

Owen was only hopeful that I was not too limited an exception to an increasingly harsh system. But we all agreed on the bottom line...that I was lucky.

Chapter Twenty-Eight

I didn't feel very lucky as I sat on the hotel room bed. I was uncomfortable...and I was scared. I was also experiencing a strange sense of claustrophobia in the cramped room.

The Riverfront Hotel in Montgomery, Alabama, had been a Sheraton at one point, but it had changed hands some time ago. And while it was not as luxurious as its Sheraton history would lead one to believe, it did have room service...and it was only a five-minute drive to Maxwell Air Force Base and the prison camp.

Karen and I had flown up earlier in the day. We wanted to spend our last hours together before I turned myself in the next morning. It was Thursday night, and I had hoped to delay until Monday before I returned to the Camp. I needed the weekend to see my family, and to resolve a few things with Karen. But I was advised that the Court required me to surrender immediately.

Once I surrendered myself, I would be confined for another ten or eleven months...a little less than the seven months on my original sentence, along with the additional four months I had agreed to serve...all depending, of course, on halfway house considerations and other release options. It was not an oppressive amount of time left, but I knew that it was enough to potentially ruin any number of dreams I had for the future.

I had experienced all this before...the first time I came to the Camp. I knew what to expect...what reality had to offer. Accepting this, I stretched out on the bed, trying to summon the courage to tell Karen what needed to be said.

I listened to her in the shower as I struggled with my thoughts. In my nervousness, I accidentally bit my lip and drew blood.

I FELT OBLIGED to inform Karen that she did not have to wait for me...that I didn't want the torture of wondering about her every day I was in jail, only to be disappointed in the end. I wanted to confess that it would even be confusing and difficult for me to sit and wait for her if the tables were turned and she was the one going away.

I wanted to let her know that I recognized all of that, and to tell her that all I wanted from her, or expected from her, was that she stay in touch with me and hopefully give me another chance when I finally came home.

I was a grown man...disillusioned by the romantic notions of confined men. During my first stint at the Camp, I had seen too many men twisted by their women at home. As I said, I had gone through it all before. And I was scared.

Karen came out of the bathroom with a towel wrapped around her, crossed over to me and sat on the edge of the bed.

"I kind of expected you to join me in there," she said, sensing my depression and gently rubbing her hand through my hair.

I looked up at her...my heart ached with confusion. It was going to be a short night. And in the morning, I realized, everything would change.

"What's wrong?" she asked, suddenly concerned.

I wanted to tell her everything I was thinking about expectations versus reality…and setting her free. But I couldn't. Instead, I blurted out, "I'm sorry." It was pretty pathetic.

"Oh, baby," she cried as she quickly reached for me and took me tenderly into her arms.

…

"I've waited long enough to find you," Karen said, holding my head and forcing me to look directly into her eyes as she spoke. "I love you…you can believe it or not, but I'll wait for you…it's not that long." Then she laughed and said, "I've been so preoccupied with you, it will take me that long to put my business back together."

I couldn't move. I didn't want to be bullshitted…at least, I'd never admit to it. But, God, her words sounded pretty good. Who doesn't like to hear that? But what's really going to happen?

I tried to speak, but Karen hushed me with her finger and said, "Just tell me in the morning how you want to handle it. Let's not waste anymore time tonight."

With the exaggerated movements of an amateur stripper, Karen pulled the towel from around her body and tossed it on the floor. "Now, we're going to have to get our fill," she announced as she yanked the bedcovers down in one motion.

She pushed me back on the bed and helped me to remove my clothes. "I'm going to start at the bottom and work my way up…," she teased, using her deep, hot-blooded voice. Then, she reached for my feet.

KAREN COULD FEEL how tense I was as she attempted to arouse me. And even as we loved, she surely felt my preoccupation with other thoughts, for her touching and kissing turned from that of erotic stimulation to soothing strokes of comfort and compassion.

I was moved by the depth of her understanding...and her unselfishness...and just as suddenly my attention focused on her alone. Karen had been a real source of strength...loving and heroic...throughout the whole ordeal. In all fairness, it was her turn to relax...to be pampered. But here she was doing her best to console my whiny ass. She was a treasure, and I was wasting time thinking about anything but her.

She smiled as she felt the shift in my attitude, and she moved to accept my sudden aggression. We continued in a burst of wordless intensity.

"I love you," I finally said, emphasizing each word clearly.

"As you should...," she replied with a smirk.

I laughed and hugged her harder. "Oh, baby...I don't want to go back there," I confessed with a sigh, rolling over on my back.

"I know..." Karen responded softly, her voice thick with sympathy.

I half-turned toward her. She had stacked two pillows under her head, and she was laughing at me.

"Hey...what's so funny?" I asked, surprised. "I'm talking about jail here..."

"But you don't have that worried look on your face anymore," she giggled.

I laughed. "You have that 'freshly laid look' in your eyes too, baby."

Karen didn't answer. She continued to smile...the same smile she wore that first morning in Savannah.

I rolled toward her and put my arms around her. "Yeah, I guess I'll make it through," I grumbled.

"Of course you will," she agreed, kissing my cheek.

We ordered some room service and cuddled and talked into the night. And although there was a touch of sadness in the air, our conversation was animated and optimistic. I was already reminding myself that things could be worse...the cardinal rule for dealing with this kind of situation.

We agreed that I would use the coming months to complete a manuscript. Karen was adamant that I preserve the memory of Eddie Walker, and make note of all the subtle changes that had taken place in my approach to life. "Of course you'll have to change the names and locations to protect the innocent," she added.

I laughed. "The names might be changed, but no one is innocent."

She promised to drive up often from St. Petersburg with Norman and Judy to visit, and she agreed to go by and see my mother…to inform her of my well-being, and to tell her a little bit about my escapades.

"But I'll leave the lurid details for you to tell her when she comes up to see you," Karen insisted.

I laughed again, and said, "Better yet…I'll send her the first draft of the book."

"I can't wait to see that myself," Karen added with a trace of apprehension…as if knowing that the story contained certain awkward elements.

I grimaced with embarrassment…but it went unnoticed in the shadows of the poorly lit room.

It wasn't that long before we found ourselves touching each other again. Already tired by strenuous love-play…and by the lateness of the hour…we stroked each other with affection, and with the casual, carefree nature of two people who had known and loved each other for a long time.

It was an extremely personal feeling, and I was overwhelmed by the warmth of the situation.

"I'll miss this," I whispered, not wanting to disturb the mood.

"Mmmm…me too," Karen replied, her eyes closed.

Sometimes the comfortable feeling of a lover's familiarity leads us to relax in unexpected ways. And under the spell we can be inspired to pursue greater exploration of the relationship. One thing leads to another, and before you know it, you embark on unchartered waters. It isn't planned in advance...and one cannot make the trip alone. Karen and I slipped into it together...

I touched her and whispered into her ear. "How will you ever go without this for so long?"

It wasn't a serious question. It was meant to tease her, and instinctively, Karen knew that. She responded to my touching by moving slowly. "I'll manage...," she answered, breathing a little heavier.

"How...?" I teased, touching her more directly.

She moaned and opened her eyes. "Well...you know," she said, her voice cracking.

"Show me," I insisted.

"What do you mean?" she asked, confused. But her body was still sensitive...she was aroused.

I parted her tired legs and reached for her hand. Lying next to her, I playfully placed a pillow over her face. I heard her muffled giggles as I took her hand and pushed it gently between her legs.

She flinched at our combined touch and withdrew her hand.

"I'll be away for a long time," I said, leaning into her. "And you'll need to conjure up wonderful fantasies to get you through the lonely nights."

Without waiting for her to respond, I retrieved Karen's hand. She gasped as I moved it against her and held it there. Then, together, we gently touched her. As she became more aroused, she became less inhibited by her own participation.

Finally, I instructed her to have any private fantasy she could imagine. "Like what...?" she asked, her thin voice wavering.

"Shusshh," I whispered. "No more talking." But I did not stop touching her. She gripped the pillow tightly over her face with her free hand, and writhed to the touch.

"That's it..." I encouraged her. "Now...just drift alone in your thoughts," I continued,

"...while I go down to check on your progress..."

She cried out as I kissed her...and exhaled heavily as I pursued her with our fingers and my hot breath. I was excited by my control over her body.

"Ohhh..." was all she could articulate in her passion. And again.

When I finally returned to remove the pillow, I found her limp...her face and hair drenched with perspiration. She trembled in my arms as I pulled the sheet over our wet bodies. And we slept our last night together...I would turn myself in early the next morning.

Chapter Twenty-Nine

I pushed myself away from the typewriter, stood erect and slowly stretched. First my back, then my arms and legs. Enough typing for one day, I thought. It was now time to get some exercise.

My return to the Camp had been uneventful. I was processed in without fanfare, but there were more than a few smiles. I was returned to my old dormitory, but assigned to a different bunk…a top bunk, like a new guy. I chuckled at the first of the many nuisance punishments I would have to endure.

It all seemed startlingly the same, although it wasn't long before I found out that in the brief months I'd been away, many changes had taken place.

Terry High-Five, my old bunkie, had been transferred to Talladega for disciplinary reasons. He had been caught with a pillowcase full of Popeye's fried chicken, which led to a shakedown of both his living and work areas.

While they found nothing of consequence in his cube or his locker, they did discover a cache of pilfered goods hidden near his work area at the base warehouse. And while they could not conclusively prove that the merchandise was Terry's, he was the most likely suspect. He was gone, to a higher level institution, within the week.

I was also informed that my old supervisor on the golf course, Bob Waters, had retired and moved to Arizona. And that things had really tightened up on the golf course work detail. Evidently, the new supervisor was strict and determined not to allow the inmate workers to get away with much.

It didn't matter to me, however, because I was now forbidden to get a job on the base. Because of my escape, I was required to work in Camp, and I was assigned a job in Food Service. Working in the kitchen did have its advantages though…like access to better food, and more importantly, having a more flexible work schedule.

I had been back for less than three months and I already followed a daily routine. When I wasn't exercising, I spent most of my off hours writing and typing. As the pages piled up, I became convinced that I would eventually accomplish my goal of completing my story.

I received constant encouragement from Karen. Every Friday at mail call, I would get a card or a letter…with a poem, or some naughty reference to the fantasy world. And she and Stormin' Norman and Judy had already driven up twice to visit me. Norman was vigorously searched and otherwise hassled each time on the orders of guard Lt. Wilson, who despite the reversal of charges against Norman, refused to believe he wasn't somehow complicit in my escape.

In the visiting yard, we made such a commotion, laughing so hard and drawing so much attention to our table…it was a farcical spectacle…we drew stares from the other gloomy families. It made me miss them even more.

It was obvious to all that I was going to make it. Not only that, but I had great hopes for the future. There were a couple of times, though, that I buckled under the regimentation…and some days went by slowly. One had to stay busy to stay sane. And I did that.

Gradually, I began to find articles in the paper and in magazines attacking the cost of the drug war and the corresponding dismantling of the people's fundamental rights over an issue that perhaps could be handled in another manner., especially for marijuana. Even television began making similar statements negating some of the overblown evils of marijuana. Maybe I had been too hasty in my earlier assessment of the press. A small portion of the media had begun to take notice...better than that, they were beginning to take a stand. Who knew where it all would end.

"THE SILVER BULLET IS PULLING IN...," a voice shouted across the compound.

The Silver Bullet was the large bus that occasionally arrived at the Camp to either bring in new inmates or to pick up individuals bound for other institutions. Terry High-Five had been shipped to Talladega on the Bullet.

It resembled a shiny Greyhound bus without any identifying markings on its sides. Sometimes it was crowded with prisoners, but oftentimes it carried only a handful of unfortunate souls... many of whom had bounced around from one jail to another on their way to their final destination. Those, like myself, who had been afforded the privilege of voluntary surrender, gratefully avoided a ride on the Silver Bullet.

Although the area around the scenic-cruiser was cordoned off, temporarily off-limits to curious onlookers, we would get as close to the bus as permitted in order that we might identify new arrivals...friends, or friends of friends. But it was actually more to relieve the boredom than for any other reason that we watched the jump-suited figures stagger off the Silver Bullet squinting their eyes.

And I'll be damned if the first one off the bus wasn't Larry Martin.

THERE HE WAS, joking with six other prisoners, and escorted by three half-smiling guards. He looked in even worse shape than when I had last seen him in Panama City. I would fix that…along with a few miles each day out on River Road.

I was elated. "Hey, Larry," I shouted as I waved, attracting scowls from his armed escorts.

Larry shaded his eyes with his cuffed hands, recognized me and grinned. He stopped to wave in my direction, but was hurried along to the receiving office by the guard.

Within a few hours, he would be loose on the compound.

"CAN'T WE PUT THIS OFF?" Larry panted, as I dragged him for a brisk walk down River Road.

"Listen, man," I said with a laugh. "Since you're only going to be here for thirteen months, we'll need every day of that to get your carcass into shape."

It was a beautiful afternoon. The summer heat had vanished almost overnight as the cooler autumn weather blew in from the north. Even Larry was invigorated as we walked along the river.

He took a deep breath as he scanned the lush riverbank. "I guess it could be worse," he grudgingly admitted.

"That's the spirit," I replied, slapping him on the back. "Keep reminding yourself of that…"

Larry smiled as we walked in silence. He was holding together well, and he would ultimately be alright. But I remembered my first day…and I knew that behind his smile lay a tremendous amount of uncertainty and anxiety, mixed with a little fear.

I knew the ropes, however, and at least I would be there to help him along. Besides, I was proud of him. He had not turned on Norman…or on me.

"Hey, Larry..." I started to say. I wanted to thank him for his unexpected courage.

"Wait a minute..." he interrupted. "What's that...?"

I looked up River Road to see a petite woman in shorts and a sweatshirt jogging in our direction. As she came closer, I recognized the hat she was wearing...my G&S Surfboard hat. It was her...Captain joggerette. I had not seen her since my return to the Camp, and I thought she'd been permanently transferred to duty elsewhere. Evidently not.

As she approached, she looked at us and flashed a surprised smile. Without speaking, she nodded ever-so-slightly and ran past us, her blond ringlets bouncing with every step.

Larry stopped in his tracks. "Holy mother..." he coughed, turning around to watch her continue up the road. Later, I would spell out the rules for him, explaining how he would not be permitted to talk to non-inmates while on River Road.

He spun around and broke into an unsteady run. I smiled and ran up beside him. "Yeah," he puffed, still wide-eyed, "I think I can get into this shit."

Then he turned around and looked at me as he pumped his arms. "The Jogging Brothers," he cracked. We burst out laughing.

"I MEAN IT, MAN...THANK YOU." We had slowed to a lazy walk, and I was emphatically trying to thank Larry for hanging tough after his arrest, and for refusing to testify against Norman and me.

He ignored my comments. Instead, he nodded his head, laughed and said, "I can't believe that you guys slipped off to a Buffett concert..." His eyes twinkled. "What happened to you then?"

We traded stories about what had happened to each of us after we'd split up. I was almost moved to tears when recounting my adventures with Don Diamond...and the beginning of my attempts at writing. Before I could tell him about Karen, he interrupted me.

"Did you really ever have any doubts about me?" Larry asked. There was a very serious edge to his voice.

I glanced briefly at my feet and replied, "Well…maybe a little, especially during the time you were incommunicado for so long. We didn't know what was up…one minute you were busted, and the next you were missing…"

"Oh…that," he said hoarsely, as he nervously looked around.

"Man," I chuckled, "where were you?'

Larry rolled his eyes and leaned close as if to tell me a secret. "I did something crazy," he confessed with a shrug.

Expecting a difficult moment and not wanting to pry, I nodded and waited for him to tell me. Seeing that I was not going to speak, he continued, "Well…I knew I was fucked. So I thought I should try to make a little money…" His voice trailed off.

I couldn't contain myself any longer. "So…?" I asked, sensing a wild story.

"So…I got offered great money to offload bales somewhere in South Carolina…"

"Skip…!!?" I almost shouted.

"That's right," Larry replied excitedly. "You know," he continued, "Skip told me that he had talked with you, but he didn't say that you knew anything about the scam…"

"What in the hell happened?" I boomed.

"I'm not exactly sure," Larry answered. "We had some delay. And they busted the boat while it was anchored out in St. Helena Sound. Shit…it was probably only a few miles from The Spot."

"Was anyone busted with it?" I asked, still dazed by this information.

"Not yet. There was nobody even on the boat when it got popped. Like I said, there was some delay…and the Captain anchored up and pulled the crew off the boat to wait somewhere until it was safe to bring the boat in."

I was confused. "Why...?" I stuttered. "I mean...what happened?"

"I was told the Feds were in the area for some other deal they busted that same night nearby...there were choppers in the air... some kind of surveillance across the water," Larry said, holding his hands up in exasperation. "There was even a boat in between the shrimpboat and The Spot...that's why the captain didn't bring it in."

Larry shook his head at the memory and said, "Shit...what a mess."

"What about The Spot?" I asked.

"They never busted The Spot. Hell, they only busted the shrimpboat two days after it was anchored...they stumbled on to it."

"Damn, man," I replied, still excited, "where were you?'

"Christ...I was out at The Spot for three fucking days...with all these fucking mosquitoes and all these guys scared shitless."

I could imagine the feeling. "How did you get out of there?"

"We had to slip out in twos and threes to avoid suspicion," Larry answered. "I went out with Skip."

"What about all the transportation...?"

"Ah, the dumptrucks went out easily...one at a time. Same with the R. V.s...although I heard that one of them got stopped on its way north." He cringed and added, "Good thing it was empty."

"It might come back to haunt everyone," I said, concerned.

Whoever stopped that motorhome would surely have taken its registration and identified the driver for later questioning. Moreover, I hadn't seen any news coverage about the bust. With that amount of marijuana aboard, it was a clear indication that an investigation was in progress.

"Yeah...that's what Skip thought," Larry said. "He's also worried that the boat captain will ultimately be identified."

"Is Skip home?" I asked.

"Skip...all of them, are on the run until things cool down."

"That could be awhile," I predicted.

"Yeah…we know."

I thought of all the months…and years…of worrying that lay ahead of them, and I was immediately thankful that I hadn't joined in.

All of a sudden, my once questionable future looked much rosier to me. "Thank fucking God," I mumbled to myself. Those guys would be carrying a heavy burden for a long time.

"Do you have any idea at all where Skip could be?" I asked, instantly remembering the feeling of being on the run.

"No," Larry replied. "But he told me that if I ever ran into you, to tell you that Eddie Walker…whoever that is…made the right decision."

I nodded my head.

"Does that make any sense to you?" Larry asked.

"It sure does," I answered. The message was clear.

I offered no further explanation. Instead, I increased the pace of our march. Larry picked up the cadence and fell in next to me. River Road lay ahead of us…worn smooth by earlier travelers.

THE END

About the Author

Tom Gribbin graduated from Florida State University, and from the University of Florida Law School. He draws on his experiences as a writer, lawyer, recording artist and touring musician, concert promoter, co-founder of an international chain of comedy clubs, and as an executive of a major entertainment company. Tom is married and lives in St. Pete Beach, Florida.

Photo by: Rebecca Gast, RockStar Image